Black Knight

Black Knight

WITCH WORLD, VOL. 2

CHRISTOPHER PIKE

SIMON PULSE

NEW YORK   LONDON   TORONTO   SYDNEY   NEW DELHI

SIMON PULSE

An imprint of Simon & Schuster Children's Publishing Division

1230 Avenue of the Americas, New York, NY 10020

This Simon Pulse edition December 2014

Text copyright © 2014 by Christopher Pike

Cover photographs copyright © 2014 by Marta Bevacqua/Trevillion Images

All rights reserved, including the right of reproduction in whole or in part in any form.

SIMON PULSE and colophon are registered trademarks of Simon & Schuster, Inc.

For information about special discounts for bulk purchases, please contact

Simon & Schuster Special Sales at 1-866-506-1949 or business@simonandschuster.com.

The Simon & Schuster Speakers Bureau can bring authors to your live event.

For more information or to book an event contact the Simon & Schuster Speakers Bureau

at 1-866-248-3049 or visit our website at www.simonspeakers.com.

Book design by Regina Flath

The text of this book was set in Garamond.

Manufactured in the United States of America

2 4 6 8 10 9 7 5 3 1

Library of Congress Cataloging-in-Publication Data

Pike, Christopher, 1955–

Black knight / Christopher Pike. — First Simon Pulse edition.

p. cm. — (Witch world ; 2)

Summary: New dangers await Jessie, who possesses extraordinary powers and the ability to

exist in both the real world and an alternate one known as witch world.

[1. Witches—Fiction. 2. Supernatural—Fiction. 3. Love—Fiction.] I. Title.

PZ7.P626Bl 2014

[Fic]—dc23

2013042274

ISBN 978-1-4424-6733-0 (hc)

ISBN 978-1-4424-6734-7 (pbk)

ISBN 978-1-4424-6735-4 (eBook)

For Abir, I Love You More

PROLOGUE

EVERY NIGHT, FOR NINE NIGHTS IN A ROW, I DREAM OF a guy I've never met. He's always working the same job. Always planning and enacting the same ingenious crime. Always vanishing at the end of the night.

Worse, he's not someone I observe from a distance. The dream is light-years beyond lucid. If it wasn't so intriguing, I'd call it a nightmare. For in my dreams I *am* him—Marc Simona, a nineteen-year-old parking attendant at a famous Hollywood theater. I see through his eyes, I think his thoughts. Indeed, I know everything there is to know about him.

Except why he haunts me.

My name is Jessica Ralle and I'm a witch. I've explained all this before. How I traveled to Las Vegas with my friends the weekend after I graduated high school. How I was initiated into the ancient game of red queen. How I died and was reborn in the mysterious realm known as witch world.

Last time, I told my story as if it happened in the past, which it did. But this time I'll tell it like it's happening now. I have my reasons, and by the time I finish this tale they will be obvious.

I had been a witch for only a month when I began to dream of Marc. At first I told no one about him. I mean, I couldn't tell James Kelter, my boyfriend, that my unconscious was obsessing over another guy. And since I couldn't even see Jimmy anymore in the real world—but only when he and I were awake together in witch world—he was jealous enough about what I was doing with the other half of my life. It wasn't that he didn't trust me. He was just . . . well, human. Hell, had the situation been reversed, I would have been none too happy.

At the same time, I was hesitant to confide in my best friend, Alex Simms. Although Alex had the genetic potential to become a witch—or to be "connected," as they called it in witch world—she had yet to go through the initiatory rite of dying and being revived—a process that usually triggered an awareness of the other world in people who had the right genetic makeup. Alex said she wasn't afraid but we both knew that wasn't true. I didn't blame her. I wouldn't have volunteered to die. Who would? The only way I became a witch was because I was forced into it.

Yet I was still hoping Alex would one day join me and become a witch, and for that reason I kept my mouth shut about Marc. I didn't want to give her another reason to be scared.

Why I hesitated to tell my father about the dreams, though, I wasn't sure. It could have been because he'd only been back in my life for a month when I began to have them. Or else it was because he'd never spoken about having a similar experience. As far as I knew, seeing through the eyes of another person while you were asleep was not a "standard" witch power. Whatever, my father still intimidated me and I didn't see him that often. Plus I wasn't the kind of person who talked about personal stuff on the phone. I was paranoid that way. I always felt like someone was listening.

So I was alone with my dreams, alone with Marc every night when I closed my eyes and fell asleep. Like I said, I felt I was inside him, that I actually *was* him. It was weird; it was disturbing and yet there was something seductive about it as well. Marc. I was pretty sure he wasn't a witch, but he was a fascinating character. . . .

CHAPTER ONE

PREMIERE NIGHT AT GRAUMAN'S CHINESE THEATRE.
Roll out the red carpet and prepare to welcome the hordes
of beautiful people in their Mercedes S-Class sedans, Jaguar
convertibles, Beamers, and Bentleys—and a bevy of other cars
worth more than most U.S. homes.

Because he was a parking attendant for Grauman's—now
legally the TCL Chinese Theatre, a name no one in Hollywood
was even aware of—the majority of people his age would have
assumed Marc Simona loved riding in such cars. The truth was
he didn't. He just parked them, usually drove them less than
two hundred yards. He never got to feel how they handled on
the open road, and besides, even if he'd been given a chance
to drive a sports car up the California coast, he wouldn't have
cared. The only thing that mattered to him was how much
trunk space each vehicle had.

The space was what mattered.

That and what kind of jewelry the owners of the cars—specifically the ladies—wore to the red-carpet events. Because Marc didn't park the cars for tips. Being a valet was just a role he played so he'd know which trunk to climb into at the end of the night.

Most people would have called Marc a thief.

He liked to think of himself as a professional.

Either way he was raking in huge bucks.

During his last trip to New York City and its famous Diamond District—he'd driven cross-country all by himself, in three days no less—he'd fenced a pair of sapphire earrings studded with diamonds and netted twenty grand in cash. The gaudy blue stones had been five carats each, and the lonely eared woman he'd swiped them from had also been wearing a gold bracelet laced with rubies that he'd sold for another ten thousand.

It amazed him that the vast majority of celebrities had no taste. He was something of an expert on the subject. He'd seen with his own eyes how difficult it was, if not impossible, for a certain category of rich or famous women to resist the temptation to drape themselves in the bulk of their jewelry box while attending a red-carpet event.

For Marc that group was easy to spot: female stars who were a few too many years past the cursed number forty, and whose phone had stopped ringing; or else trophy wives who had visited their plastic surgeons one too many times to suction off fat that would have better been shed with diet and exercise. Either group was, to Marc, the equivalent of walking pawnshops.

"Scratch it and you're dead," a producer snapped at Marc as he handed over the keys to a black Mercedes sports coupe, while another parking attendant helped the man's wife out through the passenger door.

Marc recognized the guy—Barry Hazen, executive producer on tonight's film. By all rights Hazen should have been the man of the hour. Yet Marc knew—as did anyone remotely connected to the business—that Hazen had not worked on the film at all. The guy was filthy rich. He and his partners owned a medium-size production company. All he did was write checks. He never made creative decisions. Yet, with his cash, he was able to put his name on films he probably couldn't even follow.

That was fine with Marc. Because even though Mr. Hazen was sixty years old with snow-white hair and an Armani tux, Mrs. Hazen was a thirty-year-old redhead wearing a diamond necklace with a central rock the size of a golf ball. It was so big it must have started forming back when the dinosaurs walked the earth. Marc could only dream what he could hock it for.

Marc smiled as he took the man's keys. "Have no fear, Mr. Hazen. I know a secret spot I can stow this baby where God himself couldn't touch it."

Mr. Hazen nodded his approval. "We'll be here late. Stay behind and pick it up for me and I'll make it worth your while."

"Absolutely," Marc said. He always stayed late for the after-picture party so he could prey on that one couple he'd select who would return home so tired and drunk that they'd fall into bed the instant they entered their house. But whoever that couple turned out to be—so far the Hazens looked good, but Marc knew he'd have several candidates before the night was over—he'd have to clock out before they returned for their car.

Why? The answer was simple. He had to be finished with his work so he could ride home with the couple in their trunk.

Marc hopped in the car and headed straight for Hollywood Boulevard without bothering to check the back, tearing around the block. Grauman's had been built ages ago, in the era of black-and-white films, and its parking lot could accommodate only a fraction of the valet traffic. Nowadays the best place to stow a Mercedes was in the mall next door. It had a ten-level parking structure and from experience Marc knew how early the bottom level emptied. It was perfect; it gave him more than enough privacy to keep up his lucrative side job.

He stashed Hazen's sports car in a spot he reserved for his most promising candidates. Besides being physically isolated, it was outside the range of any security cameras and had a seldom-used janitor's closet where he could store the tools of his trade and work without being interrupted.

Marc hurried to that closet and locked the door behind him. From a box hidden in the corner beneath a filthy sink, he took out a flat, two-inch-square steel case loaded with putty. Separating the Mercedes's key from the rest of Hazen's keys, he placed it inside the case and pressed the top shut.

Making the impression of the key was easy—the remainder of the process took patience and skill. Opening the case and removing the key, he reached for a tube of oily brown goo that could best be described as "plaster-glue," and squeezed it into the impression.

Marc didn't know the exact chemical makeup of the material, nor did he care. All that mattered was that it dried fast and hard, which it did when heated. That was its only drawback and the main reason why it wasn't as easy to duplicate keys as most people thought. To speed up the process he kept a battery-powered heater running in the janitor's closet. He kept extra cases on hand as well. There were nights he'd go through a dozen of them and prepare a dozen spare keys.

Yet in the end he'd use only one key and sneak into only one house—if he was lucky. A lot of factors had to come together for his plan to work. So far, after a year of parking celebrity cars and working over twenty red-carpet events, he'd managed to slip into only seven homes. And out of those seven he'd only struck gold four times.

Of course, the gold had been attached to jewels . . . so he couldn't complain.

Marc finished applying the plaster and again closed his steel case and held the top tight for a minute without moving an inch. Then, after opening it and leaving the case and the key atop the heater to dry, he cleaned Mr. Hazen's original key with a paper towel soaked in alcohol and bleach. Whenever he managed to steal something beautiful and expensive, he knew there was no easier way for the police to trace the crime back to him than if he left even the tiniest residue of putty on the original car key.

Since Hazen was his first candidate of the night, Marc was out of practice and it took longer than usual before he was able to exit the janitor's closet—six whole minutes. The process should have taken him half that time.

Damn, he thought. His boss, Steve Green—a rough-voiced ex-sailor from Australia and the head of the valet parking—was going to wonder what was taking him so long.

Yet when Marc finally did leave the janitor's closet, he did so without the fake key in hand. From practice, he knew it was best to let it dry on the heater for at least twenty minutes. The hotter it got, the harder it got.

When Marc got back to the theater, his boss did in fact ask where the hell he'd been. "Got caught behind a couple of cop cars while swinging around the block," Marc lied.

"Did they stop you?"

"Almost. I was speeding."

Green grinned his approval. He was famous for taking Jags

and Porsches out for a spin during the downtime in the middle of the movie.

Marc grinned along with his boss but cringed inside. The fact Green had noticed the delay was not good. It was reason enough to cross the Hazens off his list of candidates.

"Where'd you park Hazen's Hard-on?" Green asked. It was a common belief among the people who worked valet that most celebrity cars were phallic symbols.

Marc handed over the keys to his boss. "Next door, level G, south corner, slot nineteen, away from everyone else. You know how that asshole is about his wheels."

Green nodded as he hung the keys on the appropriate hook. "You can't be too careful with the guy who's paying for the party. He can get us all fired."

Marc relaxed as he noticed how fast his boss dropped the matter. But it was a warning he'd have to pick up his duplicating pace. At the same time, he'd have to be more selective about whom he chose as candidates.

Yet he knew he couldn't control all aspects of the heist. A large part of being a successful thief was luck. For example, how late a couple was going to leave, and how drunk they were going to be—he couldn't predict that ahead of time. That's why he had to make so many extra keys. He had to play the odds.

The time for the premiere drew near and traffic picked up. Marc found himself running back and forth from the valet booth with hardly a chance to catch his breath. However, he did manage to identify another three targets.

First came Mr. and Mrs. Kollet, who were connected to the studio that was distributing the film. They would definitely be staying late for the after-film party. Mrs. Kollet was wearing a diamond bracelet that literally dazzled Marc's eyes. As an added bonus, the couple stumbled getting out of their car and he needed only a whiff of the vehicle's interior to know they were already drunk—always a plus.

Second was Cynthia Parker, one of the most brilliant scriptwriters in the city. Although she wore a relatively modest red gown, around her neck was a string of pearls that looked like they had once belonged to a European court. The individual pearls were not excessively large but had a silver-white color that gave them what the muse in Ms. Parker might have called an "angelic sheen." Marc was careful to park her car next to the Hazens' and make a copy of her key.

Finally, there was the star of the film, Silvia Summer, and her football star boyfriend, Ray Cota of the San Francisco 49ers. They arrived late in a white Jaguar and received the loudest cheers from the gathered fans. Ms. Summer was young, but rich and successful—in the top three on the A-list of talent in her age bracket—eighteen- to twenty-five-year-olds. She'd been the lead in two hits; this would probably be her third.

Ms. Summer wore a heart-shaped emerald at the end of a gold necklace. Marc had seen plenty of emeralds in his time and knew the stone was notorious for its number of inclusions—natural flaws that showed up as dark spots under close inspection. Yet because he opened the door for her and because her breasts would have stolen the eyes out of the head of any red-blooded American male, he inadvertently got a closer look at the emerald than he planned and could have sworn it was close to flawless.

"Welcome," Marc said with a genuine smile as he shut the car door behind her. "It's an honor. I've seen all your movies. I hear you're great in this one."

Unlike most stars of her wattage level, she took the time to look him in the eye and reply. She even leaned close so that only he could hear. "I look good because everyone else sucks," she confided.

Mark had to laugh. "I heard that as well."

She paused and stared at him. She was blond and beautiful, sure, but sharp as well. He could spot her intelligence in the way she studied him, and it made him wonder if it was wise to choose her as a candidate. Stealing a necklace from a movie star was one thing—not getting caught was another. It might have been a mistake to speak to her. Her gaze continued to linger.

"You don't look like the sort of guy who should be parking cars," she said.

Marc shrugged. "It pays the bills."

Again, she came near. "For now. But there's something

in your eyes. Trust me, one day you're going to be somebody."

It was a moment, a special moment, but it didn't last. At
that instant her boyfriend swept around the Jaguar, tossed
his keys high in the air to Marc—who caught them without
blinking—and led Ms. Summer onto the red carpet and
toward the theater entrance.

Marc was fortunate to end up with the keys. Ordinarily
the driver handed them to whoever opened the driver's door.
Marc was as far from superstitious as a guy could be. Even
as a four-year-old, bouncing from one orphanage to another,
he'd realized Santa Claus had been invented to sell more toys.
But he trusted his gut and didn't feel it was a coincidence that
he'd ended up with the keys to Ms. Summer's car. He thought
somebody was trying to tell him something.

It turned out her Jaguar was the last car he parked before
the film began. Marc put it near the Hazens' Mercedes, on
the bottom level of the mall lot. He took his time making an
impression of her key, and took even more time cleaning the
original.

He had selected only four targets, which was unusual for
him—last time he'd had ten at this stage. Yet all four were
prime: They had the jewels; their connection to the picture was
such that they'd all stay late; he'd been able to make an impression of their car key; and they all had plenty of trunk space.

Now it was all a question of timing.

It was against the rules for the valet crew to watch the film, but Green was a laid-back boss and let Marc and a buddy of his, Teddy Fox, slip into the theater fifteen minutes after the movie started. All the seats were taken and they had to stand at the rear, but Marc didn't mind. He found a marble wall to lean against and rested the back of his head on the cool stone. It was a relief to rest for a few minutes and the film wasn't half bad.

It was a romantic comedy structured around a mystery. A couple were only an hour away from getting married when both their wedding rings vanished. At the start the story focused on a search for the clever thief, but it was the buried doubts about the marriage that the crime suddenly raised in the bride and groom that created the bulk of the laughs. Silvia Summer had been too hard on the film. The crowd spent most of the movie laughing out loud. Ordinarily Marc was demanding when it came to films, but even he couldn't resist chuckling a few times. He especially enjoyed the lead actress. Ms. Summer was even more stunning on the big screen.

He kept thinking how he'd like to see her again, socially. A silly thought, sure—she had a boyfriend and he was a nobody. But the remark she'd made getting out of her car—it had stayed with him.

What had she seen in him? It couldn't have been his face, although there were plenty of girls who thought he was worth a second look. It was like they had connected for an instant in some mysterious way. The simple fact was he liked her, and he found it ironic that the feeling made his desire for her necklace even greater, when it should have been the other way around.

He didn't dwell too long on the paradox. He knew the way his mind worked. He had two trains racing in the two hemispheres of his brain that unfortunately were usually on the same track and racing toward each other, which was another way of saying that he was pretty sure he was screwed up.

That was okay, he accepted it, he had to accept it; no one had given him a choice. He knew something of psychology. He hadn't had a lot of basic education but he read plenty. The fact that he had grown up without a single parent, biological or foster, and had been living on his own since the age of fifteen—often on the streets—it was a miracle he wasn't already dead or in jail.

Of course, the night was still young.

Marc rubbed his hands together in anticipation as he watched the film. He was sweating but it was a sweet sweat. He stole for money, that was obvious, but the deeper reason was the action, the rush it gave him. All the planning, all the hoops he had to jump through, the constant risk, the countless on-the-spot decisions he had to make—bundle it all together and it gave him an adrenaline high he couldn't find anywhere else. Often, he thought, he'd be a thief even if there was no payoff.

The film ended and the crowd gave it a standing ovation, partly because it was a pretty good film but mostly because the audience knew the picture's creators were in the theater and hoping they'd stand and cheer. The director and the producer delivered brief thank-you speeches, and then it was party time.

Only half the audience had passes to the party, but because the theater was so large that was still close to five hundred people. Marc knew for a fact all four of his candidates would be at the party. It was held at an elegant hotel across the street from the theater and halfway down the block. It was not unusual to hear a number of celebrities grumble as they made the short trek, although no one had to worry about traffic or lights—the cops invariably blocked off Hollywood Boulevard immediately after the film.

Marc would like to have walked with the crowd to the party and study his candidates more closely, but he had to get back to work. On average he got tipped ten bucks a car—nothing to sneeze at when he could pick up ten to fifteen cars an hour.

After ninety minutes the number of guests looking for their vehicles dropped, and Green usually let two-thirds of the valets go home. However, because Marc had been on the job a year, and Green liked him, he was always allowed to stay late.

It was at this point that Marc had to push his plan to the next level. There was no way to make a final decision on who to go home with without slipping into the party and taking a last look at his candidates. For one thing, he had to be sure they were still at the party. It was always possible a candidate could have slipped out while he was off finding a car.

The movie had ended at ten p.m. The director and producer had spoken until ten fifteen, and the party had begun at ten thirty. From experience Marc knew he could slip into the party—without a pass—from midnight on. Security grew lax as the night wore on, and besides, his valet uniform gave him a cloak of respectability. After telling Green he had to use the restroom, Marc stole into the hotel and went upstairs to the party—which was spread over three areas: a charming lounge; a massive conference room; and an exotic outdoor section that circled a delicious swimming pool.

It was a warm night—most people were outside by the pool, which glowed a haunting aquamarine while also reflecting rows of flaming torches. There were open bars inside and out and it was the rare person who wasn't drinking.

Marc spotted three of his candidates spread around the pool. The only person he couldn't locate was Cynthia Parker, the scriptwriter. She had probably split immediately after the film without his knowing. Hell, she had written the damn thing— she might have gotten up and walked out in the middle. Marc knew that most writers found it hard to see their work on the screen. They usually focused too much on how the director had ruined their material.

So he was down to the Hazens, the Kollets, and Silvia Summer and her boyfriend, Ray Cota, the football jock. Marc strolled by each couple, studying them carefully but not allowing them to see him.

The Hazens were both drunk, no question, and Marc would have considered taking them on but they were so intoxicated he worried his boss, Green, would recognize their condition and not allow them to drive home. Indeed, he might stuff the Hazens in a taxi—whether they agreed or not—and send them on their way. Marc had seen Green do it before.

Mr. Kollet was also staggering around but, surprisingly, his wife, who had smelled of alcohol at the start of the night, now appeared sober. Marc saw she was holding a glass of what looked like Coke, which made him wonder if he had misread her from the start. It was possible her husband's breath had been so strong it had polluted her aura. Whatever, she looked a hundred percent sober, which meant her diamond bracelet was probably off-limits.

Silvia Summer and her boyfriend made for an interesting mix. Ray Cota had a drink in his hand and was laughing plenty loud at every joke but he looked like the sort who could hold his liquor. Green wouldn't be worried about Ray driving home.

But Silvia Summer was a puzzle. Marc studied her a grand total of twelve minutes and saw her down two tall margaritas. Yet she wasn't laughing and socializing with her boyfriend. Indeed, she stood a few feet away, by herself, staring off into the distance. Something had upset her, Marc thought. She had been fine earlier. He could hardly believe it when, right as he was leaving the pool area, she strode to the bar and ordered a third drink.

That was a lot of booze to swallow in such a short period. She was not a big girl—her blood alcohol must have been off the chart. From a strategic point of view that was perfect. The essence of his scheme depended on the female he chose returning home too tired and too intoxicated to put her jewelry away in a secure place—like a high-tech home safe.

During his four previous successful heists, the women had invariably dumped their jewelry on top of their chest of drawers or on their bathroom counters and had then fallen into bed in a coma beside their husband or boyfriend. Tonight, all night, he had been praying that the identical scenario would repeat itself.

Yet seeing Silvia upset bothered Marc and he wasn't sure why. They'd only exchanged a few words. True, she had treated him with respect, but lots of pretty women had given him a wink and a smile. Being upset would make her careless. He should see her dark mood as a plus. Yet as he left the party, it gnawed at him that something had happened that had disturbed her.

Maybe she had hated the movie.

It only made it worse that he had *almost* made up his mind whom he had to go after. It should be Silvia Summer. She and her wide-receiver boyfriend fit most of the criteria on his self-made list. Plus it didn't hurt that her emerald was the most expensive piece of jewelry he'd seen all night.

He was probably going to steal it from her. She would

wake up in the morning and it would be gone. That would be a shame. Of course, it was more than likely she had borrowed the necklace. Few stars her age had giant emeralds in their private collection. Chances were her stylist had picked it up at a Beverly Hills store that afternoon with the understanding it would be returned within twenty-four hours. That was standard in the business.

However, Silvia would still be responsible for the necklace. Filing a police report would not make that responsibility vanish. Granted, she probably had insurance, but he'd still be putting her through a ton of grief. And there was still a chance the necklace belonged to her. For all he knew it might have sentimental value.

There were a few other details that made him hesitant to go after her emerald. The exquisite nature of the stone, its uniqueness, the fame of the last celebrity to wear it—all these points would make it difficult to fence. Even if he drove all the way to New York, it was possible he'd have trouble finding a buyer. There was no question the stone's heart shape would have to be ground away. It was even possible he'd have to break it into a half dozen smaller stones. He was no expert when it came to the craft, but he was no slouch, either. Definitely, it would be safer to break it down.

Yet it was such a beautiful stone.

It would be a pity to ruin it.

"Shut the fuck up, would ya," Marc told his mind as he

headed back to the valet station, which had temporarily moved across the street to the hotel lobby to take care of the last of the evening's clients. He knew all the cons about stealing the emerald and in the end they were all bullshit. Silvia was a near perfect candidate and she was wearing a near perfect stone.

The bottom line was what the emerald was worth. Retail, it had to cost at least five million, maybe as high as ten. That meant he could get at least a million for it in the Diamond District, maybe two million, more than all his previous jobs combined. No way was he going to walk away from that kind of cash.

It was decided.

He had to get into Silvia's trunk and soon.

"I'm beat. Would it be all right if I called it a night?" Marc asked Green as he walked up to the counter they had set up in the hotel lobby. All the guests had been previously told that this was the place to pick up their cars.

Marc added a yawn as he made his request and his boss gave him a nod. "I've still got Ted, Jerry, and Sandy running the route," Green said. "They should be enough." He added, "I hope."

"I can stay, you know, if you're worried."

Green glanced at the key hooks. "Did the party look like it was winding down?"

Marc hesitated. "Why you asking me?"

"Sandy said she just saw you up there."

Marc kept his outward composure but inside he grimaced. If he managed to steal the emerald, any unusual behavior on his part could later trigger an alarm. Green was a nice guy but no dummy. If the cops came by later and started asking questions, he might remember this exact moment.

Marc spoke causally. "I just took a quick look at the buffet." He added with a hint of guilt, "Well, actually, I sort of sampled the shrimp."

Green brightened. "Was it good?"

Marc grinned. "Fantastic. And they have a huge spread of sushi. If you're quick, you should be able to load up before they put it away."

Green shook his head. "Got to stay here."

Now was a perfect opportunity to negate any suspicion. Granted, it might cost him a shot at the emerald, but it would make it clear to his boss that he'd only gone upstairs for the food.

"Bullshit," Marc said, taking a step behind the counter. "I can handle the stragglers for a few minutes."

"You sure? You said you're exhausted."

"Hey. I'm nineteen years old. I never go to bed till four in the morning. Go now, quick, and put together a bag that will last you the rest of the week. There's only one caterer left and she won't care what you swipe. You know they just throw out what's left over." Marc added casually, "Oh, I saw some Alaskan crab fish."

"Are you shitting me?" his boss asked, a gleam in his eyes. Marc had seen Green eating crab fish a month ago and knew they were his favorite. He also knew there were plenty left.

Marc snorted. "Stop yapping and go. I did graduate from high school. I can hand out a few keys for a few minutes."

The sad truth was he hadn't graduated from high school.

"Thanks," Green said, turning for the elevator. Marc wouldn't be surprised if his boss returned with several bags of goodies. Green had a pregnant wife at home and was always complaining about how hungry she was for exotic food.

As it turned out the Hazens came looking for their car while Green was gone, and Marc had to tactfully tell the bigwig that he was too drunk to drive. Immediately, Mr. Hazen started swearing at him but just as fast Mrs. Hazen jumped in between them and told her husband to shut his trap.

"Larry, you apologize to this nice young man," she said. "He's just doing his job and he might have just saved our lives. You know we're in no shape to drive."

Mr. Hazen calmed down fast enough, although he didn't bother to offer an apology. He plopped down on a nearby chair and belched loudly. "Shit. Somebody call us a cab."

Marc signaled for a taxi that was waiting outside and opened the door for Mrs. Hazen, who slipped him a hundred dollars before climbing inside. Marc shook his head like it was too much but the woman insisted.

"It's for having to listen to my husband," she said. "He acts like an old goat when he drinks but I still love him."

"Just get home safe, Mrs. Hazen," Marc said. "I'll leave a note for your car to be sent over in the morning."

"Thank you, dear," she said.

Green was gone longer than Marc expected—a full twenty minutes. During that time the Kollets came for their car. Now the decision had been plucked from his hands. Either he went after Silvia or waited until next time. Yet he knew it was unlikely that he'd ever have a shot at such a large stone again. That was what kept him focused. If he could steal and fence the emerald, he'd be able to quit his life as a thief and get on to something important.

Whatever that might be . . .

In reality he'd be forced to quit. As it was he was already playing Russian roulette with the LAPD. Eventually the string of missing jewels would be traced back to the theater's valet service, and to him. No way he was hanging around until he got caught. Tonight's job had to be his last.

Clocking out, Marc crossed the street to the mall's parking structure and headed straight for the janitor's closet. The battery-operated heater had warmed the confined space to over a hundred degrees. Ordinarily he'd hide the heater in the corner of the closet, but since tonight would hopefully be the last time he'd use it, he decided to dump it and the extra cases somewhere outside the mall.

The decision carried with it its own risks. It was after two in the morning and Silvia and her boyfriend would be wanting their car soon. If he left the mall to dump his equipment, one of the other valets might come for the Jaguar at that exact moment.

Yet he decided it was worth the risk. He couldn't leave the tools of his trade behind for a detective to find. Collecting his used and unused steel cases, the heater, and two spare tubes of the magic plaster mix, he stuffed everything in a canvas bag and headed for the door.

He was out on Hollywood Boulevard in a minute. He had scouted the surrounding area earlier. Small details mattered. He knew of a family-owned pizza joint three blocks north of the mall. It had a large Dumpster that was unloaded every Sunday morning, which would be tomorrow, before ten. He considered three blocks the minimum distance to safely dispose of his equipment. Even if he managed to steal the emerald, and some brilliant cop quickly traced the theft back to the theater, he or she wouldn't have time to search several city blocks for clues before his stash disappeared.

Yet the three blocks were long blocks and he had to force himself not to run. Running people looked like guilty people, particularly at night, and especially when they had a bag in their hands. The whole way to and from the pizza joint, he kept thinking that Silvia would have already come for her car and split.

But the Jag was still there when he returned to the mall.

He studied it before trying out his newly minted key. The trunk was on the small size—he'd glanced at it before but had failed to scrutinize it—and there was nothing worse than getting trapped in a trunk. It had happened to him only once, but that had been one time too many.

It had been an old Mercedes, from the sixties, built like a tank, and it had not come equipped with a child's safety-release lever—the kind that were nowadays standard on most vehicle trunks as well as refrigerators. Worse, the lock on the car's trunk had not responded to his usual bag of tricks, and he hadn't even been able to push out the backseat and crawl into the interior of the car. In the end he'd spent an entire night sweating in the garage of a mansion he'd never actually seen and needing to pee so bad he'd finally pissed all over the spare tire.

He had only managed to escape the next afternoon when the owner had taken the car to get washed. Fortunately the guys at the car wash had been mostly illegal immigrants and hadn't questioned the mysterious character who had suddenly popped out of the trunk in a white shirt, black pants, and black tie—his basic valet attire—and run like hell into a nearby alley.

Since that happened, he never climbed into a trunk without carrying a mini crowbar.

Marc noted that Silvia's Jag had a high-tech alarm system but was not overly worried. The best alarms had trouble identifying a fake key. However, as a safety precaution, it was still best to pop the trunk from inside the car, from the driver's seat, after slipping the key in the ignition and turning it partway. A retired owner of a car dealership had taught him that little trick. It *reassured* the computer chip in the most sophisticated car alarms.

For the first time, Marc took out the case that held the Jaguar's copied key. It had a couple of rough edges but he was able to file them off with a small tool kit he always carried on any job. It *looked* perfect but he nevertheless held it up to the light and gave it a final exam, once again thankful his section of the parking structure was not covered by security cameras.

Then he slid the key in the lock and turned it.

Presto! It opened without a hitch.

Moving fast, Marc climbed in the car, leaving the door open, and slipped the key in the ignition, turning it a millimeter shy of starting the car. At the same time he scanned for an interior trunk release, finding one on the bottom of the driver's door beside a gas-tank release. He pressed it and the trunk popped open. Turning the ignition off, he withdrew the key and climbed out and locked the door behind him.

Time to get in the trunk. For some reason, for Marc, this part was harder than sneaking into a couple's bedroom while they were sleeping. He'd read somewhere that everyone suffered from some degree of claustrophobia—it was just a question of how much. He wasn't sure where he fell on the scale but doubted he would have made it as an astronaut.

The Jaguar's trunk was clean and empty but tight. It made sense, it was a sports car. Christ, it didn't even have a backseat. He'd known that ahead of time; nevertheless, it still annoyed him. Or perhaps "intimidated" him would've been a more accurate word.

Marc took off his valet vest and pulled out a pair of surgical gloves and a surgical cap and put them on. He'd seen too many reruns of *CSI*, *NCIS*, *CSI: Miami*—and *CSI: Lunar*, he snickered to himself—to dare leave behind any fingerprints or hair in the trunk. He even dabbed his eyebrows with Vaseline. Best to be paranoid when one damn molecule of his anatomy could strand him in the slammer for a decade.

Finally, Marc climbed into the trunk and pulled it shut.

It was dark inside and it felt stuffy. The only way he could fit in and maintain blood flow to all his limbs was to squeeze into the fetal position. He wiggled around with his back to the front and his face toward the rear. He had little room to move his arms and that concerned him. Later, when it was time to leave the trunk, he'd need his hands free if the release paddle failed. Of course there was no reason to think it should fail, but tell that to Murphy and the law named after him. Marc occasionally wondered who the real Murphy had been. The guy must have had a miserable life.

Marc was in the trunk ten minutes when Sandy came for the car. God, he thought, that had been close. He knew it was Sandy because she always sang to herself while she worked.

Sandy was a couple of years older—she'd just celebrated her twenty-first by getting drunk with the guys at work. Marc had a lot of respect for her. She hustled to park and pick up the cars and was always polite to the clients. She never bragged when she got a big tip. But what he liked most about her was that she was unimpressed with stars—it didn't matter how important they thought they were. To Sandy they were just people.

Marc was attracted to her and knew she liked him, but he'd never asked her out because of his side business. The possibility was remote, but if he ever got busted and they were dating, the cops might assume she was working with him, or at the very least knew about the thefts. There was no way he would ever put her in that kind of position. She was a classy chick. She went to college during the day, carried a full load of classes, and was going to be a dentist or a doctor—something like that.

Sandy, though, drove like a maniac. He'd never been in the trunk of a car when she was behind the wheel, and to put it modestly, it was a novel experience. Marc swore if he hadn't been crammed in so tight, he would have broken bones. She had something against the brake—she never used it, not even on sharp corners. He literally heard bones in his back and neck crack when she swung onto Hollywood Boulevard.

They reached the hotel in record time.

Ray Cota chatted with Sandy as she handed off the Jag to him. Sandy even wished Ray good luck on his upcoming NFL season. But Marc didn't hear a word from Silvia Summer.

Clearly the two were not doing well. They were on the road five minutes before Ray finally spoke to her.

"Are you going to talk to me tonight?" he asked. Marc sure hoped so. There was every possibility the car belonged to Ray, and if he didn't spend the night with Silvia, then Marc would end up breaking out of a garage and into a house with nothing to steal but sports trophies.

"What do you want to talk about?" Silvia muttered.

"She didn't give me her number because I asked for it," Ray said. "We were just shooting the breeze."

"Bullshit."

"Come on. It's late, we're both tired. Nothing happened."

"You call hustling the new phone number of an ex-girlfriend nothing."

"Karmen was never a girlfriend. I told you that."

"You also told me that you screwed her once. Oh, no, wait. I remember now. You had sex with her off and on for six months—while she was dating your best friend." Silvia paused and spoke in a slurred voice. There was no question she was drunk. "Maybe I should give Matt a call."

"Matt's in New York. All that happened in New York. It had nothing to do with what's happening between us now."

Silvia laughed lazily. "God, you're one of those guys who thinks morals are inversely proportional to the distance you are from your true love."

"Huh?"

Her tone suddenly hardened. "Karmen's here now! She's here in LA! And I go to the restroom for five minutes and you're off in the corner feeling up her tits."

"That's a lie! I didn't touch her!"

"You had your arm around her waist!"

Ray took a moment to respond. "She was as drunk as you are now. I shot out my arm to steady her. She could have fallen in the pool."

"Ha! You steadied her, my ass! Your hand slipped and groped her ass the second you got her back on her feet."

Ray had probably had too much to drink himself. His answers were slow in coming and did not win him any points. "You said I touched her tits. That's what upset you. Now you're saying it was her ass. Get your story straight, why don't you."

"Did someone crack your helmet or your head in practice or what? It doesn't matter where you touched her! It just matters that you did."

"She came on to me, I swear it. I didn't even want to talk to her."

Silvia snickered. "That I can believe! Why talk when you can just fuck? I mean, what do you have to talk about anyway? You use what's left of your skull to smash into people for a living. I can't remember the last time we had a serious conversation about anything. I'm not a hundred percent sure, but I'm beginning to think it's because you're too much of a moron to have one."

Ray's tone darkened. "You calling me stupid? I told you never to call me stupid."

"I called you a moron, stupid, but let me apologize. You're not a moron. Technically, moronic people have IQs in the fifty to seventy range. Yours has got to be at least ten points lower." Silvia paused. "I'm calling you an imbecile."

Marc felt the car swerve a little and heard Ray's voice get uglier. Still, he found it hard to keep from smiling. Silvia was pretty witty when drunk.

"You want me to take you home or not?" he asked quietly.

"I don't know. It's not like I have a lot of options."

Ray suddenly slowed. "I can drop you off right here if you want. Right there beside that homeless guy."

"Are you forgetting that this is my car? Why don't I drop you off?"

"Because you're loaded. You couldn't make it home with all that booze in your blood if you were bleeding to death."

Silvia was silent a moment then started to chuckle. "Ray, if I was bleeding to death I'd go to the hospital, I wouldn't drive home. You get it?"

"Yeah, I get it. I got it the moment we got to the theater. The way you flirted with that guy who took our keys. What did you say to him anyway? Why did he light up when you whispered in his ear?"

"I told him how cute he was and that I hoped we could hook up later because my boyfriend was a no-good, two-timing

SOB and I'd probably need some company after the film."

"And you accuse me of flirting with another girl. Bitch!"

Silvia laughed a moment then fell quiet. She spoke in a soft voice. "Just keep driving, all right? I don't want to talk to you again tonight."

Ray appeared to get the message and shut up. But then he turned on the radio, to a rap station, and a maze of high-priced speakers began to vibrate Marc's brain. The ten-inch woofer was the worst—the base sounded like thunder. All Marc could do was hold his hands to his ears and pray Silvia's house wasn't far.

In reality he had an idea where Silvia Summer lived. It was in either Pacific Palisades or Malibu; it was one or the other. He made it a point to scan the Internet to find out if a potential target lived in a house or in a high-rise condo. Climbing out of the trunk in a condo parking lot gave him no advantage whatsoever. He was fortunate that most people who could afford expensive jewelry could afford a house of their own. It was almost never a major stumbling point. He knew from his research that Silvia had a house.

The music went on for ten minutes or so before Silvia turned it off. Ray complained but she must have shut him up with a look, because he didn't turn it back on. They rode the rest of the way in silence. Marc's fear that Ray wouldn't be spending the night grew.

Then again, it was always possible Ray had picked her up

at her house in his own car and would leave her alone for the night. That would be ideal. It would be easier to sneak into the house with Silvia by herself.

Ray drove for a total of thirty-three minutes before pulling into a driveway and pushing a button that opened a garage door. He nudged the Jag inside and Marc heard the garage close behind them. It was only then Ray spoke to Silvia.

"Am I staying or going?" he asked.

Silvia opened her door. "I don't want you here."

Ray opened his door. "Sil, we need to talk. I'm . . . I'm sorry."

She slammed her door shut. "Not in the mood."

Ray was desperate now. "Can we talk in the morning? We have to talk."

Silvia seemed to think about that. "You can sleep downstairs and that's it. Come up to my room and I call nine-one-one and have you arrested. Clear?"

"That's pretty harsh."

"No. Calling the woman you say you love a bitch is pretty harsh."

They left the garage and entered the house. That was the last Marc heard of them. He knew he had reached the crucial moment. Above all else he had to be patient. He had to give them time to fall asleep. Not only to black out, but to enter a deep REM cycle, where a bomb could go off in the room and they wouldn't hear it. The smart thing to do was to stay in the trunk and wait at least an hour—two would be better.

But Marc knew he couldn't wait, at least not with the trunk closed. It had felt stuffy when he'd climbed into it, but now it felt as if there wasn't an oxygen molecule left in the cramped space. He was having trouble catching his breath. He tried to convince himself it was all in his head, that the trunk wasn't vacuum sealed, but it didn't help. As long as they had been on the road, he had felt a faint cool breeze entering from a tiny hole somewhere. But now it was like he was locked in a tomb.

He wouldn't enter the house, he swore to himself. He wouldn't even get out of the trunk. But he had to open the hood. He needed fresh air.

Marc pressed the emergency release paddle and the trunk popped open. The first thing he did was break a cardinal rule.

He climbed out of the trunk and stood up and stretched. It was dumb and he knew it. Silvia and Ray had been inside only a few minutes, and a high percentage of people were forgetful and left either their cell phone, wallet, or purse in the car after arriving home, and had to run back out to the garage to get it.

He knew he should have waited at least twenty minutes before climbing out of the trunk. If he had half a brain he would get back inside. Yet the thought of doing so made his heart pound. His claustrophobia must be getting worse—another sign it was time to move on to another line of work. He swore right then that if he got the emerald that would be the end. He'd work at the theater another month or so just to allay any suspicions and then he'd quit.

He liked boats, he loved fishing. He'd always dreamed of moving to a small island near Fiji and buying his own boat and starting a fishing service. If he could get a million for the emerald, he could make the dream a reality. Captain of his own boat—lots of chicks would go for that.

Maybe even Silvia Summer.

He still hated the fact that she was his target.

Yet he hated Ray Cota more. Silvia was right, that jock's brains were mush. Marc was confident there was nothing Ray could say to her in the morning that would keep her from dumping him.

"Yeah, she's going to dump him for you, right," he whispered to himself. The truth is all would be forgiven in the morning. It was even possible Silvia wouldn't remember the fight. She was awfully drunk.

The minutes crept by and no one came anywhere near the garage. He kept his gloves and surgical cap on. Leaving a hair or prints at the house would be just as bad as leaving them in the car. He kept his ears peeled but heard nothing from inside.

He began to pace to help pass the time. He liked to think of himself as a pro, but sitting still for long periods of time was a skill he had yet to master. He was glad this would be his last job. It would be a relief. If he ended up with a windfall, and no detectives came around afterward to ask questions, he might even work up the nerve to ask Sandy out. He realized he hadn't stayed away from her just to keep her safe. She was smart, she was doing something with her life, she came from a good family.

The truth was she intimidated him. What could he say if she ever asked about his family? That he didn't have one? A smart girl like Sandy would know a guy who grew up without parents would have to be damaged. And Marc had no illusions in that department—he wasn't normal. What guy his age would be waiting in a dark garage for a famous movie star—hardly older than himself, really—to black out so he could slip into her bedroom and steal her necklace?

If Sandy could see him now she'd run the other way.

Marc managed to wait an hour. It was the maximum he could wait—the sun would be coming up soon. He had already checked the door and knew Silvia hadn't locked it behind her. They never did—they trusted in the garage door. Plus even if she had an alarm system—say, a motion-activated one—it wouldn't be on while she was in the house.

Before entering the house, he pulled a black ski mask over his surgical cap. He had earlier gone over it with a fine tooth comb. There wasn't a hair or skin flake on it. The mask would make him impossible to identify should he be spotted.

At exactly five in the morning, Marc opened the door and entered the house. He held his flashlight in his right hand but did not turn it on. He was in a compact laundry room. A light shone above the oven in the nearby kitchen. The solitary bulb would give him enough light to move around the bottom floor.

He didn't enter the kitchen. He heard a male snoring off to his right, down a short hallway. Silvia had said Ray was to sleep downstairs and that meant Marc was looking at a two-story house.

Ray's snoring was loud. He hadn't closed the door to the bedroom. Still, the fact that he wasn't in bed with Silvia was a major plus. It would be easier to face down a screaming hundred-pound actress than a two-hundred-pound NFL receiver. Yet Marc hoped it wouldn't come to that.

Marc swung around the kitchen, near Ray's bedroom door, and found the stairs. He'd been hoping they would be carpeted but they were solid cedar. The red wood looked cool, it smelled great, yet it would creak if he wasn't careful.

He moved onto the stairway—it spiraled as it rose—using the handrail for support, trying to ease the impact of his weight. He was pleased with his progress until he was two steps from the top. It was then he put his foot on a step that creaked so loud he thought his heart would burst. The sound seemed to echo through the house.

In reality it probably just echoed through his head. Silvia's bedroom door was also open—ten feet off to his left—and he could hear her soft breathing, and listened as it didn't alter with the sound of the creaking step.

Another positive sign. She was out cold.

The upstairs floor was carpeted, thank God. Marc was able to leave the stairway and peek into Silvia's room without making a peep. Her bed was king-size, off to the right a few feet, and she was sleeping on the far right side of it, away from the bathroom and the bedroom chest of drawers.

He saw all this without turning on his flashlight but it was a collage of shadows and silhouettes. He was relieved the carpet continued into the bedroom, but without another source of light he couldn't see any details. Specifically, he couldn't see where the necklace was.

His flashlight had cost him a pretty penny. It was narrow and coated with rubber so that it could fit comfortably in his mouth if he needed his hands free. More important, it had a choice of two filters he could flip over the lens: blue and red. The blue filter cut the brightness of the light by a factor of ten. The red one reduced it fortyfold.

In the past he'd used the blue filter every time. It allowed him to see a lot better. But something about Silvia worried him. She appeared to be out cold. She showed all the signs: slow breathing, lack of movement. Yet he *sensed* something coming from her, something he couldn't put into words.

He left his flashlight off.

He stood without moving for a long time. It might have been five minutes—maybe fifteen. It felt like an eternity and still Silvia didn't move or change her breathing or give him any other reason to keep him rooted in place. Yet there was just something about her that felt . . . off.

He finally took a step into the room; he took another. He paused between each one. Despite his claustrophobia, he was skilled at breathing softly. He breathed through his mouth, not his nose. The nasal cavities were narrow and his were stuffed up from being in that damn trunk.

He stepped all the way to the bathroom and saw and felt that he had reached the end of the carpet. From the texture, through the soles of his shoes, he felt as if he was stepping onto stone tile. He wanted to get all the way inside the bathroom before he turned on his light. He had already slipped the red filter into place and he'd long ago adjusted the switch so he could turn it on without making a sound.

Unfortunately, stepping into the bathroom was like stepping into a endless void. He didn't have a morsel of light to guide him. He could be about to step on a rubber duck for all he knew, one that quacked.

He had no choice. Aiming his light downward, cupping the lens with his palm, he turned it on. The red glow shimmered like a haunted spirit. A towel on his right leaped out at him; it hung from a gold hook. That was it, that was all he saw. He still had his hand over the lens. He stood without moving for another minute. He felt he had to wait, that he had to give Silvia a chance to betray herself.

She continued to breathe softly, like a child.

He slowly removed his hand from the lens and gasped.

Lying on the bathroom counter was the emerald necklace.

Beside it was a pair of emerald earrings.

Marc couldn't believe his luck. The gems were only a few feet away. If he took a step forward he'd have them. He'd be holding his future in his hands. He could slip an earring in both pockets, pick up the necklace, and turn off the light and walk out the bathroom door, out the bedroom door, then out the front door and begin a whole new life. It was all there in front of him and there was nothing to stop him.

Behind him Marc heard Silvia stir.

She rolled over and lay with her face in his direction.

His heart shrieked in his chest but he retained enough of his wits to flip off his light. He struggled to keep his breath silent. He wasn't worried about stepping on anything. Seconds ago, even in his exalted moment, he'd taken an inventory of the floor and it was clear of obstacles.

No, his fear was of Silvia herself. Why had she taken that exact moment to move? Had she heard something? Or had she been watching him all along, assuming he was Ray come to slip into her bed?

Marc found her timing too much of a coincidence.

It was possible she was playing with him.

Or rather, playing with Ray.

Slipping the flashlight in his back pocket, he stepped forward and put an earring in both his right- and left-front pockets. He wanted to keep them separate lest they bang into each other. Granted, they would hardly make a sound if they did collide, but any noise in a silent room was loud. The necklace he picked up with both hands. His right gripped the stone, his left the gold chain. He turned and stepped to the bathroom door and looked out.

Silvia's silhouette appeared to stare right at him. Her comforter lay halfway up her arm, barely covering her invisible breasts, and the amount of light was so low he could have been in outer space. Yet he knew she was naked. It was as if he could smell her bare skin, and what a smell it was. In that instant, for an instant, he forgot the jewel in his hand.

Then he shook himself. What was he doing? He was totally exposed! He had to get out of the room! He had to get out of the house! Silvia wasn't real. Sandy wasn't real. Nor was the first nineteen years of his life. The green jewel in his hands was all that mattered, the money it could bring, the freedom. Tonight, he could be born again.

Marc turned and walked toward the bedroom door. He was about to step into the hallway when Silvia spoke at his back in a weary tone.

"Come to apologize?" she mumbled, and even half asleep she had a note of sarcasm in her voice.

Marc thought frantically. She must have seen him, and if she hadn't, she knew he was there; or rather, she knew Ray was there. If he walked away he might annoy her. She might come after him. But how could he fake Ray's voice? His voice was totally different.

He'd done his reading, however, and knew it was difficult for people to tell who someone was when they whispered, even if that person was close to them. Never mind that it would be especially hard for Silvia to differentiate him from Ray in her exhausted and intoxicated state. He decided to risk it.

"Tired, let's talk in the morning," he whispered, before quickly leaving the door. With each step he took toward the stairway, he listened frantically. Yet before he even put his foot on the top step, he heard her breathing return to a child's rhythm. She had gone back to sleep.

Downstairs, standing in the kitchen beside a rack of keys, he thought of a wild idea. It came to him out of necessity. Prior to climbing in Silvia's Jag, he hadn't thought enough about the details of his escape.

Now he realized his predicament.

In the morning—or whenever Silvia and Ray woke up— they'd immediately know someone had stolen the necklace and they'd call the police. That would be fine, that was to be expected; he would be home in his studio apartment by then, probably asleep in bed.

But it would take him time to get home. From the faint sound of waves he could hear—for the first time—out the closed kitchen windows, he must be all the way up in Malibu, beside the beach. Which meant he sure as hell couldn't call for a cab to take him home. Once the theft was reported, any detective with a brain would check with all the taxi companies that serviced rich and famous Malibu to ask if they'd picked up a guy after four in the morning. That was a given.

In his four previous thefts, his escapes had been easy. He'd just hiked a few miles out of his victim's area before catching a late-night bus. He'd never been trapped in Malibu before. The town was extremely isolated, wedged in a long strip of land between the hills and the sea. Considering how long Ray had driven before they'd reached Silvia's house, he must be far up the coast. That meant the only way out of the area was to take the Coast Highway south.

But hiking along such a main road made him nervous. Cops were suspicious of guys walking alone in the dark, never mind that the sun would be up soon. True, he could stash the necklace in a tree or bush before leaving the area. If the police stopped him and searched him they wouldn't find anything.

Yet that wouldn't stop them from remembering him. And if they dragged him in for questioning, they'd soon learn where he worked and make the connection to Silvia's missing necklace.

Hiking out of Malibu was not an option.

Shit! Why hadn't he thought of all this before?

There was an alternative. He could hide the jewels nearby, then stay out of sight until ten or so in the morning before heading home. In the daylight he'd look a lot less suspicious.

Later in the afternoon, driving his own car, he could return to the area and pick up the necklace.

The idea had pluses but it had negatives as well. He wasn't dressed right to hang out at the beach, and for all he knew he was in a private beach area. Also, once the theft was called in, the cops would be all over this section of Malibu, searching for suspicious characters.

No, the bottom line was he had to get out of Malibu.

Now. That led him back to his crazy idea.

What if he jumped in the Jaguar, this minute, and just drove the hell out of here? It sounded insane but the idea had a lot going for it.

Ray was snoring up a storm but his room wasn't far from the garage, not like Silvia's. But what if Marc softly closed the door to Ray's bedroom? In their alcohol-induced stupors, would either of them hear the garage door open and close? The fact was Marc had been impressed how quiet the garage door opened and closed when they had arrived. The house was relatively new—it had the finest equipment.

Also, he was exhausted. He couldn't imagine spending the next six hours constantly looking over his shoulder, trying to creep home. If he took the Jag right now, he could be in his apartment in forty minutes, asleep in his own bed in less than an hour. And he wouldn't have to leave the necklace behind.

Even if Silvia or Ray did hear the garage door open and realized the car and the necklace were missing, by the time they called nine-one-one and the cops were able to respond, Marc knew he would at least have made it to Santa Monica—and that itself would be a great place to dump the car before finding a safe way home.

It was decided then. He was leaving in the Jag.

Leaving the necklace on the kitchen counter, Marc crept to Ray's room and gently closed the door. Ray continued to snore like a hog. Returning to the kitchen, Marc stuffed the necklace in his pocket and removed all three sets of keys that were hanging from the rack before heading for the same door he'd used to enter the house.

Sitting in the car in the closed garage, Marc decided to keep on his surgical cap and gloves but to remove his face mask. It was still plenty dark outside, but anyone who drove by and peered in his window might notice the mask. But the medical stuff—it would probably make him look like a young doctor driving home after a long night.

Marc pushed the button attached to the sun visor and the garage door opened smoothly. He backed up and pushed the button again the instant he reached the end of the driveway. The garage shut and the window to Silvia's bedroom remained dark. He paused for a minute a short ways down the road to see if it stayed that way and it did. No other lights went on.

He was in the clear. They were both still asleep.

The house Silvia lived in was half a football field from

the ocean. Her road led directly to Pacific Coast Highway, and soon Marc was flying south with a crazy grin on his face. He knew he must look like a madman but he couldn't get rid of the smile. He had never known such joy. He had no words for how he felt. He just prayed that the feeling lasted.

The fact that no extra lights had gone on in Silvia's house gave him the confidence to drive the Jaguar all the way to West Hollywood. But he made one major change to his wild plan as he approached his apartment. Before he dumped the car, he decided to swing by the place where he hid his hoard. Now he was anxious to get the necklace out of his pockets.

His hiding place was only a mile from where he lived, in an alley behind a row of buildings that should have been condemned twenty years ago. There, behind a stinking Dumpster that was no longer used, was a red brick wall with three loose bricks. Inside the wall was a narrow space surrounded by plasterboard on three sides and cheap wood paneling on the other.

Still being careful, he parked a block from the hiding spot, casually walked over to it, hid the necklace and earrings in a brand-new garbage bag, stowed it in the wall, and was back in the Jag in five minutes.

Now he had to get rid of the car. No sweat; he left the sports car locked on a residential street four miles from where Silvia had watched her film.

He was only two miles from home. It was a relief to finally be able to take off his gloves and cap. But despite his excitement, his fatigue hit him again and the two miles felt like a long way to walk. He was tempted to hop on a bus.

But even though his legs ached, walking home on the side streets was the smart move. Now that there was a glow in the east and the sun was about to rise, and he was back in Hollywood, no one would give him a second look.

The sun rose before he reached his apartment. He was only a quarter mile from home but he had to take a piss and couldn't wait. Sliding into another decrepit alley two blocks from his goal, he quickly relieved himself against a grimy wall and pulled up his zipper.

He turned to leave the alley when he suddenly realized he was walking in the direction of the sun, when it should have been at his back. He turned again and saw a second sun. For an instant he felt utterly disoriented. He turned back to the burning disk he had seen the first time and was forced to blink.

It had moved closer in the brief span he'd put his back to it, and it definitely wasn't the warm and soothing morning sun he'd known all his life. It wasn't even yellow. Rather, it had a glaring white center and was surrounded by a blazing violet halo. Both lights were suddenly so bright they momentarily blinded him and he instinctively raised his arm to protect his eyes.

A wave of intense heat swept over him.

A massive fist seemed to slam him from head to toe, from behind, shoving him toward the lights. He felt his feet lift off the ground and assumed he was about to fall forward. But for some reason he never hit the ground.

That was the last thing he remembered.

CHAPTER TWO

I SEE THEM, THE TWO OF THEM. THE MOST POWERFUL man in the world and the most dangerous woman. I know their names, their faces. I know their history. One I loved, one I feared—as recently as a month ago, just before I watched them die. Yet here they sit, at an outdoor table in the food court of the Century City Mall, eating bowls of ice cream.

Kendor and Syn.

Once upon a time they were the oldest couple on earth, perhaps the happiest—their love born of the Iron Age, more sturdy than that period, surely strong enough to withstand the challenge of centuries.

Yet slowly, over the years, grief had eaten away at Syn. The death of a son in battle; then, six hundred years later, the loss of a daughter to the plague, along with her daughter's offspring, a boy and a girl, Syn's grandchildren. Finally, the disappearance of Syn's last child—an idealistic young man who fled from

England to the New World to escape the horror his mother was becoming.

I suspect the sight of them feels even more bizarre because of the mundane nature of the setting. I mean, they're just sitting there eating ice cream in a food court.

I'm alone in the busy mall. I almost always shop alone, and I've just exited Bloomingdale's, where I purchased a gray pantsuit from the Anne Klein section. The suit is folded in a red box and tied with a white ribbon, and when I put it on for this evening's meeting and it makes me look older and more sophisticated than my eighteen years of age, then it will have served its purpose.

The outfit cost more than I used to spend on clothes in a year. The meeting I've been called to tonight is important. It's with the Council, the Tar, the elder witches that help guide the world, the real world and witch world, from behind the scenes. My own father has "ordered" me to attend the meeting, and Cleo herself, the leader of the Council, has called and requested my presence.

The thought of going makes me nervous. It's been a month since I stood before the group of ancient witches, and I've only a short time before my plane leaves for San Francisco, where the gathering is to take place.

Yet here, suddenly, out of nowhere, I see these two titans I watched die in witch world—an important point. Although had they perished in the real world—like my boyfriend, Jimmy, did—they still could exist in witch world. But death in witch world itself is the final death, or so I've been told, the one no one returns from.

Yet I'm in witch world now.

It makes no sense that they are still alive.

The sight of them paralyzes me. I fear they will see me; I literally can't move. Yet when they do happen to look in my direction—hell, I could swear they look right at me—I see no sign of recognition. I could be just another spoiled rich girl with a new outfit tucked under her arm. They simply keep on eating their ice cream. It's like they've never tasted anything so delicious.

Maybe they didn't see me, I think.

My legs are shaking, I have to sit down. I choose a table in the outdoor portion of the food court, where I can keep an eye on them, sitting behind a wooden post wrapped in thick green vines. I can see them but I don't think they can see me.

Of course, the way they're acting, it's like they couldn't care less that I exist. I idly wonder what kind of ice cream they're eating. Kendor keeps digging into his large plastic pink bowl. It looks like he's working on some kind of chocolate dish. Syn's eating something lighter, with strawberries and kiwis sprinkled over it; and the two are so totally absorbed in their dessert, they can't be bothered to exchange a single word.

Weird. The whole scene is just plain weird.

An old man suddenly approaches them. His clothes are

fairly ordinary. He wears a pair of black slacks and a loose-fitting white shirt. His dark sandals, though, are odd. No buckles, no straps, no shine; they look like someone carved them out of wood.

The guy is tall; he's got bulk without being fat. The word "burly" suits him. His hair is long and scruffy, more white than gray. Despite his age, his crusty skin, there's a spring to his step, to the way he moves. He's clean shaven but a part of me suspects that's a recent development. He looks like the sort that's used to a long beard and whiskers. If he weren't clean shaven, he could pass for a wizard. His eyes are a rarity; cerulean blue with a hint of green. My daughter has similarly colored eyes.

The old man sits at the table with Syn and Kendor as if they're old friends. They acknowledge his arrival with a nod and for once turn away from their ice cream. The man points in the direction of the movie theaters, and to the mannequins in a store window. He talks as he directs their attention and it's odd because it's as if he's explaining what they're seeing. It's only then I realize that might be exactly what he's doing. Syn and Kendor appear dazed, almost as if they're sleepwalking.

"Did the bastard drug them?" I say aloud, when I really should be asking how the guy brought them back to life.

They stand, the three of them, and the old man deftly guides them toward the nearby escalators. They head down, into the mall's parking structure, disappearing from view.

Quickly, I grab the box containing my new outfit and jump

to my feet and follow. I'm not a big believer in coincidence—I can only assume the old man chose to parade Syn and Kendor in front of me on purpose.

If that's the case, though, he goes to no trouble to wait for me in the underground lot. I barely catch a glimpse of the man helping Syn and Kendor into the backseat of a blue SUV—opening and closing the door for them—when I have to turn and run for my own car. It's like he's chauffeuring them around, while playing a game of cat and mouse with me.

I'm lucky to catch up with them at the booth at the exit—the SUV is right in front of me. The man hands his ticket to the attendant and the guy charges him for parking, which means they've been at the mall for some time. The first ninety minutes are free. When my turn comes, I'm waved through with hardly a pause.

I tail their SUV onto Wilshire Boulevard and worry as they drive into Santa Monica. That's where I live with Jimmy—even though I'm in witch world right now, I'm still not comfortable calling him James—and Lara and my mother. For several frantic minutes I'm sure they're headed to my home but they pass by my street until they hit Pacific Coast Highway, where they go north.

A feeling of déjà vu sweeps over me.

That's the same direction Marc Simona drove last night while hidden in the trunk of that movie star's car. It makes me wonder if the dream *does* have something to do with reality, in the real world or witch world.

Yet the old man doesn't take Syn and Kendor as far north as Marc traveled in my dreams. When they reach Sunset Boulevard, he turns right and heads into Pacific Palisades, turning left at a major artery that winds through a pristine community of new and expensive homes. He parks at an adorable house that sits on a corner property atop a bluff—that gives it staggering views up and down the coast. If nothing else the old guy must have money, I think. The garage door opens and he swings into the driveway, and Syn and Kendor vanish as the door closes behind them.

I park half a block away, across the street, and turn off my engine. I have my cell with me—now that I'm a mom I always have it with me—and know I should call my father. I've already promised him that I'd drive straight from the mall to the airport to catch my flight to San Francisco so I'd be on time for the Council's meeting. My dad hates that I'm not always punctual. Now, at the very least, it looks like I'll definitely be late, if I go at all.

But what's happening is extraordinary; I feel I have to check it out. Next to Cleo, Kendor was the most important person on the Council, and the fact that he's still alive is something they'd want to know.

Now that my dad's a full-fledged Council member, he's closed his surgical practice in Malibu and moved to the Bay Area. Or so he says. It still irks me that he moved out of LA just when I returned after a ten-year absence. I can't escape the feeling he's still avoiding me and my mother, although he swears that's not the case.

The Council will be equally as interested to hear that Syn is still alive, since she practically brought them to their knees four weeks ago. As the head of the Lapras, a group of evil witches that actively works against the Council, Syn was considered their most deadly enemy.

"I should warn them. I should warn them now," I say aloud, realizing that I'm mimicking Marc's habit of talking to himself when he's alone, even though I don't have his excuse of having grown up with no one around. I wonder what that must have been like for him, if it's one of the reasons he's so reckless with his life, and so bold.

Sure, the guy's a thief and I shouldn't admire him. But the truth is, having been in his mind, I do. Yet my admiration reaches only so far. For all I know, he might not even exist.

Despite my list of strong reasons to the contrary, I don't call my father. Again, I'm not sure why but I tell myself I can explain everything later tonight in person. Flights leave roughly every hour to the Bay Area from LAX. It's not as if missing a plane has to keep me in LA all night.

Fifteen minutes go by and I decide to split. I simply don't have the nerve to walk to the door and knock. Also, it'd probably be a foolish move. The Council has to hear what I've seen, and for all I know the old man might take me hostage. For that matter, Syn could kill me. She tried to kill me the last time we were together.

I start my car—it's a brand-new Honda Accord with a baby seat in the back—and go to pull away from the curb when I see the old man walking toward me. I come close to bolting, but he raises his hand and I stay put. Still, I keep the engine running with my foot near the gas. I'm frightened, big-time—my pounding heart feels like it could crack my sternum.

He knocks on my window and I push the button and lower it. Up close his eyes are even more striking, although I see they're not identical to my daughter's. Lara's are a solid warm aquamarine; the deep blue surrounding his pupils is streaked with jagged green spikes. The colors are irregular and the feeling his eyes give off is cold.

His face is more lined than I'd thought; however, they're fine lines, and for the most part his skin is taut although rugged. He's deeply tanned; he's seen many a bright sunrise, which might just be the underestimation of the year. . . .

For I have no doubt I'm looking at a witch, and an ancient one at that. The air around him seems to vibrate and he radiates immense power. He's another Cleo or Syn; it's possible he's stronger than the two of them put together.

Yet his voice, when he speaks, is remarkably soft.

"Hello, Jessica. Do you know who I am?"

I'm not sure until he asks. "The Alchemist."

"Kendor told you about me."

I nod. "He told me enough."

"You're afraid. There's no reason to be. I'm here to help you."

"I find that hard to believe."

"Your beliefs are unimportant. What is about to happen is. And you're unprepared."

"By 'you' do you mean me or the Council?"

"I'm talking to you."

"I suppose I should be flattered." When he doesn't respond, I add, "Why did you send me that note a month ago?"

"I wanted to introduce myself."

"Why?"

"Because you're unprepared."

"What are Syn and Kendor doing with you?" Once again he doesn't respond right away, just stares at me with his icy eyes. I keep talking to hide my fear. "She killed him. We killed her. It was here, in witch world; they should be dead."

"I know."

"How did you bring them back to life?"

"I didn't."

"Gimme a break."

"Their bodies are where you buried them, in the desert sand outside Las Vegas. You can dig them up if you wish."

"So what—you're hanging out with a couple of clones?"

"You're unprepared, Jessica."

"Damnit! Quit saying that and tell me what they're doing here!"

"They're here to prepare you." He gestures to the house. "Would you like to come inside?"

"No. I can't. I have an appointment."

He studies me. "Is it important?"

"Yes." I put the car in gear. "I have to go."

He nods. "Come again, when you have more time."

Without saying good-bye, I pull away as fast as I can, gunning the engine. Nothing he said made sense, obviously, but I haven't forgotten the horror stories Kendor told me about the man. Especially the time they spent together during Julius Caesar's most critical campaign—the Battle of Alesia. How the Alchemist first gave them the secret of gunpowder and turned the tide of the battle, only to demand the heads of a hundred thousand prisoners in payment.

Of course, that was two thousand years ago, but the cold I felt radiating from his eyes tells me his character hasn't improved in the ensuing centuries.

"He's not human," I keep whispering aloud as I head toward the airport. But perhaps I'm just trying to convince myself I didn't chicken out when I refused his invitation to enter his house.

It would have been wonderful to see Kendor again.

I miss my flight, no surprise, and have to wait ninety minutes to catch another one. I'm left with no choice—I have to call my father. He doesn't react well when I tell him how late I'll be.

"The meeting will be over by the time you get here," he says.

"I know. It couldn't be helped."

"You were told how important this is. Cleo's expecting you."

"I'll be there, and I'm sure you and Cleo will wait for me if it's that important."

My father takes a long time to reply. "Watch your tone. Being Lara's mother doesn't grant you any special status. Not when it comes to the Council."

I don't try to hide the annoyance in my voice. "When have I ever asked for anything from the Council?"

"Jessica . . . ," he begins.

"Or you?" I say, before hanging up. The instant I do so I feel like a fool for overreacting. Yet my anger remains. Calling my father, I'd hoped he'd first ask how I was doing, and how Lara was. But all he seems to care about is the Tar and their conflict with the Lapras. I know his work is important, of course; I just want his family to be important too—at least some of the time.

The flight to San Francisco takes only an hour, and when I land in the Bay Area I head to the Hertz counter to pick up a car to drive to the secret address I've been given. There I discover Hatsu waiting for me.

Hatsu is a short, fat Chinese man with severe facial scars.

Seen in an alley at night, he'd probably be mistaken for a serial killer, even though he's the kindest person on the Council.

When he sees me, his face explodes in a brilliant smile and he lifts me off the ground and plants kisses on both my cheeks—all before I can say hello.

"Hatsu! You shouldn't have come," I cry.

"I wanted to." He sets me back down but keeps his hands on my shoulders. "Look at you—you're so beautiful. James is one lucky guy. I hope he knows it."

"Ha! Trust me, I make sure he does."

"How's the baby doing? Keeping you up all night?"

I make a face. "You see the bags under my eyes? I love her to death but she's a handful. But maybe it's me, maybe I'm still a spoiled teenager. I'm not used to sleeping in short spurts. It gets exhausting."

"Don't be so hard on yourself. It's a major transition for any young woman. And remember most moms are given nine months to prepare. You were given one night."

What Hatsu says is true and false. Jessica, the person I am now—or I should say the *body* I'm in now—is in reality my witch-world counterpart. It's *her* body that had Lara. But *me*, the person I think of as me—the Jessie who now inhabits the witch-world version of Jessica's body—has barely any memory of even having given birth to a daughter.

It's a complex situation and yet, ironically, it's also extremely simple. Because I went through my death initiatory rite in the real world, my memories of Jessie from the real world stayed with me when I woke up in witch world. My father explained all this to me the night I discovered I was a witch.

But he also told me that over time, a few months, I'd slowly regain the temporarily lost memories of Jessica, my witch-world counterpart. Yet for some strange reason, my twin's memories are taking their time coming back. Occasionally, while I'm living my usual "every other day in witch world," I pick up a small sliver of my other life. But the moment it pops in my head, I lose it.

I've spoken to my father about the problem, and he had some interesting insights.

"Deep down inside, it must be that you really don't want to recall another version of yourself. In other words, you don't want to be both Jessie and Jessica together in the same body. You just want to be you, Jessie from the real world, even when you're in Jessica's body in witch world."

I asked my father if such total denial was common, and he assured me that it was. Still, I wonder if I'm a rare case, or a nut job. Jimmy, for example, is having no trouble recalling his life as James. New stuff comes back to him every day—whole chunks of his other life. For example, he can recall everything that happened the night Lara was born.

Which makes me wonder if that's why he's a better father than I am a mother.

Hatsu notes my hesitation and I try to overcompensate by

speaking quickly. "I shouldn't complain. Jimmy's super great about getting up at night to feed her and change her diaper and walk her until she falls back asleep. And my mother's always around. And Whip—that kid's amazing. He's the only one who can get Lara to stop crying no matter what time of day it is. We don't know how he does it. He just has to rock her and whisper softly in her ear and she quiets right down. He calls her his little sister and he means it. It's so sweet."

Hatsu nods, pleased at what I'm saying. Yet I can tell he knows I'm putting on a front. He may be a loving and easygoing soul but not much escapes him.

"And some days you pray to God you'd never gone to Las Vegas that weekend," he says, summoning up my most common point of view in a single line. I can't help but laugh out loud.

"Ain't that the truth!" I say.

Hatsu lets me change into my new outfit in the restroom before we leave the airport. In the car on the way to the house where the Council is meeting, I give him a detailed account of what happened at the Century City Mall and outside the house in Pacific Palisades. He listens without speaking but I can feel his growing astonishment. When I finish, he pats my leg.

"You were brave to follow them back to the house."

"Was I a coward not to go into the house?"

He frowns. "From what I've heard about the Alchemist from Cleo and Kendor, I think you did the right thing."

"I didn't know Cleo had run into him."

Hatsu waves his hand. "It was long ago, during the first or second Egyptian dynasty. I don't know all the details, only that he tried to kill her and she him."

"Lovely. I'm so glad he invited me back to his house."

"Don't go alone."

"Hatsu, what I saw, Syn and Kendor—it's not possible, is it? No one who's died in witch world has ever come back to life in either world, have they?"

"No. But what you said about their dazed state might be important. The Kendor I knew would never walk around like an obedient puppy. Somehow the Alchemist must have cloned their bodies."

"How would he have access to such advanced technology? I mean, scientists have cloned sheep and goats but never human beings."

Hatsu is thoughtful. "Cleo might know. She's spoken to us of a time before the Egyptian and Sumerian civilizations, before even she was born, when there were supposedly two advanced races on earth."

"She only heard rumors of these races, she never actually saw them?"

"That's my understanding," Hatsu replies.

We arrive at the house two hours late and the meeting of the Council is already finished. Except for Cleo and my father—and Hatsu, of course—the others have left. My father hugs me but I can tell he's angry. Hatsu comes to my defense by saying I was late for an extraordinary reason.

"Listen to what your daughter has to say," Hatsu orders my father, perhaps reminding him that he's only just been appointed to the Council, and is its youngest member. Hatsu is over three thousand years old, compared to my father's modest five hundred years of age.

Once more, I repeat everything I saw, this time rehashing every word the Alchemist said. My memory's always been sharp—I give an accurate account. My father interrupts with a couple of questions but Cleo listens without speaking.

When I finish, all eyes fix on Cleo. Physically, she's changed from our time together in Las Vegas. Her red hair is shorter than before, a boy's length, and neatly combed. A petite woman by nature, she appears to have lost a few pounds in the past four weeks, making her youthful cheeks slightly sunken.

At the same time her dark eyes are as powerful as ever. When she stares at me, I feel the familiar magnetism sweep across my forehead. She surprises me by giving a smile and nodding her approval.

"The Alchemist tested you by letting you follow him," she says. "Now, at least, we know where he's located and have some idea of what he's up to."

"We do?" Hatsu asks bluntly.

"Our meeting tonight was about the Lapras and who's going to rule them now that Syn's been killed," Cleo replies. "It appears there's already a power struggle going on in the Order for the top spot. Several of the oldest Lapras have turned up dead. The feud has even spilled over into DC. Two U.S. senators have died and one Supreme Court justice."

"I thought they died as a result of natural causes," I say. The people Cleo refers to have perished in witch world, which means they'll soon die in the real world since the worlds so closely mirror each other.

"It was made to look that way so the public wouldn't panic," Cleo replies. "The Lapras have people at the top in all the major governments. Indeed, one of the U.S. senators who died was a Lapra witch."

"Fine with me," I mutter. "Let the bastards kill each other."

"That's dangerous," my father warns. "Syn's death left a massive void and it's got to be filled. Until it is, thousands of Lapras are no longer answerable to a single authority. It might sound like a positive development, but what if they break into three or four ruthless factions? If that happens they'll keep fighting until the public—in the real world and witch world—becomes aware of their existence, and ours."

"Then there will be real panic," Cleo adds. "Plus there are more Lapras than Tar—we're outnumbered ten to one. If mankind learns that there's not only witches walking the streets but that the majority of them are evil, then the whole planet could be plunged into chaos." Cleo pauses when she sees the look on my face. "It seems you disagree."

I frown. "I'm confused. I understand the danger of the Lapras' internal power struggle and the fact that our existence might become exposed. At the same time, this seems like a great opportunity to destroy the Lapras once and for all. They've lost Syn, the one witch who held them together. Now, finally, they're vulnerable. Shouldn't we take this chance to go after them?"

"We should and we will," Cleo says softly. "But we have to move very carefully."

I nod. "Go on."

"The Lapras have an old tradition. It's barbaric, childish even, but it's a tradition that's governed many societies since man first came down from the trees. To sum it up—'He who kills the king is first in line to be the new king.'" Cleo pauses. "Since you were responsible for Syn's death, that would be you."

"Whip killed her, not me," I quip.

"You were responsible for her death," Cleo says.

I laugh nervously. "You're kidding about this king/queen business, right?"

"We're not. It's why we called you here," my father says.

I feel so much nervous energy I have to stand. "Gimme a break! The Lapras would never accept me as a leader. I'm Tar—

I'm a good witch, not a bad witch. These legions of Lapras you talk about must be looking for some super-evil witch or bitch to emerge and take control. I hardly see how I fit the bill."

My father smiles. "Who knows? Once they see how stubborn you can be, they might be dying to make you their new queen."

"Very funny," I snap. "What about what I saw today? We don't even know if Syn and Kendor are really dead. Hatsu and I are assuming the two I saw must be some kind of clones. They didn't look like they could get around without help from the Alchemist. But that's just speculation. For all we know, they're still alive."

"They're dead," Cleo says. "They died in witch world and it was in witch world that we buried their bodies. I know because I had their remains exhumed last week."

I stop, stunned. "Why did you do that? I only saw them this afternoon."

"I've been aware of their presence for ten days," Cleo says.

"How?"

Cleo looks up at me. "I took the note you were sent after your trip to Las Vegas seriously. The Alchemist sent you that note and he's not known for playing pranks. I had you followed in case he was following you."

I feel annoyed. "Without my permission?"

"For your protection," my father replies for Cleo.

I remember that note, every word. It had read:

Dear Jessie,
I pray this note finds you well.
You put on a wonderful show in the desert.
One day soon we'll have to meet.
Yours, the Alchemist
P.S. Syn sends her greetings.

I feel suddenly overwhelmed and have to sit back down. "Someone help me out. I'm lost. Syn and Kendor are definitely dead but they've been walking around for over a week since they died. How exactly does that work?"

"Perhaps I can help clear up this mystery," Cleo says. "But first let me ask a couple of questions. I know you and Kendor spoke alone and at length. Did he ever mention the times he met the Alchemist?"

"Kendor told me about two encounters. One was the night he became a witch. It was thousands of years ago in England. He was fishing on a frozen lake in the middle of winter, trying to feed his family, when he accidentally fell through the ice. He came close to drowning but the Alchemist pulled him out of the water. Actually, Kendor believed he did drown and the Alchemist yanked him out only after he'd been dead for a few minutes. That's when Kendor became aware he was a witch."

"What was the other time?" Cleo asked.

"Fifty-two BC—when he was fighting with Julius Caesar

and the Roman army against the Gallic tribes in the Battle of Alesia. The Romans were heavily outnumbered and about to be overrun when the Alchemist suddenly showed up with the secret of gunpowder. He taught Kendor how to make tons of the stuff." I pause. "But when the battle was won, he demanded the heads of a hundred thousand captives. Caesar told the Alchemist to go to hell and Kendor tried to kill the bastard."

"Kendor swore he did kill him," Cleo says.

"He swore the same thing to me. But I could hear the doubt in his voice." I shake my head. "After this afternoon, I don't think there's much doubt the guy got away."

Cleo leans closer to me. "Did Kendor mention any other time he saw the Alchemist?"

I hesitate. "He was only sure of the two times. But he did say something odd when we spoke in the sewers beneath Vegas. When he was with Syn, the two of them used to dream about the Alchemist at the same time. The dreams were vivid, like the guy was actually in the room. They were also weird. Kendor spoke of seeing bright lights, objects in the sky, and hearing loud noises. But everything he saw was new to him—he recognized none of it."

"Go on," Cleo says.

"He said the strangest thing was that whenever they had these dreams, he and Syn seemed to lose time. Days, weeks—

he wasn't sure." I stop. "Wait a second. I just remembered. He told me he told you about this."

Cleo nods. "He did, once. It was long ago."

"Were the dreams important?" Hatsu asks.

"They might very well hold the answer to this riddle," Cleo says. "There are ten witch genes that we know of. Each bestows a specific power, although the powers often vary in the manner in which they manifest—or in how they combine with other witch genes that a person has. The rarest of all these genes is called the alpha-omega gene."

"Never heard of it. What does it control?" I ask.

"Time," Cleo says.

"Time? How can someone control time?" I ask.

Cleo considers. "It's been said that when the gene begins to develop, the witch who has it can accelerate and slow down time. It's rumored that one who's fully mastered the gene can even cause time to flow forward and backward—at will."

I gasp. "You're talking about time travel!"

"Essentially," Cleo agrees.

It takes a moment for the full implication of her words to hit me. "Wait a second! Are you saying that the Syn and Kendor I saw this afternoon are from the past?" I ask.

Cleo nods. "For a long time I suspected the Alchemist had this ability. Examine closely how Kendor described his dreams. He spoke of seeing bright lights and hearing loud noises. Just two hundred and fifty years ago, before the Industrial Revolution, the only way to illuminate a room at night was to build a fire or light a candle. Also, the early years of mankind were extraordinarily quiet. Imagine a time when there were no cars, no TVs, no stereos. All of us here, except you, Jessica, remember when the world was virtually silent. To us it was natural. Now imagine how loud today's world would appear to a person who was suddenly plucked from the Middle Ages. He'd jump every time someone slammed a door or hit their car brakes and caused their wheels to squeal."

"What about the objects Kendor saw in the sky?" I ask.

"Those must have been planes," Cleo says.

I hold up a hand. "Slow down, would ya? Are you saying that every time Syn and Kendor dreamed of the Alchemist and lost track of what day it was, they were transported to this time?"

"Transported in time," Cleo says. "But not necessarily to this time."

"That's crazy!" I cry.

Cleo nods slowly. "Perhaps. But isn't it more crazy to say Syn and Kendor are not dead when you saw them die?"

I shake my head. "I don't know. This idea of time travel—it's too weird."

Cleo presses the point. "You were the one who stressed how dazed they were. Consider: If they'd only been here in our time for a few days, can you imagine how new—and yes, frightening—everything would appear to them? Especially in a crowded mall? It makes sense they'd behave like children."

I want to protest but suddenly recall something that struck me as odd. "The ice cream!" I cry. "They dug into it like it was the greatest thing in the world. Like they'd never tasted anything so wonderful."

Cleo nods. "Because the Syn and Kendor you saw *had* never tasted ice cream before. They didn't even know what it was."

I hesitate. "This is still crazy."

My father speaks. "I've confirmed through DNA testing that Syn and Kendor are still in their graves. And I doubt anyone here believes that the Alchemist has the power to bring the dead back to life."

"May I ask a personal question?" I ask Cleo.

"You want to know if I possess this gene. I don't." Cleo pauses. "But you do, and so does Lara."

"How do you know?" I ask.

Cleo stares at me. She doesn't need to speak to tell me that she just knows.

"I assume the ability takes time to emerge," I tease her. The pun is intended. Yet Cleo replies seriously.

"I only heard rumors of the power when I was young," Cleo says. "My mentor told me it could take thousands of years before the ability came to fruition."

"A pity," I say. "I would have liked to have gone back in time and welcomed Columbus to America."

"He landed in the West Indies," my father corrects me.

"I was joking," I say.

"Who knows," Cleo remarks. "You might see Columbus sooner than you think."

"Huh?"

Cleo ignores me. "The Alchemist said you were unprepared. He repeated that remark twice. Then, when you asked about Syn and Kendor, he said they were there to prepare you."

"I think he was just messing with me," I say.

"The man's older than history. He doesn't waste words. If I were you, I'd take what he said at face value."

Cleo's words hang in the air and I'm not sure what they mean. Or perhaps I don't want to admit what she's trying to tell me. I reply in a quiet but defiant tone.

"I don't give a damn what he said. I've had enough of the Lapras, and I've got my own life to live. Like I told you, let the Lapras kill each other, it's not my problem."

"That might not be for you to decide," Cleo says gently.

I snort. "That's the sort of line you tried to feed me in Las Vegas. And we all saw how that turned out."

"Yes, we did see," Cleo replies. "You got Lara back alive, and you escaped with your life."

I shake my head. "Whatever you're suggesting, I'm not interested."

Cleo reaches over and touches my arm. "You're a strong-willed young woman, Jessica. The courage you showed in Las Vegas last month was remarkable. You're clever and fearless and that makes you a formidable opponent for anyone seeking to take over the Lapras. But you lack humility, wisdom—you don't know when to stop and listen." She pauses. "If you're not careful, it may be the death of you and your daughter."

I feel a flash of anger and again want to snap at her. But I stop and struggle to calm myself. Because I have the genetic gift of intuition, and can hear the truth in her words.

"Speak. I'm listening," I say softly.

Cleo nods. "If what the Alchemist says is true then it means Syn and Kendor are here to prepare you, which can only mean they are here to help you fight off others who wish to take control of the Lapras."

"But I've already told you—and I'll be happy to tell them—I don't want to take control of the Lapras! And I can't believe that fact doesn't matter to them! For chrissakes! I'm about to start college at UCLA and look at the classes I'm signed up to take. Inorganic and organic chemistry. Biology and microbiology. Physics and calculus. My schedule's solid premed. I want to be a doctor like my dad and help save lives, not practice how better to kill people. So when it comes to preparing to be the next Wicked Witch of the West—shit, I'll tell the Alchemist myself the next time I see him that someone else can have the job."

The room falls silent for a long time. Hatsu lowers his head while Cleo stares out the window at the dark watery bay and the lights illuminating the magnificent Golden Gate Bridge. My father stands and steps behind my chair, putting his hands on my shoulders. It's a casual gesture but it means a lot to me just to feel his touch. All the years he wasn't in my life, I missed his touch.

"Jessica," he says gently. "I'm afraid what Cleo's trying to tell you is that you probably don't have a choice in the matter."

My throat feels thick. "Why not?" I whisper.

Cleo squeezes my arm and answers. "We know little of the Alchemist—when and where he was born, what his abilities are, whether he's on our side or the side of the Lapras. You assume, from what Kendor told you, that he's a monster, and perhaps he is, I don't know. Yet he took Syn and Kendor to the mall today on purpose, that much is clear, and he says they're here to prepare you. We have to assume they're here to prepare you for a trial of some kind. And since the man can travel through time, we have to accept he already knows that this trial is going to take place, whether you want it to or not."

My father continues to rub my shoulders. Yet I feel as if a heavy weight from far above has descended over me. It was only a month ago in Las Vegas that my whole world was turned upside down and I was almost killed. I had been hoping for a period of peace: to raise my daughter; to love Jimmy; to go to school like a normal girl. Now I find myself struggling just to breathe, to shake off a feeling of impending doom.

"What you just said—it's quite a mouthful," I tell Cleo.

"I know."

"It's not fair," I say.

"Life seldom is," Cleo replies, before adding. "I should have warned you earlier. I knew when you had Syn killed that the majority of the Lapras would see you as a viable candidate to rule their organization. It's in their blood."

"They believe in survival of the fittest," Hatsu says.

"Promotion through assassination," I mutter, although technically it was Whip who had killed her.

"They're a brutal race," Cleo agrees.

"It still makes no sense," I complain. "Why nominate me—a recent high-school graduate who felt bad about dissecting a frog in biology class—to rule over a violent organization bent on world domination? Wouldn't they prefer someone with more blood on her hands?"

Cleo speaks. "I've already answered that question. To the Lapras what matters most is that you defeated Syn. That proves to them how powerful you are. And as far as your youth is concerned—they might see that as an advantage." Cleo suddenly stops. "Or *he* might."

"The Alchemist?" I ask.

Cleo nods. "Since you're only eighteen, he might see you as

someone he can mold as he pleases. You recall that he was Syn's mentor before she took over the Lapras."

"I didn't know Kendor confided that in you," I say.

"I figured it out on my own," Cleo says.

I sigh, or groan—it's hard to separate the two sounds and feelings in my head. "I'm still confused. On one hand you keep talking about what the Lapras want. On the other hand you act like the Alchemist is in control. Tell me clearly—who's calling the shots?"

Cleo considers. "It's true the Alchemist hasn't chosen the Lapras' leader recently. However, in the distant past, long before any of you were born, there were good and bad witches just as there are good and bad witches today. And in those days, the Alchemist did have a say on who ruled the evil witches."

"What about who ruled the good witches?" my father asks, as curious as the rest of us. This is obviously new information to everyone except Cleo. She shakes her head.

"He never came near us," she says.

"Just my luck he's decided to get politically active again," I mutter.

My father acts as if inspiration's struck. "Is it possible Lara's the reason the Alchemist is interested in elevating Jessica to head of the Lapras? Let's not forget how obsessed Syn was with the child's ten witch genes. Could the Alchemist be trying to get to Lara through Jessica? We know Syn tried a similar approach."

"That sounds logical," Hatsu says.

"Yes," Cleo says. "But I don't think he's interested in Lara. Not at this point."

"How can you be sure?" I ask.

"If the Alchemist wanted Lara, he would have taken her," Cleo replies. "It's as simple as that."

"And you wouldn't have been able to stop him?" I ask, not happy we're even discussing this possibility. Cleo gives me no comfort.

"Doubtful," she says.

"Do you know the nature of the trial I'll have to go through *if* I decide to take over the Lapras?" I ask; and I'm sure no one in the room misses my emphasis on the IF word. Cleo takes a long time to answer my question.

"We'll just have to wait and see," she says.

For perhaps the first time since I met her, I feel she is lying to me. The thought disturbs me deeply. Plus it's hard to sit so near her powerful gaze. Once again I stand and pace around the living room. Cleo's made a convincing argument for why I must obey her, but I still feel far from satisfied with her explanations and the control she wants to take over my life.

"One thing makes no sense to me," I say. "Why would the Alchemist bring Syn and Kendor from the past to help prepare me to fight to take over the Lapras? He must know I'd never listen to a word that witch-bitch has to say."

"The Syn you knew was a bitch," Cleo says. "The person

Kendor met and married was a lovely woman. And a powerful witch."

"My God, I didn't think of that," I say. It takes a moment for the implications of what Cleo is suggesting to sink in; and when they do they are so staggering, I fear even to speak them aloud. There's no need, though—I know Hatsu and my father grasp them the same instant I do.

Nevertheless, Hatsu does give voice to what we all fear.

"If the Alchemist has managed to transport an earlier version of Syn from the past, then she'll have no idea the monster she's going to change into during this time," Hatsu says.

"What a disturbing thought," my father says quietly.

Cleo sighs softly. "Who knows? It might be a blessing in disguise."

Our meeting ends on that note—almost. Cleo orders me to return to the Alchemist and accept his help and I agree. Well, sort of; I nod my head without meeting her eyes.

My father gives me a ride back to the airport instead of Hatsu. We drive for a while without speaking—my dad isn't the most talkative man. The anger I felt toward him earlier has evaporated. It's soothing being in his company.

Almost, I tell him about the dream I've been having every night about Marc Simona. Something holds me back and I feel it must be my intuitive witch gene because I want to share the puzzle with him. But I feel if I do I'll regret it later.

"Have you recovered any new memories about Jessica?" my father asks when we're near the airport.

"A few. I pick up glimpses of me and Russ hanging out together. I never knew the two of us were so close."

"You were friends. He was a great guy."

"Yeah." The sorrow comes quick. "And I had to be the one who killed him."

"You know it wasn't that way. He sacrificed his life for you and Lara." My fathers adds, "Any other memories?"

"A few, nothing important."

"There's no hurry. I took a long time to recapture my witch-world memories. It must run in the family."

I smile. "You're just saying that to make me feel better."

"How's James doing?"

"Fine. But now the role's reversed from when he couldn't get into witch world. Now he can't get out, and it drives him nuts that he can't see his son."

My father hesitates. "You haven't told him about Huck?"

Minutes before I killed Kari—Huck's mother and Jimmy's ex-girlfriend—she bragged to me that she'd had lots of lovers and that it was possible Huck didn't even belong to Jimmy.

At first, when I had returned from Las Vegas with Huck and Whip—in the real world—I'd been certain that Huck was Jimmy's son. Indeed, I used my budding intuition gene and felt it verified that he was.

But what I didn't know was how delicate an ability intuition could be. I *wanted* the infant to belong to Jimmy—largely because I knew it would break Jimmy's heart to discover he wasn't Huck's father. Thus, my emotional involvement made my intuition all but useless.

It takes only a few weeks for a baby to grow enough to take on the features of his parents. Unfortunately, for the life of me, I couldn't detect a single trait of Jimmy's face in Huck's face. So last week I took a swab of the tissue from inside the child's cheek, and gathered together hairs belonging to Kari and Jimmy, and sent the whole lot off to my father to be DNA tested.

The test verified my worst fears.

Huck belonged to Kari but not to Jimmy.

"No," I reply to my dad. "It would kill him."

My father replies with a firmness he must have picked up in medical school. *No wonder people so often complain that doctors act like God,* I think.

"You're making a mistake," he says. "Jimmy hardly saw the boy. Knowing the truth will free him up. For one thing he'll be able to focus on Lara better."

"On the surface I'd agree. Huck belongs with Kari's parents—they're the ones who should be raising him. And they would be raising him if they had a clue he was still alive. But you've got to understand Jimmy. He spent only three or four days with the kid but somehow he developed an incredible bond with him. Huck literally became the center of his universe. And then, when Huck was rescued—the same night Jimmy was permanently cut off from his son—well, it became this big heroic thing in his brain. He feels like he sacrificed his life, the life he knew, to save his son's life."

"But it's not his son," my dad says.

"He doesn't know that and I swear I don't know if he's going to care. He's always asking about Huck. What we do together in the real world. Has he got his shots. Am I taking him to the park every day. How long is he sleeping each night. Does he have colic." I pause and wipe at my burning eyes. "It's because he suspects I don't love the boy. And to tell you the truth, Dad, I don't think I loved Huck even before I found out he didn't belong to Jimmy."

"A part of you knew the truth."

"Maybe. Or maybe I couldn't look at the little guy without thinking about Kari and how she stole Jimmy away from me."

"Jessica, you have to listen to me, as your father and as a doctor. The longer you let this situation go on, the worse it will get. You know how hard it is to raise Lara and she's your daughter. There's no way you're going to have the strength to take care of Huck—especially when you have Whip to look after. It's wrong and it's a lie. You said it yourself, the child belongs with his grandparents."

I snort. "And what do I say when I hand Huck over to them? 'Oh, by the way, here's Kari's son. He wasn't dead after all. I've just been taking care of him for the last month because

I wanted to see if he began to look like my boyfriend.'" I pause. "They'll have me thrown in jail."

"You don't have to be involved with the exchange. I know people. I can make it so the child was miraculously found. The DNA evidence alone will prove it's Kari's child." My father stops. "What is it?"

I'm shaking my head. "Jimmy will kill me."

"He can't argue with the truth."

"Don't you understand? He'll kill me for having ordered the test that proved Huck wasn't his in the first place!"

"That makes no sense," my father says.

"Nothing to do with this situation makes sense! But I know Jimmy. He'll feel I betrayed him. There's even the possibility he won't believe me. That I manufactured the evidence."

"I can show him the DNA comparison. Facts don't lie."

"You can only show him a DNA comparison from the real world—show it to him here in witch world. There's no way he'll be able to replicate the test himself. Jimmy is stuck here in witch world, while Huck lives in the real world. Jimmy can never take a tissue sample of his own. He has to rely on others."

"Like you?"

"Yeah, like me," I say weakly.

My father goes to speak and then falls silent.

"Is the trust between you that bad?" he asks finally.

I hang my weary head, wishing it would fall off so I could kick it out the car door and be free of all these complexities.

"Jimmy loves me and I love him. But when it comes to Huck—no, he doesn't totally trust me. And now I've found the perfect reason for him to never trust me again, about anything."

"You're being overly dramatic. The truth is the truth."

I sigh. "Loyalty's a higher truth when you're James Kelter. Let's not forget this is the same guy who had the courage to stick a needle in his arm loaded with an overdose of drugs so he could die in the real world in order to protect me and Lara in witch world."

My father pats me on the shoulder. "I'll never forget what Jimmy did for you two. I'll always be grateful. I'm just trying to protect him from a greater pain six months from now, or six years."

I nod reluctantly. "You're right. I have to tell him. I just don't know how I'm going to do it."

"The sooner the better," my father warns.

It's two in the morning before I get home and I'm exhausted. All I can think about is climbing into bed beside Jimmy and praying that my daughter sleeps until dawn. But when I come through the front door, I find Jimmy pacing the living room, rocking Lara back to sleep. He smiles when he sees me and I give him a kiss on the lips.

"Your timing's perfect," he says. "She fell asleep three minutes ago."

"How long's she been up?"

"Not long. I changed her and fed her. She fussed a little but I think she just needed to fart. As soon as she did she settled right down."

We sit on the couch together and Jimmy hands me Lara. I still haven't gotten over what it's like to hold her. I know every mom feels her child is special, but the truth is Lara is unique—one in a billion, if not one in seven billion. As a result of the Tar carefully placing Jimmy and me in the same small town, she was conceived with all ten witch genes, supposedly the only person on the planet to have the full slate.

What that means to me as a mother is that every time I hold her, I feel I'm holding a little angel—a *real* angel. The light and love Lara gives off is difficult to describe. It hits me first in my hands, when I first pick her up, a magical warmth that makes me imagine I'm holding my hands close to a fire on a freezing night. I never lift her up without feeling instant relief, a subtle soothing, even if it's the middle of the night and I'm exhausted. Lara gives off more energy than I can ever give her, no matter how much I feed her and walk her and love her.

She feels so good in my hands right now, as does Jimmy's arm when he wraps it around me and I lean into his side. For several blessed minutes everything is perfect. The three of us are together in our own bubble and the world outside our door—or I should say "the worlds"—does not exist.

"How was your meeting with the Council?" Jimmy asks. He's tired but he looks good; he always looks good to me. He has on black sweatpants and a red T-shirt; he's a casual dresser, especially the "Jimmy" side of him, which has had a powerful effect on the "James" side. If I didn't buy him clothes I doubt he'd have anything new. He's not the sort who has any interest in impressing people.

Since shifting over to witch world, he's allowed his brown hair to grow longer, a source of great delight for me. I love to play with his curls at night in bed, love to stare into his warm brown eyes when we're talking at meals. Of course I do most of the talking, Jimmy's not someone who rambles.

Working longer hours as a mechanic than he did in Apple Valley, he's built up more muscles, although, ironically, he's probably lost some weight. To be blunt he's ripped; he looks hot without a shirt. But I wish he'd eat more. Sometimes I fear his lack of appetite is due to some worry he doesn't share with me.

I'm a fine one to talk.

I don't share most of my deepest fears with him.

"It sucked," I reply to his question about the Council meeting. I know what's coming—another example of how I can't share with him just how scary my life has become.

"Are the Lapras on the march?" he asks, taking me by surprise.

"How did you guess?"

"We're in witch world now. The newspapers are even more gloomy on this side of the veil. There are outbreaks of violence all over the place—in Africa, South America, Washington DC. I just read this article talking about the 'hidden conspiracy' that's ruining our nation. I was thinking, boy, open your eyes, guys, it started hundreds of years ago."

"But here's not as bad as Las Vegas. I sometimes forget which world I'm in."

"I hear ya." Jimmy pauses. "Tell me more about the meeting."

"Ah, it was the usual crap. The Lapras are evil and they have to be stopped."

"Did Cleo discuss who's been chosen to replace Syn?"

I sit up quickly. "How did you know we talked about that?"

Jimmy shrugs. "I figure there's got to be some kind of power struggle going on. It's got to affect the Tar. I assumed that's why Cleo called you to the meeting."

"You're right," I admit.

Jimmy studies me. Even though he's only my age, he's very perceptive—especially when it comes to me. It might be a virtue, it might be a weakness, I don't know, but I find it almost impossible to lie to Jimmy.

"So what's the verdict?" Jimmy asks. "What are they going to do? Or I should say—what do they want you to do?"

"Stay alert and see if anyone unusual approaches me."

Jimmy frowns. "I'm not sure I like the sound of that."

"I'm not worried about it." I stand with Lara in my right

hand and offer Jimmy my left. "How would you feel about putting both of us to bed?"

Jimmy stands and kisses me deeply. I fall, I fly, I melt—he's a hell of a kisser. It makes no sense, but every time I kiss Jimmy, it's as good or better than the first time.

When he finally steps back, I feel as if I'm swaying in our warm living room while drifting in outer space. I have to force my eyes open. But it's good to see him smiling at me.

"Have I ever told you I love you?" he asks.

"Never. All you care about is my body."

He wraps his arm around me and leads me and Lara toward the bedroom. She sleeps in a cradle at the foot of our bed.

Jimmy speaks. "You know, that's true. A guy would die for a body like yours."

"And you did," I say, the words escaping from my mouth before I can haul them back in. He stops and puts a finger to my lips.

"Neither of us will ever die, as long as we're together."

"You say that like you mean it."

"I know, Jessie. I know."

He's the only one who calls me Jessie in witch world.

"I believe you," I tell him, and I do.

We both put Lara down and go to bed and lie naked in each other's arms—too tired to make love, too weary even to kiss. Still, the mysterious magical bubble remains, and the fragment I think of as myself is once again whole in the arms of the guy who gave his life in the real world to save mine.

Still, the dream of Marc Simona starts almost immediately, and once again I'm swept up in the saga of his brilliantly complex escapade. Only this time when I reach the end of the night, and walk with him as he zips his fly after taking a piss in an alley not far from his apartment, the bond between us suddenly strengthens. For nine nights in a row I felt as if I was inside his mind and body. Now the feeling of identification grows a hundredfold.

I see the bright light at the end of the alley and whirl to look at the sun, puzzled how it can be in two places at the same time. But when I turn back to the original light I realize, along with Marc, that it has nothing to do with the sun. It's a light born of darkness. I know because as it grabs Marc it takes hold of me as well, and I feel myself yanked from my bed even as he's lifted from the alley. It's only then I lose all contact with Marc and see blackness. It invades my mind and body and suddenly I'm lost.

CHAPTER THREE

"HEY, CAN YOU HEAR ME? WAKE UP." A GENTLE HAND shakes me. "Rise and shine, pretty girl."

I open my eyes and see Marc Simona staring down at me. I know his face, of course, I've seen it every night in the mirror of the janitor's closet in the mall parking lot where he hides his tools.

He's handsome in a bad-boy sort of way—meaning he could use a shave and a shower. His hair is light brown, an out-of-control wavy mass streaked with dust—which I'm sure he picked up in the alley where he hid Silvia's emeralds behind that stinking Dumpster. His eyes are a clear blue, his mouth is wide, expressive; it might be his generous lips. The guy's sexy, no question. It's odd how I never noticed his muscles in my dreams. I'm not surprised he grew up on the streets—he looks like he can take care of himself.

"It's you," I whisper, my throat dry.

"I suppose," he says. "You awake?"

"Gimme a minute," I mumble, trying to straighten myself on what feels like an airplane seat. Then, blinking my crusty eyes, I give a quick look around and realize I *am* on an airplane.

Yet a closer inspection makes me wonder. There are no long aisles, no rows of seats. The walls don't curve like they normally do in the friendly skies. They're sharp cornered and dull gray, and give the give the impression we've been stowed away in a large metal box. Worse, there are only six chairs and six of us.

Still, I feel a faint vibration as if we're moving through the air or along an extremely smooth railroad track. Off to my left I see a door leading to a compact restroom. On my right is a shiny silver refrigerator. There are no windows, however, and I have a sneaky feeling we're not going to be introduced to the pilot.

Last night, when I went to sleep, I remind myself, I was in witch world. That means I'm in the real world now. The world I've known all my life. But a world without Jimmy.

"Are you thirsty? Need something to drink?" Marc asks. I realize I'm automatically assuming it *is* Marc, when I've never actually met the guy. Yet it has to be him; he looks exactly like the guy in my dreams. He even talks like him, sort of cocky, definitely cool.

However, he's not dressed in the black slacks, white shirt, and dark Nikes—the clothes he wore in my dreams. His clothes resemble a uniform. His long-sleeved shirt is dark green, as are his pants, and his ankle-high leather boots are black. He wears a bright green bracelet on his left wrist.

It takes me a moment to realize we're all dressed the same. Which means someone undressed me while I was unconscious, and probably the others. My bracelet feels like it's made of plastic; the fit is tight.

"Water, please," I say.

"Coming right up." Opening the fridge, Marc pulls out a plastic bottle and unscrews the cap, creating a popping sound. He hands it to me and nods for me to take it. "I've tried it. It won't kill ya."

Taking the pint-size bottle, I search for signs of identification—a company name, a popular logo—but there's none. Still, the water tastes fresh and I gulp down half the bottle. My intense thirst makes me wonder how long I was out.

"Thank you," I say, keeping the water.

"You're welcome." Marc sits down in the only unoccupied seat and looks to the other four as if waiting for one of them to speak. When no one volunteers, he casually leans back in his chair and sticks out his legs. He adds, "So I take it this isn't some sort of super-secret AA meeting?"

"How long did you say you've been awake?" a dark-skinned woman on his left asks in a sharp tone. Her black hair is cut short; her hairdresser couldn't have spent more than sixty seconds on the task. Her eyebrows are thick, dark, fearsome. She appears to be Middle Eastern, and it doesn't take me long to place her accent. She's from Israel.

Marc is unmoved by her nasty tone. "You already asked that question, babe."

"Answer it again for our new arrivals," she orders.

"Not very long," he says.

The woman stands and puts her hands on her hips. There's something commanding about her presence, but she's one shrill chick. She doesn't much care for Marc's laid-back attitude.

"Who are you people?" she demands of the rest of us. "What are your names? Where are you from? Why are you here?"

"I'm Brad Pitt and I'm researching a new film I'm shooting," Marc says cheerfully. "It's called *Six Suckers in a Box*." He pauses. "Any other stupid questions?"

The woman moves, freeing up her hands, standing over him. "You don't want to take that tone with me, mister," she warns.

"You don't like Brad Pitt?" he asks innocently.

Leaning over, she places a long finger near his right eye, like she might poke it out if provoked. "Answer my questions," she whispers.

"Sit back down and I'll think about it," Marc says.

The woman is clearly volatile; I fear she might hurt Marc. I feel I must intervene, and speak quickly. "Hey, I'll answer your questions as best I can. If you'll calm down and listen."

The woman throws me a nasty look. "Don't interfere."

I harden my tone. "Don't tell me what to do. Don't tell any of us what to do. This isn't an interrogation. I've offered to tell you what I know. Now sit down and behave like a human being."

"I know it must upset you that she didn't say please, but I'd do what she says," Marc adds.

The woman draws back and eyes me warily. "Go on," she orders.

"Sit," I insist.

The woman looks to the other three: a nerdy guy with sun-bleached blond hair and thick glasses; a tall black male who might have been plucked from an African jungle; and a short Asian girl with a scar on her left cheek. If the Israeli woman's searching for support, she's wasting her time. None of the others is impressed with her strident behavior. She sits back down and stares at me.

"Speak," she says.

"My name's Jessica Ralle, although most people call me Jessie. I'm eighteen years old and live in Los Angeles. I just graduated high school and plan to go to college at UCLA starting in September." I pause. "Who are you guys?"

"My name's Chad Barker and I'm a physics student at MIT—" the nerdy guy with the glasses begins.

"Wait!" the woman interrupts. "You didn't tell us how you came to be here, Jessica Ralle."

I shrug. "Probably because I have no idea. Now let Chad finish introducing himself, all right?"

The woman glares but I ignore her and turn back to Chad. "Are you one of those super-smart guys who's going to make the rest of us feel like idiots?" I ask.

Chad blushes. "Well, I'm only eighteen but I just finished my undergraduate degree and I'm about to start a special PhD program in string theory. I call it special because I'm allowed to skip getting a master's degree."

I give him an encouraging smile. I can tell he's afraid— almost as afraid as the Israeli woman. That is one tough cookie who can't stand not to be in control.

I speak to Chad. "I was right, you're a natural genius. I assume you live in Cambridge, Massachusetts?"

"Most of the year, but I'm originally from Sarasota, Florida. I'm spending the summer there. In fact, I was sleeping in late at my parents' house when I . . . well, I sort of ended up here."

"The last thing I remember is sleeping in my bed," I say. "But I was out cold, or dreaming. I don't know what time it was." I turn to the Asian girl. "What's your name?"

She hesitates. "Chong, Li. Li Chong."

"Where you from, Li?" I ask.

"Seoul."

"What were you doing before you woke up here?" Chad asks.

Li shakes her head. "Typing on a computer at work. I was there late—it must have been about nine o'clock. Then I saw this bright light and . . . I don't know what happened next."

"I saw a bright light too," Chad says quickly.

"So did I," I say. "Anyone else?" Marc and the black guy nod. The Israeli woman hesitates before doing likewise. I add, "Good. We're making progress. We have a pattern."

"We have shit," the Israeli woman snaps. "How do I know you're not all lying?"

"Jesus Christ," Marc mutters, rolling his eyes.

The woman jumps up again and points at Marc. "This guy was awake before any of us. When I opened my eyes, I saw him crawling around, checking each of us out. I closed my eyes and pretended I was still asleep. He searched the whole place."

"I would have done the same," I say.

"Me too," Chad adds.

The woman gets angry. "Don't just take his side because he's handsome. Why was he awake before the rest of us?"

"Someone had to wake up first," Chad says. "And for the record, I don't think he's that handsome."

The woman boils. "He refuses to tell us what he was doing! He won't even tell us his goddamn name!"

"What's your name?" I ask.

Marc chuckles; he's clearly enjoying the show. He speaks to the angry woman. "If you'd asked me politely, like Jessie here, I would have told you how I like my coffee in the morning and what my favorite sexual position is. But you had to start off acting like a bitch. Or are you acting? Whatever your name is . . ."

The woman sucks in a breath. It's possible she's having second thoughts, I'm not sure. She searches our faces and scowls, clearly feeling cornered. She blurts out her next remark.

"My name is Shira Attali. I was born in Tel Aviv, nineteen years ago. I'm currently stationed along the West Bank. If you have a clue where that is."

"I've heard of the place," Marc says. "Isn't it a landlocked territory located east, north, and south of Israel—right next to the Jordan River and the Dead Sea?"

Shira nods, continuing to stand. "That's where I'm from. And that's where I was standing guard when I saw a bright light and woke up here."

"What time of day was it?" Chad asks.

"Four in the afternoon."

"So you're in the army?" I ask Shira.

"Yes," she says.

"A pity you left your rifle behind," Marc says.

"Why do you say that?" Shira asks, and for once there's a modicum of respect in her voice.

Marc shrugs. "The six of us just got kidnapped. People who kidnap other people are usually bad people. A rifle would come in handy, if you ask me." He adds, "By the way, my name's Marc Simona and I'm from LA, like Jessie here. I was asleep in my bed when I saw a bright light and got snatched and woke up here. That's my whole story."

"What do you do for a living?" I ask, knowing, of course, that he's lying.

"I'm a valet at Grauman's Chinese Theatre."

I catch his eye. "You must make pretty good tips. Especially on red-carpet nights."

He takes my observation in stride. "It's a living."

Chad breaks in. "You say you got snatched. Did you feel as if someone grabbed you? Physically grabbed you?"

Marc hesitates. "Yes."

"Can you guess what time it was?" Chad asks.

"Near dawn."

"You could tell even though you were asleep?" I ask. In my dreams he knew it was dawn because he was wide awake and the sun had just come up.

"I woke up just as it happened," Marc says. "It was like some kind of huge hand grabbed me from behind. That's all I know."

"Grabbed you from behind in bed?" I persist.

"I just told you, that's all I know."

The black guy finally speaks. "My name is Ora Keiru. I'm from Sudan. I was milking a goat when I was taken here. I saw the light you all speak of."

There's a dignity in the way he talks, and he's certainly a sight for hungry female eyes. Six and a half feet tall, powerfully built—his long legs look as if they were designed for chasing down wild animals.

"What time of day was it?" Chad asks. To me it's obvious he's trying to establish a pattern to when we were abducted, and I think I see it. Yet I say nothing about the timing. I'm curious about Chad and want to see where he goes with his questions. I started out by joking about his high IQ but now I'm beginning to see he's probably smarter than any of us.

"Late afternoon, close to the evening," Ora replies.

"How old are you?" I ask.

Ora hesitates. "I'm not sure. My parents died when I was young and I've never celebrated a birthday. I live far from the city with two sisters. My country is poor but the land is beautiful and so are the people. I would not trade my home for any other place."

"What are your sisters' names?" I ask.

"Klastu and Ariena."

I can't help but notice the affection in his voice; it makes me smile. "I'll bet they're baby sisters," I say.

"Neither is a child anymore, but I am the eldest."

"Great," Marc says, and claps his hands. "Finally, we're all introduced and feeling better about each other. Now let's figure out how the hell we got here." He pauses. "Any ideas? Anyone want to speculate? How about you, Chad? It sounds like you're the brain here."

Chad smiles shyly. "I wouldn't go that far. But you're

right, we need to figure out why we're here and where here is. I suggest we start with what we do know." He stops and looks around at our metal cell. "We're in a large vehicle of some kind and it appears to be moving. The question is—are we on the ground or in the air?"

"If we were on a railroad track, we'd hear constant repetitive noises and feel slight bumps from the track," Marc says.

"The fast trains in Japan are supposed to be almost silent," I say. "They use powerful magnets and sort of float along."

"They don't float," Chad corrects me. "The magnets are used to reduce the friction with the track and give a smoother ride." He pauses. "And there's not a lot of places in the world that have them."

"So you think we're in a plane?" I ask.

Chad considers; I can see the gears turning inside. "Even on the smoothest flight in the world you feel some slight rises and falls as you hit air pockets. But I've been awake ten minutes and not once have I felt a sudden drop in elevation—not even a tiny one."

"Does that mean a jet's out of the question?" I ask, and it strikes me then that, except for Shira, we're all behaving pretty rationally—almost too rationally. I tell myself that my inner calm comes from the fact that I'd been warned by Cleo that weird shit was right around the corner. But the reasoning feels thin to me.

It makes me wonder if we've been drugged.

It also makes me wonder why I don't feel more bitter about my kidnapping, *especially* after my talk with Cleo. I've no illusions that my abduction is not somehow connected to the Lapras' need for a new leader and the Alchemist's mysterious desire to be involved in that selection.

Yet a part of me accepts that what's happening now is little different from what happened to me in Las Vegas. The bottom line is I was born with seven witch genes, and because of that fact I'm cursed to have a "destiny," perhaps an important one— and all my bitching to the contrary is not going to change that fact. When I think back to everything Cleo told me last night, in witch world, I realize that's what she was trying to tell me.

"Get over it, girl."

It does sort of help that I have Marc along for the ride.

The guy is a lot cuter in person than in my dreams.

Yet why do I have anyone with me? I know from being inside Marc's mind that he's no witch. Hell, I can tell by scanning the room that I'm the only witch present. If I'm about to embark on some test of witch powers to determine if I'm fit to lead the Lapras, then the company I'm keeping makes no sense.

"Ask me after another ten minutes," Chad replies to my question about us being in a jet. He adds, "It is possible we're in the back of a large truck."

"It'd have to be on one hell of a smooth road," Marc says.

"It could have a high-tech suspension," Chad argues. "I've

read how such systems are currently being tested. Once a person's aboard such a vehicle, and blindfolded, they can't tell whether they're moving or not."

"You're all assuming we're moving," Shira says. "I'm not so sure. That vibration we feel—it could be anything."

Her remark appears insightful, and the room falls silent. Yet I know it's not true. Since I awakened to my witch status in Las Vegas a month ago, I've become much more aware of where I am at any moment. It's like a GPS signal has become activated in my brain. I'm not saying I can tell where we're at, but I know—*absolutely*—that we're moving rapidly. For that matter, I know we're high up in the sky, extremely high.

"We're probably in a jet," I say. "And we're probably up so high there's almost no air. That's why we're not hitting any air pockets. People who flew in the Concorde used to say they never felt like they were moving. That's because it flew above fifty thousand feet."

"The Concorde got grounded years ago," Marc says.

"That's irrelevant," Chad says to Marc, although it's clear he's impressed with my remark. "I think Jessie's onto something. The military has jets that can fly miles higher than the Concorde. If we're in one of those craft, we could be going faster than the speed of sound and not even know it."

Marc shakes his head. "Sorry, Chad, Jessie, I don't buy it. I've never been much for government conspiracies."

"Then maybe it's time we stopped and talked about *who*

has abducted us," Chad says. "Let's look at the facts. You may have noticed I've been trying to keep track of when each of us was abducted. Accounting for the different time zones, it looks like we were all picked up at exactly the same time, even though we were spread all over the globe."

"Shit," Marc mutters in amazement as the truth of what Chad is saying sinks in.

Shira points to Marc and me, but speaks to Chad. "Don't you find it odd that those two are from the same city?" she asks.

"Not really, not unless they know each other," Chad replies. "You don't, do you, Jessie? Marc?"

"No," Marc says.

Shira points at me. "Then why did Jessie say, 'It's you,' the second she woke up?" she demands. "When Marc was standing over her?"

I shrug. "Did I say that? I don't remember. I was out of it. I thought Marc was my boyfriend waking me up."

"You were awake," Shira says firmly.

Chad raises his hand. "For now can we please just trust each other and assume everyone is telling the truth? It'll make this go a whole lot faster."

Shira gives me a dirty look. "Fine. Go on."

Chad continues. "The reason I want us to consider that a government's behind our kidnapping is because of the exotic way we were all knocked out. I mean, none of us got hit on the skull or belted in the nose. None of us had a cloth dipped in ether pressed to our mouth. No, we all saw a bright light and some of us felt like it grabbed us. That sounds pretty high tech to me."

"Are we talking about the U.S. government here?" Marc asks.

Chad shakes his head. "They're a leading candidate but it doesn't have to be them. It could even be a rich corporation. My point is that it took special tools—which means plenty of cash—to pick us up within a few minutes of each other, knock us out, and stash us in this cell."

To me, it sounds like Chad's describing the Lapras, but I keep the idea to myself. Even though none of them *feels* like a witch to me, I wonder if one or more of them is and doesn't know it. Their ignorance might camouflage their powers, even from my intuitive gene.

Whatever, if none of them is aware of witches then my breathtaking tale of what happened to me in Las Vegas is unlikely to go over well. Shira, for one, would probably try to kill me the first chance she got.

There's a lot of anger in that woman—or girl. I wonder at its source. I have to keep reminding myself she's only nineteen. She doesn't act like a teenager. But I suppose being in the army could do that to you.

"Why would someone go to all this trouble to grab us?" Marc says. "What's special about us?"

"That question is key," Chad says with energy in his voice. "Let's give it a closer look. If we can figure out what makes each of us unique, then we might be able to figure out the motive behind our kidnapping."

Marc shakes his head. "There's nothing special about me. All I do is park cars for a living."

"Is that all?" I ask. "You don't have any hobbies?"

"No."

"A second job perhaps?" I persist.

"No."

I recall what Silvia Summer told him the night of the movie premiere. I feel an irresistible urge to goad him. "You don't look like the sort of guy who should be parking cars," I say, quoting her word for word.

Marc meets my gaze without flinching. Yet I can tell I've scored a hit. At the same time I wonder if I'm playing with fire. Marc is one cool customer, I have to grant him that, especially when he answers.

"You're not the first person to tell me that," he replies.

"Do you live alone?" Chad asks.

"Yes," Marc says.

"I assume you work at night or on the weekends. What do you do with the rest of your time?"

"Pick up pretty girls."

"You can't think of a single thing that you can do better than anyone else?" Chad asks.

Marc grins at me. "Pick up pretty girls."

"All right," Chad says, turning to Ora. "I can tell by looking at you that you've had a hard life and that you're probably stronger than the rest of us put together. Is there anything else unique about you?"

"Unique? I do not know this word," Ora says.

"Special," Chad explains.

Ora is thoughtful. "I am Chita. That's the name of my tribe. There are many of us who live in my part of Sudan. But nearby are the Kirus—another tribe. One of their villages borders my village. That makes it a dangerous place to live."

"The Chitas and the Kirus don't get along?" Chad asks.

"They're always fighting, always killing each other."

"Why?" Chad asks.

"For land. For cattle, goats, and women."

Chad considers before asking his next question. "Do you lead your village when you fight the Kirus? Are you a warrior?"

Ora stares at him. "I have killed many Kirus since I was a boy."

"Do you have guns?" Shira asks. "Any AK-47s?"

Ora nods. "I have seen that gun you speak of. I have fired it. But now, on both sides, we have no bullets so we fight by hand, or with spears and knives."

Shira's question is shrewd. I know from reading that AK-47s are the most common weapon arms dealers smuggle into Africa. The machine gun is renowned for its reliability. It seldom jams even when dunked in water or coated with mud. It would be the perfect weapon to own in a dusty land like Ora's.

Chad appears to think the same as I do. He turns to Shira.

"It sounds like you know your weapons," he says.

"I told you, I'm in the army," Shira replies.

"Doesn't everyone, male and female, have to serve in your army?" Chad asks.

"For two years. Then, later, we can be called up at any time if our homeland is threatened."

Chad speaks carefully. "Have you seen action?"

Shira hesitates. "Yes."

"Interesting," Chad says.

A vein on Shira's head pulses with blood. He's touched a nerve. "Why do you say that?" she demands.

Chad raises a reassuring hand. "I meant no offense. I just find it curious that here we're a group of six teenagers and two of us have been in battle. At least two of us." He turns to Li. "Tell us about yourself?"

Li fidgets. "I'm not important. I work long hours in a packaging firm. Sometimes on the weekends I volunteer at a hospital."

Chad's ears perk up. "What do you do at the hospital?"

"Help take care of the sick."

"Are you in training to be a nurse?" Chad asks.

Li hesitates. "Yes. Or a doctor, I'm not sure."

"Li, may I ask a personal question?" Chad says. "I notice

the scars on your face and the one on your hand. May I ask where you got them?"

Clearly Li doesn't want to answer. Lowering her head, she says quietly, "Bad men beat me."

Chad goes to speak and then pauses, glancing at Marc and me. It's as if we all share the same thought. Li may live in South Korea now but *where* did she grow up? Besides the scars, she's extremely short, a sign she suffered from malnutrition at an early age. North Korea, probably the most intolerant place on earth, is well known for starving its population. And its police routinely arrest people for no reason and beat them senseless.

"Li . . . ," Chad begins gently.

"I live in Seoul," Li interrupts, repeating herself, stopping his questioning—or what to her might feel like an interrogation. Sensitive to her distress, Chad quickly backs off. He turns to me.

"What makes you special, Jessie?" he asks.

"My good looks."

Chad smiles. "That's a given. Anything else?"

I shake my head. "I honestly don't know. I'm your average teenage girl, spoiled, lazy, but looking forward to starting college. Like Li, I'm interested in medicine. I'm mainly going to take premed classes. But I do sort of have an interest in the occult."

Chad blinks. "The occult?"

I let the remark slip as a feeler of sorts but I don't get any special *buzz* back from the group. "I just like to read about weird shit is all. Near-death experiences. Out-of-body travel. Ghosts. Vampires. Reincarnation."

"Remember any past lives?" Chad teases.

"Maybe. Oh, in this life, I have an awesome boyfriend named Jimmy."

"Who isn't here to protect you," Marc says with just a shade too much enthusiasm.

I smile sweetly. "Don't sweat it. I'm pretty good at taking care of myself."

"Tell us more," Chad says, watching me closely, maybe too closely. I remind myself again how intelligent he is. He might guess I'm playing a role.

I shrug. "There's nothing else to tell."

"Do you live with your parents?" Chad asks.

"With my mom."

"And Jimmy," Marc mutters, making his own assumptions. "You've got one cool mommy."

"It's true my mom's super cool, but I live in a guesthouse behind the main house," I say, lying. The reverse is the truth. Jimmy, Lara, Whip, and I live in the main house. My mother likes the guesthouse—she enjoys the privacy, in witch world and the real world.

"Where are you at in LA?" Marc asks.

"Santa Monica."

Marc nods. "I know the area."

"I'm sure you do," I say.

Chad glances back and forth between us. He is damn smart; he's picking up the connection between us, even more clearly than Marc. Yet I can tell my remarks have Marc puzzled.

"Why don't you tell us about yourself," I say to Chad.

He's reluctant to let me off the hook but he can see he's not getting anywhere with me. "Like I said, I have a degree in physics from MIT and I'm going to do my graduate work there. But I've also taken a lot of classes in biology, and for a while I was thinking of trying to get into a brand-new PhD program Harvard has just created on the physiology of the brain. I've always been obsessed with how the human mind works."

"And why yours works so well," I say. "Come on, let it out. What is your IQ?"

Chad reddens. "Only assholes brag about their IQs."

"A hundred and fifty?" I say. "One sixty-five?"

He grins. "It's higher. But it's not important."

"I disagree," I say. "Maybe it's very important. You yourself pointed out that Ora and Shira have both been in battle. Li, too—she's obviously faced down some pretty tough characters in her time. That means at least half our gang has had to claw their way through life. Then we have you, Chad, with your one-in-a-million IQ. You've got to admit that can't be a coincidence."

"Exactly what kind of coincidence are we talking about?" Marc asks.

"Well, we all speak English," I say.

Marc waves his hand in dismissal. "Nowadays, with the Internet, everyone speaks English."

I stare at him. "I get the impression we're an extremely capable group. And I don't just mean when it comes to fighting."

"You're talking about survival," Chad says, intrigued.

"Exactly," I reply.

Marc shakes his head. "I don't see how Jessie and I fit in."

"Sure you do," I tease. "Any idiot can see how quick you are on your feet. Don't deny it—you're a natural-born flirt, among other things. To top it off, you're courageous."

"Huh?" Marc says.

"Weren't you the one who just offered to protect me?"

Marc appears to warm to my idea, or else to my flirting. Still, he frowns and I realize he's not gotten over his confusion at my insight into his secret life. Frankly, I don't care, I feel confused myself. Our gang makes for an interesting mix but what does it have to do with what Cleo told me last night?

The bottom line question is—why have I been abducted and thrust together with five admittedly capable teenagers instead of five powerful witches? The others are certainly exceptional, but put us together in an arena and I could wipe them all out in a minute. I'm not bragging, it's just the way it is.

Which means I'm missing something somewhere.

"Are you saying we've been hand picked by a secret branch of the government or an evil corporation to be trained as spies?" Marc asks.

"Jessie's just pointing out that our group is special." Chad comes to my rescue. "What we're going to do when we reach our destination—how we're going to be used—I'm sure none of us has any idea."

Shaking his head, Marc leans back in his seat. "If you ask me, we're talking out of our asses. This situation is just too weird. Chances are we've been kidnapped by a bunch of aliens. And when we get to their home world, they're probably going to lock us in a cage and make us fight to the death—just to see who's the last one standing."

"That's not funny," Chad says seriously.

Marc closes his eyes. "I'm just saying I don't think all of us are going to get out of this alive."

CHAPTER FOUR

WHEN I WAKE UP THE NEXT MORNING, I'M BACK IN witch world, back in my bed with Jimmy lying beside me in Santa Monica. The last thing I recall about the real world was searching the cell we were locked in for a possible escape route. But there was no way out.

There wasn't any food, either, just plenty of bottled water. The restroom came with a working toilet but there was no shower or towels or blankets. We continued to toss around ideas of what was happening to us, but eventually we started talking in circles and I finally followed Marc's lead and laid back in my seat and dozed off. At least I think I naturally fell asleep. For all I know our captors gassed our metal cabin.

Jimmy takes care of Lara in the morning, letting me sleep in, then goes off to his part-time job as a mechanic at a gas station in Venice—one town over. Ordinarily he might take Whip with him—who's in love with cars and actually helps

Jimmy fix whatever's broken—but Whip's on vacation with Alexis at Florida's Disney World. For that matter, Whip's there with Alex in the real world.

Whenever Whip's away, I always worry that someone might spot his tail, but Alexis is pretty clever when it comes to dressing him. The truth be told, just as Jimmy's a better father than I am a mother, Whip probably has more fun hanging out with Alexis than me. I tell myself it doesn't bother me but the fact that it has me reassuring myself sort of invalidates my rationalization.

Whatever, I'm always happy when Whip's having fun. The kid's not had exactly an easy life, not with Syn as his mother.

My mother takes Lara from me at noon and I use the free time to drive out to Pacific Palisades, once again parking down the road from the luxurious home where the Alchemist brought Syn and Kendor—or their earlier incarnations. I sit and stare at the house for an hour, remembering Cleo's orders to make contact. Hoping the Alchemist will take the initiative and come outside and invite me in, and praying the guy stays away and leaves me alone.

In the end I don't knock on the door and I know it's because I'm scared. But the reality of the situation influences my decision. Definitely something remarkable is going on in the real world and I'm sure I'll need help soon. But until our "gang of six" gets to where we're going, I figure I don't know what kind of help to ask for. So I decide that's good reason enough to wait, and drive away.

I don't go home. Instead, I decide to swing by Grauman's Chinese Theatre to see if I can pick up any information on Marc Simona. I'm almost certain my dreams about him were accurate, and yet I'm not sure if the events I saw happened in witch world or the real world or both. There's a strong chance it's the latter. Events in witch world usually reflect what happens in the real world but—and this is a huge *but*—the reflection isn't always perfect.

For example, Marc might have worked as a valet the night of the film's premiere and hidden away in Silvia's trunk, but it might have been a ruby bracelet he stole rather than an emerald necklace. And Silvia's boyfriend might have been an NBA guard rather than an NFL running back. Since my transformation into a witch a month ago in Las Vegas, I'd seen such random differences again and again.

However—and this is a huge *however*—occasionally the variations between the two worlds are striking. I don't run into it too frequently but it happens often enough to keep me on edge.

In witch world Jimmy and my next-door neighbors were a lovely elderly couple named Betty and James Gardner who went to bed early every night and hardly made a sound. In the real world three young women rented the same house and threw wild parties every Saturday night, and the Gardners were dead.

From researching the obituary section of old copies of the *LA Times* newspaper, I knew they'd died two months ago in a traffic accident, which probably meant they would soon die in witch world.

Probably but not *definitely.*

All that was definite was that if you died in witch world you always died in the real world, usually the same day, absolutely within two or three days. That was why the sight of Syn and Kendor had thrown me for such a loop. I'd seen the witch-world version of Syn stab Kendor in the heart, and had watched as Whip had stung Syn in the heart.

Cleo's explanation for their return had been bizarre, to say the least, and yet it had rung true to me. All the little clues Kendor had dropped, and all the ones I had picked up watching the dazed couple—Cleo had tied them together in a neat tidy package.

Yet I still wondered why she'd made that strange remark about me seeing Columbus. I'd just been making a joke but as far as I knew Cleo didn't joke. And if the Alchemist didn't waste words, Cleo didn't either. She'd been trying to tell me something, but what? She'd made it clear that my alpha-omega witch gene would take thousands of years to spring to life. There was no way the gene could come to my rescue in the near future—certainly not in the next few days.

At the theater, I park in the back lot—which is almost empty in the middle of the day—and hurry to the front. Soon

I'm standing on Hollywood Boulevard. I haven't been to this part of town in years and yet everything looks familiar, as if Marc's memories have slightly merged with my own. The valet booth is nearby and I immediately recognize his boss, Steve Green, the laid-back Australian with the pregnant wife. He doesn't look busy and I walk up to him and flash my brightest smile.

"Hi, I'm Alexis Simms and I work for the *LA Times*," I say, using my best friend's name. It's an old habit of mine, which grew out of the fact that Alexis almost always uses my name when she's in a questionable predicament. I continue, "My paper is thinking of doing a personal-interest piece on what it's like to be a valet for the stars. We're looking for a single candidate to focus on. I was wondering if you could help me?"

The man gives a friendly nod while checking me out. "You look a little young to be a reporter," he says in his thick accent.

"Want me to run back to my car and get my ID?"

"That won't be necessary. I can't imagine many people would be interested in what we do. We park cars for people and later in the night we fetch their cars. It's mundane work."

"Mundane? You've got to be joking. Why, in one night, you meet more stars than your average person could hope to meet in ten lifetimes. I think it must be exciting, Mr. . . ."

"Green, Steve Green. I must admit when I started here, twenty years ago, I got a kick out of the red-carpet nights. But now each premiere is the same to me." He pauses and laughs. "I'm afraid I'd make a lousy man for your article."

"Is there someone else you can recommend? A handsome young guy perhaps. You know the public—you're nobody unless you have a pretty face."

Mr. Green considers. "There's someone you might want to talk to. His name's Marc Simona. He's nineteen, a hard worker, and tons of the starlets stop to flirt with him. Why just the other night Silvia Summer—I'm sure you've heard of her— told Marc he should be up on the silver screen. She may have been stroking his ego but I was standing nearby and it sounded like she meant it."

"Interesting," I mutter. In my dream Silvia had acted like Marc could do better than park cars, but she hadn't said the precise line Mr. Green was quoting. It was possible the man was exaggerating, or else he was repeating Silvia's remark verbatim as he'd heard it here in witch world—when my dream of Marc had taken place in the real world. In other words, in the real world, Silvia might have said almost the same thing but not quite. Once again the variations between the two dimensions fascinate me, as much as they disturb me.

Even more critical is when Mr. Green says Marc met Silvia. It was only last night, which means I had dreamed about what Marc was going to do over a week in advance.

It's only then that I realize that for the first time in ten nights, I didn't dream about Marc last night. I suppose there's no longer any point now that I'm physically with him.

But no longer any point to whom? Or to what?

"He sounds like a perfect subject for my article," I say. "Is Marc working tonight?"

"He'll be in tomorrow evening. If you give me your card, I can have him give you a call."

"That's all right, you know us conniving reporters. I'd rather catch him at work when he's not looking. In fact, please do me a favor and don't tell him I'm going to stop by. I want to observe him in action before I slide over and interrogate him."

Mr. Green is amused. "I'm afraid I can't promise that. All valets live by a secret code. We always cover each other's back. But I'll encourage him to do the interview. Marc's easy to talk to, especially if you're a pretty girl."

"Thank you for your time," I say, backing up. "And good luck with the baby."

The man blinks in surprise and I quickly realize my slip.

"How'd you know my wife's going to have a baby?"

I force a chuckle. "I told you, I work for the *Times*. We have a policy of never going to an interview unprepared. Thanks again for being so helpful."

I get out of there in a hurry.

Having lived and breathed so many nights in a row inside Marc Simona's mind and body, I know exactly where he lives—just two blocks shy of the alley where he stopped to take a piss as the sun came up. The same spot where the bright light snatched him from the face of the earth. I drive to the alley hoping to find clues of how it was done. But studying the area, I only manage to find the spot where Marc took a piss. Only two blocks to go and he couldn't hold it. Just like a guy, I think.

I didn't start the day thinking that I'd try to meet Marc's witch-world counterpart. For one thing, until I spoke to Mr. Green, I wasn't a hundred percent sure which version of Marc I'd been observing in my dreams. But now that I know it was the real-world Marc, the temptation to speak to his witch-world counterpart is powerful. Of course, via Mr. Green, I've already set up a tentative meeting for tomorrow night. But with so much happening, that feels like a long ways off.

I drive to 14742 Twenty-second Street, near La Brea, and park fifty yards down the block from his studio apartment. He lives in unit twenty-seven—I can see his front door from where I'm sitting. The building is badly run-down and I know Marc chose it because of the cheap rent, and the fact that it's close enough to the theater that he's able to walk or jog to work. Marc's never played formal sports but I know he's in excellent shape. It's kind of spooky knowing so much about him.

Yet at the same time I know nothing. What's our connection? Why did I dream about him? Why was he chosen to be kidnapped with me? It's like someone's moving us around like pieces on a chessboard. Cleo told me how ancient the Alchemist is but could he really be behind all that's happening? I wonder. . . .

Climbing out of my car before I lose my nerve, I stride toward Marc's door, taking a flight of stairs to the second floor. The wood on the door is chipped and could use a fresh coat of paint. To the left of it is a sliding-glass window, and through a crack in the curtains I'm able to see Marc reclining on the couch with a can of beer in his hand, watching TV.

I'm surprised to see he's watching *Casablanca*. The movie's almost over and Humphrey Bogart is telling the love of his life, the incredibly gorgeous and extraordinarily talented Ingrid Bergman, to get on the plane and leave him for another man. It's like Marc has seen the movie dozens of times. He mouths aloud Rick's famous last words to Ilsa, "Here's looking at you, kid." Marc busts up at the scene but wipes at his eyes as well, before taking a gulp of his beer.

Is he crying? I always cry when I watch that scene. It looks like we have more than one thing in common. *Casablanca* is my favorite movie as well.

I can't knock. I don't know what to say, how to explain that we're trapped together in a metal cage in an alternate world. Even if we hadn't been kidnapped, there's not much chance he'd believe I'm a witch. Not unless I lifted him to the ceiling with one hand. I've already been through that with Jimmy, though, and dislike demonstrating my powers.

Yet it's good to see him in his natural environment. I have to admit he's awfully cute. If it weren't for Jimmy . . . well, there's no point in thinking about that. Jimmy gave up his normal life to save me and we have a kid and I love him and . . . it's enough. I don't need another lover.

I suspect there's a good chance Marc's gloating over the emeralds he stole the night before. Although I hate whenever I get ripped off, even when it's something small, I have to admit it was kind of cool how he jumped in Silvia's Jaguar and used her own car to escape. It took a lot of guts.

Unknown to Chad and the others, Marc might be the real survivor in the group. I'm stronger but Marc's got instincts. He knows how to get out of a tight spot. Under normal circumstances he'd make for a dangerous adversary.

"See you tomorrow," I say softly, thinking I'm not being entirely accurate. It's Sunday in witch world and when I wake up tomorrow morning it will be Sunday in the real world. So, in a sense, I'll be seeing him today.

Walking back to my car, I wonder if we'll still be locked in that strange compartment.

CHAPTER FIVE

I AWAKEN TO FIND THE SUN IN MY EYES. THE GLARE IS blinding—I have to raise a hand and squint through my fingers to see where the light is coming from. A section of our cell wall has been pulled aside as if it were a sliding doorway, and through the yellow glare I catch a glimpse of acres of green and hear the sound of a trickling stream.

"What the hell?" I mutter, glancing at my partners. Although I was the last one to awaken before, I'm the first one this time around. Marc stirs in his seat at my remark but doesn't open his eyes. The others are out cold. Chad, Shira, and Li all sit with their chins resting on their chests, while Ora lies with his huge head hanging back over the top of his seat, snoring loudly. The guy is so big he can hardly fit in the chair.

I stand and stretch, feeling a momentary wave of dizziness. Since I never feel dizzy when I wake up, and since the rest of the gang has yet to open their eyes, I suspect someone pumped an odorless gas into our cell before we landed. For sure, I have no recollection of us touching down.

I step to Marc and gently shake him, whispering, "Marc, wake up."

He opens his eyes and frowns when he sees it's me. "I was just dreaming about you," he mumbles.

"What was the dream about?"

"None of your business." He notices the missing section of the wall and the bright sunlight. "Shit. Did we crash-land?"

"I'm pretty sure our landing spot was chosen very carefully. Get up, I want to look around. And don't wake the others."

Marc stands uneasily; I have to help steady him on his feet. "Why not?" he asks.

"Because I don't trust them."

"But you trust me?"

"Don't fool yourself. Come, let's take a look outside."

Outside is unmistakably a jungle. The green foliage is extraordinarily dense; it rises sharply a half mile to our right and a mile on our left. Which means we're somewhere in the middle of a valley. The stream I heard from inside the cell is to our left—running east, in the direction of the rising sun— and it has enough kick in it to be labeled a river. Although it's clearly early in the day, the air is warm and humid.

"What the fuck?" Marc gasps as he takes in the scenery. "Where are we?"

"Somewhere we've never been before. Close your eyes and listen. What do you hear?"

He indulges me and shuts his eyes. "Running water. What am I supposed to hear?"

"Keep your eyes shut. Listen. What else do you hear?"

He shrugs. "Nothing. Can I open my eyes now?"

"Yes." I take a step away from him, scanning the surrounding hills and the sky. Although the sun is bright, we're seeing it through a thin haze—a mist perhaps that rises from the damp foliage.

Marc comes up at my side. "What's wrong?"

"We hear the river but that's all we hear. This is a jungle. It should be swarming with insects and birds. But there's nothing. If it wasn't for the running water, this place would be as silent as a tomb."

"That's silly. There's got to be insects. There's no place on earth that doesn't have insects. Maybe this area's just been sprayed with a powerful insecticide."

"And the birds?"

"You don't always hear birds," Marc says.

"Really? How many jungles have you been in?"

"As many as you. None. Look, we just got here. Don't start jumping to conclusions."

"I'm puzzled is all." I point in the direction of the river, to a man-size stone standing at the edge of the water. "That rock. See it? There's something pinned to it."

Marc is wary. "It doesn't look like something that grew here."

I pat him on the arm. "Stay here, I'll check it out."

Marc brushes away my hand. "Like you're in charge."

"I didn't mean it that way. I was just trying to say . . ." I don't finish for obvious reasons. I was about to say it's better if I check out anything weird because I'm a witch and am better able to protect myself. Like that would put him at ease.

Together, Marc and I walk to the river. It's only two hundred feet away and we struggle to get there. I've never hiked in a place before that didn't have even a semblance of a path. We have to skirt a few trees but worse is the thick grass and shrubs. Every square inch of ground is covered with life. We hike less than the length of a football field and yet Marc's sweating by the time we reach the rock. I think it annoys him I'm hardly breathing.

Fastened to the gray stone is a wooden plaque etched with six lines. Despite the fact they're written in an elaborate flowing script, the words are in English and are easy to read.

It takes me a moment to realize I've seen the script before—when I was with Kendor in the desert outside Las Vegas. He took me to a delicious pool of water hidden within an outcrop of rocks he said used to belong to a tribe of Paleo-Indians. At one end of the pond was a stone wall covered with petroglyphs, and littered with words written in this style, only in an unknown language Kendor had to translate for me.

At the time Kendor had implied the Alchemist had been involved with the creation of the Paleo's petroglyphs, although he hadn't elaborated on the point. Yet standing before the wooden plaque with Marc by my side, I'm more and more convinced the Alchemist must be behind our abduction.

The message on the plaque reads as follows:

To protect the righteous and slay the wicked
Six of six are called to the Field
To live
To fight
To die
One will survive

"What the fuck?" Marc says.

"You've got to stop saying that. I have a feeling this place is going to be full of surprises."

"To hell with that. Do you know what this message is saying?"

"Yep. We've been put here to fight to the death."

"Fuck that shit!"

"I told you . . ."

"Shut up, Jessie!" Marc steps back, shaking his head. "This is too much. Who would set something like this up?"

"Somebody who wants to see who's the strongest."

"I don't know what you're talking about. Are you saying this honestly means something to you? I mean—what is it with you, Jessie—you're not acting at all surprised."

"I'm as surprised as you are."

"Bullshit! I may not have Chad's IQ but I know people. And from the second you woke up in that tin can, you haven't so much as blinked. I've been in some pretty hairy situations in my life and like to think I've got balls. But right now, standing next to you, I'm the equivalent of a whimpering schoolgirl. While you . . ." He doesn't finish.

"Go on," I prod.

"You know what's going on here. Don't deny it."

"I don't, honestly. I don't know where we are or who put us here."

He stares at my face. "But you're not surprised we're here. Admit it."

I shake my head but don't speak. When it comes to my lying, Marc's almost as good—or bad, depending on your point of view—as Jimmy at picking up when I'm being evasive. Somehow he can see right through me. He puts his hands on my shoulders as I glance at the ground.

"Tell me what you know," Marc presses.

I raise my head. "We're in a place called the Field. We're

here with five other groups containing six people each. The six of us here—Shira, Chad, Li, Ora, you, and me—have been selected to work together to defeat the other groups."

Marc takes back his hands. "Why do you assume we're supposed to work together? So far Shira acts like she'd love nothing more than to stab me in the back."

I hold up the bright green bracelet on my wrist. It appears to be made of plastic but it's not. Because I can't break it off and I have the strength of twenty men when I draw on the power of my witch gene.

"This bracelet is bright green because it's designed to identify us," I say. "I doubt it has any other purpose. Our uniform is green for probably the same reason—although if that's the case we're lucky because it blends in with the surroundings."

"Are you saying we're the green team and the other groups we run into will be wearing red, brown, yellow, blue, or purple?"

"Yes. I mean, it's possible they'll have on green uniforms as well but I'm confident they'll have different-colored bracelets."

"How can you be so sure?" Marc asks.

"Because it's logical," Chad says, causing both of us to jump. People are not normally able to sneak up on me, which makes me wonder again if Chad and his buddies might not be latent witches, just unaware of who they are.

"How long have you been standing there?" Marc demands.

"Long enough to follow your argument," Chad says,

stepping closer to the plaque and briefly taking off his glasses to clean them on the hem of his green shirt. Already, I've decided the long sleeves will have to go—it's just too hot and humid. I keep eyeing the river, wishing I could strip down and take a dip.

If I do go for a swim, though, it will be quick. My antenna is on high alert. We're in an unknown environment surrounded by hostiles. The plaque made that clear. It wasn't by chance that it was placed in the one spot we'd head to before going anywhere else—at the edge of the river. The person or people who organized this contest wanted us to know the rules of the game right from the start.

Chad studies the plaque for a full minute before speaking. "Whoever etched this had a steady hand," he says finally.

"Who gives a damn about his hands?" Marc snaps. "It's the message I'm worried about."

Chad wipes at the sweat on his forehead and gives Marc a weak smile. "If it's any consolation I'm as freaked out as you are."

I groan. "Would you two quit acting like I'm not scared. I'm supposed to start college in a couple of months. Instead I'm stuck here in a wild jungle like some idiotic character in *Battle Royale*."

"Is that a book?" Chad asks.

Marc speaks. "Yeah. I read it, I liked it. It's one of those gladiator-inspired novels where everyone kills everyone else."

"Glad you enjoyed it," Chad says before turning back to the plaque. "This last line, 'One will survive'—it can be taken two ways. It can mean that only one of us will survive or it could mean—hopefully—that one of the six of six will survive."

"Meaning a whole group," I say.

"Exactly," Chad says.

"I wouldn't count on it," Marc mutters.

I punch him in the arm. "Hey, what's with all the gloom and doom? You were the life of the party on the way here."

"That was before I knew I'd been chosen to amuse a group of rich assholes," Marc says.

"Is that our latest theory on who brought us here?" Chad asks.

Marc shrugs. "Unless Jessie's got a better one, which wouldn't surprise me. But consider the opening line here. It says, 'To protect the righteous and slay the wicked.' A line like that could only have been written by two types of people: a religious freak or a sadist. Personally, I think this is some kind of elaborate sadistic ritual designed to amuse a small group of sick minds."

"It's an interesting idea," Chad says. "But if we're here for entertainment, the trees should be loaded with video cameras and omnidirectional microphones, monitoring our every move."

"Who says they aren't?" Marc says.

I scan the trees. "I don't see any cameras."

"Give it time," Marc says.

Chad speaks up. "Hey! What if we're on the Internet and don't know it? Think about it. A fight to the death would easily draw a hundred million hits on YouTube."

"The whole world would watch," Marc agrees. "Shit, I'd watch if I weren't here."

"I for one would stop watching if the hero kept swearing every other time he spoke," I say.

"Since when did you become such a prude?" Marc asks.

"I'm not a prude," I say.

"Since when is he the hero?" Chad asks, insulted.

I have to laugh. "We're off to a great start. If we're being watched, no one's going to bet on our group winning. We may as well lie down here and surrender."

No one responds for a moment but I notice the guys have slowly turned back to the plaque. My remark was supposed to be a joke to lighten the mood but it seems to have had the opposite effect. Probably because Marc's right—I'm the only one who has a clue what's really going on.

Marc and Chad are both brave young men. But that's the problem—they're men, they're *human*. In a crisis they can't call upon genetically enhanced powers to protect themselves. I'm scared too but I know what I'm capable of. There might be other witches in the Field—there probably are—but I know I'm not going to be defeated easily.

"I hope we can win," Chad says softly.

I pat him on the back. "Seriously, with your huge brain and Marc's diabolical mind, we're way ahead of the curve. Let's wake up the others. We've got to explore this area. If there's thirty people out there plotting to kill us, we'll be sitting ducks if we stay here. I say we refill our water bottles in the river and head for the high ground."

"What about weapons?" Marc says. "Shouldn't we make some kind of weapons?"

"Out of what?" Chad says. "Jessie's right. We need to see what the Field has to offer in the way of supplies and defensive positions. I'm for climbing out of this valley."

Chad heads back toward our gray cell, which lies wedged between a half dozen trees at an awkward angle. It looks like a cargo carton that was casually dumped from the sky. The idea disturbs me for some reason. For all I know we may have been flown here alongside five other metal containers, in the very same craft.

I go to follow Chad but Marc grabs my arm, holding me in place, and speaks softly in my ear. "I'm not fooled, Jessie. There's something you're not telling us."

I turn and stare into his blue eyes, inches away. "Same with you."

"How are we going to protect each other if we don't trust each other?" he asks.

"Trust takes time. You of all people should know that."

He raises an eyebrow. "Why me of all people?"

"Because while I've got my secrets, you've got yours."

Marc squeezes my arm harder and sharpens his tone. "I said it a few minutes ago but I wasn't sure until now that it's true. I'm scared, Chad's scared, but you're not. Not the way an eighteen-year-old chick fresh out of high school should be."

With my free hand, I reach over and mess up his already unmanageable brown hair. "I'm glad you think I'm fresh," I say, before effortlessly shaking free of his grip and walking away.

By the time we reach our open cell, the others are beginning to stir. Shira jumps up fast when Marc gently shakes her awake and immediately demands to know who gassed her. I should have been the one to awaken her, I realize. But Marc smiles at her fury; and I swear he's determined to push Shira over the edge.

"It was those damn Nazis," Marc replies, a joke that only he finds funny. Shira glares at him and shoves him aside and this time I don't blame her. After all, there was probably a good reason her family ended up in Israel.

Ora drinks four of our ten remaining bottles of water—we had twenty-four total—for breakfast, while Li spends over ten minutes in the bathroom. In the end Chad has to knock on the door to get her to come out. Li also drinks a lot of water; for such a small thing, she has a huge thirst.

We show the others the plaque. We have to take them to

the river to see it—the thing is practically embedded in the stone. None of them is too happy to read what it says. Then again, I'm just glad no one gets hysterical. I suspect the gang as a whole was already prepared for the worst.

Yet when I think about it, I realize why none of the others is shocked. Shira serves in the army in one of the most violent parts of the world. Ora, also, lives on the edge of civilization and the Stone Age, and is used to fighting to stay alive. And Li—we don't know much about her except that her past was undoubtedly brutal.

"Looks like I'm not the only one acting suspicious," I can't help but whisper in Marc's ear after the others read the plaque and slowly absorb the enormity of our predicament. Of course, Marc is quick to point out that Shira, Ora, and Li come from vastly different worlds than we do.

"They're used to violence," he hisses at me.

"I didn't exactly grow up in Candy Land."

"Do tell?"

I push him away. "Would you shove it?"

Even though Shira doesn't overreact, she does insist on giving orders as to what we're to do next. It's like she assumes she's in command. Since she wants to climb to the top of the nearest hill, none of us puts up an argument. But I can see we're going to have trouble with her in the near future.

We refill our water bottles in the river, carrying four each in dark green backpacks our benefactors have thoughtfully provided, and begin our hike. Except for the bottles and packs, there's absolutely nothing else we're able to salvage from the cell that would be of any use to us. Yet as I walk, I marvel at how snug my brand-new black boots fit. It's as if someone molded them to my feet.

I'm glad we're on our way. Since finding the plaque, I've been anxious to get moving. I'm glad Shira and Ora appear to share my anxiety. This very instant, I think, someone could be stalking us.

I immediately rip the sleeves off my shirt—Marc and Ora follow suit—and store the extra material in my pack.

"Who knows, we might need it for bandages," Marc says as we plow up the nearest hill. Shira is in front, naturally, leading the way, with Ora by her side. Chad and Li walk in the middle, and from what I can hear it seems Chad's managed to get her to open up a bit. Marc and I bring up the rear.

"The others may not act scared but they are," I warn. "You might want to curb that loose tongue of yours."

"On one condition."

I groan. "How did I know you were going to say that."

"Why did you say, 'It's you,' when I woke you up?"

"You're as bad as Shira."

"It's a legitimate question."

I hesitate. "I dreamed about you before we were brought here."

"No shit. Really?"

"Cross my heart and hope to die."

"And you say I've got a loose tongue."

"Sorry."

He pauses. "What was the dream about?"

"I saw you at work, parking cars. Then I saw you hiding in the trunk of a car."

Marc stops midstride and I have to ask myself why I bother to taunt him. However, my loose mouth may not be so reckless after all. At some point I'm probably going to have to tell the others I'm a witch. I'm just hoping I've earned their trust by then. Preparing Marc ahead of time with a few hints might not be a bad strategy.

"What was I doing in the trunk?" Marc asks.

I smile. "A girl can only wonder."

The thickness of the foliage is staggering, and by the time we reach the top of the hill the gang's breathing heavily and our green uniforms are soaked with sweat, except for Ora's. He's obviously used to strenuous exercise and warm temperatures. I notice him collecting sticks as we walk, a few that could be used for staffs, and long strands of dried-out reeds. I can tell how alert he is, his eyes always scanning in all directions, and am glad he's up front.

Naturally, I don't get winded like the others but I'm not immune to the heat. Just a small reminder that changing into a witch did not make me a superhero.

At the top we find another—taller—hill waiting for us,

and if the terrain had not suddenly opened up we probably would have sunk to our knees and begged for mercy. Fortunately, the worst of the jungle seems confined to the valley. The trees and shrubs suddenly thin and there are actually areas where we're hiking through tall grassy meadows.

Near the top of the second summit, flat slabs of rock are added to the environment, and by taking a winding course over the stone we're able to escape the skin-scraping branches and the worst of the vines and bushes.

The rock is a deep black, obviously volcanic in origin, and it's etched with lines and grooves that remind me of currents and ripples, making it easy for me to imagine a molten river that long ago froze in place.

At the summit we're treated to a staggering view.

We're on an island. Off to our left is the ocean. It's east of us, five miles away, and in front is a vast expanse of rolling land that leads down to the water. In places it's thick with trees. Other spots are either covered with grass or more black rock.

A churning river flows down the center of the expanse, a much larger and aggressive body of water than the one we left behind. From our vantage point I'm able to count five separate streams that feed it; and I have to ask myself how we'll ever be able to cross it—if we're forced.

The coastline is enchanting: the white sandy beach, the crashing waves, the towering stones that look like ancient statues that disintegrated due to the passage of time or neglect.

The swells are a force, the waves easily ten to fifteen feet high, and they send up massive jets of foam as they strike the fallen rocks.

Yet for all its beauty, it's not the coast that holds our attention. Far to our right and in front of us is a dark mountain crowned with a smoking cloud of black smoke shot through with burning red streaks. It takes time for the truth to sink in. We've been left to fight an unknown foe on an island with a highly active volcano.

"That's odd," Chad says.

"What is it?" Shira demands.

Chad shakes his head, his face already showing signs of sunburn. "This island—I don't recognize it. I mean, there are dozens of active volcanoes in the world but I've never seen one like that before." He gestures to the terrain below. "I've never seen pictures of a place like this, which is weird. I'm no expert when it comes to geography but I should at least be able to tell what part of the world we're in. But . . . I can't."

"This is looking more and more like *Lost*," Marc says. "Did any of you watch that show? It was awesome. It was about a bunch of people stranded on an impossible island."

"I do not know this show," Ora says seriously. "But I do not own a TV."

Marc pats him on the back. "Right now, buddy, I envy you. Because you have no idea how bad this can get."

"Shut up!" Shira snaps. "This isn't TV. We're here—this

island is real. We have to figure out how to defend ourselves."

"Good luck with that," Marc says.

I speak. "Chad, like you said, there's dozens of volcanic islands spread all over the world, and we've only seen a portion of this place. We've only just begun to explore. I'm sure we'll figure out where we are eventually."

Chad nods. "I suppose. It just caught me off guard is all, seeing that cinder cone. It looks like it's about to blow."

"I don't want to stay up here any longer," Shira says. "We're too exposed. We could be seen from miles away." She nods to the expanse in front of us. "We have to go down."

"We don't know who's down there," Marc says. "It might be safer to go back."

"No, Shira's right, we can't go back," Ora says. "We need to find another source of water and a strong place we can defend." He points to our right, along the edge of the cliff where we stand. "I see shadows along the side of this ledge. They might be caves."

"A cave can turn into a perfect place to get trapped," Shira warns, although she speaks to Ora with respect, like one warrior to another.

Ora nods gravely. "It depends on the cave. Let us decide after we have seen what is there."

We don't head straight in the direction Ora pointed. Shira insists we hike down lower, decrease our visibility, before turning west, to our right. Since I can't dispute any of the choices

Shira and Ora are making, I keep my mouth shut. For the most part Marc does likewise, until Ora stops and picks up a long sleek piece of volcanic rock and asks Marc if he can carry it in his pack.

"What's wrong with your pack?" Marc asks.

"It is full," Ora says. He has been collecting rocks since we reached the summit.

"All right but don't get carried away," Marc says, accepting the stone. "These babies are heavy."

"Why do you call the dark stones babies?" Ora asks.

"A figure of speech, my friend," Marc replies.

An hour later we encounter—to our relief—the birthplace of a stream that literally bubbles out of the side of a sloping stone wall. I'm not entirely surprised to find it. Like Ora, I've been mentally mapping the lines of water that feed the central river far below and knew there had to be a source nearby. But I'm as happy as the others to replenish my water bottles. The heat and humidity are forcing us to drink almost constantly.

I sit beside Li as we take a short break, although Ora has continued on, saying he wants to scout an area that's caught his interest. Marc and Chad strip off their shirts, boots, and socks, and stretch out in the flowing water, which is delightfully cool. Even Shira takes off her boots and soaks her feet.

But I stay with Li because I'm worried. She's been falling behind all day and now looks on the verge of collapse.

"How are you feeling?" I ask.

She nods as she sips from her bottle. "Fine."

"You're not fine. You're beat. We're all tired but you looked tired before we left that cage behind. Tell me, what's wrong? I won't tell the others if you don't want me to."

Li hesitates. "I'm diabetic."

That's what I feared, especially since we haven't seen any fruit trees all day. Not even banana trees, which grow practically everywhere.

"Type one or type two?" I ask.

"Type two. I can control it mostly with diet if I can eat a little every hour. But I do take medicine."

"Insulin?" At least she's not type one, I think.

"No. I take other medication, but I don't need shots."

"I don't suppose you woke up with your pills in your pockets?"

Li shakes her head. "No such luck. I get dizzy without the meds."

"Can you manage the condition in an emergency? If you do get enough to eat?"

Li nods. "I can get by. But I need protein, not fruit. And I have to rest often."

I squeeze her hand. "Is it okay if I explain your condition to the others? They might wonder why you keep falling behind."

Li watches as Marc splashes Shira when she turns her

back to him. For an instant Shira smiles, before whirling and shouting a foreign obscenity at him. Marc splashes her again, in the face.

"I'll try to keep up," Li says.

"All right. I'm sure we'll find something to eat soon." I say this to give her hope, but also because it makes no sense that those who have organized the "Field" would not give us enough food to stay alive long enough to fight.

Ora reappears thirty minutes later with news. He's found a series of caves. Better yet, he says one of them has a narrow opening and is well hidden behind a row of trees. Shira acts skeptical but her interest is piqued when Ora reassures her that it has a back door.

"The cave digs deep into this side of the hill," Ora explains. "And the opening at the rear leads to the other side of the hill."

"You discovered all that in half an hour?" Marc asks.

Ora nods. "I move fast when I'm alone."

The hike to the cave takes only a few minutes; and once again I'm impressed with Ora's eagle eyes when he points out the opening. The entrance isn't merely camouflaged—it's virtually invisible. The trees help but it's the low entryway that makes the cave next to impossible to spot. We have to drop to our hands and knees to crawl inside. If I had been searching alone, I would have missed it.

Ora's discovery is a good reminder for me. I may be the only witch in the group but each of us has something to contribute. I'm glad we've established a hidden base of operations within walking distance of fresh water. It's my hope that having a *home* of sorts will help our gang bond.

Yet we have a problem. Because the upper lip of the stone entrance extends almost to the ground, the interior is extremely dark. We're fortunate the narrow cave opens to a decent-size cavern, but move us ten yards away from the opening and we start walking into walls.

"We need flashlights," Marc grumbles.

"Torches," Ora counters.

"You've been collecting sticks and volcanic rocks," I say to him. "Can you make us a torch?"

Ora hesitates. "We need another ingredient. But I think I know where to find it." He turns toward the entrance. "I'll be back soon."

I move to follow. "I don't want you wandering out there alone. I'm going with you."

"I can move faster when I'm alone," he repeats.

"Trust me, I won't slow you down."

No one else volunteers to accompany us, probably because they're beat. As Ora and I hike away from the cave, heading west toward the distant volcano, I ask what he's looking for.

"Tar," he says.

For an instant I think he's talking about Cleo and the Council. Then I realize he's using the word the way most people do.

"Have you seen some?" I ask.

He stops and shifts his bundle of long sticks and rolled-up dried reeds into one arm and points with the other arm toward an area near the base of the hillside.

"Do you see it?" he asks.

As a witch, all my senses are naturally magnified. Still, I'm unsure what I'm searching for. One thing, though, the area's choked with trees, and there's a weird kind of fog. . . .

"Is that smoke? Has someone built a campfire there?"

He accepts my ignorance of the outdoors gracefully, although I catch a faint smile. "What you see is steam, not smoke. It can confuse the eye in the bright daylight."

"We're looking at a hot spring?"

"Yes. It's probably caused by lava flowing beneath the ground, mixing with water. But sometimes the lava rises all the way to the surface."

"How did you happen to spot it?"

He touches his nose. "Smelled it."

The hike to the hot spring takes time. It's two miles away and we frequently run into sudden sharp drops that force us to circle around and find another way down. If I were alone I'd jump—I can easily leap off a five-story building—but I don't want to startle Ora.

Yet there's something almost mystical about the guy. Of all the people in the group, I suspect he'd be the first to grasp what I am. Now that we've spent more time together, I'm virtually certain he's a latent witch, who only needs to be awakened. Unfortunately, because it takes an initiatory death rite to bring about the change, I'm not anxious to test my theory.

The biggest obstacle to "connecting" a potential witch to his unique genetic code is not knowing whether or not the person in question possesses the healing gene. The power to heal is first and foremost a power to heal oneself. Those who have it usually survive the initiation rite. Those who don't often die. That's why Jimmy—in the real world, in Las Vegas—died while gambling to come to our aid in witch world.

If only he hadn't injected himself with an overdose of opiates behind my back! I'm far from a master healer but chances are, if I'd been with him, I could have kept him alive. Of course I never would have let him take the risk in the first place, and that's why he didn't tell me what he was doing. Until it was too late.

The guilt I feel over his sacrifice never leaves me. Never.

Ora brims with abnormal strength and I've no doubt that, besides being a latent witch, he has the crucial gene for speed and strength. His endurance is phenomenal; I can see why he wanted to go alone. We don't walk toward the spring, we jog; and yet I see his surprise at how easily I keep up with him.

"You remind me of Ariena," he says.

"Your sister—that's kind of you. How old is Ariena?"

"Fifteen. But she's strong, very strong. She walks ten kilometers every day to the well, and back again with a large jug of water on her shoulder."

Ten kilometers is six point two miles. That means his sister walks over twelve miles a day in the heat, and here I bitch about having to get up and feed Lara during the night. No matter how tough I like to think I am, hanging out with Ora is turning out to be a humbling experience.

The odor of rotten eggs hits us half a mile from the hot springs and grows almost overpowering as we plow through the steam toward its source. From high-school chemistry I know the smell is the result of sulfur mixing with the hydrogen in the water. Not that I care—it stinks and it irritates my eyes. But Ora is quick to point out that such hot springs are good for the health.

"In my country they are highly prized. People travel many kilometers to find one. There's a spring near my village. Take a bath in it and all the scars from spider and snake bites melt away as if by magic. The water also makes a barren woman fertile and old men virile."

I give him a look. "I'm sure everything you say is absolutely true. Just as long as you understand I already took a bath back at the stream, and that I'm not about to take another one."

Ora lets loose a hearty laugh. "You're a special girl, Jessie. One day you will make a lucky man a wonderful wife."

"I don't know how to break it to you, Ora. But in my country us girls aspire to do more than make a man happy." I'd been pinching my nose during the last portion of our hike but

I suddenly stop and lower my hand. I sniff the stinky air. "Hey, I think I smell tar."

Ora is pleased. "Good, we have to find it. Be careful where you put your feet. There may be boiling puddles hidden in these trees."

"Do you know the name of these trees?" I ask as we creep through the steam-filled jungle. "I'm surprised they can survive hot stinking steam."

Ora frowns. "I am also surprised. I've never seen such trees."

"They sure as hell don't grow in my neighborhood," I say, studying the trees more closely. They have thick trunks; the dark brown bark looks as if it could be used for armor. The leaves, also, are unusual—red instead of green, and shaped like spiraling vines.

We locate a supply of tar a minute later. Unfortunately, it's not gathered into a convenient pit but is thinly spread around the rim of a steaming pool. Ora doesn't mind. He squats and quickly begins to wrap the dry reeds around the end of one of his staffs, tying them tight. I kneel by his side.

"Let me help," I say, trying not to cough but not having much luck.

"No. The gas bothers you more than me. You should wait away from the boiling pools."

"I don't want to leave you."

"I'll be all right. I don't need long. Once I wrap all the

reeds around the sticks, I can soak up the tar. You'll see, it'll burn for hours."

"I believe you. But remember the plaque. We may not have seen anyone else yet, but this island is supposed to be swarming with others who were probably shown a similar plaque. If I were them, I'd assume the only way to get off this island is to kill the rest of us."

Ora stops working and stares at me through the sweltering steam. The whites of his eyes are red from the irksome gas, but there's genuine concern in the depths of his gaze. He's hardly spoken about the plaque.

"Do you believe it?" he asks.

"I'm afraid I do."

"You think we're here to protect the righteous and to destroy the wicked?"

"I'm not sure about that line, although I won't be surprised if we run into some pretty nasty characters. But I'm confident this is a trial of some kind."

Like Marc that morning, Ora senses something amiss.

"You don't question the instructions like the rest of us. You seem to accept them." Ora stops. "Tell me, did someone warn you this was going to happen to us?"

I find it difficult to lie to such trusting eyes.

Plus there's a logic in confiding in him.

It will help me gauge how the others will react.

Maybe. Hopefully. Yet Ora is unique. . . .

"I wasn't warned that we'd be thrust together as a group. But yes, I was told by a very wise woman that I'd soon be facing a trial of some kind. Most likely a trial of life and death."

He returns to wrapping the reeds atop the sticks. Yet he's not done with me yet. "Who is this wise woman? Why did she choose to tell you this secret?"

I hesitate. "Ora, what I'm about to tell you next will sound crazy. You'll have trouble believing it. In fact, you won't believe it if I don't prove it to you." I pause. "Drop what you are doing and stand."

Unlike your average American boy, he instantly obeys. I step directly in front of him. "Try knocking me over," I say.

"I might hurt you."

"Trust me, you can't. Do it."

He reaches up and gently shoves me in the chest. I instantly grab his wrists, and he tries to break free, and boy do his eyes widen in shock when he realizes he can't. He fights harder, using all his strength, until I casually throw him down on his butt. He stares up at me in wonder.

"*Who* are you?" he whispers.

I kneel by his side. "It's a long story, one I'll tell you soon when we're alone and away from these stinking pools. But to put it bluntly, I'm a witch. I have special powers. I was born with these powers but I only discovered what I am a month ago. I'm stronger than a dozen men put together. I can move faster than your eye could follow, and can change the way I look whenever I wish." I pause, thinking of how long it took for me to convince Jimmy. "Do you believe me?"

He doesn't hesitate. "Yes."

"I'm glad. For now, it's important that you keep this secret. The others aren't like you, they won't understand. They may even think I've been planted here to kill them. But I promise you, Ora, my only goal now is to protect the rest of you from harm."

"I trust you. I promise to keep your secret."

I'm curious. "Why do you trust me?"

He continues to gaze at me. "I can feel your heart, Jessie. You're kind and good. I knew it the moment you first spoke."

"You're able to sense whether people are good or bad?"

"Yes."

I stand. "That's an amazing gift to have. I want to hike down to the main river, check it out. But I still should be able to keep an eye on you. Even if I'm a couple of miles away, I'll see if anyone else tries to sneak up on this spot."

"Another witch?"

"It's possible. I suspect there are witches in the other groups. But if anyone outside our gang comes after you, I'll head them off." I offer my hand. "Here, let me help you up."

I effortlessly pull him off the ground.

"You're going to the river to look for fish," he says.

"Yep. We have to eat something and I haven't seen much in the way of fruit trees."

"Li needs to eat soon."

"Did she speak to you?"

"She doesn't have to tell me, I know she's sick." He pauses. "Can you tell me what the problem is?"

I hesitate. "She asked me to keep her secret but I know I can trust you with it. She has diabetes. She's used to taking medication each day. Her condition isn't serious, not yet, but it will get serious if she doesn't raise her blood sugar. Protein is what she needs, and fish would be perfect."

"Do you need me to teach you how to catch them? Or can you use your . . . powers?"

I smile at the reverence with which he says the word. "I should be able to snare any that swim by, and I have my pack to store them in. Plus it looks like you'll be able to build us a fire to cook them with so hopefully we'll be all set."

"We have to be careful where we light a fire," Ora warns. "At night it can be seen from far away."

"How about during the day? Are you worried about the smoke?"

"The torches I'm making shouldn't give off much smoke. But if we build a fire in the cave to cook with, it might make it hard to breathe." He pauses. "It might be better if we eat the fish raw."

An idea strikes me. "Let's worry about that when I get back. For all I know, the river is as empty as the trees." I turn toward the river, adding, "Work as fast as you can."

Once free of the foul-smelling steam, I survey the landscape, searching for any sign of movement. The stretch of land from the base of the volcano to the sea is at least ten miles, maybe more, and for all I know the island is more than twice that in diameter.

On the far side of the river is a dense forest area, and behind it stands a rocky cliff that even I'd find challenging to scale. It's possible the other five groups could be hiding in those trees, or in caves buried in the cliff.

But only if the island is on the small side. That's what frustrates me most. I have no sense of the land—its shape, its proportions. A map of it would be every bit as valuable as one of Shira's army rifles.

Like Chad, I wish I'd studied more geology and geography during my long hours at the library. Yet common sense would dictate that the volcano that dominates my view has probably gone through active and quiet phases over time, and was undoubtedly responsible for the creation of the island. Given that, the chances are that it's sitting—roughly—at the center of the island; and if that's the case our respective groups have been given a huge field to do battle in.

There's no way around it, I decide. At some point I'm going to have to climb the volcano and see all the island at once. Then I'll be able to create my own map. But it's a task I'll have to save for later. Even with my witch-enhanced strength and speed, I'm not looking forward to hiking to the top of that cinder cone.

The land between where I stand and the central river is an open field. If I switch to high gear I can cover the mile and a half in less than a minute. Unfortunately, if any witches happen to be watching, I'll be exposing that I possess one of my main abilities. Knowledge is power and I hate to give away any secrets.

Yet I fear to leave Ora alone for long. For that matter, I'm worried about the four I left behind at the cave. They've read the plaque; they're properly spooked. But do they really comprehend the extent of the threat? I doubt it. How can they when they don't even know that witches exist. . . .

What to do? Fly like a witch on a broom and let every other witch know who I am? Or hike to the river like a normal eighteen-year-old girl?

I stand undecided, the passing time eating at me.

But it's because of the pressure of each passing second that I come to the decision I do. At some point, without consciously realizing it, I've begun to feel very protective of my group. It might have come over me when I spoke to Ora a few minutes ago. It doesn't matter, I suddenly realize I have to get back to the others as fast as possible.

I take off like a bat out of hell.

Gasping for air, I reach the river in way under a minute.

I'm greeted by a pleasant surprise. The water is full of fish. My entire education on fish rests with what I've seen spread out on ice at the local grocery stores I've visited over the years.

I know what salmon, tuna, swordfish, and halibut look like—my favorite four fish—but that's about all. These fish are different somehow, but close enough to my favorites that I don't hesitate to jump in at the edge of the river and start grabbing whatever swims by.

The poor fish. They've never met a hungry witch before. I'm way worse than a grizzly. Still relying upon my speed gene, I fill my pack in no time. Indeed, the fish are still alive and kicking as I race back to Ora. I feel kind of guilty about that. I should have smacked their heads on a stone before I stuffed them in my pack. Next time.

Ora is still at work when I return, but I'm surprised how many torches he's assembled. He has a half dozen sticks topped with tar-soaked reeds stuck in the ground. Since he insists on making a few more, I grab one of his torches, a bundle of his smaller sticks, and two sharp pieces of volcanic stone.

"What are you doing?" he asks.

"I'm going to cook the fish here," I reply.

Ora's quick; he understands in an instant. Using the shelter of the steam, I can cook all the fish I want without attracting attention. I leave him behind again for a spot far enough from the stinking pools that I don't pass out, but still close enough to the cloud of steam to hide the smoke of my campfire.

Earlier, Ora had explained that he'd been collecting the slender volcanic rocks to fashion them into knives. But they serve another purpose. When I chip them together above the tar-soaked reeds, they quickly ignite my torch, which I in turn use to light my hastily assembled pile of wood. However, I don't use the torch itself to cook the fish. I worry its black fumes might contaminate the meat.

Ora's already sharpened one of the narrow stones and I'm able to remove the scales, cut off the fish heads, slice open the sides, and pluck out the bones without much fuss. Still, I wish I had a pan, but the tip of a particularly hard stick appears to be all but fire retardant and I use it to roast a half dozen fish at once. I am, after all, cooking for six.

Ah, the aroma of the roasting fish drives me mad! I can hardly wait to dig in. Indeed, the rude bitch that I am, I don't bother waiting for Ora to join me. I scarf down twice as much fish as I've ever eaten in all my life. Tasting like a cross between swordfish and tuna, it's absolutely delicious.

Ora soon appears and insists we head back to the cave. He eats as we walk and I'm glad that at the last minute I cooked an extra two fish because he eats three. The other fish I've wrapped in the torn sleeves of my shirt, which is the best I could muster, and stored them in my backpack.

On the return hike I give Ora a condensed version of what happened to me in Las Vegas. He listens spellbound—often he forgets to chew his food. Unlike Jimmy when he was told the tale of my witch-world connection, Ora doesn't interrupt me once, and when I'm finished he doesn't ask any questions. I'm left hanging.

"Well, what do you think?" I finally ask.

He looks over at me with his big brown eyes. "You've been blessed," he says.

"Now, none of that religious fanaticism," I tease, poking him in the stomach. "I can't stand it. I'm just a normal teenage girl with seven abnormal genes."

But he grabs my hand. "I'm not a fanatic. I speak the truth. You've been blessed."

I shake my head. "By God! Ora, I don't think . . ."

"I know what I know. You are special." He adds, "The Field makes more sense to me now."

"Good, I'm glad. That's what matters, that you understand what's going on here."

He shakes his head sadly. "You know it's not so good. The rest of us, who are not witches, are going to get slaughtered."

The truth of his remark is so obvious, I wonder why I refuse to accept it in my own mind. I want to protest, to say I'll protect him no matter what. But who am I fooling? I can't defend five people twenty-four/seven against five hostile groups. The only way my team members can truly be safe is to put each of them through the death experience and see who survives.

Like any of them is going to be fool enough to let me try such an experiment on them. . . .

I respect Ora too much to give him false hope. I don't know how to respond to his remark. I just look away.

A hundred yards short of the cave, a flash of movement

catches my eye. It comes from the trees on the far side of the central river. Ora sees it as well; he cups his palms around his eyes to reduce the glare of the sun. His sight is exceptional. To me it's another sign he's a witch.

"What do you see?" I ask, craving a second opinion.

"Someone short with white hair."

"Who the hell could it be?"

His face darkens. "I'm not sure it's human."

"Of course he's human. Witches are human beings. We've just got a few extra special genes is all. He's probably an albino."

Ora continues to peer at the distant trees. "Whoever he is, he moves fast."

"What color is his uniform? I saw gray."

Ora nods but that's all.

We walk the rest of the way to the cave in silence.

To my immense relief—I had not even realized how much I was worrying about them—the group is safe, and they cheer when I unveil the cooked fish. All of them except Li, who sits dozing in the corner. I wake her up while Ora lights one of his torches.

"How are you feeling?" I ask, worried. Her eyes struggle to stay open.

"Weak," she mumbles.

"Your blood sugar's low. You need to eat. I've brought fresh roasted fish—the perfect food. Eat, come on, force it down if you have to."

Li's too feeble to raise her hands, and I end up breaking off bite-size pieces of fish and feeding her like a child. Her strength returns quickly, though, and ten minutes after her first swallow she is sitting up with clear eyes and holding the fish in both hands. I fetch her a bottle of water and she bows her head in gratitude.

She sighs. "I haven't gone so long without food in ages."

"When was the last time?" I ask so that only she can hear. The others are focused on their fish and are ignoring us. I can't say I blame them. None of them has eaten in over two days.

"In prison, in the North," Li says, her lower lip quivering at the memory. There's no question she's capitalizing the "North" as she speaks.

"You escaped from North Korea to South Korea?" I ask.

She hesitates, nods. "Two years ago."

"Were you in prison at the time of your escape?"

"Yes. We . . ." She falters. "It's not easy to talk about."

"I'm sure it isn't." But I feel I need to question her, need to understand why she's been placed in my group. I speak gently, "Who is *we*? Your parents?"

"My parents were killed when I was twelve. There was just me and my twin sister, Lula."

"Does Lula live with you in Seoul?"

"She . . . Lula, she died when we were in prison. In North Korea they don't need a reason to arrest you. Lula died while she was being tortured." Li pauses. "I was in the room."

"Oh God. I'm so sorry."

She wipes away a tear. "We were close. We did everything together. It's been hard without her."

"How did you escape from the prison?"

"A group of us escaped. A guard helped us, he came with us. We headed for the Chinese border. We knew it was dangerous but it was the only way. Sometimes the Chinese send you back and you're tortured and then shot. Sometimes the Chinese kill you at the border. They always say it's an accident but we know better."

"And sometimes they help you escape to South Korea?"

Li hesitates. "They helped a few of us. But most of our group—they didn't make it."

"How about the guard who helped you escape?"

Li shakes her head.

I have more questions but don't want to push her too far in her weakened state. In the same way I feel Ora's unique, I know there's something unusual about Li. She's sick, she can hardly fend for herself, but I sense a hidden strength in her. Once more I'm forced to reflect on how easy my life has been.

Up until the day I was introduced to witch world.

The gang gathers around Ora and his burning torch. It gives off little smoke and the orange light is somehow soothing in the dark cavern. Yet our situation is anything but. The group quizzes Ora and me about what we saw on our hike, and we tell them the truth, although I leave off the part about running sub-one-minute miles to the river and back.

We tell them about the figure we saw, the albino racing through the trees. Ora had told me ahead of time that they had to know. Their lives were as much at stake as our own, he insisted. I sense Ora wants me to open up about being a witch but I also know he won't break his promise to keep my secret.

Shira starts to pace at the mention of the albino. "Are you sure he was alone?" she asks.

"Yes," I say firmly.

"I'm not sure," Ora adds. "There may have been two."

Shira snaps, "Surely you can tell the difference between one or two people."

"He moved fast and the sun was in our eyes," Ora says.

"It's unlikely there would be more than one albino on the island," Chad says.

"It's unlikely there would be any," Marc says. "You said the guy was short. How short?"

"A meter and a quarter," Ora replies. "Four feet tall."

"Oh Christ," Marc says. "He can't be human. You know what? This sounds exactly like that last *Predator* movie. The one where a bunch of fighters from different countries were transported to another planet and used as wild game."

"For godssakes, we're not on another planet!" I cry.

"How can you be sure?" Marc demands.

I snap at him. "Because the sun in the sky is the same sun

that's always been in the sky. Because the plants are identical to plants we've always seen. Got it? We're on planet Earth. . . ."

Marc interrupts. "You're the one who pointed out that there's no insect or bird life on this island. Explain that, Ms. Logical."

For some reason all our eyes automatically swing to Chad. He stands peering at the light coming through the low stone rim of the entrance, before turning back to us.

"The sun's sinking behind the volcano," he says. "It'll be dark in an hour, which means we're still on a planet with a twenty-four-hour rotational cycle."

"Thank you, Chad," I mutter.

He raises his hand. "But I agree with Marc on one point. There are mysteries here I can't explain. Where *are* the birds and insects? Where are the fruit trees? The river's loaded with fish and I'm glad, but what kind of fish did we just eat? And who exactly is running around on the other side of the river?"

"He must be a member of one of the other five groups that's been put here to kill us," Shira says. "It's the only explanation. And it's the only thing that matters. Yes, I know what the rest of you think of me. That I'm a trigger-happy Israeli who's trying to export a war that belongs back in her own country. I can see it by the way you look at me. But that plaque was put there for a reason—to warn us. I'm sure the others were given identical plaques and are right now making plans to destroy us. That's why we have to prepare. We have to make weapons to defend ourselves, and send out scouts to see what the enemy is up to. It's the only way."

"I agree," Ora says.

Marc's annoyed. "Didn't you just hear Chad? The sun's about to set. What do you want us to do—go outside and stumble around in the dark until someone puts an arrow through our chest?"

"The dark might be the safest time," Shira says.

"If the overcast evaporates it might not be so dark," Chad warns. "We were abducted four days shy of a full moon. On a clear night, with no artificial light around, the moon can be pretty bright."

"So much the better," Ora says.

Marc stands. "Wait a second. Say we do decide to scout the other side of the river. Say we send out a couple of people. How do they protect themselves if they run into a hostile group? The other gang could kill our people or kidnap them. They could even torture the two to tell them where the rest of us are in this cave."

Shira sneers. "Would you rather cower here like a frightened child?"

Marc shrugs. "Probably, yeah."

Shira spits on the floor. "Coward!"

Marc stays cool. He speaks to the rest of us. "Think about it. Why not hide out here a few days and let the other groups go at it? It's possible they'll wipe each other out, or at least fight until just one is left standing. Then we can emerge from our hideout and snuff the bastard." He adds, "The best offense is a strong defense."

"You've got the quote backward," I mutter.

"Shut up, Ralle," he says.

Chad speaks. "What Marc says has merit. Except for one problem."

"What?" Marc asks.

"If Ora and Jessie saw the albino, what are the chances he saw them? The albino was running through shady trees. Ora and Jessie were standing high atop our side of the valley. Worse, they were only a hundred yards away from our hideout."

"Damnit, Jessie," Marc growls. "You should have hiked around the top of the hill and come in the back way."

"I was in a hurry and didn't want your food to get cold," I say, trying to deflect my blunder. Marc's right, unfortunately; I was careless. Ora and I both were.

"Waiting for the enemy to attack is no way to win a battle," Shira says with conviction. "Someone will come, if not today then tomorrow. They'll search every cave along this cliff until they root us out. Then we'll be cornered. And don't think our escape route will save us. If I were them, the first thing I'd do is check if there was more than one way in and out of this cave." She stops. "We stay here and we'll die. It's that simple. And I don't intend to die."

Shira's words are powerful because she's a soldier. She

thinks like one, she acts like one. I suspect it's why she was chosen to be a part of our group. A bitch with fire—we need someone like her. Even Marc appears moved by her speech.

"We still come back to the issue of weapons," he mutters.

Ora speaks. "Several of the rocks I've collected can be sharpened into knives by grinding them against a slab of stone. The same with the sticks I gathered—they can be sharpened into spears. But it will take work."

"Hard work and time," Chad warns. "If we plan on sending out a scouting party tonight, we'd better get started now."

Shira grins and pulls out a wickedly tipped black stone from her back pocket. "I started the second Jessie and Ora left to catch fish."

"Hold on," Marc complains. "Who's brave enough or dumb enough to volunteer for this so-called scouting expedition?"

"I'll go," Shira says.

"I'll go with her," Ora says, his eyes seeking me out. He knows they will need my protection.

"Count me in," I say.

"Good," Shira agrees, slapping me on the back. "Three will go, three will stay. A wise use of our resources. No one will be left alone."

Marc and Chad glance at Li, then at each other. I don't need to be a telepath to know what they're thinking. They're worried Li can do nothing to protect them, and that the group's two warriors—Ora and Shira—are leaving together. Of course, they'd feel worse if they knew what they were losing with my absence.

"Are we sure we should split up?" Marc says, floating the idea.

Chad says what no one else wants to, choosing his words carefully. "I can stay with Li and look after the place."

Marc doesn't speak but looks at me. His suspicions haven't abated—if anything they've grown. Yet I can tell he doesn't want me to leave with Ora and Shira. There's a fear in his eyes but it's not for himself. I must be tired; I take a minute to understand.

He's worried about me.

We set off four hours after sunset. It's taken us that long to make a rudimentary set of spears and knives. Even with Ora extorting us to put more muscle into the task of grinding the sticks and stones, the weapons end up crude. My knife, and Ora's, are the only two sharp enough to slice open a piece of fruit.

Or an enemy's belly.

Our spears are better, naturally; it's easier to sharpen wood than stone. Yet several of Ora's sticks are slightly bent and I worry how straight they will fly when thrown. The others may hope to hang on to their spears, but I plan on hurling them with as much force as possible. That's why I bring half a dozen.

They'll be my arrows; my arm will be their bow.

Marc gives Ora a hard time about not teaching us how to construct bows and arrows, even after Ora explains, several times, how difficult it is to find the materials to make them. The string has to be strong and flexible at the same time, and the bow has to be made out of wood that can bend and not break. In the end Ora tells Marc we'll be lucky to live long enough to have bows and arrows. That shuts Marc up.

Marc's no coward, though. When it's time to leave, he insists on coming. He jokes that he doesn't want to be caught dead with the two nerds in the group, but he's definitely coming to look after me. I don't object—it'll give me a chance to cover his back.

As Chad promised, the moon is two nights shy of being full and the lunar glow blazes across the wide expanse beneath our cave; the river, in particular, sparkles beneath the white light. It's bright enough that we're able to hike with our torches unlit.

The river's our main obstacle, obviously, and Ora suggests we head west two miles, toward the volcano, which will take us above three separate streams that feed the river.

"The last few streams make the river strong," Ora explains as we hike down from our ledge. "The farther upstream we go, the better chance we'll have of wading across."

"Two miles at night is a long detour to take," Marc says.

"That would be true if we knew where we were going," Shira says wisely.

"I assume we're searching for the albino pygmies," Marc says.

"We're looking for anybody who wants to kill us," Shira says.

Her attitude annoys Marc. "So we shoot first and ask questions later? We're not willing to talk?" he asks.

"Don't be a fool," Shira says.

Ora speaks to Marc. "We have to assume anyone we meet on this island wants us dead. They may pretend to be on our side, and offer their hand in friendship. But I believe the plaque—only one will survive."

"I'm glad we're listening to a few crazy lines written on a piece of wood by a total stranger," Marc says. "You guys treat that plaque as if it were your bible. Don't you find that strange?"

Marc's question is, of course, the most important one of all. It's surprised me the group hasn't discussed the proclamations on the plaque at greater length. Myself, I have an excuse. I know the Lapras are in the midst of a power struggle and that the plaque was written in the Alchemist's handwriting. With the exception of Ora, the others know nothing.

Yet I understand why my group has largely accepted that they'll have to fight to survive. The complexity of our abduction, the mystery of the Field, even the haunted wording on the plaque itself has convinced them that they're dealing with a power bigger than themselves.

Yet Ora surprises me by putting forth a theory that's far simpler, and perhaps more accurate.

"It doesn't matter whether we believe the plaque or not. All that matters is what the other groups believe. Before this night is over, we'll know. Talking about it can't help us."

Ora leads us along the foot of our side of the valley, trying to make use of the cliff's shadows. Essentially we're hiking uphill toward the volcano, and it haunts our night. Even with the bright moon, the red glow from the smoldering magma flickers through the dense smoke that hugs the cinder cone, creating the illusion of a devil's ruby crown.

A devil who watches over the Field and waits.

Only when we're two miles closer to the volcano does Ora turn us toward the river. Here, the expanse has narrowed and it's not long before we're standing at the edge of the roaring water.

Marc eyes the river uneasily. "How deep do you think it gets?" he asks me.

"I'm not sure. But it's colder than you'd expect," I reply, remembering my afternoon fishing expedition.

"If it rises above our waists, we'll have trouble staying on our feet," Ora warns.

"You talking about your waist or ours?" Marc asks.

Ora is the first to plunge in but we don't let him go far

before following. Slick pebbles litter the floor of the river and I struggle not to slip. Because we hold our spears and unlit torches over our heads, our hands and arms are not free. The stone knives and water bottles in our packs add to our weight. Despite my witch-aided strength, I find the crossing difficult and worry about the others. Especially when the water does reach to our waists.

"We have to go back!" Marc cries as we near the center of the river.

"Shh! We can't go back!" Shira snaps.

"This is as deep as it gets!" Ora calls over the roar.

"How do you know?" Marc demands.

"I know," Ora says.

He's right, the worst is over; suddenly the water begins to sink down below our waists. But the cold liquid has left its mark and I shiver at the loss of body heat. Still, the night is warm and once we reach the far side I quickly recover. For several minutes we huddle by the shore, catching our breath, unsure which way to go.

"We have to hike into the trees, get out of sight," Shira says.

Ora nods. "We're exposed here. But if someone waits for us in the trees, they will have seen us already. Better we hike by the river. If they try to attack, they'll have to cross the open field and we'll see them coming."

"Ora's right," Marc says. "We can't hike through that jungle without lighting our torches. Fire them up and a blind bat would spot us."

Ora wants my opinion. "Jessie?"

"There's no good choice, but I feel naked out here with that bright moon. Let's compromise. Let's hike to the edge of the trees and turn down toward the ocean."

"You want to hike all the way to the beach tonight?" Shira asks.

I shake my head. "Let's play it by ear."

Whoever is in the trees might let us pass, I think. Or they may try to murder us the first chance they get. The sad truth is I can't imagine any of the other five groups wanting to talk. Clearly Shira and Ora have infected me with their cynicism.

Or else Cleo did before I was even brought here.

The tree line is a mile from the river. Reaching it, we find the jungle thick but not as impenetrable as in the valley where we landed. There are patches of open meadows and the trees themselves seem less tropical. I finally spot a few I'm able to identify: ferns, oaks, maples. I find it odd that the plant life should change so radically from one side of the river to the next.

We hike two miles down the sloping valley and are almost opposite our home base—which is high on the other side of the river—when I see two white flashes deep in the trees. They come from behind but in the blink of an eye they're in front of us—moving faster than any witch I've ever seen, not making a sound.

Then they vanish, only to reappear as bobs of white even deeper in the jungle. As best I can tell, we're seeing the heads of two albinos. Their white skin seems to react to the moonlight, creating an eerie aura.

Marc's stunned. "How do they move so fast? They're like ghosts."

"They're not ghosts," Ora says solemnly, glancing at me. Marc notes how he keeps looking to me.

"Then what are they?" Marc demands.

"Quiet!" Shira warns. "They're stalking us."

"Then let's stalk them," Ora says, again looking to me for approval.

I nod. "Let's give it a try."

Ora lights his torch and we follow him as he plunges into the trees. The "ghosts" shift once more to our left, toward our original course, toward the sea. Suddenly there are three, instead of two, white bobbing orbs. They keep their distance but don't dash away.

Yet they keep us running; we're not given a chance to catch our breath. After fifteen minutes of chasing them, Marc signals he has to stop and rest. Shira, too, is winded; she sags against a tree. And the burning torch shows the sweat glistening on Ora's strong face.

"We should stop," Ora says.

"You're the one who wanted to go after them," Marc gasps.

"They're playing with us," Ora says. "Leading us."

Shira is tense. "Into a trap?"

Ora nods and again looks to me. "What should we do?"

I point in the direction of the now *four* white heads that can be glimpsed through the woods. "They're clearly waiting for us to follow them. It's like they're taunting us. It could be a trap, but we hiked all this way to learn something and so far . . ."

I let my voice trail off. The time has come, I realize. I can't keep my secret hidden forever, not and protect the others. I say the words that I know I'll never be able to take back.

"Let me go on alone," I say.

Ora hesitates. "That might be best."

"What?" Marc cries. "Are you insane? We don't know a damn thing about who they are. For all we know they're blood-sucking vampires. If they get their hands on you they could rip you to shreds."

I put a hand on Marc's shoulder and try to speak in a calm tone. "Trust me, it's better if I go alone. I'll be all right."

Marc drops his spears and grabs my arm roughly and pulls me toward him. "No, no way! You're losing it, Jessie."

"For once I must agree with Marc," Shira says.

I let Marc hold on to me but speak to both of them. "I haven't been honest with you guys. I know more about this Field than I let on. I know why we're here and I have an idea who organized it. But right now it will take too long to explain everything I want to. For now I need you to just accept that I can handle myself when it comes to these creatures. I'm faster than a normal person, stronger. Ora can vouch that I'm telling the truth."

Ora nods. "I've seen what Jessie can do. We should let her go on ahead."

Marc cannot take his eyes off me, or his hand. It's like he's seeing me for the first time and recognizing me from long ago—both at the same time.

"You really did see me in the trunk of Silvia's car," he gasps. "How?"

"I'm a witch," I say.

"Huh?"

I lean over and kiss his cheek, carefully removing his fingers from my arm. "I'll tell you everything before the night is through. I promise."

That's it—that's all I tell him. Without another word, Ora hands me his torch and I set off after the four ghosts. My exit is abrupt, blindingly fast, enough to shock both Marc and Shira. I hear their startled gasps trail off behind me.

The forest—it now feels more like a forest than a jungle—suddenly thickens and the moonlight is largely smothered by the branches and leaves. I need the torch to keep from running into trees. It's hard to hold on to it and the spears at the same time, and catch up with the damn ghosts.

My breath burns, my chest heaves. The tall grass is the worst obstacle. My soaked boots feel caught in quicksand and I imagine I'm running the wrong way up an escalator. My endurance is exceptional—my witch gene for speed and strength sees to that. But I'm still human, basically, I'm not a machine, and I suspect the ghosts are trying to wear me out.

Is it possible they're not from our world?

Of course they can see me coming. My torch couldn't be a more brazen beacon. Its flames whip around the branches and my trailing hair as I struggle to increase my pace. But the ghosts are monitoring me—running just fast enough to keep their distance. More and more I believe that I'm being led into a trap.

It comes in an unexpected form. In a ghastly vision.

One moment I'm racing through a tidal green wave and the next I emerge into a meadow. The grass is curiously low, the space is strangely circular; almost as if the area has been prepared ahead of time. Hell, it's definitely been prepped. In the crackling light of my torch, I see red, red everywhere, a literal carpet of soaked blood and hacked flesh.

The meadow is filled with bodies.

Five bodies. Severed arms, legs, and heads.

"Oh God," I whisper, and it is a prayer. For those who lie scattered at my feet, for what they've suffered, and for my own sake, that I don't soon join them.

Three of the dead wear brown uniforms, with brown bracelets on their wrists—at least on the two guys whose hands and arms are still attached. Their partner was a girl, with short red hair, freckles, and cute dimples. Her lonely head lies near my foot. None could have been older than myself.

Another body belonged to a girl wearing a dull red uniform with a bright red bracelet. She's been hacked far beyond death; her killer was clearly a sadist.

Or else he was bent on sending a message.

The fifth body is the least damaged—a blond girl, no more than sixteen, dressed in dark blue. She has only a single chest wound and almost looks as if she's sleeping. But dead is dead.

The bracelet of the red-haired girl—it's fallen from her severed arm and I pick it up and examine it, specifically the inside, which I've been unable to see on my own bracelet because it's on so tight. On the portion that would have pressed against her veins, the inside of her wrist, is a narrow oblong shape filled with a smooth dark stone.

I have to assume my own bracelet has the same material inside it. The bracelet is heavier than it should be, and stronger. Setting down my torch and spears, using both hands, I try as hard as I can to break the bracelet. But it remains intact.

What the hell are these bracelets made of?

I still think we've been forced to wear them as a form of ID. But I suspect the dark stone, set so close to the veins and blood that flow in and out of our hands, has another purpose. The stone, when I touch it with my fingertips, feels *strange*. It gives me a chill despite the fact that it isn't cold.

"Jessica Ralle," a husky voice says.

He's just there, no warning, standing in the center of the meadow, dressed in dark blue pants, his chest bare, like his feet, a long bloody stick that resembles a machete in his right hand. He holds his weapon casually by his side, red drops dripping off the sharp tip.

I don't need special genes to know he murdered several of those who lie dead at our feet, and the fact that he's heard my name means he must be a witch. Yet it's my intuition that warns me of his enormous physical strength and tremendous speed. I feel his power with an unseen sense—it pours off him like invisible radiation.

Yet something in his expression confuses me. He's no ordinary psychopath. He doesn't smile and he doesn't gloat. Perhaps it's his blue eyes—the centers appear frozen, fixed on a goal only he can comprehend.

He's a handsome hulk, as tall and muscled as Ora, but tan, with long, curly blond hair that reaches past his shoulders. From his accent, the way he said my name, I can tell he was born in a Scandinavian country. He looks older than me—twenty, maybe twenty-one.

He seems to read my mind. He nods.

"I am called Nordra," he says.

I pick up my spears and stab the nonburning end of my torch into the ground and leave it there. The moon pours its light into the red-streaked meadow; I can see more than I want or need to see without assistance.

I hear movement behind me; two guys approaching. And behind Nordra, in the trees, I see the silhouettes of two girls. All dressed in dark blue, all carrying machetes, clearly all members of the same team. They come only so close, remaining outside the bloody meadow.

"How do you know my name?" I demand.

"Who has not heard of the witch who slew Syn?" Nordra asks, taking a step closer, his bare foot stepping on a mutilated hand. "Although I must admit I'm surprised. I mean no offense, but I heard so many stories, I expected more."

The two guys behind me continue to move; they're obviously positioning themselves. I know they have machetes but what else do they carry? It would be politically correct to let them make the first move, but the blood dripping off Nordra's machete screams out what a fool's move that would be. The truth is to fight this monster I need a machete of my own.

Whirling, tossing a single spear from the bundle in my left hand into my free right hand, I take aim and let fly at the guy nearest to me. I don't aim for his heart but lower, six inches beneath his sternum, and put a ton of velocity on my stick.

The spear pierces him like a hot knife going through a warm loaf of bread and pins him to a tree. Before his buddy can react I strike again, hitting the second guy in the same spot, the tip of the spear once again sinking into the trunk of a tree behind him.

My entire offensive takes a grand total of three seconds, and I'm left with two pinned male butterflies screaming in agony just beyond the edge of the meadow.

I don't know whether to cringe or celebrate.

I do neither. I don't have time to be human.

My victims drop their machetes and I hurry and pick up the one closest to me. Turning back to Nordra, I expect to catch him leaping toward me. To my amazement he hasn't moved an inch, nor has his expression changed. However, his two female helpers have backed up.

The first part of my plan has worked. I have a machete; it feels good in my hand. It reminds me of the staff Syn gave me when I fought Russ. The wood is heavy and hard enough to be petrified.

Just as important—two of Nordra's people are dying and their cries are scaring the shit out of the rest of his team. If Nordra himself didn't appear so damn inscrutable I'd feel a whole lot better.

He adds, obviously impressed with my swift work, "But maybe you will deliver," he says.

"These people you killed, they weren't witches," I say, trying to make it sound like a statement of fact, when in reality I'm looking for facts.

"You must know there's only one in each group."

I shift to his right, the cries of my victims beginning to die down as they choke on their own blood. The pitiful sounds continue to work their sick magic on Nordra's backup. His girls keep retreating deeper and deeper into the trees.

"Then why bother with the humans?" I say, taking a casual dip to untie my boots. Slowly, while I circle, I work free of them and kick them off, along with my socks. Barefoot may not be best while hiking miles in the woods, but when it comes to a hand-to-hand fight in a meadow, the extra traction of feeling every blade of grass can make the difference between life and death.

"Why did you kill the two behind you?" he asks.

"They were sneaking up on me."

Nordra gestures to the bodies. "These ones were in my way."

"What about me?" I ask.

He speaks seriously and for all the world he sounds sincere. "You and I, we can work together. Dispose of the deadweight assigned to us and then go after the others. It would be faster that way."

By "others" he means other witches. The deadweight are those who aren't connected, people like Marc and Ora. Normally I'd think how tragic it is how little regard Nordra has for human life, but from where I'm standing, only a few feet in front of him, his remarks seem perfectly natural. He's a throwback to a Viking warrior, who lives to kill, nothing else.

"You must know only one can survive," I say, testing to see whether he's read the same plaque.

Nordra nods. "In the end there would be only the two of us. Then, and only then, would we fight."

"Why should I trust you to let it go that far?"

He gestures over his bulky shoulder. "As a sign of good faith I'll slay what's left of my group. You will do likewise." He pauses. "I know you have brought three of them with you."

"Your offer is tempting. It would simplify matters. But what do you need with me? You're obviously very strong."

For once he appears troubled. "The other witches on this island—their powers are strange and unpredictable."

"How so?"

He shakes his head. "Join me and I'll tell you what I have seen. Otherwise, we fight, we fight now."

"Like I said, I'm interested. But I don't know you."

He grows impatient. "Surely you've heard of Nordra. My word is my bond. Ask any witch, Tar or Lapra."

"Which are you, Tar or Lapra?"

"I am my own person. But enough talk. Decide."

"Give me a minute to think."

For the first time he acts concerned. "There is no time. Viper hunts nearby. I have seen her handiwork and smelled her trail. It will take the two of us to stop her." He pauses. "Surely you have heard of her?"

"I know Viper. And I'll help you fight her. But leave the other members of my group out of this."

"No!" Nordra says viciously. "Humans cannot help. Dispose

of yours and you will have my trust. That's my final offer."

"Very well," I reply, sliding the tip of my machete into the ground and transferring a spear into my right hand. "My answer is no."

Nordra nods. "So be it."

He attacks; he comes straight at me with his machete raised. I barely have time to get off my spear. He's ten yards away. I aim for the center of his bare chest and let it fly with six times the speed of the finest fastball in Major League Baseball. In other words, almost as fast as a speeding bullet.

He swats the spear away as if it were a fly.

I reach for my machete; he knows I will reach for it. But it's a feint. He's coming too fast. I'll have time to grab the weapon but not enough time to raise it and block his initial blow. So I let it be and instead rise up on the balls of my feet, spinning like a cyclone on the big toe of my left foot and suddenly lashing out with my right foot. It's a move Herme, the son of Syn and Kendor, taught me, and it can be devastating if it's not expected.

Nordra did not expect it.

My heel crashes into his sternum and shatters it.

He staggers back with the wind knocked out of him and probably fragments of bone rammed into his chest cavity. I'm amazed he's still standing. The blow should have killed him. Herme had assured me it would kill anybody if done correctly.

Yet somehow, in the space of seconds, Nordra transforms

from a pale dying Viking back to a tan Nordic god. He sucks in a deep shuddering breath and I hear his sternum crack—his healed sternum. I finally realize what I'm facing. A witch who doesn't merely possess the healing gene, but one who can almost instantly heal himself.

I drop my spears and grab the machete. The only reason I was able to plant my foot on his chest is because I fooled him. Already I can see he's not only stronger than me, he's faster. Never mind that he's an experienced killer when I'm just a month free of high school. True, Herme has tutored me on how to defend myself, and Kendor—despite his denial to the contrary—taught Herme, but I'm still a beginner when it comes to fighting other witches.

Nordra knows that. He smiles as he watches me resume my circling. "You should have struck immediately after your kick. That was your chance. You won't get another."

"Syn felt the same way," I taunt.

"Kendor was with you when you faced her."

"True. But Kendor was dead when I killed her."

Nordra nods as if he's going to continue to talk but then he leaps toward me, rising five feet off the ground. Ducking, I do the ridiculous, the least expected. I run under him, slicing at his left knee. My machete makes contact but it's not a true sword. It's not sharp enough. I bruise him, badly, but I don't take off his leg.

Yet I remember his own advice. He heals too fast. I can't

take even a one-second break between blows. Our backs are to each other when I whirl and try to take off his head. But he ducks, I miss him, and my momentum sends me into an out-of-control spin.

I'm too close to him, I know the danger. Yet I have no time to regain my balance. I catch a blurred image of him raising his machete. He's obviously a master at decapitation and he's going to take off my head. I can't get my machete up in time to block the blow. I can't duck. I can't do *anything*!

Except jump. Even spinning out of control, I'm still able to bend my knees and flex the muscles in my legs enough to send me soaring upward. A fraction of a second slower and I would have been cut in two. I feel the breeze of his slashing machete on the bottoms of my feet as I rise.

The jump works, it extends my life—an extra two seconds. From ten feet above the ground, I look down in search of a miracle, only to find Nordra directly below me.

Yet he's made a second error. In his lust to separate my head from my torso, he swung too hard, putting every last fiber of his being into his blow. As a result it's his turn to be caught spinning out of control due to excess momentum caused by a bad miss.

The fact that I have just cut into his left knee also helps. His healing ability isn't truly instantaneous—it's just awfully fast. His injured knee is still a problem, it's still healing. I know because he staggers as he spins.

This is one of those rare instants where his size and strength are a disadvantage. I'm only half his size. He may be fast but he's not nimble. Bottom line—he can't duplicate the height of my leap into the air.

I don't strike at his head. It's the obvious move and even in the midst of his wild gyration he still possesses enough smarts to raise his machete to block such a blow. Instead, as I descend, I place the tip of my machete on the top of his massive skull. I'm not trying to draw blood—I'm trying to line up my fall.

I drop directly onto his shoulders, my legs gripping his neck. I don't know who's more shocked—him or me—that my crazy move has worked. I'm sure he's never had to "play horsey" with an opponent before.

I grab his head. I have it in my hands, I'm ready to snap his neck. He's completely vulnerable and there's no reason for me to hesitate. He's a murderer. His latest victims lie strewn in pieces all over the meadow and I'm sure they're only a fraction of the people he's killed in his life. He deserves to die.

Yet I do hesitate. Throwing spears at his creeping minions, pinning them to trees, even letting them die slow, painful deaths, that didn't bother me as much as it does to hold Nordra's head—his life—in my hands. It makes no sense.

Yet it does make sense, unfortunately. Soldiers often talk about how in battle they can shoot and kill the enemy at a distance. But to come right up to them, to stab them with a bayonet, or worse, a knife, to hear and feel the blade go in another person's body, it can overwhelm even battle-tested marines.

Yet I don't have the luxury of being overwhelmed.

Logic intercedes.

If I don't kill him, he's going to kill me.

Slipping my right palm beneath his chin, I grip a handful of hair at the base of his skull and viciously rotate his head farther than it has any right to go. I hear a bone crack and am only a millisecond from snapping every vertebrae in his neck . . .

When his machete swings up and strikes my left wrist.

The sharp end hits my green bracelet. Had it struck anywhere else, it would have taken off my hand. Still, the blow is painful and I hear a loud pop. Pain rockets up my arm. I figure it's my own bone breaking and fear I've waited too long. With his free hand Nordra reaches up and grabs me by my shirt and tosses me over his head as if I were as light as a pillow. I know what awaits me when I strike the ground.

Death. He will decapitate me when I land.

Yet something miraculous happens. I take forever to hit the ground. Well, maybe not forever but a long time. I wonder if it's because I'm about to die. If my brain can't cope with the grim reality and has overloaded and shorted out and caused the last second of my existence to last and last.

If I'm objective, though, I'd have to say time is suddenly moving at quarter speed. I take four seconds to hit the ground, and in those seconds, Nordra scarcely moves at all. I don't know why, I'm dumbfounded. When I do strike the ground, I hear the stone inside my bracelet click against itself and realize that Nordra must have broken it with his machete.

But I pay it little heed because when I land time returns to normal. For me, not for Nordra. He's still acting like a figure that's been caught on film and replayed in slow motion. He sees me, that's clear. His eyes swell with rage and the veins in his neck pop. I know I broke one of his cervical vertebrae but I don't know which one. Obviously I didn't get the top joint, which would have killed or paralyzed him. The bastard's still moving, still preparing to cut off my head.

But I have time to escape, four times more time than I should have. Not being the sort to look a gift horse in the mouth—or question all the weird shit that keeps happening in my life—I jump up and race to the edge of the meadow, grab my spears, boots, and socks, and run into the trees. I keep the machete. Whatever's happened to Nordra, or me, I figure I'll be seeing him again soon.

Twenty minutes later, I find Marc and Ora in the worst way possible—by following Shira's screams. Whatever happened to time in the meadow has stopped here in the forest. And it's clear I'm not the only one who ran into a witch.

Shira lies writhing on the ground with Marc desperately trying to put out her burning shirt by smothering the flames with his own shirt. Only the fire won't die and Marc is getting his own hands burned.

Meanwhile, Ora stands pinned to a tree by a spear that has pierced far inside his left shoulder. It sickens me to see my own dirty trick used against my own people. Ora isn't bleeding heavily but is clearly in pain, although he hides it well. Yet it's obvious his inability to help Shira is causing him more grief than his wound.

"Stand aside!" I snap at Marc as I push him out of the way and reach for the water bottles in my pack. The reason Shira's shirt keeps burning is because it's been sprayed with molten lava. I don't think Marc knows that.

"Get out your water!" I order Marc as I pour my own supply over the flames. The instant the liquid hits the lava a jet of steam strikes us in the face and Shira's shrieks echo through the forest. I keep pouring, though, going through a dozen pint-size bottles before the flames are finally out and the lava loses its ghastly red glow.

Yet a mass of bloody flesh has taken its place. The left half of Shira's chest and a large portion of her left side, down to her waist, is severely burned. I want to try to heal her—I have the gene for healing. Unfortunately, I've used the power only sparingly: to cure Lara's colic and Jimmy when he had a bad flu. I doubt I can summon enough juice to cure Shira.

The lava intimidates me the most. In large swabs it's

literally fused with burnt skin and I can hardly tell the black flesh from the black rock.

Shira's cries begin to die down. It's a mixed blessing. I want her to black out and escape her agony but fear she'll go into shock. Marc shares my concern.

"We can't let her lose consciousness," he warns. "We have to keep her awake."

"Who'd want to live through this?" I mumble, the adrenaline-fueled rush I had felt after escaping Nordra being replaced by a feeling of despair. It was childish but I'd actually felt excited running back to my partners. I felt pumped up—ready to share what I'd learned and help plan how we'd strike back. Clearly the intoxication of escaping death had gone to my head. Now I wished I had never left my friends alone.

I don't even know what happened to them—who attacked them, and if the person is still in the area—and I'm surprised to discover I'm in no hurry to know. It won't change a thing, I try to tell myself. But the truth is far more disturbing.

I'm a pitiful leader.

I must have closed my eyes without realizing. Marc shakes me and I reopen them. "Do something!" he shouts.

"What do you want me to do?"

"You told Ora this afternoon you can heal. Heal her!"

I glance behind where Ora stands pinned. "But Ora . . . We have to get him free." I start to stand. "We have to pull out the spear."

Marc yanks me down. "Pull out that spear and he'll bleed like a stuck pig. We have to be prepared when we take it out. But right now you have to save Shira."

"Shira," I whisper. I realize then I'll never be a doctor. I can hardly bear to look at her wounds. The lava has burned through to her rib cage. I see charred bones poking through black crusty skin. The stumps of veins that have been cauterized by heat. Open veins that bleed freely; the sticky blood trickling over her scorched belly and soaking the top of her pants. A wave of nausea sweeps over me and I fear I'll vomit.

"I can't," I moan.

Marc takes my hands in his. "Look at me, Jessie."

I do as he says and suddenly I realize how grateful I am that he's not hurt. That's something, I tell myself. Yet the thought also fills me with shame.

"I can't," I repeat.

Marc squeezes my hands. "I know what's been driving me crazy since I met you. You have magic. Even before you told us you were a witch, I knew you were special, maybe even more special than you realize. You can heal her, Jessie, I know you can. So does Ora. After that bitch attacked us, and Shira was crying and I was freaking out and Ora was stuck to the tree, Ora told us it would be all right. He said, 'Jessie will come back. Jessie will save us.'" Marc pauses. "You can do it."

"Was it Viper?" I ask as if the name has meaning to me, and it does in some primal way. It's as if I've been dreaming about her along with Marc, only when it came to Viper they were nightmares that I blocked out and forgot about. Until now.

"That's what she called herself," Marc says. "She could have killed all of us but she didn't. She said she wanted to wait until you were here so you could watch us die."

"She's evil," Ora says solemnly. "But you're a good person, a great person. What Marc says is true—I have faith in you, we all do. Help Shira. If you can't save her, at least stop her pain. Don't worry about me. I can wait."

"I'll do what I can," I say, turning back to Shira, instinctively placing a hand on her forehead and another on the center of her chest. Closing my eyes, I feel as if the moon suddenly swells in size and brilliance before I realize I'm seeing it all inside—some kind of mysterious light. It's not hot or cold but it moves and is alive and I sense it carries life within it. In the midst of my despair my intuition is finally able to speak clearly. The light has come to us because I've dropped my badass attitude, because I've been humbled, and most of all because I only care about helping Shira.

Beneath my hands I feel her body relax and know her pain is receding. I open my eyes the same instant she does. Looking up at me, her face calm, she smiles. She has a nice smile.

"Thank you," she whispers.

I lean over and speak in her ear. "In another world I'll find you. I'll call and introduce myself. You won't know me at first but I'll know you, and maybe we'll have a chance to be friends."

Her eyes fall shut. "Be sure to call, Jessie."

I kiss her cheek and feel unshed tears burn my eyes.

"I promise, Shira," I say.

She dies. She dies to the real world.

CHAPTER SIX

WHEN I WAKE UP IT'S NOON, IN WITCH WORLD, AND the house is empty. That's okay, I'm back home, the nightmare's over. I can't believe how much relief I feel! It's like I want to run around the house and scream how great it is to be alive!

A pity I'll be back in the Field come tomorrow.

There's a note from Jimmy. He's taken Lara and my mother to Griffith Park Observatory.

I use the bathroom, shower, don't bother with makeup. A lot fewer people use makeup in witch world than in the real world, I don't know why. For breakfast I have scrambled eggs, bacon, and toast, and thank God it's not fish. I drink three cups of strong coffee with plenty of sugar but only a pinch of milk. Finally, with hot food in my belly and caffeine fortifying my blood, I feel ready to tackle the day.

It's unusual for Jimmy to leave without saying good-bye. I must have been sleeping deeply. I never stay in bed until noon.

Then again, in the real world, in the Field, I didn't get to lie down until near dawn. I barely made it back to the cave to make what I like to call the "soul switch." It's during the two and a half minutes when the sun is rising that a witch's mind moves from one dimension to the other. If you're not in bed asleep during that narrow span of time, you black out where you're standing.

I call Cleo after I finish my breakfast. I've had her private number since Las Vegas but have never called before. I sit on the living room couch with a pad and pen nearby in case I need to take notes. The woman doesn't waste words, I remind myself.

My heart pounds as I dial the number. Cleo answers after one ring and cuts straight to the chase. "Jessica. I've been waiting for your call. I've heard you're in the Field."

"How did you find out?"

"Your competition's been calling their contacts and asking about you. Specifically, they want to know how many genes you have and what powers you've developed."

"Nordra and Viper?"

"Yes."

"Anyone else?"

"If there is anyone else, they're being discreet." Cleo pauses. "How's it going?"

"I lost one of my team. Shira Attali from Tel Aviv."

"A pity. Are you all right?"

"Physically I'm fine, but I've had a few close calls. Nordra and Viper are not nice people."

"Tell me," Cleo says.

I relate everything that's happened since I woke up in the transport cell with my gang. As usual Cleo listens without interrupting. I try to give as much detail as possible, but toward the end I feel I've talked too long and rush through my battle with Nordra and Shira's death.

When I finish Cleo asks, "Why didn't you call yesterday when you were first taken?"

"I didn't feel I had enough to report," I say.

"Nordra and Viper contacted their people right away. They were better prepared than you." Cleo pauses. "Still, you have done well so far."

"All I've done is stay alive."

"That's the main point of the exercise."

"Looks to me like it's the only point." When Cleo doesn't respond, I ask, "What can you tell me about Nordra and Viper?"

"They have at least six witch genes each. To be taken to the Field you must have at least that number. As to their strengths, you have already met Nordra. You know he's fast and strong and heals quickly. To kill him you'll have to strike a single fatal blow."

"Have you scanned his DNA?" I ask. My own DNA has been scanned but I've never been "formally" told by the

Council which witch genes I possess, although I'm aware of five of them.

I have healing—which can involve the healing of others or myself; intuition—which can manifest as insight, intelligence, or wisdom; speed/strength; cloaking—which means I can assume the appearance of other people; and the time gene—which I only heard about from Cleo the other night.

The other two are a mystery to me, and my lack of knowledge of them frustrates the hell out of me, particularly at a time like this when I need every edge I can get.

Unfortunately, the Tar's Council usually withholds the details of a witch's genetic makeup because they have a strict rule that a witch should develop his abilities naturally, over time. They feel that if a person knows he has a latent ability, there's a good chance he'll focus on developing it prematurely. In other words, the Council feels even good witches can be seduced by the desire for more power.

Yet my father gave me plenty of hints about my abilities in Las Vegas, and Cleo did tell me about my ability to alter time when I saw her in San Francisco. Given the fact that I'm fighting for my life in the Field, I'm hoping that Cleo will ignore their protocol altogether and tell me everything she knows about me, along with any secret information she might have on Nordra and Viper.

"The Council has not had a chance to scan Nordra's DNA," Cleo replies. "But we know he has heightened hearing and vision—far beyond what most witches possess. He also has the intuitive gene, which in him manifests as cleverness. He came right at you when you fought but watch out for his tricks. He can be clever."

"Why is his self-healing ability so phenomenal?"

"It runs in his family. Long ago I fought an ancestor of his. She'd recover from the most severe wound in a matter of seconds."

"Where did you fight her?"

Cleo hesitates. "In the Field."

"So you—"

"Focus on the task at hand," Cleo interrupts.

I feel a flash of annoyance, which I often do around Cleo. I love the woman, and my respect for her is immense, but I dislike having to answer to her. I've never made a choice to be beholden to the Council, but my father has told me that as a good witch—one who's not a Lapra—I'm automatically Tar and required to obey the Council. And since Cleo leads the Council, she's technically my boss.

"What about Viper?" I ask. "Like I said, I didn't meet her face-to-face but Marc and Ora—two of my people—told me her gang struck with spears while Viper sprayed Shira with molten lava without warning. Marc says she just waved her hand and the lava flew through the air."

Cleo speaks seriously. "Viper's a psychopath. She enjoys inflicting pain and she has the tools to do so. The depth of her cruelty's impossible to overexaggerate. We think it's a result of being connected at the age of six. No other witch in our history has ever been awakened so young. She grew up wild on the streets of Tokyo, closely connected to Yakuza, the Japanese mafia. She's strong and fast and heals quickly. Her telekinesis is extremely potent. There's any number of ways she could have used it to burn Shira with the lava."

"She must have had a container of lava nearby," I say.

"Perhaps. But there's plenty of lava on that island. Avoid confronting her near a hot spring. Also, we've heard numerous reports out of Japan concerning her cloaking gene."

"I have that one."

"You can alter your appearance and you've made a good start at using the gene. But Viper's ability is highly developed. She can make herself invisible."

"Shit!" I gasp.

"It's a problem. But keep in mind she's young—all the contestants in the Field are young, fifteen to twenty-one. Viper's only sixteen and to be able to turn invisible at her age is unheard of. I'm sure it requires all her strength to disappear, and I doubt she can keep it up for long. Also, even when she's invisible, you should be able to see an outline of her in the moonlight. Plus, in the bright sunlight, you should see a faint shadow on the ground. For that reason, it's best to catch her out in the open beneath the moon or sun. Otherwise, you've got to hear her coming."

"What if she's carrying a knife or machete? Will they be invisible too?"

"If they're touching her skin," Cleo says.

"She sounds like a nightmare. But Nordra's got to be a psychopath as well. Most of his victims were dismembered."

Cleo speaks firmly. "That's not his style. Viper probably did that to his victims after they'd been killed to send a message to all the other witches in the Field that she's coming for them."

"To scare us?" I ask.

"If you like, yes."

"Lovely," I mutter. "I told you about the ones we call the 'ghosts.' What's their story?"

"The fact they're fighting in the Field is a surprise. I haven't seen a 'ghost'—the Council calls them by the same name—since Ancient Egypt. Kendor told me that he and Syn spotted a few of them outside Rome not long after the death of Caesar. The ghosts have only been seen in groups, never alone. They're extremely telepathic, even when young. It was the belief of the ancient Tar that they somehow function together as a hive mind."

"You mean they don't see themselves as individuals?"

"We're not sure. Our knowledge of them is sketchy. I've heard rumors of them being seen in odd places—high in the Andes and the Himalayas. There was one report they had been spotted in Antarctica. But that was back in the eighteenth century."

"But who are they? What are they?"

"They're human beings, like you and I, witches. My mentor told me they were highly respected during the Atlantean era, although reclusive. It was my understanding they never socialized with normal people. Perhaps their appearance kept them apart or the fact that they don't speak."

"They're mute?"

"Their telepathic gifts are apparently so great they have no need to speak. I wouldn't be surprised if their vocal cords have atrophied due to lack of use."

"They sure can run. I got the impression they were trying to lead me to Nordra so he could kill me."

"That's probably their wisest strategy—to hope the rest of you wipe each other out. Whatever you do, don't underestimate them just because they appear physically weak. To have survived for so long, and stayed hidden, means they must be intelligent."

"Do you know anything about the other two witches on the island?"

"No. Try to discover their names and I'll find out what I can." Cleo adds, "For all we know, Nordra or Viper might have already killed them."

A silence settles between us. For my part, Cleo's hit me with a ton of information, most of it unpleasant, and it's taking me time to absorb. But what Cleo's thinking I have no idea.

"I need to understand more about the Field," I say finally.

"I can understand why a group of witches would be put on a secluded island to battle for superiority. But why have we been assigned the others?"

"The Field exists to test your leadership qualities as well as your power. The majority of people in the world are not witches. A true leader has to be able to command both—witches and humans."

"Hold on. Surely the Tar don't use the Field to pick who's going to be next in line? I mean, you didn't become the head of the Council by fighting in the Field?"

"I'm the head of the Council because the others treat me as the head. I have no official position."

"But was that always the case in the past?"

"The Field is ancient. I first heard of it over ten thousand years ago, from my mentor. Back then there were no Lapras, which isn't to say there were no evil witches. In that time, the Field was used to pick a single world leader."

I've never heard Cleo admit she was so old.

"One who would lead both the good and the bad witches?"

"One who would lead the whole world," Cleo replies.

"When was it last used?"

"Long, long ago," Cleo says.

"Were the contestants always sent to an island?"

"They were sent to the island where you are now, with the identical number of witches and non-witches. Six groups of six."

"What was it like when you were a contestant?"

Cleo hesitates. "I can't answer that question at this time."

"Why not? You've already admitted you were there."

Cleo tries deflecting the question but she just raises more. "You're wondering if your partners might be potential witches. That's for you to discover."

"Come on, Cleo!" I complain, for all the good it does me.

"No."

"Then tell me this. The rules of the Field—they were presented to us on a plaque. It said, 'To protect the righteous and slay the wicked. Six of six are called to the Field. To live. To fight. To die. One will survive.'" I pause. "What the hell does it all mean?"

"Understand, long ago, the selection of a new leader was considered a momentous event. Whoever was chosen *did* protect society from the wicked. And in those days there were a lot more witches than there are now, and many were evil. To be blunt, the plaque means what it says."

"It makes no sense that someone so young, no matter how powerful, should emerge victorious from the Field and assume leadership of the whole world."

"Surviving the Field is the first step to leadership. Other tests follow, and by the time they're completed the person isn't so young."

"I see," I say, although I'm not sure if I do. "What about the last line on the plaque? If I win, if I kill all the other witches, can other members of my group also survive?"

Cleo takes time to answer. "I was your age when I asked my mentor that same question. He told me that there was no reason a good-hearted witch should harm his or her own people. Yet he said there had never been a time when a normal person had survived the Field."

I think of Marc and my throat constricts; it makes my voice tight. "There's always a first time," I whisper.

"True, Jessica. I know you'll do everything in your power to protect your people. That's who you are. Now, it's essential you accept the Alchemist's offer. Go to the house he led you to. He's already told you that Syn and Kendor are waiting to prepare you. You've already lost a day in witch world by not working with them on Sunday. Don't waste another."

"How can you be so sure they can help me?"

"Kendor told you once that you have the identical genetic makeup as Syn. And you can be sure he trained her to use all her abilities. You could have no better teachers than the two of them." She pauses. "But be careful. Never reveal to them Syn's future. We cannot be sure what year the Alchemist has plucked them from, but it's probably from before she turned toward the darkness."

"Kendor doesn't even know me now. Why should he help me?"

"The Alchemist must have told him why he's in this time. Also, for whatever it's worth, Kendor only knew you for a few days in Las Vegas, yet in that short time he loved you. And I think you loved him."

"That was then," I protest, wiping away a tear.

"Love is never lost, Jessica. Not even time can erase it. Go to him and you'll see. He'll welcome you and help you." Cleo pauses. "I'm sure Syn will do the same."

"I'll do what you say."

It's not easy to knock on the door of the house the Alchemist led me to in Pacific Palisades. I'm not afraid for my life—I doubt the sorcerer would have gone to so much trouble just to kill me. I'm more worried about meeting Syn and Kendor. I don't share Cleo's confidence that they'll be happy to see me.

Syn answers the door. I've forgotten how beautiful she is. Her skin's a light brown, smooth and radiant, and her black hair is cut shorter than I remember; it barely touches the shoulders of her white summer dress. She smiles when she sees me, and with just a glance in my direction her dark eyes seem to cast a spell.

"You must be Jessica," she says.

"Yes. How do you know my name?"

"William told us to expect you," she replies, opening the door wider. "Please come in."

The house is lovely, rich; the architect clearly designed it with one mandate in mind—to take advantage of the ocean views. Syn leads me to a large living room, where the windows reach to a second-story ceiling. Polished cedar frames the glass rows. Most people would label the style modern. The sofa and chairs are white leather, the tabletops are made of thick stone. Yet the abundance of wood on the walls and stairway adds a cozy feel.

Syn beckons for me to have a seat as Kendor enters from the backyard. Whatever age he's been plucked from, his clothes have not changed much. He has on the same black leather pants and boots, although his short-sleeved shirt is gray and looks like it was purchased at the mall where I first spotted them. Like before, his dark blond hair is long and uncombed, and if there's a more sexy man on the planet, I've never met him. Like Cleo, Kendor has an aura of immense power, yet he approaches me shyly, bowing and kissing my hand. He introduces himself and welcomes me to their home.

Together we sit in the center of the room, forming a peculiar triangle. I don't know who looks more uncertain—them or me. Yet I sense they're glad to see me, although I must admit my own emotions are more complex. My last vision of Kendor was of him falling to the floor, his heart pierced, with Syn standing over him with a bloody knife.

I glance around. "Are we alone?" I ask.

"William has been gone two days," Syn replies. "He did not say when he would be back."

"William?" I repeat, turning to Kendor. "Is that another name for the Alchemist?"

Kendor nods. "I am sure the man has many names."

I smile nervously. "Well, I've only got two. Jessica Ralle. You can call me Jessie if you want."

"And you know us?" Kendor says carefully, questioning.

"Yes. You're Syn and Kendor."

Syn frowns. "How long have you known us?"

"What did William tell you?" I ask. "I mean, I'm not trying to be evasive. I'm just wondering. . . . Do you know where you are? What year it is?"

Kendor and Syn exchange a dark look. Kendor answers.

"William has explained these things to us. We are from what you would call the sixth century, and he has brought us forward in time fifteen hundred years to prepare you for the Field."

I do a quick mental calculation. Syn and Kendor met and married around 47 BC, and had a son, Robere, in AD 386. Unfortunately, when the Huns attacked Rome in 431, Robere was pinned to a tree by a javelin and died. The Kendor I knew, the one I met in Las Vegas last month, told me that Syn grieved over the loss of her son for ages.

Yet I'm hoping Syn's healed over the past century. Because it was the repeated loss of her children and grandchildren over the long years that led to her eventual obsession with evil.

"Pleasure for pain," she used to call it.

"You know about the Field?" I say.

Kendor speaks. "I know of it, Syn does not. But most of

what I know has come to me from rumors and legends. I never fought in it."

"Not like Cleo?" I say, fishing.

Kendor is impressed. "You are friends with Cleo? That is good. We were not told that. I am surprised she spoke of her time in the Field. It was a secret she hid from me for a long time." His face darkens. "She never got over what happened there."

"Pardon me," Syn says. "This may sound rude but I must ask. How long have we known you in this time? What is our relationship?"

The way she phrases the questions, it's clear the Alchemist hasn't told them that they're dead in this time. Hell, I think. The two must be wondering why their present-day incarnations are not around to tutor me.

I hesitate. "Not long. But we're friends."

"True friends?" Syn asks.

I'm not sure what she means by "true." Nevertheless, I'm surprised at the quality of their English. Except for a faint accent I can't place, they could be understood by most people in town.

I recall that Kendor once told me he was able to pick up languages easily and that Syn had a photographic memory. Still, except for the absence of contractions, their phrasing is remarkably modern. I remind myself they were probably living in Sicily when the Alchemist swept them into our time.

Also, they're not dazed like when I saw them at the mall. It makes me wonder if this is their same "time trip" to my century. What I mean is, this could be the third or fourth time the Alchemist brought them to the twenty-first century, while two days ago could have been the first time. It's a weird idea but that's the problem in trying to analyze a time traveler's state of mind. I mean, how can I get things straight in my own head when I'm dealing with people who are not living linear lives?

"I like to think so," I reply carefully.

"When did you see us last?" she asks.

"Not long ago. Maybe four weeks ago."

Syn frowns. "William refused to explain why our counterparts in this time are unable to prepare you for the Field. I did not press the matter but I assume that must mean we are already dead—at this time. But you say we are not. Perhaps you can better explain why we are here?"

"Is it a hardship for you to be here?" I ask, wanting to change the subject. "I imagine it would be exciting to travel through time, and confusing. Most of what you see must seem strange."

"Strange and wonderful," Kendor says. "William took us to a place where 'jets' take off into the sky. They are so big, so heavy, and yet they seem to float into the air. To us they look like magic."

I smile. "I saw you eating ice cream. How was that?"

Kendor grins. "I could eat it all day and have nothing else."

"That's great," I reply.

"Why do you avoid my question?" Syn asks suddenly.

I consider. Syn and Kendor are both perceptive. Lying to them is risky. I decide the more truth I can tell the better.

"You know the Alchemist better than I do," I say. "I only met him for the first time two days ago. I'm not sure why he's gone to all this trouble to bring you here. I've been asking myself the same question. It's not like I'm an important person."

"You must be important to be fighting in the Field," Syn says.

I shrug. "I have many powers but most are undeveloped. To be blunt, the reason I came here today is because I was hoping you could show me how to use them. In the other world I'm already in the Field and fighting for my life."

Kendor studies me. "You remind me of Syn. What are your gifts?"

"I'm supposed to have seven but can only use four: intuition; speed and strength; healing; and I can cloak myself." I stop and shake my head. "Cleo said I have the ability to alter time but told me I won't be able to use it for a long time. So I suppose it can't help me at this time."

"It can take a long time," Syn agrees quietly.

Kendor stands. "The day moves on. Let us see what you can do. And while we test you, tell us everything you know about your opponents. Since you are already fighting in the

Field, I doubt you need to be told how dangerous it is. Still, I feel I must tell you. Cleo herself barely made it out of there alive."

"I understand. Only one can survive."

He nods. "Only one."

Kendor leads me into the backyard and I expect Syn to follow but she leaves us alone. Perhaps she thinks her husband is the master warrior, and I don't need her help. Maybe she doesn't like me, I don't know. Certainly she is wary. Although Kendor appears to have accepted the switch in time, I can tell Syn resents having her life interrupted by the Alchemist.

We have that much in common.

Neither of us can stand to be controlled.

The curious thing is that I know, from having spoken to Kendor in Las Vegas, that both of them will have only the faintest memories of having been in our time.

Kendor has available an assortment of primitive weapons: swords, spears, bows and arrows, handheld iron shields. He tests how I handle each one and suddenly stops when I pick up a sword and feel its balance before I move into a fighting stance.

"Who taught you to do that?" he demands.

Herme, Kendor's son, recently taught me the basics of sword fighting, and naturally Kendor taught him, despite the fact that Kendor had specifically told me that his son had wanted nothing to do with the fighting arts. When Herme had begun to teach me, I'd asked him why his father had lied. Herme had smiled and shaken his head and said, "My father trained me every day straight, for ten years, before I told him no more. Yet to my dad, a decade of hard study was equivalent to nothing."

Since Herme isn't going to be born to Syn and Kendor for over a thousand years—their time—I'm not sure how to respond.

Yet Kendor is wise. He suddenly puts a finger to his lips.

"Shh. Tell me what you can when you can," he says.

I'm touched. "We just met. Why do you trust me?"

Kendor catches my eye. "Because you are my friend."

We start with the sword and he drills me hard. He shows me a move once, twice, a maximum of three times, then he expects me to know it. He attacks with his own sword and if I don't use what he has taught me he cuts me. Literally, he doesn't mind hurting me, and it's not long before my pants and blouse are stained with blood.

He gives me little time to recover, to heal, sometimes none at all. He seems to think that fighting in pain is the best way to learn. At one point, exhausted, I beg for a break and he responds by stabbing me in the thigh. Herme has given me lessons for a month but in two hours Kendor teaches me more than his son.

Kendor switches to the spear, knowing it's the most handy weapon available on the island. At first he has me throw it at various targets. Then I become the target—he throws the spears at me, forcing me to knock them away. His throws grow faster, more fierce. He aims for my heart and if I were to miss blocking the stick I'd die. Pain isn't the only tool he uses to teach. It's clear he feels fear works even faster.

All the while he asks me what I know about Nordra, Viper, the ghosts. He's curious why time seemed to slow down when I fought Nordra. He assumes it's a sign my time gene is becoming active, although he agrees that is very unusual.

But I don't think the time change had anything to do with my gene. I suspect it had to do with the fact that Nordra cracked the stone in my wrist bracelet an instant before everything went into slow-mo. It couldn't have been a coincidence.

Yet why should a rock change the flow of time?

Kendor also seems particularly interested in how Viper was able to move the lava with her mind. "You can use that same power," he says suddenly.

"Telekinesis? I've never shown any sign of having that ability. None whatsoever."

I see a gleam in his eyes as I reply to his remark.

In an instant I know what he has in mind.

"No!" I shout at him. "Don't do it. Don't try throwing any of your spears any faster at me."

"Why not?" he asks casually.

I shake my head. "I know what you're thinking. That if I'm not fast enough to physically block a spear, then my telekinesis will magically kick in and I'll be able to swat it away with my mind. Don't try it, it's too risky."

"You should trust me to know your limits."

"I do trust you. It's just, right now, I'm too exhausted."

"All right," Kendor seems to give in. "Tell me what you know about this power you and Viper share."

"Not much. By definition, 'telekinesis' means having the ability to move something with your mind."

"The ability is greater than that. Telekinesis controls all forms of movement. Whether a person moves an object or his body—it is all the same thing, it is just a question of degree. When fully developed, this gene allows any witch who has it to teleport himself to any place on the planet."

"Can Syn do that?" I ask, stunned.

"Ask her."

"Maybe I will." I gesture to his assortment of weapons. "Are we finished for the day?"

"Almost. I want to show you something special. A place I have discovered in your time." He turns for the house. "We will need to take that vehicle you call a car."

I chase after him. "Do you know where you want to go?"

"Up the coast."

Together we drive north through Malibu and beyond to a cliff that attracts him for some strange reason. The setting sun glares in our eyes as we climb out of the car. The cliff doesn't frighten me. I figure if worse comes to worst, he'll throw me off the side and I'll be forced to land on the rocky shore on my own two feet.

Yet the instant we near the ledge, he suddenly attacks me. He stuns me with a blow to the head and before I can recover he pulls out a rope and ties my ankles and wrists together. It takes him seconds to immobilize me and that is not the end of his abuse. Yanking me by my hair, he drags me to the edge of the cliff. A ragged glance warns me I'm looking at a fall of over two hundred feet onto jagged rocks and crashing waves. Wherever he got the rope, it wasn't at Home Depot. Try as I might, I can't break free.

"I cannot teach you how to survive the Field unless your faith in me is complete," he says, holding me as I teeter at the edge of the cliff.

"Kendor, please!" I cry. "You're making a mistake. You've got me—I can't break free. I won't be able to control my fall." I feel him pushing me forward. "Don't! If I hit my head, I'll die! Kendor!"

"Then you will die," he says, and shoves me off the cliff.

I fall and time fails to rescue me. It refuses to slow down and I fall fast, the jagged edge of a large boulder waiting to crack open my skull. My terror is absolute, equal in every way to when I lay frozen and helpless on that morgue table in Las Vegas, in my first night in witch world, while Syn and her assistant prepared to slice me open as part of an autopsy. Now, as then, I know I am going to die.

I *am* going to die.

The black blade of the rock rushes toward my face. My forehead will hit first and after it cracks, the cartilage of my nose will shatter and pieces of bone along the ridges of my eyes will splinter and be rammed into the gray matter of my brain. Then I will die.

I *am* dying.

The boulder is twelve feet away when I feel a bolt of electricity rush up my back. It's as if lightning has struck the base of my spine and sent a current capable of electrocuting me. The bolt is blindingly fast. From a dozen feet above the boulder till six feet above it the charge manages to rise from my tailbone to my brain.

Whether it fries or opens every channel in my nervous system along the way, I'm not sure. All I know is that I suddenly *know*—with the kind of absolute faith Kendor just mentioned—that I have the power to stop myself from falling. It doesn't matter that it probably takes years to activate the first stage of the telekinetic witch gene.

Kendor obviously knows a shortcut.

The exploding power in my spine bursts out the top of my head and surrounds me like an invisible cocoon and I stop falling. I halt a mere six inches above the brutal edge of the boulder. Hanging there, too stunned to breathe, I feel a wave rear up and wash over me, rinsing out a large portion of my blood stains. Yet the wave fails to move me, to even shake me. I have the power, I'm in control.

To a degree.

I'm able to use the same energy to burst free of the ropes but I'm not so confident in my ability that I try levitating back to the top of the cliff. After all, it's supposed to take centuries to learn to fly. Instead, I hike up like your normal rock climber and find Kendor waiting for me by the car. I look at him and shake my head.

"You bastard," I say.

He laughs. "I assume that word has a different meaning in your time than in mine."

I want to kill him but hug him instead. "Yeah. In our world it means I love you."

When I get home, and Jimmy sees the condition of my clothes, he wants to know what happened. I beg off and tell him I have to shower and change first. Then we can talk, I promise. But when I'm clean and wearing fresh clothes, I notice the time. Marc will be at the theater, working, but he's probably going to get off any second. Since I'm going to be playing the part of a reporter, I figure I'd better catch Marc at work, not at his apartment.

Rushing out the front door, I call over my shoulder to Jimmy that I'll explain everything as soon as I get back. I know I'm being rude but I've got a lot on my mind. I figure I can make it up to him later.

I arrive at Grauman's Chinese Theatre none too soon.

Parking in the adjacent mall, I rush onto Hollywood Boulevard in time to see Marc pull up in a black Lexus and hand the keys to a waiting couple, who give him a generous tip. He watches them drive off and approaches his boss, Mr. Green, and points to his watch. Obviously he's asking if he can punch out for the night. I don't hesitate; I hurry to the valet station, hoping Mr. Green will introduce me to the witch-world version of Marc Simona.

"Mr. Green, remember me, Alexis?" I call as I flash my most winning smile, brush aside my troublesome maroon hair, and try to sound older than I am. Unfortunately, when I climbed out of the shower at home, I didn't know I was headed back out and have on a frumpy pair of blue jeans and a red sweater my mother knitted for me last Christmas. I look more like a struggling college student than an *LA Times* reporter.

Mr. Green is happy to see me. "Of course! Marc, this is that reporter I told you about. She's writing an article on what it's like to mingle with the beautiful people. I wanted to tell her how most of them are not so beautiful on the inside but decided you were the one she should talk to, since you're the only one the actresses flirt with."

Marc snickers, although I can tell he's checking me out. "Get off it, boss. You afraid to say what you really think 'cause you know it's going to cost you your job?"

It's a friendly jab and Mr. Green laughs.

"Hey. You don't have a wife and a child to support." Green

pauses. "Marc, meet Alexis. Alexis, Marc here is the only valet who works here who's got even a remote chance of making it to the big screen."

"Really?" I say. "So you're an actor?"

Marc shakes his head. "He's jerking your chain. I couldn't act to save myself. And I've got nothing to tell you about being a valet to the stars. I park their cars, I pick up their cars. The nice ones tip me, the jerks don't, that's it. That's all I know." He turns away. "Nice meeting you, Alexis. Sorry I couldn't be more helpful."

"I heard Silvia Summer asked for your number," I call.

Marc stops, turns, looks at Mr. Green. "You told her that?"

His boss is a picture of innocence, and in reality I am exaggerating. "I didn't say a word," he replies. "Let me buy you coffee," I offer quickly. "I know a place not far from here that makes the best apple pie in the world."

Marc checks me out again, debating. "Where?"

"Come with me and I'll show you."

"Why don't I follow you in my own car?" Marc asks.

"Didn't you walk to work?" I say.

Marc frowns. "Not today. But how did you know . . . ?"

"She knew Dina is expecting," Mr. Green interrupts.

What's passing between the two—it's a conversation that would only happen in witch world. The average person in this world knows nothing about witches. But people in important positions, and those on the other end of the spectrum, people close to "the streets"—they know that certain people are "connected," and that those are people you've got to treat carefully. Right now, Mr. Green's suggesting it would be a mistake to say no to me because I might be one of them. The two keep glancing at my eyes, trying to pick up a vibe. These two have definitely heard about witches, even if they don't call them that, or know exactly what we can do.

Marc nods. "All right, coffee it is. But you're paying."

I smile. "It will be my pleasure."

I take him to Jerry's Famous Deli in West Hollywood, a favorite of mine. It's always open in witch world—never mind that it's closed in the real world—and has the best sandwiches and desserts in all of LA. Syn and Kendor had invited me to stay for dinner, but because it was already late I left their place without eating.

Now I realize how starved I am and order a turkey sandwich on rye with lettuce, tomatoes, cheese, and a touch of mayo. The sandwich comes with a four-inch stack of turkey and half a plate of awesome fries. I dig in like a ravenous animal, Marc watching me closely, wary but not scared.

"You're not really a reporter, are you, Alexis?" he says not long after the food arrives. He has coffee and pie but only because I ordered it.

"Nope. And call me Jessica, that's my real name." I take another bite of my glorious sandwich. "Hand me the malt vinegar, would ya? It's a thing I picked up from my dad when

I was a kid. He's from England and you know how they like their fish and chips. Always malt vinegar, never ketchup on fries."

"What's your father do?"

"He's a doctor, among other things. A famous heart surgeon."

"Maybe I've heard of him. What's his name?"

"Oh, we don't share the same last name."

"I'd think being a famous doctor would be enough," Marc says, probing, not reacting to my evasiveness. He's heard the drill before: *Don't anger the connected.*

"Not for my father. But I don't want to talk about him. I want to talk about you."

Marc shrugs. "What's there to talk about? I told you being a valet to the stars is nothing special."

I catch his eye. "And you know by now I don't give a shit about what you do for a living, although your side work interests me. How much do you think you're going to get for that rock you lifted off Silvia Summer?"

My goal is to shake him up, blow his mind, so when I get to what counts he'll be ready to listen. My question stuns him but he hides it well.

"I don't know what you're talking about," he says.

"Don't worry, I'm not a cop. I'm just curious is all."

He has guts in both worlds. He stares me down.

"What do you want?" he demands.

I take my time answering. "Do you know who I am?"

"No. Maybe. Who are you?"

"I move in a certain circle, one you've heard of. Don't act puzzled, you know what I'm talking about. Just be straight with me and you'll have nothing to worry about." I pause. "Agreed?"

He shakes his head. "I didn't steal no rock from Silvia."

"You're lying. Stop. Or you'll piss me off."

He has remarkable control. He sips his coffee. "Tell me what you want," he says.

I soften my tone. "This might surprise you, but I'm here to help you."

"Why?"

"Let me ask a few questions. When was the last time you got sick?"

"Huh?"

"The last time you had a cold or flu?"

"I can't remember."

"Do you ever get sick?"

"Sure. It's just been a while."

"How long is a while? Back when you were a kid bouncing from one orphanage to another?"

I'm hitting hard and fast but he remains cool. "I haven't caught a cold or flu in years," he says flatly.

"When you cut yourself, do you heal fast?"

"What kind of question is that?"

"Answer it."

"Yeah. I'm a fast healer."

"You're fast, period, aren't you? You're a thief. You have to get in and out of a house quickly. Have you ever been caught? Have you ever had to fight your way out of a nasty situation?"

"You're talking bullshit."

"Have you ever lost a fight in your life?"

"No!"

Smiling, I sit back and take another bite of my sandwich, chewing slowly, enjoying the food. I casually throw out my next question.

"How would you like to be connected?"

He draws in a breath. "I'm not sure what you're asking. I barely know what that's all about. I've just heard rumors and stuff."

"What's the weirdest thing you've heard?" When he doesn't respond, I prod him. "Come on, I told you I'm here to help you. What have you heard?"

He looks around, checking to see if I've brought backup, before leaning forward. "Is it true that people like you can do supernatural shit?"

"It's true. Go on, what else have you heard?"

He shakes his head and sits back. "Nah. This is too weird."

I put down my sandwich and it's my turn to lean forward. "Tell me the craziest story you've ever heard, and I promise you I'll tell you whether it's true or not."

He picks up his fork, pokes at his apple pie, changes his

mind, and puts the fork back down. He looks at me, really looks at me, deep into my eyes, and I finally feel I'm seeing the Marc I know in the Field. *Something* passes between us. I don't know what to call it. Recognition?

"I've heard stories that you people can travel from this world to another world," he says. "A world like this one but different too."

"Interesting. That's also true," I say.

"You're not messing with me?"

"This other world—it's as real as this one. And just about everyone you see here, they exist there as well. When you go there it's like you meet the person you see in the mirror every morning." I stop. "That's why we're talking right now. Because of that other world."

"I'm not following you."

"I know you there. You're a friend of mine. That's how I know so much about you in this world. I know how you rode in the trunk to Silvia's house. I know how you stole her car when you left her house. I know stuff only a friend could know." I pause. "I'm right, aren't I?"

He's shaken, finally; there's no way to stay cool with what I've just hit him with. "All right, Jessica, say I believe you. Where do we go from here?"

"To be blunt, we've got a long ways to go. You see, in this other world we're in danger. We're trapped on an island where we're being forced to fight for our lives. Six people on the island are like me, they're connected. Another thirty are like you. I was brought there because I'm connected. You're there because you've got street smarts, you're a survivor. On the island there's six groups of six, six teams fighting each other. Only, our team is down to five people. Last night we lost a brave woman named Shira."

Marc's confused. "When?"

"This part's hard to understand, listen closely. Shira died last night in the other world. Everyone who's connected goes there at dawn, and lives a whole day there, before returning at dawn to this world. You go there too, everyone does. But only the connected are aware of both worlds. Do you understand?"

Marc struggles. "How do I go there if I don't know I'm going there?"

"Because you're not really going anywhere. Witch world and the real world are parallel dimensions. Mirror images of each other. I live one day in witch world and the same day over again in the real world."

"Why do you call it witch world?"

The odd thing is I'm talking to him in witch world. But I don't want to get into that with him, not yet. I can tell he's already overloading and I can't blame him. When my father explained all this to me, it took him half the night, and here I'm trying to ram it down Marc's throat in a few minutes.

"To be connected means to be a witch. A person with special genes that give you special powers. I only became a witch a month ago. No, I should say I only became *aware* I was a witch a month ago. I've always been a witch. It's a genetic condition, the next step in human evolution."

Marc holds up a hand. "Whoa, slow down. You say we're together on this island, fighting to stay alive. But if these two worlds are so similar, how come we're not doing something like that in this world?"

His question is insightful. I would have taken a lot longer to spot the flaw in my explanation.

"Normally people do pretty much the same thing in both worlds," I reply. "*Before* they become aware of both worlds. After you're connected, all bets are off. And to make our situation even more complicated, the fact that we're on the island changes everything. We've been whisked away to fight like gladiators."

"Like gladiators in Ancient Rome?"

"That's it. They used to start with a hundred slaves in the Colosseum. They'd pair off and fight to the death. The next round there'd be only fifty slaves, then two dozen. Until finally two slaves would face off against each other and fight for their freedom, for full Roman citizenship, lots of babes, and tons of gold. I know it sounds kind of far-fetched, but our Field is kind of like that."

"Field?"

"That's what it's called, not that it matters. There's a reason I'm telling you all this. Normal people don't do so well in the

Field. They almost always die. Usually, as the contest reaches its climax, it's only witches that are left alive."

Marc looks like I've sucker punched him in the gut. "Then the other me is fucked," he mumbles.

"No! I think you've got a chance, a good chance to survive. Because I think you're just like I was a month ago. You're a witch who doesn't know he's a witch."

"What are you talking about? I ain't no witch."

"I think you are! That's why I asked the questions I did. You never get sick. You heal rapidly. You're fast, you're strong, you're shrewd. These are all signs you have witch genes. To be sure, we'd have to try to connect you. Then you and I could really help each other in the Field. We could survive together." I pause to catch my breath. "Are you following me?"

"Have you told my counterpart in the Field all this?"

I hesitate. "No."

"Why not? He's the one on the island. He's the one who needs these powers to stay alive."

"You're not getting it! You are him! You're the same person here as you are there!"

"Then I'll ask again. Why haven't you told him what you just told me?"

The answer is because it's easier to spot a witch in witch world than in the real world. Our powers are stronger here, more obvious. I want this version of Marc to try to connect in this world for that reason. He obviously has the healing gene; that's why he doesn't get sick.

Plus connecting him will work better here than in the real world. Better in the sense that if he lets me take him through the initiatory rite—here, where we won't be disturbed by Viper or Nordra or God knows who else—he'll stand a better chance of surviving. Plus Herme can help me administer the right drugs. Bottom line, I don't want what happened to Jimmy to happen to Marc. I don't want him to die in either world.

Well, that's not exactly the bottom line. If he dies here in witch world, he'll die in both worlds. But if he dies in the real world, there's a good chance he'll survive in witch world.

I don't think I should tell him that detail.

"It's complicated," I say.

"I'm afraid you're going to have to do better than that."

"We've got our hands full in the Field. We're both having to guard our group day and night. We don't have time to perform the initiatory rite that will connect you to both worlds." I pause. "But we've got time here. We can do it tonight if you're feeling up to it."

"What do I have to do?" he asks.

I reach out and take his hands. "You have to die."

Two hours later we say good-bye near the theater when I drop him off beside his car. Despite our long talk he's not ready to trust me with his life. But the strange thing is he's willing to think about it. He wants to meet me tomorrow night.

"Here or at your apartment?" I ask.

"And I suppose you know where I live?"

"You bet," I say.

He leans over my open window. "You really are a witch, you know that, Jessica."

"Jessie," I say.

"Is that what the other Marc calls you?"

"Yeah."

He gives me a quick kiss on the lips. "Good night, Jessie."

He gets in his car and drives away. I don't know why but I don't want to let him go. It's late, I'll be fighting like a bat out of hell to stay alive all day tomorrow in the real world. I desperately need to rest. But I want to go after him. It's like the one kiss wasn't enough.

I drive home like someone over the legal limit. I know Jimmy's going to be waiting up for me, and that he's going to take my head off. But he's not in the living room when I walk in the house. For that matter, he's not in the house. A spasm of fear grips me and I rush to the guesthouse and peek through my mother's bedroom window and see Lara fast asleep not five feet from where my mom's passed out. The sight cuts my anxiety in half but I'm still freaked.

Until I hear Jimmy park out front and walk toward the

porch. When he comes inside, when I see his face, my fear explodes. I've never seen him look so mad.

He doesn't look at me, just stalks by. I try to hug him but he shakes me off. I don't know what's wrong but I'm starting to get a bad feeling. I follow him out back, where he's standing in the yard and staring up at the moon. It's bright in witch world, too.

"What is it?" I ask. I've never really had Jimmy yell at me before. He's not the type. When he gets annoyed he just falls silent, goes off by himself. But I have a sinking feeling I'm going to see a new side of him tonight. He keeps staring at the moon. His face should be white, I think, white as the moonlight. But it looks red to me.

"Talk to me," I plead.

He snorts. "Talk? Talk to you? What's there to talk about?"

"I don't understand . . . ," I begin.

"What's his name?!" he screams at me, loud enough to wake my mother, Lara, and half the neighborhood. The sheer volume of his voice makes my heart skip. And what he's asking, why, it makes it break.

"Marc," I whisper.

He turns on me, God does he turn on me. "His last name, Jessie, I want to know his last name. I know his first name. How could I not? You've been moaning it in your sleep every night for the last week."

"I have?"

"You know what? Fuck you, I don't care what his name is. Go stay at his house tonight. Anywhere but here. I'm going to bed." Jimmy turns and walks toward the house. I try to follow but he locks the door. Coming in, a few minutes ago, I set my keys down on the coffee table. I run around to enter through the front door but he's locked that as well.

I start crying. I love Jimmy, he's the love of my life. I can't believe he won't talk to me, listen to my side of the story. I realize what must have happened. I originally came home covered in blood and then rushed back out without explaining where I was going. He must have chased after me, followed me to the theater, then to the deli, and then back to Marc's car, where he saw Marc kiss me good-bye.

But it had been a casual kiss! I hadn't kissed him back! Why would Jimmy kick me out of the house because of that? It makes no sense, at least not to me.

Damn him!

I reach out and grab the doorknob and break the lock.

Storming inside, I find Jimmy already in bed, lying on his back, staring at the ceiling, the light still on. He acts like I'm not there.

"Let me explain," I beg.

He doesn't say anything.

"You owe me that much," I say.

He rolls over, puts his back to me. "I don't owe you shit."

"It's not what you think."

Nothing. He says nothing.

I step closer to the bed. "If I've been moaning his name for the last week, how come you only blow up tonight?" I ask.

My Jimmy, he's such a sweet guy. But he replies with such bitterness, it's as if his few words poison the air. "I guess seeing your girlfriend with another guy can do that to you," he says.

I see something then, something that was never supposed to see the light of day. A piece of paper lying on top of the chest of drawers. The piece of paper from the lab my father used to test Huck's DNA. The paper that confirmed Jimmy isn't the baby's father.

The clinic my father used must have automatically mailed it to me. Or my dad might have sent it to me assuming I'd be the one to open it. Or else my father *deliberately* mailed it to our house hoping Jimmy would open it and discover the truth. Mailed it to our house in *witch world*! When I sent it to the clinic in the real world, where Huck lives.

My dad has only come back into my life in the past few weeks. I don't know the man as well as I like to think. I don't really know how far he'd go to interfere with my life.

At the moment it doesn't really matter.

Now I've got two reasons why Jimmy is blowing up tonight.

"I didn't order the test on Huck because of Marc," I say.

"Right."

"Jimmy, I'm going to talk now and I need you to listen.

Just for a few minutes. When I'm done, if you want me to leave, I'll leave. It will be up to you. Okay?"

He doesn't respond. I sit on the corner of the bed. I sit because my legs are shaking so bad I'm ready to fall over. I'm still crying and want to stop but I can't. I fight to keep my voice even as I speak.

"Something scary is happening in the real world. I should have told you about it but I didn't want to worry you. Two days ago I was abducted. I'm still not sure who kidnapped me. It could've been the Alchemist, it could have been the Lapras. It could have been someone we've never heard of. In a way it doesn't matter. Right now I'm stuck on an island with thirty-five other people. I'm in what's called the Field and I'm fighting for my life. Marc is there with me."

I tell Jimmy everything from beginning to end. Halfway through my story he rolls onto his back and stares at the ceiling. When I get to my fight with Nordra he stares at me. I wish at some point he'd take my hand but that doesn't happen, although his expression darkens when I explain how Kendor tied me up and threw me off the cliff. He finally interrupts.

"What was he going to do if your telekinesis hadn't kicked in?"

I shrug. "I don't know. It did. I'm grateful I've got another weapon to work with."

"Why did you meet with Marc tonight?"

"To explain what's happening to us in the real world."

Jimmy snorts. "Like he'd believe you."

"He did."

"Gimme a break."

"Believe what you want. The guy's intuitive. He knew I was telling him the truth."

Jimmy gives me a hard look. "You still haven't answered my question."

"Marc, Chad, Ora, Li—they're all talented, smart, brave. But against witches like Nordra and Viper they can't do a whole lot. I wanted to meet with Marc—with witch-world Marc—to see if he'd let me try to connect him."

"You don't know if he's a witch."

"They might all be potential witches. That might be the reason they were selected. There's certain signs—I don't know. But it would be tricky to try to connect them in the Field. Too much is happening—we're too exposed. But I knew Marc was from around here, and I figured if I could reach out to him, make him understand what's at stake, he'd take the risk."

"So just like that, on your first date, you asked him if he wouldn't mind dying for you?"

"Please, it wasn't a date. But to answer your question, yes, I told him that's what he'd have to go through to get connected."

"What did he say?"

"He said he'd have to think about it. He's not bullshitting—he's not that kind of guy. He's seriously considering it. We're going to meet again tomorrow."

"How would you do it, if he does say yes?"

I sigh. "I don't know. I could ask my father to fly in. Or I could ask Herme for help."

"You might do better to bring him straight to Kendor."

I force a smile. "Are you saying that because you're hoping Kendor will try to connect him by throwing him off a cliff?"

Jimmy doesn't smile back. "Everything you've told me has scared the total shit out of me. We're back to where we were a month ago. You're waking up in another world I can't go to and you're surrounded by danger. Tonight, when we go to sleep, how do I know if you're going to be dead or alive in the morning?"

"If I die on the island there's a chance I could still wake up alive here. You did."

"Great. That makes me feel a whole lot better when it means my son will be left without a mother. And Huck's still my son, Jessie; that piece of paper doesn't change a thing."

I nod, although I privately think it changes everything.

"You're right. Huck needs me," I say.

Jimmy keeps up the hard stare. "If Huck needs you so much, why did you take a swab of his cheek and mail it off to be tested by your father?"

I hesitate. "Before I killed Kari, she mocked you. She said, 'If I cheated on Jimmy he never knew. Or, I should say, he never asked. He's a nice guy but he's too naive for this world.'" I pause. "I'm sorry, it stuck with me. I had to know."

"Why?"

I shake my head. I don't know what to say.

Jimmy sits up suddenly, grabs my hand, his touch far from tender. His eyes bore into me. "Listen, you're not turning Huck over to Kari's parents. They're the reason she grew up so twisted. They're worse than she was. There's no way my son is growing up in that house. Do you understand me?"

"Yes."

"Swear to me, Jessie. Swear you're never giving him up."

I nod quickly. "I swear."

Jimmy's eyes linger; he still doesn't trust me. He lets go of my hand and lies down on his back. He speaks to the ceiling.

"You're probably waiting for an apology. All the stuff you're going through—I'm not dumb, I know it's a thousand times more important than our personal problems. Like I said, I'm terrified of what might happen to you. I doubt I'll sleep tonight, I know I won't."

I wait. "But?"

He glances over. "But think what I went through tonight. I get home and find this letter from this clinic in San Francisco. I open it and find out my son doesn't share any of my genes. Then you come home drenched in blood. But you don't talk to me. You take a shower and run back out the door. So I follow you and what do I find? You're meeting another guy. You're flirting with him. You take him out to eat. You talk for hours. Then, when you drop him off at his car, you guys make out in the parking lot."

"We didn't make out. He kissed me good-bye, a light peck on the lips. And I didn't kiss him back."

"Why?" he asks.

"Why?"

"Why did he kiss you? This guy you just met?"

"I don't know, he just did."

"How many times has he kissed you on the island?"

"Never."

"So his witch-world persona is more of a stud?"

"Jimmy . . ."

"Don't bother. What I'm saying is that was my night. That's how everything looked from my point of view. So you can see why I don't feel like apologizing."

I swallow thickly, tears rolling over my cheeks. "And if you wake up tomorrow morning and I'm dead, will you regret it?" I'm acting like a child, I know. If he won't give me love, I at least want his pity.

Jimmy rolls over, turning his back on me again.

There's a million things he could say.

But he says nothing.

CHAPTER SEVEN

CHAD WAKES ME IN THE MORNING IN THE FIELD. Because I've slept on a stone floor, I sit up feeling stiff as a board. A torch burns in the corner of our cave and I notice Chad's forgotten to shave. Oh, right, I remind myself. They don't hand out razors in the Field.

"How did you sleep?" Chad asks.

"You'd be amazed," I reply, thinking of the whole day I lived while the rest of them were unconscious. "How's Ora doing?"

"He's healed. He's out scouting with Marc."

"What? That's impossible," I gasp. I healed Ora as best I could before we recrossed the river, and then again back at our cave. But the best I could do was stop the bleeding and take away some of his pain. The last I saw him, before I dozed off, the wound to his shoulder blade was still ugly.

"Li worked on him when you were asleep," Chad says.

"None of us ever saw anything like it. The wound healed right in front of us. Ora doesn't even have a scar."

Li's a witch! Fantastic!

"Where's Li right now?" I demand.

"Just outside. Keeping watch."

"Tell her to come here. I need to talk to her alone."

"Gotcha," Chad says, jumping up. I'd filled him in as best I could about my true identity while I was working on Ora—Marc backed up my miraculous claims—but I know Chad still has a million questions. He's a good guy, though, very mature. He never gets impatient and he doesn't mind taking orders from me.

Li appears a minute later and sits beside me, not far from the torch. I ask how long Ora and Marc have been gone.

"An hour. They said they were heading for the hot spring to cook more fish," Li replies, her eyes tired.

"How are you feeling? Are you getting enough to eat?"

Li shrugs. "The fish helps but I'm missing my meds more than I thought I would. I'm dizzy and have a pounding headache. I just want to close my eyes and sleep."

"Maybe you should."

"That could be dangerous."

She's talking about falling into a diabetic coma. Her condition is more serious than I realized. Yet she was able to heal Ora. I'm missing something here.

"I heard about what you did for Ora. Why didn't you tell me?"

"Tell you what?"

"That you're a witch."

Li shakes her head. "I'm not a witch."

"Are you saying you don't experience another world when you go to sleep at night?"

She looks at me funny. "What other world? Are you talking about Seoul?"

"No. Let's back up a minute. How long have you been able to heal?"

She hesitates. "Since Lula died."

I remember her sister had been tortured to death in a North Korean prison. Li had told me she had been in the room when her sister died. A bizarre idea suddenly pops in my head.

"Li, you said Lula was your twin sister. Was she an identical twin?"

"Yes."

"What I'm going to ask next—please forgive me for forcing you to remember such a painful time. But you said you were close to Lula when she died. What did you feel right then? The exact instant she died?"

Li blinks away tears. "Sad. Pain in my heart."

I feel like a jerk for pressing. "Anything else?"

Li lowers her head. "It's hard to say with words. When Lula died, I felt her come inside me. Like we became one. Then I felt her leave, go to another place, but not so far that I couldn't still feel her."

"And after that you could heal?"

Li looks up, catches my eye. "Lula is the one who heals. She healed Ora last night. I felt her near."

Her remarks strengthen the bizarre theory that's forming in my mind. The key to activating the witch genes is the death experience. Technically, Li never died. But her sister did—her genetically *identical* sister. It's my belief that the two were so close that Lula's trauma triggered in Li a partial awakening of her genetic potential.

My father, no one on the Council for that matter, has ever discussed such a possibility with me. But clearly Li can heal. She can heal better than I can. Yet it's equally obvious that she can't be a complete witch. She has no awareness of witch world.

"How many people have you healed?" I ask.

"Only a few, since I came to Seoul. People I know, or the parents of close friends. I don't want people talking about me."

"Have you ever tried to heal yourself?"

Li is puzzled. "I don't think I can. Lula, if she wanted to help me, she would help."

"You heard what happened last night. This place is very dangerous. We're going to have to keep moving, keep fighting, just to stay alive. We need you at full strength. You assume you need your medicine to get better. But I think if you and I— and Lula—work together, we can get rid of your diabetes, or at least make it better. Do you want to try?"

Li looks around as if searching for her sister.

"What do I do?" she asks.

"Lie down on your back in front of me. Lie as close as you can, let your side press against my knees. I'm going to put my left hand on your forehead and my right hand over your pancreas. You put both your hands over my right hand and just close your eyes."

From studying *Gray's Anatomy*, for the premed program I plan to take at UCLA, I know the pancreas is located not far above the belly button. As Li wraps her fingers around my right hand and closes her eyes, I immediately feel a heat radiating from her palms. It's extremely hot and we have scarcely begun.

"You might feel Lula nearby or you might not," I say. "It doesn't matter. All that matters is that you feel the energy flowing through your hands and mine, flowing into your body. Right now it feels like heat but that can change. You might feel magnetism as well. Just relax into it and let go. Don't try to make the energy come. It flows by itself."

"Lula," Li whispers, sweat forming on her brow. "She's here."

"Then let Lula take over. Your sister loves you. Let her help repair your body so you are no longer sick."

The weird thing is I see another version of Li, dressed in stylish clothes and with longer hair. Closing my eyes, my vision of her sharpens and I suspect I'm seeing Lula as she appears in witch world.

Whoever she is, she holds up her palms in my direction and they give off a warm pink light, which washes over me like a soothing shower. I feel Lula is not just helping her sister, she's soothing me, and I realize how great their potential is. The sisters' healing genes might be two of the most powerful on earth.

I don't know how long we sit under the shower of pink light. It's so comforting—I feel no desire to stop. But at some point I appear to wander into a dream, with Jimmy and Marc in it. The two are arguing, I'm not sure why, I only wish they would stop. Jumping between them, I stick out my arms.

It's then I awaken with a jolt.

Li is sitting up beside me.

"Are you all right, Jessie?" she asks.

"Never mind about me. How do you feel?"

Smiling, she puts her hand over her abdomen as if she were feeling a kicking infant inside. "It feels good. I feel good."

I lean over and hug her and whisper in her ear. "I think I saw your sister," I say.

"She saw you. She told me so."

We help each other to our feet, both of us feeling dazed from the healing. We go outside to check on Chad and find him talking to Marc. Both stand inside the shadows of the cliff so neither is visible from the valley. The sun's a lot higher in the sky than I expected and I realize I must have slept late.

Marc looks me over in his usual lustful manner. "How's sleeping beauty?" he asks.

"Rested. How come you came back alone? Where's Ora?"

"He's still at the hot spring and he's not alone. We made contact with the leaders of two other groups. Kyle, a freaking rock star from London, and Sam, a fashion designer from New York City."

"You're positive they're witches?" I ask.

"They sure know a lot of weird shit if they're not. Yeah, I'd bet they're for real. They want to meet with you, form an alliance, have their groups join ours. At least that's what they say. But me and Ora—we didn't want to give away our hiding place. That's why I came to get you, so we could meet on neutral ground."

"You left Ora out there alone?" I ask.

Marc shrugs. "What choice did I have? There was no way I was giving away the location of this cave."

"You should have stayed with him," Chad says.

"In your bookworm opinion," Marc says.

I speak. "You three stay here. I'll see what this Kyle and Sam really want."

"Hold on, sister," Marc says. "Ora ain't exactly where you think and I'm not saying where he is unless I get to come along."

I fret. "I don't like leaving Chad and Li alone. It's not safe."

"No place is safe on this crazy island," Marc says in a tone that makes it clear he's not going to back down.

The two of us set off at a brisk clip, heading toward a spot that Marc says is "near" the hot spring. We've barely left the cave when he wants to know if I spoke to his double.

"I did," I say.

"How did it go?"

"He says he'll think about it."

"Think about dying? Boy, Jessie, you must have been mighty persuasive."

"Is he telling me the truth?"

"Did you tell him my secret?"

"Yeah, that you think I look like the first girl you ever got a crush on. I saved it for last, when I dropped him back at his car."

"How did he react?"

"He kissed me."

"Then he's thinking about it."

"I'm serious, Marc. Will he go through with it?"

"If it was me, I wouldn't. Not with what he knows."

"It is you, damnit. Are you saying he's just bullshitting me?"

"What do you want? You just met the guy and you ask him to die for you so he can help save you on a mysterious island in another universe."

"Joke all you want. You don't change into a witch in the next day or two and you won't be leaving this island."

"I have an idea."

"What?"

"Listen without jumping on my case. You say I'm him and if that's true then I do know him. I know the way he thinks, how to make him trust you."

"How?"

"Have sex with him."

"Go to hell."

"Listen! If he's like me, he's a lot more romantic on the inside than on the outside. Once he sleeps with you, he'll feel all protective and shit. Look at us, we've only kissed once and I'm out here risking my life so I can watch your back."

"I kissed you on the cheek, once, and I was being friendly. Besides, I have a boyfriend."

"Jimmy? It's not like you have to tell him that."

"By 'him' which one do you mean?"

Marc shrugs. "If it was me, I wouldn't tell either of them. Look, I'm just trying to give you a heads-up on the way he thinks. But I still say we're better off trying it here. At least I know for sure that my ass is fried if I don't do something desperate."

I stop him. "Talking about dying is one thing. Doing it is something else. We can't kill you and then change our minds. If we do it, we have to go all the way."

Marc considers, staring at the forest on the far side of the river. When he speaks next, his voice is somber. "I know why you want my twin instead of me. Your logic make sense, but it's not the reason. You figure it will be easier to kill him than me."

"I don't feel that way."

"You do. You care about me and I care about you, and it doesn't matter if you have a boyfriend or not. For an all-powerful witch you're not very good at hiding your feelings."

I go to make a wisecrack but my throat constricts. What he says is true. I do care about him, more than I want to admit to myself, and it terrifies me. Because he might die. Because of Jimmy . . .

Marc can see I'm struggling and takes my hands. "No matter how much you work my counterpart, he's never going to know you the way I know you."

I nod, regrettably. "But we can't do it here. We don't have the meat lockers or the drugs or whatever we're going to use. And we don't have the time. I can't be watching over you for hours with Nordra and Viper circling us."

"But we do have one thing here that you don't have in witch world."

"What?"

"Li. You were passed out when she worked on Ora but I saw what she did. You helped him plenty but she closed that wound so perfect a doctor would never know he'd been stabbed. If Li can't bring me back to life, no one can."

"Li can heal but she's not a true witch."

"I thought you said it was the healing gene that was the key?"

"It is. But Li doesn't know what it means to be connected.

247

I don't trust her to guide you through the process. I hardly trust myself. But at least in witch world I've got people who can help us."

He puts his hand over my shoulder. "You're scared, admit it. It's because of what happened to Jimmy."

"Yeah." I'd told Marc how Jimmy had overdosed in Las Vegas.

He pulls me closer, hugs me, kisses me on the side of the head. "It's all right, Jessie. We do it here or we do it there. But we both agree we've got to try it. Okay?"

I sigh. "We'll do it."

We continue on our way and Marc fills me in on what he knows about the witches who want to be our allies. Turns out that nineteen-year-old Kyle Downing of London is already known to us. He's a rock star. His debut CD has already produced three hits and both Marc and I have seen his videos on MTV. His music taste is eclectic—a cross between grunge, goth, rock. On TV he wears dark and white makeup, black leather, acts like a vampire in need of a bloody hit. I seem to recall reading something about him being the new bad boy on the block.

Sam Verra, Marc tells me, is an ambitious gay fashion designer who is extremely well read, lifts weights, has run the New York City Marathon, has numerous tattoos, and seems to be overall just a nice guy. Marc says he trusts him more than Kyle.

"Because he's gay?" I ask.

"No. Sam's just got a genuine quality to him. He definitely grew up in Brooklyn. He's got the accent and knows the town. You'll like him."

"They sound like an odd pair. I wonder if Kyle's used his powers to get ahead in the business."

"If I were him I would have," Marc quips.

"It's important because the Tar frown on that sort of thing. It might mean Kyle's a Lapra, and if he is we can't believe a word he says."

"What about that razor-sharp intuition of yours? Can't you tell when someone's lying?"

"It doesn't work so good on other witches. Particularly if they've got a lot of witch genes, like all the witches on this island."

"Great," he says sarcastically. I sock him.

"Hey, my intuition is for real. For example, I know you were lying when you said you cared about me."

"I wasn't lying."

"You were. You don't just care about me. You're crazy about me."

He laughs but his face reddens. I know it's not easy for him to talk about his feelings.

Yet he lied to me to come along. Turns out Ora and company are hidden inside the same cloud of steam where Ora and I spoke the previous day. However, the spot makes sense; except for the strong sulfur smell, it's a great place to hide.

Ora introduces the newcomers. Kyle is more elfin than he appears in his videos. Pale, blond, with unhealthy blue eyes, he outweighs me by twenty pounds if he's lucky. His accent is thick; he sounds like an early Beatle, which makes sense since he says he grew up in Liverpool. But he has a charming smile and he seems genuinely happy to meet me.

Kyle's uniform is a dull red, his bracelet bright red. He says his group is down to five and two of them are seriously injured—courtesy of Viper.

Sam's group has been cut in half; there are only three of the brown gang left. Nordra's people blindsided them, Sam explains, although he managed to take out one of Nordra's clan. Going by Sam's timetable—and the bodies I discovered in the meadow—he ran into the monster before I did.

"Did Nordra offer to form an alliance with you?" I ask Sam. The guy is more reserved than Kyle, definitely more wary, which I can appreciate. He's not as big as Ora but he's got muscles and it's clear from his description of his encounter with Nordra that he must have the speed and strength gene.

Yet he holds his left arm awkwardly. He says he's fine but his sleeve is bloody and his arm looks a little crooked. It's clear he doesn't have the healing gene, a dangerous defect when it comes to the Field. For some reason I just assumed all the witches I'd have to fight would be self-fixers.

Unless Sam's lying. They could both be lying. For that matter, they *should* be lying. As the rules say, only one will survive; and I'm confident they've seen the same plaque we have.

"Are you joking?" Sam says in response to my question. "Nordra's like a force of nature. He smashed into our camp and started hacking away. I was lucky to take down one of his people at the start and pick up a machete. None of my group would have escaped if I'd been unarmed."

"Are your people far from here?" I ask.

Sam gestures vaguely. "Not far."

Kyle steps up. "I can see already the direction this is heading. None of us trusts the other." He turns to Ora and Marc. "Would either of you be offended if we borrowed your leader for a bit? There're things we best discuss in private."

Ora doesn't mind but Marc's suspicious. "Leaving us out in the cold is a lousy way to gain our trust," he says.

Kyle grins and slaps Marc on the shoulder. "It's a witch thing, it's nothing personal." He stops and looks at me. "But it would help move our plans along, if you know what I mean."

I nod. "Ora, Marc—I'll talk to them alone. We'll sit over there on those rocks. You'll be able to see us at all times."

Kyle leads us to the boulders. It's a small thing but the fact that he walks in front shows that he doesn't expect to get stabbed in the back. Me, I'm wound tight as a spring. Besides having Ora's sharpest knife hidden beneath the tail of my shirt, I have the machete I stole from Nordra's minion poking out the top of my backpack. Sam keeps his machete handy as well. He walks beside me but keeps enough distance to have time to raise his weapon—should I attack.

We sit in a rough semicircle. Kyle pulls out a bottle of water and takes a deep drink before offering us some. We decline. Kyle shakes his head.

"This is no way to start a friendship," he says.

"We're not friends," Sam says bluntly. "We're three people who have common enemies. Nordra, Viper, and those damn ghosts. Let's at least be honest about that. We need each other if any of us is to survive."

Kyle is amused. "That might be true about you and me, Sam. But Jessie here, she's got a reputation. The high-school witch who took down Sinful Syn. It sounds like even Nordra likes her. Assuming you weren't jiving us about his proposition?"

"It was a serious offer on his part," I say. "He'd kill his people and I had to kill mine to show good faith. Then we'd go after everyone else until the two of us were left. Then we'd fight."

"Sounds like true love," Kyle says.

Sam snorts. "Nordra's afraid of Viper. That's the only thing motivating him."

Kyle doesn't agree. "I told you, most of what you've heard about her is rumor. She's not a snake, she's not a dragon. She can't breathe poison or vomit flames. She's got telekinesis is all. She can fire off whatever shit is handy, nothing more."

"And turn invisible," Sam growls.

"I thought that talent didn't bother you," Kyle says.

Sam doesn't dispute Kyle's remark, which naturally stirs my interest. "You can see through her cloak?" I ask.

Sam hesitates. "I think so."

"You're not sure?" I ask.

"A witch in New York can turn invisible and I can spot her night or day. But I don't know about Viper. Haven't run into her yet."

"So you have the witch gene that controls the senses," I say. "How's your hearing? Your sense of smell?"

"I'm not here to divulge my entire repertoire," Sam says.

Kyle groans. "Here we go again. No trust. It's because of the rules of the game. No matter how we play it, in the end we've got to kill each other." Kyle stands and gestures with his hands to make his point. "Well, I say fuck the rules. Let's make up our own game. Sure, Nordra and Viper have to go. They're murderous lunatics. And the ghosts—I'm not sure about them yet. But who says we have to behave like barbarians with each other?"

"Maybe the people who put us here," I say. "Maybe they don't let us out of here until there's only one of us left."

Kyle holds up his hand. "I'm right there with ya. Besides our lack of trust in each other, that's the key. But Sam here might have found out a way off that will let us say 'fuck the plaque.' A way off this island."

Sam grumbles. "I wouldn't go that far."

"Tell Jessie what you saw," Kyle says. "Go on, Sam, you told me. We've got to start building some kind of bond here or we're just spinning our wheels."

Sam glances in the direction of the volcano before answering, and there's something in his voice, in the way he gestures and now and then looks me in the eyes, a quiet sincerity, that makes me feel he's being honest. I can see why Marc trusts him.

"I think it's clear by now that we were each dumped here in different locations. The director behind this sick charade probably wanted each of our groups to have a chance to get settled before the fun began. That's the way I see it at least—that we're here to entertain some pretty sick witches."

"With your special sight," I say, "have you seen any sign that we're being watched?"

"Nothing," Sam admits. "I've not seen a single camera or microphone. That puzzles me and it probably means my theory is crap. I don't know, you tell me when I'm done talking. My group set down west of here, near the base of the volcano, a mile or so higher than where we're sitting now. Right away I decided I needed to get the lay of the land, maybe spot where each cell had been dropped. I hiked to the top of the volcano, or at least close to the top. The smoke pouring off that lava gets pretty nasty when you get near the peak. Anyway, Jessie, I was able to see your cell buried in the valley on the other side of this hill. And I spotted Kyle's cell farther over, on the beach."

"They put you right beside the sea?" I ask Kyle.

Kyle nods. "When I read the plaque, I assumed everyone was somewhere along the coast. That's where my group started their search. But we didn't get far before Viper hit." He pauses. "A quick point before Sam goes on. I can only talk so long. I've got to get back to my people. They're defenseless without me. Worse, I've got two girls who are hurt bad. That tall African guy, Ora, he told me you've got a superhealer in your group. I need to borrow her if that's okay with you?"

"Let Sam finish talking and then I'll decide," I say to Kyle before turning back to Sam. "Did you see where any other cells put down?"

"No," Sam says. "But I assume they're on the other side of the river. It makes sense in a weird sort of way. Three groups on this side of the river, three groups on the other side. Anyway, let me tell you what else I found up on the peak. For one thing it's taller than it looks. I started a mile above sea level and had to hike at least another two miles higher. I put the volcano's high point between sixteen to eighteen thousand feet. I suppose you know what that means."

"There's snow up there?" I ask.

"Yeah. There's more on the back side than this side because of the direction the wind blows the fumes. But the snow's thick. The runoff from it is the main source of water for the river. It starts close to the top as a trickle but it picks up water fast."

"I've been wondering where all the water was coming from," I say. "What's on the other side of the island?"

Sam briefly closes his eyes, as if trying to figure out how to explain something I might not understand. Then he opens his eyes and looks me right in the eye.

"There is no other side of the island," he says.

I frown. "You mean the volcano's right on the coast? That's odd."

"It's light-years beyond odd. There's a black wall running along behind the volcano. It's set a quarter of a mile down from the peak. I circled around to it because, like I said, I had trouble breathing with all the fumes at the top and couldn't go any higher. That's when I ran into it."

"What's the wall made of?" I ask.

Sam shakes his head. "It's like nothing I've ever seen before."

"Until he came here," Kyle interjects. "Until we all came here."

"Hold on a sec," I say. "I'm not following you guys."

Kyle nods to Sam. "Tell her everything."

Sam holds up the brown bracelet on his left wrist. "Have you had a chance to examine what's on the inside of this contraption? I have and so has Kyle since we've both lost people who've lost their arms. There's a dark stone pressing against our skin."

"I've seen it," I say.

"That's what the wall's made of. I can't tell whether it's rock or metal. For that matter, I can't tell you what it feels like because when I touched it something strange happened. I was standing there one second and a moment later I felt like I'd been standing there forever. And I mean forever, like years had gone by without me moving." He pauses. "I know it sounds crazy but that's what happened."

"You must have blacked out," I offer.

Sam's voice trembles. "I wish I had. That wall creeped me out and it wasn't just because of what happened when I touched it. Like I said, there's a lot of fumes and smoke near the crater. Most of it blows our way but there's still plenty near the wall. But even with it cluttering up the air, I still should have been able to see over it."

"How high is the wall?" I ask.

"I assumed it was around thirty feet. I know what you're thinking, there's no way I could see over a thirty-foot wall. But I'm saying I couldn't see over it even when I hiked away from it—up the side of the volcano—and stood over a hundred feet higher."

"Wait, I'm confused," I say. "Are you saying you hiked a hundred feet away from the wall and couldn't see over it?"

"No. You heard me right, you just don't want to accept what I'm telling you. I hiked a quarter of a mile away from the wall, toward the peak, which left me standing a hundred feet higher than the wall."

"And you still couldn't see over it?" I asked.

"Nope," Sam says.

"The fumes and the smoke were in your eyes," I say.

"Nope. I just told you, there wasn't enough to block my vision. I either should have seen the other side of the island and the ocean beyond, or I should have just seen the ocean. I saw neither."

I shake my head. "I'm sorry, I'm still not following you."

Sam takes out his own water bottle and takes a long hit. "Believe me, Jessie, I sympathize."

"Damnit! What did you see?" I demand, exasperated.

"Nothing. I couldn't see anything."

I continue to shake my head. "That makes absolutely no sense."

Kyle speaks. "Don't be too hard on the boy. Whatever that wall is, it's not natural. It not only screwed with Sam's head, it warped his eyesight."

"But when you first brought it up," I say to Kyle. "You acted like it was our way off this island."

"I didn't say that exactly," Kyle replies. "Anyway, Sam's not done with his story. Tell Jessie what else you found up there."

Sam shrugs. "A cave loaded with quartz crystals and huge amethysts. There's writing on the walls and painted pictures. I even found a few primitive tools. I assume they're from previous contestants."

"Could you read the writing?" I ask.

"Nope."

"Have you been back there since day one?"

"Nope," Sam says, rubbing his injured arm. "Been a little busy."

"It's broken, isn't it?" I ask.

Sam sighs. "Yeah."

Kyle stands. "I think it's clear we've got to have another look at this wall and that cave—if we're to have any chance of escaping from this island."

"How is that clear?" I ask.

Kyle points to his red bracelet. "Whoever put us here felt it was crucial that all of us walk around with a piece of that wall touching us at all times. Now, I don't know about you two but that strikes me as a hell of a coincidence. Or maybe the word I'm looking for is it's a hell of a clue. It doesn't matter how I say it—that wall's important. We need to check it out some more, and we need to examine that cave as well. I believe the people who were here before us might have figured a way off this island, and they might have left the answer on the walls of that cave. That might be what Sam was looking at."

"A way to cheat the Field?" I ask.

Kyle nods. "That's what I'm thinking."

"It's a possibility," Sam agrees. "And, if nothing else, the cave will give us a strong base to defend. From up there you can see anyone coming from miles around."

"Except Viper," I mutter.

"I'll see her," Sam says.

"We're stronger together," Kyle says. "Nordra and Viper—even they would be afraid to take on three witches at once. My plan is we merge our people together and hike to the top of the volcano. It's the only plan that makes sense. We help each other. We still need to sleep and we can only sleep if we've got someone we trust standing guard."

"What if Nordra and Viper form an alliance?" I ask, noting how slyly Kyle had slipped the word "trust" into his proclamation.

"More reason we should band together," Kyle says. "But that ain't going to happen. Nordra's heard enough stories about Viper to know she's poison."

"You seem to know a lot about them," I say. "May I ask who your source is?"

Kyle grins. "I've been waiting for you to ask that. You want to know if I'm with the Lapras or the Tar?"

"I figure someone must be greasing your wheels," I say. "A nineteen-year-old kid whose first album's gone triple platinum."

"And you figure the Tar aren't in the habit of making young punks like me famous," Kyle says. "I'm not going to lie to you. I'm guilty as charged. I've got plenty of Lapra friends, and one of them in particular did help me get my foot in the door. She got me my start, but it was my talent that made me famous. And for your information, I have just as many friends who are Tar."

"So what you're saying is that you belong in neither camp?" I say. "Or do you belong in both?"

"Both, neither—what difference does it make? You know this line from my CD? 'I walk where I want and talk to the whole lot.' That sums up how I feel about both them groups. And from what I've heard about you, Jessica, you're no different. You hate being bossed around as much as I do."

He must have been talking to someone high up; it's like he knows me. I stand and face him. "You still haven't told me who your source is for all these fabulous insights."

Kyle shrugs. "And I'm not going to. As long as I keep my mouth shut, they'll keep feeding me what I need to know."

"Did your source tell you the way out of here was on top of the volcano?" I persist.

Kyle claps at my question. "Maybe, maybe. Let me make a suggestion. Tomorrow morning, when you wake up in witch world, why don't you call your source and see what they have to say about me. I can tell you what you're going to hear. That I'm the brand-new bad boy on the block. That all I care about is sex, drugs, rock'n'roll. And it's all true. But there's one thing you ain't going to hear—that Kyle's a killer."

Sam stands. "Then why are you here?"

Kyle waves his hand in dismissal. "I don't know, Sam. Why are you here?"

I feel Sam tense, and worry he might lash out—his broken arm notwithstanding—and the last thing I need right now is a testosterone-fueled fight. I step between the boys.

"How do we formalize this alliance of ours?" I ask.

"Like I said, two of my players are badly wounded," Kyle says. "You loan me your superhealer, let me take her back to my beach house, and I'll be eternally grateful."

"And then you'll form an alliance with us?" Sam asks.

"I believe I just said that," Kyle replies.

"I want Sam healed first," I say.

"My people are seriously hurting," Kyle insists. "Every minute they lose—it might be the difference between life and death. Please, Jessie, let me borrow your healer chick. I'll protect her as if she were one of my own."

I frown. "You plan on taking Li with you? Without me?"

Kyle gestures toward the volcano. "Sam's people are already stuck partway up the mountain. I'm sure he's as anxious to get back to them as I am to get back to my gang. You can meet back up with Sam at his home base. And once Li heals the rest of my team, we'll circle around this valley and rendezvous with all of you at roughly the halfway point."

What Kyle's suggesting sounded reasonable. Each of us three witches has to get back to our people. They're vulnerable without us. At the same time, merging our groups as swiftly as possible will give us even more protection.

Still, I feel troubled. I dislike sending Li off with Kyle. I don't know him and by his own admission he isn't the most caring soul on the planet. On a selfish note, her healing ability gives our group a big advantage. Yet I don't want the blood of his wounded on my hands. If nothing else, Kyle's concern for his people sounds genuine.

"One thing I don't understand," Sam says to me. "Why was your group given two witches?"

"Li's not a witch," I reply. "Just an amazing healer."

"How's that possible?" Sam insists.

I shrug. "I don't know. I just know she closed Ora's wound without leaving a scratch."

"That works for me," Kyle says, anxious to get moving. He proposes I hike back to my camp with him and then he'll escort Li to his home base. Meanwhile, he suggests I pick up Chad and catch up with Sam, who will be leading Marc and Ora up to his camp.

"I'm okay with everything except the last part," I interrupt. "Marc and Ora will accompany us back to our camp."

Kyle's puzzled. "You're just making them cover the same ground twice."

"He has a point," Sam agrees. "Hell, if you carry Chad on your back, you'll catch up with us in no time."

"Marc and Ora are staying with me," I repeat. "Sam, from what you've told me, I have a good idea where you're located. But call out if you see us walking past your camp. Kyle, come with me and the others."

Sam is fine with my change. "I appreciate your caution. I'll be waiting for you."

I walk over to where Marc and Ora are waiting and explain the plan. Marc doesn't like it; he doesn't like Kyle. But Ora can see the wisdom in joining forces.

"We can't fight this creature we can't see," Ora says.

"What if Li doesn't want to go with Kyle?" Marc asks. "Or do you figure she'll do whatever you ask? Because if that's true then you better know you're taking on a dangerous role."

Marc's words are true, of course, that's why they sting. Once I assume control of the group, it will be hard to back away from the position, unless I make a wrong decision and someone gets hurt or dies. But I see no alternative.

"Someone has to decide," I say.

We set off, the four of us walking close together. Kyle talks openly about his abilities. He admits to having strength/speed, intuition, healing, and the cloaking gene.

"But the only one I can heal is myself," he says. "That might be because I've never practiced on anyone else. And intuition—I think with me it's more like being a crafty little bugger. I almost always can tell what other people are thinking, and I know how to get out of a tight spot."

"You sound like a guy I know," I say, glancing at Marc.

"I've just begun to get a feel for the cloaking gene," Kyle continues. "I feel when I'm on stage I can make the crowd fall in love with me. I'm serious. I just look into their eyes and wish for their love. It's got to be more of a magnetism thing with me."

"The charisma just drips right off you," I say.

Kyle laughs. "True! But it don't do me any bloody good in this place."

"What else do you have in your little bag of tricks?" I ask.

"I'm not sure. I've been scanned by a bigwig Lapra but all he'd do was confirm the powers I already knew about. But I know I have more, he told me that much. He said I'd pick them up as I went along."

"How many did he say you have altogether?" I ask.

Kyle brightens. "Six! That's a pretty fair number, don't you think? How many do you have?"

"I don't know," I lie. "The Tar scanned me but they don't give out that kind of information."

Kyle nods. "I've heard their rules. 'Your abilities have to mature naturally, in the fullness of time.' What a load of crap. I felt like strangling the Tar twat who told me that shit."

"Tar twat?" I ask.

"That's what the Lapras call them in London," Kyle says.

I'm not so worried about revealing the location of our cave now that we're abandoning it. We find Chad and Li waiting inside, huddling around a dying torch. Li looks better from the healing we did earlier; the energy boost seems to be holding. When I explain about Kyle's wounded team members, she quickly volunteers to go with him before I ask. She's such a giving person—I wonder if that's why she's such a gifted healer.

We part with Kyle and Li minutes later, after agreeing on a clear rendezvous point. Yet just before he leaves, Kyle pulls me aside.

"I know I kept saying that we've got to start trusting each other," he says. "I don't know how we're going to survive unless we do it. But I've got a problem with Sam I've got to tell you about."

"What is it?" I ask.

"He told me how he lives with his mom. He said he's studying to be a fashion designer and spends Monday through Friday at Parsons College. On the weekends he volunteers at a shelter for disabled children." Kyle groans. "Do you see what I mean?"

"You're worried he sounds too good to be true?"

"Aye. He sounds like a goddamn saint. Now, to his credit, I had to drag this information out of him. He didn't brag about it or nothing. But that thing about his arm bugs me too."

"Why?" I ask, although I can guess what Kyle's going to say.

"How many witches do you know who don't have the healing gene? I've never met one. I mean, how did he survive the dying-and-coming-back-to-life rite?"

"Half the people who lack the healing gene survive the rite."

"That's bullshit."

"My father told me that and he wouldn't have lied to me."

"Right, your father the doctor. It's true, half the witches

without the healing gene survive if they're in a hospital with a heart surgeon and cardiologist looking over them. When you come from the poor side of town, that fifty percent drops to less than ten. Trust me, I grew up broke."

Kyle's info is disturbing but enlightening.

"Sam might have had outside help," I say. "Is his mother a witch?"

"According to him she's an ancient witch. But that raises another question. If she's so old, why did she wait so long to have him?" Kyle pauses. "I swear to you, Jessie, I'm not the least bit homophobic. I have plenty of friends who are gay. Only I don't know anyone who's as perfect as Sam."

"You're the one who proposed the alliance."

"What was I supposed to do? The guy can see for miles and he's got the equivalent of X-ray vision. He proved it to me and you've got to admit those are pretty handy powers to have when you've got a bitch like Viper stalking you. I want Sam to be as pure and holy as he acts. I want to give him the benefit of the doubt. All I'm saying is keep an eye on him."

"And on you," I add.

Kyle nods. "Point taken. I'll be keeping an eye on you as well. One thing you've got to admire about Nordra. He puts it to you straight. Maybe none of us is going to get off this island until there's only one of us left."

I flash a grim smile. "It's something to think about. Maybe it will be just you and me at the end, going at it."

Kyle looks me over and grins. "With a body like yours—I'll bet you know how to kill a boy and still leave him smiling."

Kyle leaves with Li. Marc, Chad, and I—we gather together our spears, torches, and water bottles and set off for Sam's camp. Sam gave me precise instructions. Follow the base of the hill two miles west of the hot springs, until we see a large white boulder in the center of the river, then go a quarter of a mile farther and search the rolling terrain for his gray cell. He told me it was lodged behind a lonely cluster of thick trees.

Sam warned me the two miles would be mostly uphill and I am prepared. But Marc and Chad start complaining not long after we pass the hot springs.

"You'd think after having so many fights to the death here, there'd be a few well-worn paths," Marc says. "I've almost twisted my ankle a dozen times."

"I don't think the Field's been used in a while," I say, scanning the area for even a hint of a shadow. Since hearing from Cleo about Viper's powers, I feel like my paranoia has increased a dozenfold. I find I can never relax. But I try not to let my fear show. I add, "At one time there must have been trails. But they got overgrown."

"I don't know," Chad says. Next to Li, he's the weakest one in the group. Sweat pours off his brow and he's breathing hard.

"Why do you say that?" I ask.

"Just an observation that nothing on this island is the way it should be," Chad says. "Remember the jungle we landed in?

It was like the deepest, darkest part of the Congo. But then we hike over a single hill and suddenly the jungle thins out and we've got trees on the other side of a magnificent river—trees that look like the sort you find in North Carolina. Maple, oak, walnut, olive. I didn't see any of those trees in our valley."

"What are you saying?" I ask.

"That this island is a bizarre collection of various ecosystems," Chad says. "Yet each ecosystem is incomplete because there are no bugs or land animals."

"None that we've seen," Marc says. "I'll bet we run across a squirrel or a rabbit any minute."

"I'll take that bet," Chad says.

"You sound so confident," I remark. "Why?"

Chad stops and gestures to the wide expanse below. "This island reminds me of the old simulations the Pentagon used to do in the event of a nuclear war. They believed the first thing to be wiped out by a radiation blast would be people and large animals. The last land creatures would be insects, especially cockroaches. A cockroach can take twenty times the radiation of a human being. But even a cockroach would not outlast a tree."

"That's crazy," Marc says. "In a nuclear war the trees would immediately catch fire."

Chad nods. "They'd catch fire and burn to the ground. But their roots would survive because they're underground. Over time, as the background radiation declined, they'd start to grow again. In the same way millions of species of fish would survive because they're underwater. Sure, certain species might die off, but many years after a full-fledged nuclear war it's easy to imagine you could have a planet where not a single land animal walked the ground but the seas were still full of fish."

"Sort of like our river," I say, feeling a creepy sensation as I contemplate what he's saying. It's almost as if I sense the truth of his wild scenario.

"Yeah. Like our river," Chad agrees.

"So what are you saying?" Marc asks.

Chad shakes his head. "I need to see that wall Sam talked about."

Marc waves a hand. "I think our buddy Sam had too much smoke in his eyes when he ran into that wall."

"I hope so," Chad says, giving me a dark look.

We reach Sam's home base after a ninety-minute hike. His two remaining team members are brother and sister—Billy Bob Kelly and Mary Jo Kelly. Billy is eighteen, Mary is fifteen. Both have red hair, green eyes, a ton of freckles, and strong Kentucky accents. Billy appears in good shape when we arrive but Mary is lying down. Sam explains how she got knocked on the head when Nordra's people attacked.

"She has signs of a concussion," Sam explains. "Billy stayed up with her all night to make sure she didn't slip into a coma. She's better off today than yesterday but I'm not sure if she can climb to the top of the volcano. Not unless Li can fix her."

"You didn't mention that you had wounded," I say.

Sam nods. "When we first met, before I knew you better, I didn't want you to avoid us because of Mary. So I kept my mouth shut."

I squeeze his good arm. "I would have done the same thing. Let me work on Mary and see what I can do. Kyle and his people have got to be at least an hour behind us."

"You know he wanted to rendezvous with us higher up on the volcano," Sam warns.

"He'll have to wait," I say.

Mary has a lacerated left side, probably a few broken ribs. Nordra's people did not only cut her with their machetes, they pounded her torso. Yet the blow to her head is clearly more serious. She hardly responds when I enter their cell and examine her. I wish Li were present. Not only is she the more effective healer, using the healing ability doesn't seem to drain her the way it does me.

Still, I can't let the girl lie suffering.

As usual I place my left hand on Mary's forehead, my right over her heart. Closing my eyes, I pray for the magic to come and help the girl, and it's not long before heat begins to flow through my hands. Yet the light doesn't come, and when I try to make it come, the current pouring out of my fingers begins to fade. I try not to try, the old paradox I face every time I heal, but it's hard because even though I've only just met Mary, connecting to her in this way makes me feel close to her.

Definitely I feel her pain. My head aches as I work on her and when I'm finished I have to sit for several minutes with my eyes closed before I have the strength to stand.

Mary's fallen asleep but I sense it's a good sleep so I let her be. Stepping outside in the sun, I find Sam waiting by the door. I felt his eyes on me the whole time I treated Mary but didn't mind. Had the positions been reversed, I would have kept an eye on him.

"How is she?" he asks.

I shrug. "Better than before. But well enough to hike to the top of the peak? I doubt it. Hopefully, Li can do more for her than I can."

"You don't need to do that," Sam says.

"Do what?"

"Feel guilty about what you have no control over."

"An old habit, I guess."

Sam gestures to the landscape below. Even though we're a lot farther from the shore, I can still see the waves breaking against the dark rocks, and wonder what it would feel like to dive in that water and swim out past the swells and just float on my back and stare up at the blue sky. It seems forever since I totally relaxed.

Sam speaks. "On the way here, I got to know the people in my group. We had a whole day to talk about our lives. And when we landed here and I read the plaque, I swore I wasn't going to let anything happen to them. I'd die first before I'd let one of them get hurt." He pauses. "Then Nordra came and suddenly half my family was gone."

"Your family?"

"It's silly, I know, but that's how it felt. They were each special in their own way." He stops and sighs. "They were here one moment and gone the next. I blamed myself for taking the route I chose. For taking them with me. For not killing Nordra when we were face-to-face. It ate at me all night, and then again all day, in witch world. But then my mother told me something about the Field that helped me accept what was happening. She said, 'The Field is like life itself. It forces you to face your fears. Only, in the Field you face them in days rather than in years.'"

"Your mother sounds like a wise woman."

"She's the greatest person I've ever met." Sam pauses. "She knew I'd end up here."

"How?"

"I don't know. But that night I went to bed, the night I was taken, she kissed me good night and I saw tears in her eyes."

"Kyle told me she's been around for a while."

"Thousands of years. She's one of the oldest witches in the world."

"Does she have much contact with the Council?"

"She belonged to it a long time ago. But now she keeps to herself."

"And your father?"

"She's never spoken about him."

"That's odd."

"Not if you know my mother." Sam pats the granite boulder we're leaning against. "She's like this rock, nothing touches her. She just watches the days go by." He stops and corrects himself. "At least she used to."

"The plaque could be wrong. We might be able to get out of here."

"Do you believe that?" he asks.

"It's easier to believe it than to accept that we're doomed."

Sam nods. "You sound like my mother. I wish you two could have met."

"Maybe one day we will. While we're waiting, let me take a look at your arm."

"Bad idea. I saw you staggering when you stood up after working on Mary. Save your strength. I can wait for Li."

"You still think she's a witch?"

"I think they're all witches. It's just a question of whether they know it or not."

I hesitate. "Have you thought about connecting one of your people?"

Sam considers. "Billy's the only one left I could try to convert. But this is a far from ideal environment."

"How about in witch world?"

"I've got his address. I thought about going to see him. But he's going to school in North Dakota. It would take time to get there, and then what would I say? 'Hi, my name's

Sam. If you let me kill you in this world, it might help save your life in another world.'" He shakes his head. "How about you?"

"I suppose I feel the same way you do," I lie.

I've already warned my people not to tell Sam or Kyle where they live, or even to give out their last names. If Sam and Kyle are not who they're pretending to be, they could wipe out my gang by killing them all in witch world.

Sam isn't put off by my vague answer. He smiles faintly, to himself, and I get the distinct impression Billy has never been to North Dakota in his life.

We spot Kyle and his group two hours later, a mile above us. I'm not surprised that he's crossed onto the volcano where he has. The cliff that houses our old cave runs into the ground near where he's led his people, and it tells me that Kyle, like Sam, knows the island a lot better than I do.

I'm disturbed when Sam tells me that Kyle has only two guys with him, and one short Asian girl.

"Odd he'd leave his girls behind," I say.

"Maybe Li wasn't able to help them," Sam says.

Mary is feeling better and is able to hike, although at a slower pace than we'd like. Her brother, Billy, carries her pack for her and holds on to her hand, practically dragging her up the side of the mountain. Already the two merged groups are feeling the effect of the thin air. Except for Sam and myself, everyone's panting.

With no cliff left to hug, we're far more exposed. The trees are few and the grass is sparse. The higher we climb, the more often we cross over large black plates of frozen lava. The rock is actually easier to traverse. But to our dismay we spend most of our time trudging through a loose mixture of gravel and dirt. Kyle and his people patiently wait for us, yet it takes us over an hour just to climb up one mile.

Half the day is gone and the peak is still far off when we finally do reach Kyle and his people.

Li sits with her head hanging as we approach. She doesn't even look up to say hello. I order Kyle to tell me what happened. My tone is demanding. He raises his hands defensively.

"It wasn't Li's fault," Kyle says. "I watched her work on them. She did everything she could and they seemed better. But when we set off, Teri's wound reopened and she bled out. Then, half an hour later, Nicole complained of chest pains so we sat down and took a break. She closed her eyes and seemed to doze off for a few minutes. But when we tried to wake her, she was dead."

"What was wrong with Nicole to begin with?" I ask, studying Kyle's two male partners. Both are dark, black as Ora, but smaller, skinny. One has a French accent, the other sounds like Kyle. Pierre and Keb. They stand near Li as if protecting her. For some reason, Li refuses to look at me.

Kyle speaks with bitterness. "Viper struck Nicole's side with a staff. The bitch must have cracked her rib cage. Nicole probably got a punctured lung. During the night I know she was spitting up blood."

"I don't get it," I say. "Ora was fine after Li worked on him."

"It's possible treating Ora drained Li," Sam suggests.

"She freaked out when we lost the girls," Kyle says to me. "Started raving in Korean and shit, acting like she was the one who killed them. I tried talking to her but . . . she doesn't know me and I don't think she trusts me. Maybe you can help her. Whatever you can do, Jessie, do it fast. Hanging out on the side of this mountain is like waving a white flag in surrender. You can bet Nordra and Viper are eyeing us as I speak."

"I'll talk to her," I say. I walk toward Li, kneeling by her side, Ora at my back. With her hair hanging down, I can't see her face. I pull it aside and put my hand on the back of her neck. "Li? Li, look at me, it's Jessie. Tell me what's wrong."

She's a long time answering. I wait a minute, two—it's like someone's cut out her tongue. I'm tempted to shake her but finally she turns in my direction. Yet it's like she doesn't recognize me at first. She blinks rapidly, then stops, gives me a glassy stare.

"I'm sorry," she whispers.

"It's not your fault. They were dying. No one could've saved them."

She closes her eyes. "They were all right."

"What? Are you saying you healed them?"

"Lula said they were fine. But . . . they died."

I stand and trudge back to Kyle. Sam and Marc are sorting through our supplies, looking for cooked fish. Ora stays with Li. I speak in Kyle's ear, wanting only him to hear.

"After you left your cell, was it possible you were attacked?" I ask.

Kyle acts surprised. "No. No one touched Teri. She just started bleeding. And no one touched Nicole."

"Could Viper have been there?" I press.

"If she was, I didn't see her." Kyle suddenly stops. "Shit!"

"What is it?" I snap.

Kyle's fingers grip into fists. "Just before I went to wake Nicole, she made a peculiar breathing sound."

"Define peculiar."

Kyle struggles with himself. "Fuck. She sounded like she was choking a little in her sleep. That's why I went to wake her. But what if she was being smothered?"

"Viper?" I say.

Kyle closes his eyes and lowers his head. "Some fucking hero I turned out to be. I let that bitch kill Nicole right in front of me."

We continue our hike toward the volcano's peak. Li is too depressed, too upset, to heal either Sam or Mary. I have no choice but to work on both of them. Luckily, Sam's fracture is hairline and I'm able to fix it. But Mary barely responds to my touch this time, possibly because I treat her after Sam. Healing always drains me. As a result, Mary continues to be the weak link in our train. She lags behind with her brother, forcing us to make frequent stops so she can rest.

"I don't want to be the one to say it," Kyle tells me as we tread over a slick plate of black rock. Sam, Ora, Chad, and Marc are up front. Kyle's boys—Pierre and Keb—keep Mary, Billy, and Li company at the rear.

Up ahead, a quarter of a mile, steam rises from the ground. We're approaching another hot spring.

"You want to dump Mary," I say.

"I don't want to dump anyone. But we've got to think of the group. We can't risk ten lives to save one."

"To save two. Billy's never going to leave his sister."

"Then that will be his decision. But we've got to increase our pace if we're to reach the cave before dark, not keep taking more breaks."

"You have the nerve to just leave them behind?"

Kyle isn't insulted. "I told you I'm no saint. But this isn't about me. This is about you. Whether you accept it or not, the group's already appointed you our leader. Even Pierre and Keb—they just met you but I swear they trust you more than they trust me."

"You're exaggerating."

"I'm being blunt." Kyle reaches out and grabs my arm, stopping me. He's a strong devil. He lets the last of our gang trudge by before he lays into me. "You defeated Syn. You had that rep before we were taken to this godforsaken place. And you went one-on-one against Nordra and survived. You're already making the big decisions. You're the boss! Now start acting like it. Make the tough call and get us off the side of this mountain where every witch who wants to kill us can see us."

"I didn't kill Syn," I mutter.

"What?"

"Her five-year-old son killed her. I just happened to be there."

Kyle blinks. "No shit?"

"Still want me to be the one to condemn Mary and Billy to death?"

"Yes."

"You're a cold bastard, you know that?" Kyle doesn't reply, just looks at me, waiting. I snap, "All right, I'll think about it."

Kyle nods in the direction of the hot spring. "Don't take long," he warns, before his expression suddenly shifts to shock. He turns and calls to the front of our pack. "Sam!"

Sam's already waving to us. "I see them! Get up here!"

We rush to the front. Marc, Ora, Chad—they don't understand what the big emergency is. "What are you witches seeing?" Marc demands. That's the first time he's called us that.

Sam answers. "Ghosts are hiding behind boulders up ahead. There are two on our right, two on our left. But for all

I know all six of them are here." He pauses. "They let me see them on purpose."

"You sure?" Kyle asks.

"No question," Sam says. "They didn't peek over the rocks. They let their gaze linger. They wanted us to spot them."

"We know they're fast and telepathic," I say. "Anything else?"

"They heal quickly," Kyle says.

Sam speaks. "They always move in packs. Always have a leader. That will be their witch. We catch him, they won't know what to do."

"How do we know which one's the leader?" Marc asks.

Sam studies the large black rocks that litter the steaming pools. I smell sulfur and recall Cleo's warning. Be wary of Viper anyplace there's exposed lava. I ask Sam what he sees but he answers Marc's question.

"I'll be able to spot their leader," Sam says.

Kyle snorts. "So you're a telepath. You never told us that."

Sam is annoyed. "Like you told us half of what you can do."

I raise my hands. "We'll fight about our powers later. What do we do now?"

"We need to make a decision," Kyle says. "Do we try to take them or let them go?"

Sam cups his hands around his eyes and again scans the terrain a half mile up. But this time I feel he's searching more with his telepathic mind than his extraordinary vision. "If it helps with the decision, their leader is on the far left, away from the others, alone behind a rock."

"You can see him?" Kyle asks.

Sam shakes his head. "I can feel *her*. She's the only one who hasn't deliberately revealed her position."

"They're protecting her," Chad says.

"Cut off the head of the snake and the snake dies," Marc says. "Knowing her location gives us a big advantage. Here's my plan. You three act like you're heading for the ghosts who've shown their heads, then make a radical left turn and take her down."

"So we're talking about killing her?" Chad says.

Marc shrugs. "We can't exactly ask her to join our team."

Sam speaks. "If we do take her hostage, we might be able to force the ghosts to work for us."

Kyle shows interest. "How? By torturing her?"

Sam ignores him. "We need to decide. Kill her or try to take her alive?"

All eyes go to me. Kyle's right, they're already depending on me to make the final call. Yet I feel we're rushing our decision.

"You're all acting like we're the hunters here," I say. "This could be a trap. Look at last night. The ghosts led me straight into Nordra's arms."

"She's right," Marc says, reconsidering. "The ghosts could be working with Nordra or Viper."

Sam nods. "I suspect the ghosts would know if Nordra or

Viper are in the area. But I doubt they've formed a partnership with them. The ghosts are extremely reclusive—they'd never trust an outsider."

Sam's comments fuel my doubts. What he says tallies with what Cleo told me about the ghosts. Yet it troubles me that they've decided to face us all at once, particularly in broad daylight. They must have something up their sleeve.

"I don't like leaving the rest of our people exposed," I say. "And that's exactly what we'll be doing if the three of us go after the ghosts."

"Us three" has come to mean "Us witches."

Ora holds up a spear. "We're not defenseless."

For a moment the arguing stops, although Kyle continues to pace impatiently. Sam appears thoughtful. He breaks the silence.

"I agree it could be a trap. But I think we stand a better chance of fighting our way out of a trap if the three of us stick together." He turns to me. "Sorry."

"I agree with Sam," Kyle says. "Let's take the spears and strike fast and hard. Kill whoever gets in our way and then take their leader, dead or alive."

Again they look to me to make the call. But I can see they're through talking. It's time to act.

"All right, all three of us will attack," I say. "We'll take the machetes. But we're leaving half the spears with the rest of our group."

Kyle goes to protest but thinks better of it. Quickly our spears and machetes change hands. I pull Marc, Ora, and Chad aside.

"I need you to do what I say and not ask any questions," I whisper to them. "Take six spears and set one lying flat atop each of those six boulders." I point to the ones I've chosen. "Set the sharp ends pointed uphill. Do it a minute after we leave."

"Jessie—" Marc begins.

"Just do it," I cut him off.

Kyle, Sam, and I are set. We each carry a machete in our right hand, a bundle of spears in our left. As a backup, we have knives in our belts.

Our plan mimics Marc's suggestion: rush the more obvious ghosts before veering left toward their witch. The only change is Kyle insists we kill any ghosts that raise their heads.

We line up like gladiators of old.

I tell them we'll go on a count of three.

"One . . . two . . . three!" I cry.

We explode out of the blocks, and I'm relieved to see that Sam and Kyle have no trouble matching my speed. Kyle may even be faster. The ghosts react to our attack by scurrying away like startled insects. Yet their retreat was planned in advance. They all head to our right, away from their leader, and they make clever use of the surrounding terrain. Just when one ghost appears to make a tempting target, he or she ducks behind a rock. Kyle wastes three spears and screams in disgust.

"Shit!" he says.

"Forget them! Their leader's on the move," Sam yells.

"Where?" I snap.

Sam does a quick mental scan. "She's heading down the mountain and farther south, half and half."

I nod. "Gotcha. Kyle, cut straight across at this altitude, stay above her. Sam, chase after her, keep on her tail. I'll run halfway back toward our group then cut south. That way we'll have her boxed in. Now go!"

We set off like three missiles homing in on a flying target. The head ghost is every bit as fast as us but it's three against one. She clearly didn't expect Sam to spot her. Already I can see her darting in and out of the maze of boulders and steaming pools. She's at a terrible disadvantage because she can't veer up or down the side of volcano. She'd just run into Kyle or myself. To stay ahead of us, she has to keep running in as straight a line as fast as possible. Yet that makes it almost impossible for her to hide.

I know we're going to catch her.

I want her caught, alive.

Suddenly I hear a chorus of cries at my back.

A bolt of terror and guilt shoots through me and I almost trip and fall. Even before I turn I realize I should have listened to my gut. That we were the hunted and not the hunters. That the ghost leader knew exactly what she was doing.

Twisting my head, I see a nightmare.

Nordra and his two girls, in their blue uniforms, are racing toward the center of our group. Nordra carries a machete; his partners each have a bundle of spears. Ora runs out to meet them, Chad and Marc a few steps behind him.

The girls' sticks are either bent or else they're lousy shots. Their spears fall harmlessly to the ground. Still, the hail of sharp sticks intimidates the others, causing them to huddle helplessly; and it looks like my friends will be taking the brunt of the attack.

All thought of the ghosts vanishes. All I care about is getting to Nordra before he reaches my friends. Having already run halfway back to the main group, I'm closer to them than Sam or Kyle.

Nevertheless, I call to my fellow witches as I turn and race toward Nordra. I hear Sam shout in reply but don't know what he says. My heart shrieks in my head. I saw what Nordra did to those people in the meadow and know he'll show my people no mercy.

Ora is fifty feet from Nordra, on a head-on collision, when he stops to throw a spear. He puts every fiber of his strong muscles into the heave and his form is superb. Unfortunately, Nordra's reflexes are blinding. Seemingly without breaking stride, he plucks the spear from midair and snaps it in two, tossing it aside.

Ora manages to draw his knife but that's as far as he gets. Nordra doesn't even raise his machete as he races by. The beast slugs Ora in the chest, knocking him to the ground. I'm two hundred yards away but I'm still able to hear the bones and cartilage in Ora's sternum crack.

Marc and Chad are more successful. Their spears go wide on their first throws, but they're fast learners and hit both of Nordra's girls on their second attempts. Chad's spear strikes one in the leg; Marc's pierces the other's chest, and there's no question he's delivered a fatal blow.

Perhaps that's the reason Nordra goes after Marc, I don't know. It seems crazy but I wonder if Nordra's seen me talking to him, if he knows I care for Marc. Whatever the reason, Nordra plucks Marc off the ground and, using both arms, holds him over his head as if he were made of foam rubber.

The dramatic pose is for my benefit.

Once again, Nordra has come to make me an offer.

"Jessica Ralle!" he calls as I rush to Chad's side. "I would speak to you!"

Chad whispers to me. "What do we do?"

"Get back with the others."

"I'm not leaving you!"

"You can only hurt me by staying. Go!"

Chad accepts that I mean what I say. He withdraws to the others, who at least have picked up their spears and look ready to fight. Even Mary has grabbed a spear and stands beside her brother, Billy. Nordra's attack may have startled them but they're not cowards.

I just wish Sam or Kyle would get here.

I stick the tip of my machete in the ground and spread my arms. "What can I do for you?" I call.

Nordra walks toward me, taking long, slow strides. He continues to hold Marc aloft as if he were a prize fish, and I have no doubt he'll snap him in two if I say or do the wrong thing.

In all the scenarios I've run through my head since coming to the Field, this is my worst nightmare. I feel helpless and, already, a sense of devastating loss. But loss of what? A friend? No, it feels much deeper than that, and it's only then I realize how much I care for Marc. If I could trade my life for his I'd do it in an instant.

But Nordra doesn't want my life, not yet.

He wants me. He wants me to kill with him.

Nordra halts fifty yards away. "The deal remains the same," he says.

"Put him down and we'll talk about it," I reply.

Nordra chuckles as he shakes Marc high in the air. "Sure, I'll put your boyfriend down. But in how many pieces? The answer is up to you, Jessica Ralle."

Boyfriend. Nordra has been spying on us.

Sam appears at my side, gasping for breath. I fear to turn my head to search for Kyle. There's no need—Sam says he's only seconds away. But we don't have seconds, I tell Sam. He nods and stares at Nordra and Marc, his sharp eyes searching for an opening of some kind.

"We can take him without Kyle," Sam whispers. "Rush him from opposite sides."

"He'll kill Marc," I reply.

"He's going to kill him anyway."

I hear the finality in Sam's statement and know it's true. Nordra's never going to let Marc go, no matter what I promise. He's already told me as much. His deal hasn't changed. I have to sacrifice my people to show he can trust me.

"Do you have a secret power you haven't told me about?" I ask.

Sam sighs. "Nothing that can help us now."

I can see Nordra growing impatient and half expect him to begin torturing Marc to hasten my response. Still, I take a moment to scan for the spears I ordered placed atop the boulders. There's one almost directly behind Nordra, slightly off to my right. But it's a hundred yards—the length of a football field—from the tip of the spear to Nordra's back.

"I'll make you a counteroffer!" I call out. "Put down my friend and together you and I will leave here. I'll help you find Viper. I'll help you kill her. That's all you care about. Besides me, she's the only one who can threaten you."

Nordra nods his approval. "An interesting offer, Jessica Ralle. I am tempted. But there's a problem."

"What's that?" I ask.

"I don't trust you."

"We've come to this island to kill each other. We're never

going to trust each other. But once I give my word I keep it. If I say I'll help you kill Viper, I'll do it. Besides, she's my enemy as much as she is yours. Once she's dead, you and I can fight. Think about what I'm offering. With Viper and me dead, who will be able to stand against you?"

Nordra considers while Marc squirms in his hands. I can't look at Nordra without seeing Marc's eyes, which never leave me. I know what's he's trying to tell me.

"Don't worry about me. Kill him."

But all I can do is worry, when what I need to do is focus—focus on the spear. It seems so far away, so out of reach. After Kendor threw me off the cliff and shocked me into activating my telekinetic witch gene, he had me practice by moving objects with my mind. My near brush with death had gotten my juices flowing and I was able to reach out and grab anything at hand with a simple thought. Unfortunately, the object had to be close. My grasp reached ten yards, no more.

Kendor had told me the limitation was self-imposed.

"Distance is in the mind. Size is in the mind. Now that your power is alive, you can move mountains."

"You sound like Yoda," I said.

Kendor had been puzzled. "Who is Yoda?"

"The Jedi Master in the Star Wars *movies."*

"What is a movie?"

Of course, I knew a man plucked from the sixth century would have no idea what a Jedi Knight or a movie was. It didn't matter—I believed Kendor's wisdom was timeless. Throwing me off the cliff had been as hard on him as it had been on me. He had known it might kill me, but he'd done it anyway because he knew if my latent power could be activated, I'd be almost impossible to kill.

Kendor had that kind of faith in me.

It's time I showed my faith in him.

"Distance is in the mind," I repeat to myself.

Sam glances at me, understanding. "So says my mother."

"I will make you a counterproposal," Nordra calls. "But I will still need proof of your sincerity."

"What kind of proof?" I ask.

"Kill the witch standing beside you."

"And if I refuse?"

"I will tear your boyfriend in two," Nordra says, suddenly pulling Marc's arms and legs in opposite directions. Marc lets out a choking cry and it's all the more horrible because I know he wouldn't make a sound unless the pain was unbearable.

Marc's howl deepens the nightmare for me, and yet, at the same time, it's like the spark that lights the torch in my dark dungeon. Raging hatred for Nordra explodes in my gut and starts a fire that blazes through every nerve in my body. My heads burns, my thoughts feel hot enough to melt lead, and with a fury I've never felt in my life, I reach out for the spear with my mind, lift it three feet off the rock, and send it rocketing into Nordra's spine.

The spear passes right through Nordra, dropping to the ground ten feet in front of the groaning bastard, the sharpened wood soaked in blood. A red stain swells across the chest of his blue uniform and the life drains from his limbs. He drops Marc as if he were a sack of flour. It's possible the spear has in fact severed Nordra's spinal cord.

I truly hope so because I'm about to rush toward him, my machete held high, and cut off his head when . . .

A piercing scream erupts behind me. Turning, I see Mary engulfed in flames, and for a second I'm convinced my burning brain has accidentally hit one of my own people with a bolt of fire.

Then I see the strangest sight. It starts a few feet behind Billy, who is struggling in vain to smother the flames that have engulfed his sister. The lava beneath the steaming water—in a thin red coil that resembles a burning snake, it rises from the center of the hot spring and swiftly wraps three times around Billy's body. Before he's even aware it's there, the witch who holds it in midair relaxes her grip and the lava drapes over him like a chain made of molten mercury. His brown uniform instantly ignites and in the blink of an eye he's a flaming mirror of his burning sister.

I feel as if the whole world has gone insane.

Sam shakes me hard. His words bring me back to reality.

"It's Viper!" he cries. "Everyone! Get away from the pools! Run!"

I see her, Viper, for the first time. No doubt she crept up on us while cloaked, but now that she's using another weapon, her telekinesis, she's had to drop the invisibility. I've been told that even ancient witches find it hard to use two powers at the same time.

Viper, for all her badass rep and evil nickname, cuts a pathetic figure. She's short, her dark hair is short—it looks like it was cut by a barber with a rusty pair of scissors. She's so thin her black uniform fits her like a blanket, and her pale face is scarred. At first glance it looks like a bad case of acne, but then I realize the marks were caused by an infected needle.

Maybe she was tortured as a child. Maybe she developed a drug habit as a teenager. I don't know and I don't care. She looks awful and she is awful and I'm going to kill the bitch.

I reach for the lava with my mind. I envision a tidal wave of molten rock pouring over her head. But no tsunami arises. The clouds of steam whirl from my psychic assault but I can't grip the flowing lava the way I could the solid spear. I can't get a lock on it; the glowing magma literally feels like it pours through my mental fingers.

All right, I tell myself, I'll lift up a boulder with my brain and flatten Viper that way. Pound her into the ground. Unfortunately, I'm not given a chance to concentrate. Suddenly I realize why Kyle never made it to my side.

He's already squared off against Viper, trying to use his speed and his machete to take her down. But every time he makes a stab at her, she sends forth a hail of splattering lava, and only Kyle's incredible reflexes keep him from ending up like Mary and Billy.

Speaking of which, Mary suddenly stops flailing and drops to the ground with a spear in her back. I scan the area expecting to find one of Viper's people attacking from behind, but all I see is Ora raising a second spear. It takes me a moment to understand. I had assumed Ora was down for the count. Instead, he's back on his feet and trying to do the most merciful of all things—put Mary and Billy out of pain.

"Ora!" I shout. "Aim for Viper!"

He looks at me like he's already thought of that and tried it half a dozen times. Indeed, he probably did exactly that while I was talking to Nordra. Yet, whether for good or bad, Ora takes my orders seriously and turns and runs toward Viper, holding a spear ready.

"Don't get near her!" I cry. "Stay away from the pools!"

This time Ora doesn't listen and I understand why. The sight of Billy writhing in the worst pain a person can suffer overwhelms us all. To be transformed into a human torch—I can't even look at Billy and not feel the same rage that's overcome Ora. Yet I'm the one who ordered him to kill the bitch when I should have kept my mouth shut and dealt with her myself.

Forgetting Nordra, forgetting even Marc, who's still trying to find his feet, I grab my machete and rush Viper. I'm grateful

I've got Sam by my side and that Kyle's already trying to take Viper down.

But Viper sees me coming. Over the two hundred yards that separate us, our eyes lock and she smiles faintly, nods, and there's something so evil in the simple gestures that I know in an instant what she's thinking. She's got three witches closing in on her and I'm their leader. It doesn't matter that I've just taken down Nordra; he's just demonstrated exactly how she's going to stop me.

By going after those Jessica Ralle cares about.

Viper turns toward Ora, who's closed to within a hundred feet, and raises her right hand while making a peculiar swirling motion with her left. Behind her a two-inch-thick stream rises into the air like a long red hose poking from a steaming sauna. The stream curls over Viper's head, flecks of ash spilling onto her hair, yet it doesn't appear to bother her. On the contrary, it's as if she's flexing a muscle she's anxious to strike with.

The stream suddenly narrows, projects; it's like Viper has fired a laser from an invisible gun mounted three feet above her skull. It's only when it strikes Ora in the chest, splashing over the front of his body, that it reverts to its original form— molten lava.

Ora screams and explodes in a ball of flame.

"Now you die!" Kyle cries, falling on her with his machete held high. It seems inevitable he'll kill her. By going after Ora, Viper's left herself wide open. Besides, Kyle's only three steps from Viper, and he's about to chop at her slender neck with his sharp machete. A half second more, at the most, I think, and her head will be flying through the air.

Viper vanishes from sight.

Kyle swings and hits empty air.

"Damn!" I swear, leaping toward the hot springs.

Sam grabs me from behind. "Jessie!"

I try shaking him off. "She can't have gone far! Look for her!"

Sam holds on. "Ora! We have to help Ora!"

I want to tell him we can't help Ora, not now, not while we have a chance to put an end to Viper. I should probably also say I'm deliberately not looking in Ora's direction because I can't bear to see him suffer. But it would all sound so feeble because we can all hear him screaming.

I turn to Marc, who has finally regained his senses.

"Grab a spear, a machete, anything," I order. "Kill him."

Marc gasps. "But Li . . ."

"He can't be saved! Kill him!" I cry.

Marc does have the strength to look in Ora's direction. His face pales but he nods. "I'll do it, Jessie. Just kill that bitch."

Ora's screams haunt me all the way to the steaming pools. Until they abruptly fall silent. Once again, I don't look, I can't. Sam, Kyle, and Chad huddle around me.

"Can you see her?" I ask Sam.

He's scanning the area. "No. It's the steam. I can't find a

trace of her shadow. She must be weaving through the pools."

Chad speaks. "The steam might block Sam's vision but it can help us. An object, even an invisible object, if it passes through a cloud, it leaves a visible trail."

"What exactly are we looking for?" Kyle demands.

It's Chad's turn to scan the hot springs. "There's a breeze blowing downhill, slowly pulling the steam with it. Look for any place where it suddenly parts or spins uphill. That will be a sign Viper's nearby."

"She's shrewd," I warn. "She might not run. She might not disturb the steam at all."

"Then we'll listen for her," Sam says.

We break into two teams. Sam goes with Kyle. Chad comes with me. I'm armed with a machete and a knife. Chad has a knife and a spear. We move silently around the bubbling pools, the stench of the sulfur almost suffocating.

Of course it's always possible Viper's tricked us and has doubled back on the rest of our people. But somehow I don't think so. Easy access to the lava is still her most potent weapon, and I don't believe she'd give it up unless we drive her away from the pools.

We hear a sound at our backs and whirl. It's Marc, breathing hard; he's run fast to catch us. Putting a finger to my lips, I caution him to remain silent and he nods. But I can tell from his miserable expression, and the blood on his machete, that he carried out my last order.

Ora is dead.

Marc may have killed him but it's Viper who's the murderer.

I swear to myself I'm going to take her down.

The steam is thick. We can see each other, and the narrow pathways through the pools, that's it. Then Chad taps me on the shoulder, points to a trail of footprints in the crusty black soil. The prints belong to a small barefoot woman. Like Nordra, and myself for that matter, Viper must have set aside her boots before going into battle, counting on the extra traction and quiet steps the absence of footwear would give her.

Together, we track the footprints. But we've not gone far when we come to the edge of the hot springs and a flat sheet of black stone. It's covered with a faint coat of ash; still, Viper's footprints are now unclear. We see a partial print of her left foot, hike another twenty feet before we see a print of her right toes. Chad tries his best to resist but the fumes cause him to cough, giving away our position.

I motion for us to stand still, listen. I think I hear something off to our left. Marc is on my left. He gestures, silently asking if he can whisper in my ear. I nod and he leans close to my head.

"Behind us," he says. "To our . . . Aaah!"

A stone knife magically emerges from the steam the instant the tip penetrates Marc's lower back. He cries out in pain and I immediately slash behind him with my machete, hitting nothing but thin air. Yet, over Marc's moans, I hear movement. Gesturing to Chad to help Marc, who's dropped to the ground, I anxiously scan the area behind us.

The steam is still thick; we're on a rock plate, prints are hard to find, and my eyes are aching from the fumes. I can't rely on my vision, I have to listen, have to block out whatever sounds Marc is making.

But my guys are true heroes; Chad knows what I'm doing. He clamps his hand over Marc's mouth and Marc quietly reaches up and pulls it away, nodding that he knows he can't so much as groan.

If Viper was fleeing I'd see movement in the steam, but it sticks to us like a shadow. It's unfortunate the steam's robbed me of the glare of the sun, that I can't spot the outline of her shadow. It's as if she's planned everything ahead of time. First she waited until we were at our most vulnerable, when Nordra attacked. Now she's probably celebrating the fact that I've split up our team of witches to search for her. That might have been an error on my part, I think. Marc's already wounded and . . .

I hear someone draw in a sharp breath. The guys are behind me, this sound comes from in front of me. What would force her to take an audible breath? The sound is coming from at least ten feet away, closer to fifteen. I hear a faint rustle of clothing.

Viper's about to attack!

Attack from a distance!

She must have picked up a spear! A spear that will only become visible after she's thrown it at my chest!

That's why she attacked Marc with a knife. She didn't want to mess with me at first. No, she used the knife to give me the impression that was the only weapon she had beside her telekinesis—which she can't use while cloaked. She tried to plant the idea in my mind that she would have to come close to hurt me. And she has come close but only close enough to make sure her spear doesn't miss.

I have one chance and I take it. From holding my machete up high, I swing it around like an overthrown bowling ball and let go of my grip. The sharp stick flies through seemingly nothing but steam—until it strikes.

Viper suddenly appears, the stump of her left arm gushing blood. My machete's caught her wrist. Her severed hand, the fingers gripping one of our own spears, lies bloodied on the black rock. Viper stares down at it, stunned, then glares at me.

The hatred in her eyes shouldn't shock me and yet it does. She's stalked us and she's murdered us. Yet she's outraged we've fought back. It's like she's never been spanked before and doesn't know how to deal. Well, I do, I know exactly what I'm going to do to her.

I leap toward her. She vanishes.

I stop, think.

She's wounded, she should try to escape.

But she's furious, she wants revenge.

Which fact will drive her next decision?

I retreat to Chad and Marc, pick up the machete Marc dropped, scan for drops of blood. There's a mass of red where Viper's hand has fallen but I can't find any other bloody drops. Forcing an arrogant smile, I wave the machete in the air and act like I don't have a care in the world.

"Come out, you coward!" I shout. "Let's put an end to this now!"

I don't mean what I say. I'm trying reverse psychology, hoping she'll reject my challenge. My first priority has to be Marc and Chad. Marc's been stabbed and Chad is tending to him. They can't help me but—even missing a hand—Viper can probably find a way to use them against me. Just look at what Nordra did.

Far to my right I hear running steps. I even see the steam twist and whirl as someone races through the stinking cloud. Finally I glimpse a trail of blood. But I don't go after her. Viper will just make me pay by circling around and cutting Chad's throat.

I kneel beside Marc and Chad.

"How bad is it?" I ask.

Chad's already torn off the sleeve of his shirt and is using it as a bandage. "She struck near his kidney but I think she missed," he says. "Pressure's slowing the bleeding. I doubt she hit a major vein or artery."

I put my hands on Marc. "I'll do a quick healing."

Marc stops me. "Wait until we get back to the others."

"Okay. As long as you let me carry you."

Marc looks disgusted. "No way."

"Way," I insist.

Chad nods in the direction of Viper's severed hand. "Is she capable of growing another one?" he asks.

I pick up Marc, being careful to hold his bandage in place.

"I don't know," I say, and I don't.

On the way back we pass where she lost her hand.

But the hand is gone.

Yet she's left her black bracelet lying on the ground.

I tell Chad to pick it up and put it in my pocket.

Nordra is gone. In the confusion, no one saw him leave. I'm stunned that he was able to recover from such a deadly blow. My spear must have somehow missed his heart and given him a chance to heal. I can only hope he's no longer a hundred percent.

Both Nordra's girls are dead, which is a surprise. Apparently Chad hit the major artery in the girl's leg when he struck with his spear. While the rest of us were dealing with Viper, she bled out. It's a small victory but we'll take it.

I do a healing on Marc while Sam digs graves for Ora, Mary, and Billy, who are so badly burned they're unrecognizable. The graves are shallow and Sam digs alone. The healing I did on his arm is holding.

Kyle is off with his guys, Pierre and Keb, collecting the leader of the ghosts. He swears he wounded her, tied her up, that he just has to collect her. In all the commotion I've almost forgotten what triggered the attacks.

I manage to stop Marc's bleeding but the wound remains open and I don't like the smell of it. I suspect Viper's knife had poison on the tip. I keep the suspicion to myself but Marc senses something's wrong. He says he feels a weird burning sensation.

"Where?" I ask.

"All over," he says.

I wish Li could work on him but she's afraid she'll make him worse. I don't press her. The attacks have only made her more anxious than before. For the life of me, I don't know what's wrong with her head.

Kyle and the others miss our brief memorial service. Sam says a few words about the courage of Mary and Billy, but when it's my turn to talk about Ora, I choke up, and Chad has to speak for our group.

"Ora was a warrior at heart. He knew how dangerous it was to get near Viper but that didn't hold him back. I saw his face as he charged her. He knew he was about to die but he wanted to protect us. That was the only thing that mattered to him. We only met two days ago but I can honestly say I never knew a braver soul." Chad kneels and picks up a scoop of dirt, pouring it over the mound of Ora's grave. "Rest in peace, my friend. We'll miss you."

Dear Chad—I know his words are partially meant for me.

Chad knows I'm plagued with guilt. It does no good but I keep replaying in my head how I should have made my order clearer. I had wanted Ora to throw his spear at Viper from a distance, not approach her. Yet Chad's trying to tell me that Ora was going to sacrifice himself no matter what, and maybe he's right. I kneel beside Chad as he puts his hand on Ora's grave and hug him.

Kyle finally returns with the ghost, carrying her in his arms. She's badly injured. It appears Kyle not only speared her in the lower back but cut *both* her Achilles tendons with his machete. Even before he pulls me aside, I'm suspicious about her wounds.

"I know what you're going to say," he blurts out.

I'm furious with him. "That you're a sadist?"

He balls his hand into a fist and pounds his leg. "Damn you! We talked about this. You need to make tough decisions. You still don't get it, do you? We're at war. It's kill or be killed."

"Then kill her! Put her out of her misery!" I glance to where Kyle's dumped the ghost beside Sam. Her gray uniform is soaked with blood; half is dry, the rest is fresh. I add, "You deliberately cut her tendons so she can't run."

"And I keep cutting them. Do you know a better way of restraining her? It's not like when we came to the Field we were each given a kit equipped with handcuffs, ankle chains, and rope. No, they gave us a plaque that said only one of us is going to survive." Kyle stops and throws up his arms in frustration. "But if you want her dead, then you kill her."

"There's no need to continually mutilate her!" I snap.

"I just explained why it is necessary!" he snaps back.

"What did you do while we were fighting Nordra? Spear her to a tree and slice her tendons?"

"I came as fast as I could."

I hesitate. "I'm not calling you a coward."

"No. Just a sadist. Thank you. Thanks a lot."

"I'm just saying that most of her wounds are fresh. You're not letting her heal. You keep cutting and stabbing her."

Kyle lowers his voice. "How else do we keep her from running back to her buddies? Oh, and before you do answer please keep in mind that it was the queen of the ghosts here that led us into the trap that killed Ora, Billy, and Mary. It's not like these cute little albinos are innocent."

I shake my head. "I don't know how to keep her captive. I just know that we're not going to keep slicing up her body so she keeps bleeding. We do that and we're no better than Nordra or Viper."

Kyle stares at me. "Who said we are better?"

I look up at the volcano and sigh. The edge of the sun has touched the cinder cone's rim, its light scattering and dimming as it passes through the heavy smoke. An eerie orange shadow falls over the graves and I fear we'll be digging more if we don't find shelter before dark. I explain our predicament to Kyle but he's one step ahead of me.

"I spotted a cave when I went back for the ghost," he says. "I didn't have time to check it out but I sent Pierre and Keb to give it a look and they said it goes way back into the mountain."

"It sounds perfect," I mutter.

Kyle hears the double meaning in my tone. "Maybe too perfect?"

I tell Kyle I want to talk with our ghost. He doesn't object. We both know she can't talk. But Sam's sitting with the wounded creature and I wonder if he'll be able to make contact with her. I sit beside them while Kyle organizes the rest of the group to head for the cave.

"Can you pick up her thoughts?" I ask.

"Only the ones she chooses to share," Sam says. "She has a highly disciplined mind. She's in terrible pain and in unfriendly hands but she's still calm."

"Is that good?" I ask.

"Personally I'd like it if she was more afraid of us. You know we underestimated her earlier. She knew Nordra and Viper were about to attack. She and her people helped them by dividing us at a critical time."

I frown. "Have you changed your mind? Do you think the ghosts are working with Nordra and Viper?"

Sam shakes his head. "I think the ghosts have mental radar, that they have a rough idea of where everyone is on the island at all times. But they're physically weak. The only way they can defeat any of us is by moving us around like pieces on a chessboard. Force us to kill each other."

I study the ghost leader as Sam speaks. The females appear to be as tall as the males—four feet. Her hair is pure white but her skin has a pink tinge. Her red eyes make her look sickly, at first glance. As I study them closely, I feel a sudden anxiety and quickly look away. Sam notes my reaction.

"She can plant thoughts and feelings in our minds," he says.

"To what degree?" I ask.

"That is the big question, isn't it? She might have trouble controlling us because we're witches. I know she's tried to plant the idea in my mind to walk away and leave her alone. So far I've been able to block her. But I wouldn't want to let her get too close to the others."

"Have you tried telling her we'd like to be friends?"

"After Kyle shot her with a spear and hacked up her legs? Yeah, I told her and it went over great. She trusts us even less than we trust her."

"And you don't trust her at all," I say.

Sam's worried. "Our plan to use her to control the other ghosts could backfire. They know we've got her, which means they'll be tracking us. It could make them more determined than ever to lead Viper and Nordra to our doorstep."

"What are you suggesting?" I ask.

Sam leans over and whispers in my ear. "Either leave her here or kill her now."

I groan. "Does she have a name?"

"Jelanda."

"Let me try talking to her. Tell me if she responds to what I say." Sam nods, and I move closer to the ghost and again her eyes fasten on mine. But this time I meet her gaze straight on and feel her psychic probing as fingernails poking the front and back of my skull. I gesture to her bloody heels.

"This isn't what I wanted," I say.

Sam pauses before giving her reply. "Are you the leader of your group?"

"Yes."

"Kill the one who injured us and we will believe you," Sam replies for her. I note her use of the words "us" and "we." I wonder if she has any sense of individuality.

"There's been enough killing. We want a truce. If your people leave us alone, we promise to leave you alone."

"You are asking for a treaty?"

"Yes," I say.

Jelanda glances in the direction of our graves. "Your group is weak, vulnerable. Why should we treat with you?" Sam stops and frowns. "I'm sorry, Jessie. I'm not sure of that last phrase."

"It doesn't matter, I know what she meant." I lean toward her. "We are stronger than we appear, and you are our prisoner. You have no choice but to deal with us."

Jelanda smiles and her eyes are cold.

Sam translates. "She says, 'None of you will survive.'"

I sit back on my heels, barely resisting the urge to break her neck. I tell myself I'm being civilized. At the same time my heart warns me I'm making a mistake. That I should kill her now before she destroys us all.

CHAPTER EIGHT

IN THE MORNING, IN WITCH WORLD, JIMMY SHAKES ME awake minutes after dawn. My body—this body—has slept but my mind feels like it has gotten no rest. Because it hasn't. I was awake most of the night in the Field.

Watching, waiting, standing guard.

I groan and roll over and cover my head with my pillow. "Let me sleep," I beg.

"Lara's awake," Jimmy says.

"I don't hear her," I mumble.

"Her eyes are open. She's looking around, looking for her mommy."

"Give her to my mom."

Jimmy hugs me from behind and kisses my ear. "I love you."

"If you loved me you'd let me sleep."

"If you get up we can have sex. And we can do anything you want to do."

My eyes pop open. "Anything?"

He kisses my neck and gently bites my skin. I must have been a vampire in a past life. Touch my neck, kiss it, lick it—it doesn't matter, I turn into a slut.

"Anything," he swears.

I throw off the covers and stand up. "Let me pee and take a shower. Remember, you said anything. Get naked."

"Should I get naked before or after I give Lara to your mom?"

"Right now I don't care."

An hour later we're holding each other in bed and I feel myself drifting down lazy currents, floating, falling back asleep. I know I have no right to be happy. The Field is only another sunrise away and so is death. It's impossible to imagine a more ridiculous time to feel joy and yet it's here—in Jimmy's arms. It's always here because he's always here. I know he loves me and what's sad is I always knew I loved him even more.

But now I know nothing.

Except that it's good to hold him.

My eyes are shut. I hear him speak.

"You have to tell me what's happening," he says.

"You don't want to know."

"Has anyone died?"

I sigh. "That's what people do in the Field. They die."

Jimmy goes in the kitchen and makes coffee. When he returns, I can hear myself snoring but he drags me into a sitting position and forces me to drink two cups—scalding hot but sweet. At some point my brain turns back on and I start talking.

I tell him everything that's happened.

When I finish, he sits in silent shock.

"Say something," I tell him finally.

"You have to stay alive, Jessie."

"I'm trying."

"Do whatever it takes."

"I can't betray the ones who trust me." I pause. "I can't betray you."

Jimmy knows what I'm saying. "You're worried Marc's going to die. You want to see him again today, try to convince him to do it."

I hesitate. "Yes. But—we've talked about it—it's tricky. I'd be asking him to risk his life. He doesn't know me like the other Marc."

"Let him get to know you. You have to work fast. Get him to fall in love with you."

"You don't mean that. Last night . . ."

"Last night was last night. I didn't understand then what you're going through. And I was being selfish, I was thinking of myself. Now . . ." Jimmy takes my hand. "You have to stay alive," he repeats.

My body trembles with the shock of what he's telling me to do. The sacrifice he's willing to make to keep me safe. The absolute love he has for me. I feel awe, I feel shame, I feel him—my Jimmy.

I squeeze his hand. "I might not be home tonight."

He nods. "I know."

I want to visit with Lara before I leave the house. I want to hold her in my lap and kiss the top of her head. I love the smell of her head. I don't know why but it often smells like honey to me, although the shampoo I use to wash her hair has none in it. Other times she smells like flowers. Jimmy likes to boast that our daughter is a constant source of aromatherapy.

But I don't stop to play with my daughter. I fear if I do, hours will go by and there's much I have to do. Also, I'm afraid if I hold Lara even one more time, it will be to acknowledge that I might never see her again. My reasoning makes no sense but it's how I feel.

After dressing, I leave the house quickly, giving Jimmy a painful kiss good-bye. I'm halfway to Kendor and Syn's house when I pull over to the side of the road and call Cleo. She's quick to answer.

"You're still alive," are her first words.

"How do you know? I could have died in the Field and I'd still be alive here in witch world."

"If you had died there, you wouldn't be calling." She pauses. "Give me an update."

"Wait. I need to speak to my father."

"He's away on important business."

"It's crucial I talk to him."

"Why?"

"I've been thinking about Huck. I sent his DNA to my father to be tested and the lab sent a form back stating that Jimmy isn't his biological father."

"I heard."

"Did you hear that the lab report was accidentally sent to our house—our house in *both* worlds—and that Jimmy accidentally read it?"

"I'm sure that upset him. I'm sorry."

"Are you? The more I've thought about it, the more I've realized my father doesn't make mistakes. He's too controlled, too careful. That report was sent to our house on purpose. I *know* that. But what I don't know is if the report is even accurate."

"Why do you doubt it?"

"Because my father has plans for me. Important plans for my future. He's desperate for me to free up more time, which means giving up Huck. You know the connections my dad has. It would have been a snap for him to have a lab send out a false report." I pause. "It would have been a snap for you."

"You think I would mislead you in such a manner?"

"I don't know what to think."

"I would never do that to you, Jessica."

I feel my eyes burning. I wipe away a tear.

"It's just driving me crazy, you know, the way it's eating at

Jimmy. He only saw the letter last night, and this morning . . . this morning he didn't say a word about it. Here it's killing him and he says nothing to me. Except that I have to stay alive."

Cleo speaks gently. "He must love you very much."

"Yes, he does. I'm sorry, what I said, I know you wouldn't lie to me like that. It's just hard, thinking that my father might."

"You'll talk to him when he gets back."

I hesitate. "Is he all right? Where he is?"

"He's alive. That's all I can say. Now give me an update."

Pulling myself together, I recount my adventures in the Field—in a more condensed form than I told Jimmy. When I'm finished, Cleo asks a few seemingly random questions about Sam and Kyle. She appears to be searching for something. I finally interrupt and ask what's bothering her.

"I told you, to be in the Field they have to have at least six witch genes," she says. "So far they haven't told you everything they can do."

"I'm no better. They have no idea I can.cloak." I pause. "Do you know anything about them from your sources?"

"Both are known to the Council. Kyle Downing, because of his music. And Sam Verra, because of his mother, Larla."

"Sam told me she was once a member of the Council. But it sounds like she turned her back on you guys. Why?"

"Larla has the same streak you and Syn share. She's always been wary of authority. She hates being told what to do— not that many people would try with her. At her age, she's a formidable presence. We first met thousands of years ago and in all that time she's always been a loner. Her thoughts are her own. I wouldn't be surprised if she's passed that quality onto her son."

"Do you know who Sam's father is?"

"I can't speak about that, and it's irrelevant. What you want to know is if you can trust him. I'll run background checks on him today but I already know of one disturbing report. Sam was arrested last year in connection with the murder of his longtime boyfriend, Michael Edwards. Michael was found strangled to death in a workroom at Parsons, where they were both students. Sam was arrested because he had motive and opportunity. He was working late at school that night and he freely admitted to the police he was upset that Michael was planning to leave him. But Sam swore he was innocent." Cleo pauses. "Eventually he was released due to lack of physical evidence."

"The way Michael was choked—was there any sign excess physical strength was used?"

"Yes. The detective in charge of the case noted that in her files. Of course, she was unable to explain the cause of the damage to Michael's throat and trachea."

I swallow. "Sounds like a witch killed him."

"Clearly. I can tell by the way you talk about Sam that you trust him. But you must keep this incident in mind." Cleo pauses. "Now Kyle, he's had a checkered past. He's been arrested twice on drug charges and once for assaulting a police officer. But he's never been to jail. Each time the charges were dropped."

"The Lapras?" I ask.

"We assume Lapra influence. We know for a fact a highly placed Lapra executive secured a recording deal for him and launched his career. You've seen how often his music videos play on MTV. Someone pays for that time."

"Kyle freely admits to being rock'n'roll's latest bad boy."

"What better way to divert your suspicions than to admit to being corrupt? He's not gotten as far as he has so fast without being ambitious. That doesn't necessarily make him evil. Still . . ."

"You want me to keep an eye on both of them."

"A sharp eye," Cleo says.

"How about Viper's hand? I lost fingers when I fought Russ but they grew back. Can her hand regenerate?"

"You lost the tips of your fingers. A hand is another matter, and it sounds like you severed it above the wrist. It would take a master healer to repair such damage and Viper is too young to possess such ability. You've definitely wounded her but keep in mind there's nothing more dangerous than a wounded animal."

"Any thoughts on Nordra?"

"I know you felt pressure to protect your people from Viper's attack, but you erred when you wounded Nordra and didn't finish him. Now both are still out there. Don't repeat your mistake. Viper and Nordra must know where you're heading. They'll be waiting for you at the top of the volcano."

"What can you tell me about that dark wall?"

Cleo hesitates. "You have to see it for yourself."

"But you've seen it already." When Cleo doesn't respond, I realize I've hit a nerve. I speak carefully. "Kendor told me that the Field was hard on you. That you barely survived."

"The Field is hard on everyone."

The way Cleo says "everyone" strikes me as odd. I experience a flash of insight. Even before I quiz her on the point, I know the truth.

"You weren't a witch when you were put in the Field," I say. "Your mentor connected you there."

Cleo takes forever to respond. "Yes."

"He sacrificed his life to save you." For the second time Cleo refuses to reply, and I feel a sharp pain in my heart. I force out my next words. "Is it true only one can survive? That there's no hope for the rest of my team?"

Cleo repeats what Jimmy told me.

"You have to stay alive, Jessica."

Syn greets me at the house in Pacific Palisades and leads me into the living room, where Kendor is waiting. Immediately I know something's changed. The feeling in the air is much more serious.

Yesterday, there had been a degree of unreality to our meeting. They had hardly spoken about the fact they had been shuffled through time. Sure, Syn had asked about what their present-day counterparts were doing—and I had lied when I'd given the impression they were still alive—but the sheer weirdness of their situation had not been discussed.

And I had let it go. I was there for a purpose, I had told myself. To learn from two experienced witches how to stay alive in the Field. I had been relieved when Kendor had quickly started my training. There was no way I wanted to talk about his dying. I feared I would get emotional.

Now, today, it's like the two are more aware of their surroundings, and I can't help but wonder at the progression. From dazed zombies at the mall, to compliant instructors yesterday, to . . . what today? For the first time since they died last month, I feel like they're totally in the room.

Syn eyes me suspiciously. "Who are you?" she asks.

I sit up straight. "You asked me that yesterday. My story hasn't changed. I'm Jessica Ralle. The Alchemist—the old man you call William—brought you here to help train me for the Field."

Syn shakes her head. "Nothing you say explains why we are here. And this place." She looks around as if it's haunted. "I do not like it."

"Yesterday you seemed at home," I say.

"Yesterday was a long time ago," Kendor remarks.

I feel as if there's no point in trying to lie to them. These are the Syn and Kendor of old—two of the sharpest minds the world has ever known. I feel their eyes on me, studying. If I lie they'll know it.

Yet I try to stall until I can get a better idea of what's happened to them. "You're witches. It's natural for you to experience every day twice."

"That is not what we mean," Syn says.

"Yesterday was tomorrow," Kendor explains. "We moved through time again. Maybe it was the Alchemist, maybe a bright light, we do not know. But we were in the future, your future."

I remember how I saw a light before I was abducted.

Marc saw the same light. I saw it through his eyes.

"How long were you in this future?" I ask.

"Long enough," he says.

"See anything interesting?" I ask.

Syn and Kendor exchange a look that chills me to the bone.

"The question is why we are moving through time at all," Syn says. "It is an extraordinary event. It makes sense that there should be a profound reason behind it. But today, and the day we saw you last, all we did was wait for you to arrive so we could train you to survive in the Field."

"Not that the Field is not important," Kendor says. "But it seems someone wants to give you an edge."

"Someone wants you to survive," Syn adds.

I nod. "There may be some truth to that. The training you gave me with the sword, the telekinesis you helped activate—it's already saved me from a ton of grief."

"We are grateful we have been of some help," Syn says. "Yet you seem as puzzled as us why we are here."

"All I know is what I've told you," I say.

"Did you know that we are dead in this time?" Syn asks.

I hesitate. "Yes."

"Why did you lie the other day?" Kendor asks.

"I didn't want to upset you by telling you such shocking news."

Syn never takes her eyes off me. "Was there another reason?"

"I was there when you both died."

"Were you responsible?" Syn asks sharply.

I feel a sudden wave of anger. It catches me off guard but it's real, and very powerful. "No, you were responsible," I snap.

Syn tenses, as if she's ready to stand, to strike even. She fights for control. Taking a deep breath, she shakes her head. "I do not believe it," she says.

"Can you tell us what happened?" Kendor asks.

"I'd rather not," I say.

"Why not?" Syn demands.

"Before you died, you and I were friends," I tell Kendor. "You told me all about your life. How you fell in an icy lake as a young man and were saved by the Alchemist. How you helped Caesar defeat the Gauls at the Battle of Alesia. How you first saw Syn in a Roman crowd and fell in love with her. You also told me you had vague visions, only you didn't know at the time what you were seeing. But these visions, they were of now, which tells me that everything that happens between us in this house—you will forget it when you return to your time." I pause to catch my breath. "That's why there's no point in explaining everything to you."

There's a long silence in the room.

"Were we friends?" Syn finally asks.

"No," I say.

Syn smiles faintly. "That I can well believe."

"Perhaps we should concentrate on the task at hand," Kendor says, taking my remark about them forgetting everything to heart. He asks me to tell them what's been happening in the Field.

So for the third time that day I recount my adventures on the island. Syn and Kendor have never heard of Sam and Kyle but listen patiently as I describe them in detail. Like Cleo, they don't appear to trust either of them.

"They know the rules as well as you do," Kendor says when I finish. "It is natural they should approach you and suggest an alliance, especially after seeing what Viper and Nordra are capable of. But never forget that all alliances in the Field are temporary."

"I don't believe that," I reply. "Kyle's a wild card, it's true, but Sam genuinely seems to care. I feel I can trust him."

"There are witches who can make you fall in love with them," Syn warns. "Take a person born with the powers of magnetism—or what you probably call 'cloaking'—and telepathy. Once his abilities become active, they feed off each other, making him almost impossible to resist. He could tell you to jump off a cliff and you would do it."

"You're exaggerating," I say.

"She is not," Kendor says. "That combination of abilities is rare but we have seen it. Such a person could appear to do almost nothing and yet control the entire Field." He pauses. "Whose idea was it to climb to the top of the volcano?"

"Kyle's," I say before stopping to consider. "Well, it was Sam who told us how it was either the wall or the cave that held the key to escaping the island. But . . ." My voice trails off.

"But you are not sure why you are hiking to the top of the volcano," Syn says, finishing for me.

They have made their point.

Obviously, I don't know how to answer.

Like the man I used to know, Kendor tires of talking and wants to dive back into training. Taking me out to the backyard, he tests what he taught me the previous day. He uses the length of the grass to throw spears at my chest. However, today he orders me to deflect them with my mind. His methodology is intense; there's no room for error. If I fail to block a spear I'll die.

Kendor is worse than a drill sergeant. After a continuous

thirty-minute barrage, I feel my mental grip begin to waver and swipe away a spear with my hand. The next one I manage to deflect with telekinesis, but the one after that I have to knock away with my other hand. I feel myself weakening and fear Kendor will step up his assault. But he suddenly stops and congratulates me.

"I have never seen anyone use that ability for so long," he says.

"Even Syn?"

"Even Syn. Have you tried lifting your body into the air?"

"Not since you threw me off the cliff."

"Have any of your opponents levitated?"

"No."

"Viper?" Kendor presses.

"Her ability to hit us with lava is killing us. That and her invisibility. I wish there was some way to see through her cloak."

"There is a reason the power is referred to as 'cloaking.' The person is still there, no witch can ever be totally invisible. The key is to be attentive to what is around you." Kendor pauses and gives a sly grin. "Darling?"

Suddenly I'm aware we're not alone. I feel a presence off to my right, six feet away. As I turn in that direction Syn appears and laughs at me.

"I did not make a sound. Good work," she says.

I shake my head. "I wouldn't have become aware of you if Kendor hadn't given me that hint."

"Perhaps," Syn says. "You might have better luck with Viper if you improve your own ability to cloak. I understand you can mimic the appearance of others?"

"It's one of my strengths."

Syn is unconvinced. "It is one thing to fool a human. It is another to fool a witch." She turns to her husband. "I will take over her training for now."

Syn leads me into the house, to the bedroom where they appear to sleep. There's a floor-to-ceiling mirror, and like when Herme—her son, ironically—gave me my first instructions in cloaking, Syn leads me through a series of grueling steps designed to fool even her.

What I find fascinating is how much her lessons on cloaking remind me of the problems special-effects experts run into while creating realistic scenes on a computer. I've always been fascinated by CGI and I've studied it on the Internet.

For example, Syn orders me to mimic her face, with her standing beside me, and I get everything right except for her hair. When I turn my head and toss *her* hair, it refuses to flow naturally. Syn being Syn, she scolds me that I'm not trying hard enough.

Pointing out that CGI experts have the same problem fails to illicit her sympathy, possibly because she's never seen a movie before, but more likely because basically she's a tough bitch. Yes, her husband did throw me off a cliff to teach me a lesson, but at least with Kendor I had fun. With Syn work is work, she is all business.

Yet after spending several hours in her company, I finally put on a face that even she has to admit is flawless. The trick, she teaches, is not how well I mold my features but how strong my belief is. Herme taught me something similar but his mother's standards are far more stringent.

"Believe you are who you pretend to be and no one will question your identity," Syn says, summing up her philosophy.

I nod. "I'm grateful for the time you've given me. But I'm puzzled why you haven't let me try to turn invisible."

Syn acts as if my complaint is childish. "Because you're incapable of doing that right now. But more important, you have not been listening to what we have been trying to teach you. You need to reflect on what we told you earlier."

"I'm afraid I don't understand." I say.

"That is why you need to reflect on it."

"All right, if it's reflection you want, then answer this. When you and Kendor spoke about being shuffled in time, you went out of your way to say you had been in *my* future, not simply in *the* future. Was that a slip of the tongue or were you trying to tell me something?"

"What does 'slip of the tongue' mean?"

"What were you trying to tell me?" I demand.

For the first time since I have met her—in this time frame and when I knew her in Las Vegas—Syn appears flustered. It takes me a moment to figure out why.

"You're worried about me!" I gasp.

Syn shrugs. "Naturally we are concerned for your safety. The Field is a dangerous testing ground."

"No, it's something else, something you saw when you went into the future. What did you see? My dead body?"

Syn hesitates. "Not exactly."

"Damnit! What did you see?"

Syn gazes into my eyes. No one knows better than I do how easily she can cloak her expression, but clearly she feels the time for disguise has passed.

"Before I answer your question, tell me why you fear me."

Like me, she's asking for the truth. A blunt answer isn't hard to find. "Because you change as you grow older. You become a monster."

Syn sucks in a painful breath. "Why?"

"Grief. Pain over the loss of those you love."

"I have already lost my son."

"You will lose others." I pause. "I'm sorry."

She sighs. "So am I, Jessica."

I don't speak, I can't. I wait.

Finally, Syn answers my question.

"A month from now, Kendor and I were at your memorial service," she says.

Without saying good-bye to either of them, I flee the house, jumping in my car and driving aimlessly. When I finally stop, I realize I have driven to the jagged part of the coast where

Kendor threw me off the cliff. Getting out of the car, I step to the edge and stare out at the sea. My confusion is as deep as the ocean is vast. Two questions torment me. . . .

Did they attend my funeral in the real world or witch world?

Can the fact that I know the future allow me to change it?

If I die in the real world, where the Field is taking place, then it's possible I'll still be alive in witch world. Jimmy died from an overdose of drugs in the real world and I still see him every other day in witch world. Yet, to me, with the exception of missing Jimmy and Lara, the real world is where I feel most comfortable and if I should perish in the Field, then at best I'll go on living half a life.

However, it's possible the Alchemist gave Syn and Kendor a glimpse of my future so they could alert me to alter my course. But how exactly am I supposed to do that?

Kendor had gone out of his way to warn me that all alliances in the Field are temporary, while Syn had said that I still wasn't hearing what they were trying to teach me. Were the two trying to give me hints as to how to alter my future? Were they saying I absolutely had to stop trusting Sam and Kyle? If I did that, I'd be essentially alone on the island, with no one to help me fight off Viper and Nordra. And Marc . . . he would almost certainly be killed.

"The Field will not change who I am!" I shout at the sea. The words just explode out of me but I feel they must have originated deep inside. Because I know they are true.

I'm not going to become a perverted and plotting beast in order to survive the Field. If I do that, if I betray everything I believe in and everyone who is counting on me to protect them—just to save my own skin—then my life will hardly be worth living, in either world. Because then I'll become what Syn is destined to become.

I'll become the monster.

My hands shake. I take my cell out of my pocket and dial Marc's number. His voice sounds thick when he answers and I suspect I've woken him from a nap. With his other half wounded and suffering in the Field, he might be feeling more tired than usual, I don't know.

"Still want to meet?" I ask.

"I haven't thought about anything else all day."

"When and where?"

He chuckles. "You know where I live?"

"I told you I did."

"Then come over now."

By the time I get there, Marc has spruced up for me. He has on a nice pair of beige slacks, an apricot shirt, and a brown sports coat he paid good money for—unless he stole it. Not many guys can get away with apricot anything—it's too close to pink—but on Marc it works. Or maybe the clothes have nothing to do with it.

I feel like a slob. I haven't changed from my training, and

a few of Kendor's spears nicked me. As a result I've got blood-stains on my bare arms and pants. Marc raises an eyebrow when he answers the door.

"What's wrong with you witches? You don't take showers when you move from one world to the other? Too busy waxing down your broomsticks?"

"Cute. Don't tell me you're a surfer?"

"I'm world class and I'll teach you if you explain why you're covered in blood."

"It's just a few drops." He's not buying it. "I just came from practicing how to kill the bad guys in that other world."

"Is that your blood or your trainers'?"

"Mine," I admit.

"You don't have a scratch on you."

"Told you, I heal fast. Are you going to invite me in or what?"

He's amused. "I was going to take you to my favorite restaurant but they won't let you in dressed like that."

"So take me to that mall where you park your extra cars. Buy me a new outfit, I know you can afford it."

"Whoa! You sprang for the tab last night. I would never have figured you for an expensive date."

I smile. "You have no idea."

He lets me take a quick shower at his place then we go to the mall, where I pick out a tight pair of black slacks that show off my butt, a silk blouse that matches the color of his shirt, and a black leather jacket that's both chic and country at the same time. Marc insists on a pair of brown boots that catch his eye, and make me four inches taller.

"I don't like to have to bend over to kiss a girl," he explains as we head for my car. He seems to like that I drive.

"Ha! Sounds like you've got the whole night planned," I say.

"Me? What about you and my twin?"

"I'm not sure what you mean," I say.

"You know exactly what I mean. My problem is I don't know what kind of relationship you two have got going. You've only known me a few days. Ordinarily I don't trust people I've just met."

"Not so. You trust me with your life."

"Probably because I've got no choice. Tell me what kind of personal information he gave you about me?"

"His first rule was that I not tell you anything he said."

"There you go! That cannot be true! I wouldn't shut my own self down just to please a fresh piece . . . a brand-new girl I just met."

"Were you about to call me 'a fresh piece of ass'?"

"No, ma'am! I'm not ghetto, I don't talk that way."

"Liar. You're comfortable in all kinds of environments and know how to adapt to wherever you're at and whoever you're with. You're a chameleon."

Marc considers quietly. "Did he tell you how to get to me?"

"No."

"You swear?"

I smile, poke him. "He didn't have to. I already know."

His favorite restaurant is in Santa Monica, not that far from my house, across the street from the beach. It's a few floors up and we get an outside table that allows us to view the sunset. The waitress swings by and Marc orders steak while I ask for swordfish and a large margarita. I just have to give the waitress a sharp look and she doesn't bother asking for ID. Only in witch world.

Noting the exchange, Marc asks for a beer and when the waitress is gone he leans near the table's center candle and asks if I just used my powers on that poor unsuspecting girl.

"What I did with her was hardly a miracle. This is a pricey restaurant and I picked up that she's used to serving powerful people and knows not to question them. My look was just a look."

"But only because you were able to feel her out?" he asks.

"That's one way of looking at it. Why do you ask? Afraid I'm going to make you do something you don't want to do?"

"Duh. In case you've forgotten, you talked about me dying for you last night."

I speak seriously. "The 'dying' is for both of us. Actually, it's more for you than me. Unless you get a hundred times stronger fast, you'll be toast."

"Jessie . . ."

"Another thing. I wasn't given a choice to 'connect.' It was thrust on me. But you do have a choice. I'm not going to force it on you."

Marc sits back in his chair. "I take it things aren't going so well in the Field?"

"They've gone from bad to worse. I lost a good friend yesterday and you're barely hanging on."

"Why?"

"You were stabbed in the lower back, probably poisoned. We're holed up in a cave not far from the top of a volcano and you have a high fever."

"Shit," he mutters.

"Exactly." Our drinks come and I take a deep drink of my margarita. After all I've been through, I need something to calm my nerves. I add, "Anything else you want to know?"

Marc sips his beer. "Who stabbed me?"

"Viper. She snuck up on you while invisible—the bitch. You didn't stand a chance. I chopped off her hand if it's any consolation."

"I'd feel better if you'd killed her."

"You're not alone."

Marc smiles and shakes his head. "This is what my twin told you to tell me? Tales of invisible witches with poisonous knives? I don't think you're lying, but I've got to warn you that you're ruining my appetite."

I shrug. "You asked, I didn't want to lie. But you're right, we should talk about something more cheery. Have you figured out who you're going to sell that emerald to?"

Marc quickly glances around and leans close. "Shh. Wrong part of town to be talking about a missing jewel. There was an article in the *LA Times* about the theft. The reporter seemed to know more than he should."

"You know you can't keep it up."

He raises his palms in mock surrender but keeps his voice low. "No one knows that better than I do. That was my last job using my valet cover. And I've decided I'm going to break down the rock into medium-size pieces before I fence it. The jewel's too well known, too easy to trace."

"Marc . . . ," I begin.

"Don't say it," he interrupts.

"What?"

"That I could be doing a lot more with my life."

"It's true. You're smart, you plan everything carefully, but it's all a question of odds. Eventually you'll get caught and sent to jail. Imagine living a decade behind bars? It would be such a waste."

"Of course I wouldn't have to live the way I do if I'm connected. Is that what you're saying? I could make all the money I want just by turning on a few well-hidden genes."

"Money is the worst reason in the world to become a witch."

"Spoken like a true, spoiled, rich girl."

"Hey, for your information I grew up wearing the same five pants and three skirts to school for all of my junior and senior years."

"I thought you said your father's a heart surgeon."

"He is, but that's a long story, and I'm not here to talk about how tough it's been for you or me. We talked enough about our lives last night. I'm here because we've got a problem."

Marc sips his beer. "And because you're crazy about me. Let's not forget that."

"It's more the other way around but whatever." I take another gulp of my drink and signal to the waitress to bring me another. "Let's enjoy our dinner and talk business later. I've been through a lot since we last met. I need to unwind."

"I can see that," Marc says as he watches me finish my margarita.

I've finished my second drink by the time our food arrives so I order a third. I know I'm acting reckless but figure that since my memorial's only a few days away . . . what the hell.

The swordfish tastes divine and Marc lets me have a bite of his steak and it isn't bad. By the time we leave the restaurant, I'm blabbing away about Las Vegas and how great I am at twenty-one, blackjack. Marc figures I'm drunk and really mean twenty-two, red queen. It is, after all, the game of choice in witch world.

We walk over to the Santa Monica Pier, to the end, and for the second time today I stare out at the sea and wonder how long I've left to live. The thought is sobering; I stop talking. Marc puts his arm around me and I lean into him. He feels like the other Marc, whom I'm sleeping beside in the cave so I can keep an eye on his fever.

"You want me to go through with it," he says. "You want me to die."

"For a short time, yes."

"You know how crazy that is?"

"Yes."

"How would we do it?"

"When I was driving to your apartment, I spoke to a friend, Herme. He sells drugs and medical equipment to doctors. He knows what to give you to stop your heart and he knows what to do to restart it."

"Is he a doctor?"

"No. But he's old and has a ton of experience."

"I thought your dad would be there."

"I can't get ahold of my dad."

"It's sort of a bad time for him to go missing."

"I can't argue with that."

Marc stares out at the dark sea. "How much time does it take?"

"It's different for everyone. How long they have to be dead. How long they take to connect. Let's just say the sooner we start the better."

"Jessie."

"You're not ready, I know."

"I'm sorry, really. I know you're trying to save my life as much as your own. Maybe more. It's just the thought of lying down on a table and some stranger sticking me with a needle that will stop my heart—it freaks me out. I can't handle it."

"I understand."

Marc pulls me close. "What should we do?"

"Take me to your apartment."

"Is that what my twin told you to say?"

"It doesn't matter. Take me."

I drive back to his apartment, slowly, making sure I don't run any lights or miss any stop signs. We park on the street, and as we walk to his front door, he grabs my hand, and for a moment I'm able to pretend that I'm with Jimmy. That I'm about to make sweet love with my wonderful boyfriend.

But when we get inside and begin to kiss, it's not Jimmy.

It's Marc and he feels so good it's hard for me to feel bad.

We end up naked in bed and I feel I'm drowning in a sea of sensation. Minutes go by where I can't stop myself, nor can he, and it's okay, it's better than okay. It honestly feels like it was meant to be.

But when he stops to put on a condom, everything in the room seems to slow down. It's almost like when Nordra attacked me and time dropped to a crawl and I was able to escape with my life. Once again it's like I'm being given a chance to avoid a fatal wound. And Marc seems to sense that. Even though he sits with his back to me on the edge of the bed, I know his mind the same way I knew it in the dreams I had of him before we met. And I know he knows there's someone else in the room with us. He turns and faces me.

"You don't want to do this," he says.

"I do."

He drops the condom and moves close. "You can't do this."

I stare at him. I shake my head. "I have to."

He shakes his head. "You don't have to."

"But you said, he said, it was the only way to get you to do it."

"He never said that. I would never say that and he knows you a lot better than I do. He loves you. You don't have to do this."

I struggle to breathe. "I don't understand."

"I'll do it. I'm telling you I'll do it."

"No."

"What do you mean no? That's why you're here. We have to do it. It's the only way to save us both." He reaches for his pants. I stop him.

"No," I repeat.

"What's wrong with you, Jessie?"

"It's you, it's us, it's me. You love me, maybe I love you, I don't know. But it's too dangerous."

"Of course it's dangerous! You're talking about me dying. But it's just as dangerous if we do nothing. I get it, I finally get it. So why are you suddenly afraid to go ahead with it?"

"Because you don't understand. If you die in this world, what we call witch world, you die in both worlds. But if you just die on the island, in the Field, you can still be alive here. I can still see you here."

Marc takes a moment to digest what I've told him. Granted, it's a hell of a lot to absorb in the space of a moment.

"Even if we both die in the Field, I could still see you here?"

"Yes," I say.

"Are you sure?"

"It's complicated. I'm not a hundred percent sure."

He stares at me sitting naked before him. "What should we do?"

"Well, for one thing, we shouldn't call Herme."

"That's not what I'm talking about."

"What are you talking about?"

"Your boyfriend. He was there last night, in the deli, I saw him."

"You did? How? I didn't even know he was there."

Marc waves his hand. "It doesn't matter." I reach for him but he holds me back. "He's here now."

Sitting back, I glance anxiously around. "Where?"

Marc smiles sadly and shakes his head. "He's sitting right here, between us. You know it and I know it."

Without thinking, I pull up the sheet and cover my breasts.

"What should we do?" I say.

"I asked first."

"Yeah, right. How about we do what we're doing in the other world? There, I'm sleeping beside you. Can I sleep beside you here?"

"Just sleep?"

"Would that be all right?" I ask, sounding like a child.

Marc leans over and kisses me on the forehead.

"It would be perfect," he says.

CHAPTER NINE

I FEEL HEAT AND SWEAT AND HEAR THE SOUND OF RUN-
ning water. For a long moment, I don't know why, I refuse to
open my eyes. I feel like if I allow myself to fully awaken, I'll
regret it. I'm like a child who can't bear the idea of having to
get out of bed in the morning and go to a new school where
I don't know anyone and I'm sure I'll be too stupid to understand what's being taught.

Only my feeling of dread is a hundred times worse.

It's only when I hear Marc speak that I open my eyes.

"Jessie," he says. How odd it is to hear him say my name in
a dark cave in the Field in the real world when moments ago
I was in his bed in witch world. In the faint light that comes
from the cave entrance, he looks like he's aged fifteen years
since we went to sleep in his apartment. He's beyond sick, he
looks like he's dying.

Yet he smiles at me. "Sweet dreams?" he asks.

"How are you feeling?" Sitting up, I put my hand on his forehead, feeling a fever I'm afraid to give a number to. He's on fire.

"Great," he answers.

"The truth."

"I'm screwed," he says, groaning as I help him sit up.

"Is it your wound or the fever?"

He rubs his eyes, blinks, trying to get them to focus. "You were right. That knife must have had poison on it. My heart's racing and my blood feels like it's full of acid, that it's eating me alive. If that makes any sense."

"I'll do another healing," I say, reaching out with my hands. But he takes my hands and presses them together and shakes his head.

"You've been healing me all night."

"Let me try, it can't hurt."

"I'm serious, Jessie. All night, when I'd have a spasm of pain, you'd pull me closer, hold me tighter, and the pain would subside. That's probably why you look so worn out."

"I'm fine."

"Liar." Marc pauses. "How did it go with my twin? Since I haven't turned into a superhero, I take it he chickened out."

Before answering, I check out the cave where we spent the night. Li lies asleep beside a thin stream that spills from a pile of rocks near the narrow entrance and flows toward the rear of the cave, which I have yet to explore.

Li is having her own nightmares. Twisting and turning in her sleep, she occasionally groans and whispers her sister's name—"Lula."

Lying flat on his back ten yards deeper inside the cave, Chad snores loudly. Except for Li and Chad, there's no one else around, although I can hear Sam and Kyle talking outside. I can't pick up their exact words but it sounds like an argument.

"I was the one who chickened out," I reply.

"He wanted to go ahead with it? Why didn't you let him?"

"It was too risky."

Marc struggles to hide his annoyance. "Jessie! We're way past risk in this hellhole. You should have let him try. I mean, what do either of us have to lose?"

I lean over and kiss him on the same spot where he kissed me last night. "Trust me, it was the right decision."

Marc studies me closely. "You're with him now. We're together."

I hesitate. "In a manner of speaking."

He sucks in a breath. "What about Jimmy?"

"Jimmy knows."

"God."

"I thought the same thing." I stand and offer him a helping hand. "Can you walk?"

"I'm not dead yet," Marc says, although he leans against me as he staggers to his feet.

"Wake up Chad and splash some cold water on your face.

Try to eat what's left of the fish. I've got to talk to the boys."
I head for the cave entrance but pause and look back at him.
"You know, for such a tough guy, you sure can be a gentleman."

I'm paying him a compliment but he acts disappointed.
"Does that mean we didn't go all the way?" he asks.

I laugh. "I don't kiss and tell."

Outside, I quickly lose my smile. Kyle and Sam aren't just
having an argument. They're in a heated discussion concerning
how Pierre and Keb died. The two bodies lie sprawled against
a black boulder that pokes from the ground a hundred yards
behind the cave opening.

Below us, in the opposite direction, chained to a pointed
rock with ropes of vine, is Jelanda, the head ghost. She's been
watching me since I exited the cave.

"What the hell happened?" I demand in the glare of the
morning light. The sun has just risen above the rim of the sea,
but exposed as we are on the side of the volcano, it seems particularly bright. The entire expanse below us—the river, the
trees, the cliffs—are bathed in orange light.

"Pierre and Keb were on guard duty with Sam," Kyle says,
not bothering to hide his bitterness. "They'd been ordered to
watch the peak while Sam was supposed to be keeping his eyes
on anyone approaching from below."

"Damnit, what happened?" I snap.

I've never seen Kyle so uptight. "I don't know, that's the
problem. I took the first shift and everything was fine. Then

Sam relieves me in the middle of the night and I wake up at dawn and all of a sudden my two guys are dead."

"Wait a second," I interrupt. "I was supposed to take the second shift. How come neither of you woke me up?"

"That was my decision," Sam says. "You looked exhausted. I wanted you to rest. Besides, I thought Pierre and Keb could help each other stay awake. They only had to keep a lookout in one direction. I was scanning ninety percent of the island."

"Funny how you didn't see anyone sneak up on them," Kyle says.

Sam shoves him in the chest. "Stop that shit right now! No one in this group killed them. It had to be either Nordra or Viper, or one of the ghosts."

"You didn't hear anything?" I ask Sam.

He looks miserable. "I could hear them talking, up until about an hour ago, but I wasn't listening to what they were saying. Then they got real quiet. I didn't think much of it. It was only when it got light that I went to check on them."

"You couldn't see them from here?" I asked.

"No," Sam says. "I moved their bodies to where they are now so we can keep an eye on them. But when I first checked on them, they were around that bend you see there. I stationed them there so they'd have a clear view of the peak, and anyone coming at us from the north. I—"

"You had no right to station them anywhere without asking my permission," Kyle interrupts.

Sam snorts. "Like you owned them."

"They were my boys! They were in my group!" Kyle cries, very upset. "I was responsible for them!"

I move between them. "Keep your voices down! We don't have to tell every enemy we've got exactly where we're camping out." I pause and speak to Sam in a gentle tone. "So it got light and you went to check on them. What did you find?"

Sam shrugs. "They were just lying there, dead."

"You must have examined them. How did they die?"

"They have bruises on their necks. Both their Adam's apples look like they've been crushed." Sam pauses, fidgeting. "They were probably smothered."

Cleo's words come back to haunt me.

"Sam was arrested last year in connection with the murder of his longtime boyfriend, Michael Edwards. Michael was found strangled to death in a workroom at Parsons, where they were both students. Sam was arrested because he had motive and opportunity."

"The person who attacked—was he strong?" I ask.

Sam nods. "He or she was definitely a witch."

The coincidence is disturbing, to say the least. Yet it's also very convenient—if someone is trying to set Sam up for Pierre's and Keb's murders. But who would know about Sam's past? I know because I have access to Cleo, who has almost unlimited resources. Does Kyle have an equivalent source?

Yet even if Kyle did know, how did he manage to exit the

cave without Sam seeing him and murder the guys? It doesn't seem feasible, which means either Sam did kill them or one of our foes managed to sneak into our camp without Sam hearing or seeing a thing. Sam, with his supersensitive eyes and ears . . .

"Look, we can talk about this until we're blue in the face," Sam says. "We're not going to figure out what happened. We're on a clock here. It might look like we're over halfway to the top but it's deceptive. The higher we go, the steeper it gets and the thinner the air is. We're going to need the whole day to reach the cave and the wall. We should gather our stuff and just go."

"No. I want to bury them," Kyle says.

"Didn't you hear what I just said?" Sam asks.

Kyle's furious, hurt. "We had time to bury Ora, Billy, and Mary! How come Pierre and Keb are worth less? Because they came here with me?"

Sam goes to yell a reply but in the end they both turn to me. He might be the greatest actor on earth but I could swear Kyle's pain is the real deal. I feel like crying with him. It's difficult to say no to his demand, yet I have to think of the greater good.

"Marc's sick and injured and Li's not at full strength," I say. "And Sam's right—it's going to get harder to hike the higher we go. We'll move Pierre and Keb into the cave and have a brief service. But we're going to have to forgo digging graves."

"I'll move them," Kyle snaps, bitter. "Funny how you picked this morning to start making the tough decisions. I wonder what your choice would have been if it'd been Marc or Chad who died."

Kyle stalks off and Sam pats me on the back.

"Don't let him get to you," he says.

I shake my head. "No, he's right. I doubt I would have made the same decision if it had been my friends. I suppose that makes me a shitty leader."

"It makes you human," Sam says.

We're underway twenty minutes later. Unfortunately, Marc doesn't last long on his feet. Whatever Viper coated her knife with, it not only added fire to his blood, it interrupted the healing process. None of my witch powers has much effect on it and I'm forced to shred the remainder of my shirt sleeves to construct a bandage that applies steady pressure to the wound. I can't believe he's still bleeding.

Marc complains that he won't be treated like a baby, but there's no punch to his fight and in the end I have to insist on carrying him. He knows he's slowing us down and finally lets me lift him onto my back. The extra weight is taxing but there's no way I'm leaving him behind.

Kyle has his own weight to deal with—Jelanda, the ghost queen. He uses a combination of vines and strips of cloth from Pierre's and Keb's uniforms—he removed them before he laid his guys to rest—to keep her tied, but his main tool is the spear he presses to her back. Even though battered, Jelanda appears less weary than the rest of us.

I hate the bitch, she gives me the creeps. Whenever I glance in her direction, she gives me a twisted smile, like she's waiting—just waiting for us to die.

Chad walks beside Marc and me. He gathers from our talk that we're seeing each other in witch world and wants to know why I haven't tried to contact his twin.

"You live on the other side of the country," I say.

"You could at least call," Chad says.

"And tell you what?" I ask.

Chad considers. "Right. I don't suppose a complete stranger raving about being my friend in another dimension would go over too well with my other self."

"Chad," Marc mutters behind my head. "Get a clue. Jessie's not calling you because you're not hot like me. Why, you wouldn't believe what the two of us are doing in witch—ouch!"

I had just pinched his leg. "Considering the fact that you're nothing but deadweight in this world, I'd stop bragging about how hot you are." I add, "Besides, brains are a lot more sexy to me than swagger."

"It's only called swagger if you can't deliver," Marc says. "And you of all girls know otherwise. . . . Ouch!"

I pinch him again. "Quiet."

Chad laughs. "I hope we get out of here alive. I know we've had it rough but, for me, this has been the only real excitement I've had in my life. I keep thinking what a great bedtime story my time here would make if I ever had grandchildren. I'd give each of us hero names. Ora the Warrior. Shira the Brave. Chad the Wise. Li the Healer. Jessie the Powerful. Marc the . . . Hmm, what's so special about Marc? I can't think of anything."

When Marc doesn't reply, I say, "Marc the Survivor."

"That makes me sound like a coward," Marc complains.

"It makes you sound lucky," Chad corrects him. "I'm going to use that name. My grandkids will love it."

"I'm sure they'll love you," I say.

A pity they both hear the note of sorrow in my voice.

Yesterday we had to deal with two types of terrain: the loose gravel, which was worse than walking through sand; and the flat sheets of frozen lava, which were so sleek we were constantly slipping, skating. Today we have a third type—row after row of giant rocks. Because they're usually separated by large gaps, we keep having to make treacherous leaps from one to the other.

Whatever psychological breakdown Li suffered when she failed to heal Kyle's people, it's made her a much more timid hiker. As a result Sam is frequently forced to carry her while we navigate the maze of black boulders. They're all made of the same ancient lava belched out the top of the volcano, but some are so huge, I'd swear they look like something the cinder cone once choked on.

Choked. Strangled. Murdered.

It disturbs me how much I've begun to doubt Sam. Cleo's

information about his past isn't easy to ignore. But it's not just how it connects to Pierre's and Keb's deaths that disturbs me. Kendor and Syn's mysterious warnings haunt me as much if not more. Kyle, too—I find I can't look at either of them the same way I did before.

It strikes me then how insidious the rules of the Field are, and it makes me wonder who created them and what they were thinking—*if* the old tales Cleo told me are true, if the Field ultimately has the high purpose of choosing the perfect leader. The more I dwell on the questionable morality of the people behind the contest, the more I wonder if they are even human. Or witches.

Something about the Field makes no sense.

The hike wears on, harder and more painful with every step we take. Veering south, at Sam's direction, we begin to follow the river up the side of the volcano. The closer we stay to the water, Sam explains, the less we have to deal with the loose gravel and the intimidating boulders.

Naturally, since we're approaching its source, the river has shrunk in size and strength, but its roar still fills the air, making it all but impossible to listen for the approach of an invisible foe.

Carrying Marc makes me vulnerable. I don't have instant access to my arms and hands. And his heavy breathing, and occasional groans, cloud my hearing as much as the river.

Yet I feel Viper near, as clearly as I sense Nordra has already gone ahead and waits for us at the peak. And the ghosts—they follow a mile behind, scarcely bothering to hide their trail. Sam sees them first but soon I spot them as well, darting across the side of the volcano, flashes of their white skin peeking over the edges of the black rock.

Kyle tries driving them back by stabbing his spear deeper into Jelanda's spine, but she can't cry out in pain because she can't talk; and besides, for all we know, her suffering calls her comrades to come closer. Her only response to Kyle's torture is to look at me and grin.

"None of you will survive."

I wish Kyle would just let her go, or else kill her; I don't see the point in keeping her around.

Syn and Kendor's warnings have infected me in the same way Viper's poison has infected Marc. The main reason I feel vulnerable is I feel Sam or Kyle, or both, are just waiting to kill me.

"How was I?" Marc whispers to me through a haze of pain and fever. The heat of his skin against mine is hotter than the rays of the naked sun pouring over my head.

"I told you, you couldn't get it up," I tease.

I feel him smile. "I can get it up right now and I'm about to die. Come on, tell the truth, how many times did we do it?"

"It depends what you mean by 'do it.'"

I feel his smile widen. "So you're the naughty sort?"

"You couldn't tell?"

"I was hoping. Who came more times, me or you?"

"Me, of course. A girl can come all night."

"So it was great. I was great."

"Nah. I told you, you couldn't get it up. I had to get my vibrator out of my bag just to keep the night from being a total disaster."

He kisses the side of my head through my sweaty hair.

"The next time you see Jimmy tell him I'm sorry. I know that once you've had a guy like me nothing else will ever satisfy you."

"Keep dreaming, Marc. That's what you're good at."

He begins to black out from the pain. "As long as you're there in my dreams," he mumbles.

At last we reach the base of the cinder cone, which crowns the top of the volcano proper like a brown clown's hat topped with a flickering red light. The crimson glow of the boiling magma is constant but its light wavers with the shifting clouds of steam and smoke. Talk about fire and brimstone. There are moments when the fumes are almost suffocating. But then the wind will suddenly shift direction and I'm able to breathe easily.

The size and force of the river has suddenly shrunk to a tenth of what it previously was. Sam kneels at its edge to take a drink.

"It's time we crossed to the other side," Sam says.

"Why?" Kyle demands, suspicious. I'm not the only one suffering from paranoia. Since the loss of Pierre and Keb, Kyle doesn't even pretend to trust Sam.

Sam goes to speak but first has to cough. "Isn't it obvious? If we stay in the path of these fumes we won't make it to the top."

I scan the face of the cinder cone. The incline is a minimum of forty-five degrees, even steeper closer to the crown. Its surface is made of deep fluffy ash, which will be a demon to wade through.

"I don't see any sign of the cave," I say.

"Me neither," Kyle adds.

Sam gestures. "It's around the left side. We'll reach it before we come to the wall. But we've got to start circling around now, before we climb any higher."

"That will lengthen our hike," Kyle says. Technically he's right. Circling the base of the cinder cone will require us to walk farther than if we were to circle it closer to the top.

Sam shakes his head in disgust. "Try hiking straight up if you want. I won't stop you. But a small thing called 'lack of oxygen' will."

Kyle is unsure. "The wind keeps shifting. Who's to say the south side will be clear?"

"I'm not a bloody weatherman!" Sam shouts. "I can't tell which way the wind's going to keep blowing. All I know is the last time I was up here, I made it to the top by hiking up the south face. And if that isn't good enough for you, then climb up here, get yourself gassed, I don't give a damn."

Chad speaks. "I have to agree with Sam. The direction of the wind has shifted a dozen times since we came to this island.

But it's always come back to an easterly direction, down toward the sea. Also, a few of you might have noticed how the trees all lean slightly toward the ocean—another sign of the direction the wind favors. The south and west sides of the cinder cone should be more breathable."

"I'm sold," I say, studying the sun as it moves closer to the top lip of the volcano. "But we've only got another two hours of light left and we've still got at least four miles to go. We've got to increase our pace."

"What are you suggesting?" Sam asks.

"Cut Jelanda loose. That way Kyle can carry Li while you, Sam, carry Chad. We're witches. It's our job to help out the others."

"Says who?" Kyle mutters.

I step in front of him. "You're the one who pushed me to lead this group. Now you don't like my orders? What's your problem?"

Kyle glances at Sam before answering me. "You have the gall to ask what my problem is? How about I'm scared shit-less? You didn't know Pierre and Keb, I did. They were mates of mine and someone killed them. Sam says he's innocent and you want me to believe him. All right, for the sake of argument, let's say I do. Then who killed my friends?"

"It could have been the ghosts," Chad says.

"We know they're in the area," Sam says.

"Because you keep torturing their leader," Chad adds.

Kyle wipes at his eyes, his voice choking from something

other than fumes. "That's good, that's great, put Pierre's and Keb's deaths on me. Why not? I'm the asshole in the group. But if it is my fault I got my mates killed, then I'll be damned if I'm going to surrender the one thing I stole from the ghosts that made them kill Pierre and Keb."

His words shake me because they explain so much that should have been obvious—why Kyle's refused to let Jelanda go, or kill her for that matter. It's clear he feels he's paid too high a price to catch her.

"She's slowing us down," I tell him. "Either way, she's got to go."

Kyle shakes his head. "I'm stronger than I look. I can drag her along and carry Li at the same time. I swear, I'll keep up. We can't let the White Queen go."

"Why not?" I persist. He sounds so sure of himself.

"Think how old her race is," Kyle says. "They go back before recorded history. But what do we know about them? Next to nothing. They move in packs and they're telepathic. That's it. Oh, wait, there's one more thing. They're so damn old because they're so damn good at surviving. All of us, let's be honest, we see them as the small and weak ones. We're not afraid of them like we are of Viper and Nordra. But I think they want it that way. I think it's all a setup. You ask me, they're the most dangerous creatures on this island."

"No one fears the enemy that's right in front of you," Chad mutters, nodding.

"Exactly!" Kyle cries, yanking on Jelanda's chain. "Look around, we're all afraid, and we have a right to be." He points at Jelanda. "Now look at her, she's not scared, not at all. Because she knows something we don't. That's got to be the reason."

I consider. "All right, you've made your point. You can keep her prisoner as long as you can carry Li and keep up with Sam and me. Now, enough talk, let's move."

Crossing the river turns out to be a curious experience. It's a mere stream compared to the raging rapids we had to wade through our first night on the island, but I find it almost as difficult as that initial attempt. I have Marc on my back, of course, and the air is thin and filled with fumes, but none of these factors equals the *chill* factor. The water is the direct runoff of melted snow and should be freezing, and yet it feels colder than ice, much colder. Splashing as fast as I can over the slippery stones hidden three or four feet below the rushing surface, I almost feel as if I'm taking a dip in a giant flask of liquid nitrogen, or some such exotic fluid that's only found in chemistry labs. My feet and calves go numb in seconds and from the yelps I hear from Sam and Kyle, I'm grateful we have Marc, Chad, and Li secure on our backs. I swear the water would have killed them. I hate the bitch but it's hard to watch Kyle drag Jelanda through the stream. It's not until we've hiked far from the river that I finally build up enough body heat to stop shivering.

"That was cold," Marc mumbles in my ear, slipping in and out of consciousness.

"Sleep, darling," I whisper, and he does go back to sleep.

We circle a quarter of the cinder cone, reaching what we believe is the center of the south side, when suddenly the fumes all but disappear. What a relief! From our new angle it's clear that Sam was right and the majority of the steam and smoke is being blown directly east, toward the sea, the direction we came from.

Yet the air is extremely thin and our lungs labor to extract enough oxygen to keep our blood from turning into molasses. Plus the terrain has changed once again. There's snow on the ground: not everywhere, but in patches long and deep enough to slow us further. Gazing down at the distant sea in the dimming light, Chad estimates our altitude at nineteen thousand feet. The sudden drop in temperature backs up his estimate.

"We're three and a half miles above sea level," Sam says. "I've never heard of an island with such a tall mountain."

"Actually, if you measure Mauna Kea on the big island of Hawaii from its base to its peak, it's a lot higher than Mount Everest," Chad says. "It's over six miles high."

"Bullshit," Kyle says. "Everyone knows Mount Everest is the highest mountain in the world."

"I meant if you measure Kea from its oceanic base," Chad explains. "Its base is a couple of miles underwater."

Kyle's tired and annoyed. "What does such scientific trivia have to do with our situation?"

Chad shrugs. "It's a good reminder that where we're at isn't on any map I've ever seen."

"How high up is the cave?" I ask Sam. I still can't see the opening and it's going to be dark in less than an hour.

"You don't see it until you're practically on top of it," Sam says. "It's like someone built it that way."

"What about the wall?" Kyle asks.

Sam's face darkens. "Let's deal with that when we get to it."

Finally, the last stretch of our long hike. Soon we'll arrive at our goal and soon we'll know if it was worth the effort. What am I hoping to find? Answers? Sam's already been to the cave, and the wall for that matter, and he doesn't seem to know anything we don't. The truth be told, I worry we've come all this way because we didn't know where else to go.

Yet the dark stone embedded in our bracelets gives me hope we might discover something vital. Especially since the wall is supposed to be made out of the identical material.

I search for the magical wall as we hike toward the invisible cave entrance. I don't see it, either, and wonder how a wall as massive as Sam described isn't visible when we're so close to it.

The last half mile of our hike is brutal. The cinder-cone ash is like quicksand. Every step I take forward, my leg sinks up to my knee. The incline is as bad as climbing a ladder. Even with my unnatural strength, I gasp for air and feel as if my heart is going to explode in my chest. The freezing air is devoid of moisture. I drink but my thirst remains. I never imagined I could be so cold and so thirsty at the same time. God do I miss my shirtsleeves.

Marc stirs. I lean my head back and let him press his cheek to mine. He's so hot I feel like crying. "Hey, babe, how ya doin'?" I say.

He coughs. "Are we there yet?"

"Almost."

"Great."

"How are you feeling?"

He coughs some more. "Great."

"I'm going to help you. When we get to the cave, I'm going to torture Li if I have to but she's going to heal you. And if she refuses, I'll heal you myself."

"No."

"You're not going to stop me."

"It's not what I need." He coughs again; he doesn't seem able to catch his breath. "You know what I need."

"Don't think of that. We can't do that here. We need peace, we need quiet, we need to be safe."

"You did it and you weren't safe."

"I'm not going to risk your life."

He turns his head and kisses my damp cheek. I didn't know I'd started crying, silly me. I guess I didn't know how much I loved him. He speaks in a fading whisper.

"There's no risk. I'm dying, Jessie. I'm going to die."

I want to argue some more but he passes out.

He suddenly feels so heavy on my back.

Like the way people are supposed to when they're dead.

Please, God, no. Please spare his life. I'll do anything if you do. Anything. Kill me if you want but save him.

I keep praying although I'm fairly certain that if there is a God, He's not the sort who actually answers prayers from everyday people or witches like me. I think of all the billions of people throughout history—and even people I know personally—who have prayed in life-threatening situations, like ours, and not a single one of them has ever been treated to a bona fide miracle.

Still, it makes me feel better to fix my mind on a higher power. It beats thinking of Marc dying. I love God, I remind myself, I do believe in Him.

I just don't know if I trust Him.

The sun sets in the middle of our final push. But it's strange, I can't say exactly when it fell beneath the horizon. It just seemed to wander to the left of the peak and disappear.

The moon, though, when it rises, is brilliant. It's big and round and its white light seems to sparkle when it strikes the side of the cinder cone.

Higher than the moon is the haunting red of the molten peak. It dominates the sky, throwing off red sparks that rise straight up and then slowly curve and fall downward and flame out as they strike the path before us. All along I knew the volcano was active, but I never considered that it might suddenly spew out a shower of lava and roast us alive. There's a peculiar rhythm to the spray of sparks. It comes in pulses, like a beating heart, and it makes me wonder if the volcano is alive in some way.

Definitely, I feel something powerful watching us.

"There it is!" Sam calls from twenty paces in front of me, pointing. He stops and sets down Chad and lets the rest of us catch up. Kyle also lets go of Li, but I continue to hold on to Marc. He's still out and I worry he may never awaken.

Sam is pointing to a black hole a hundred yards above and fifty yards off to our left. Seen from the side, the cave opening is hard to focus on. I blink and lose it for a moment until I blink again. It appears as tall as a man, circular; maybe unnaturally so. I can understand why Sam feels it might have been cut into the side of the cinder cone.

"What's our plan?" Kyle asks.

Sam nods. "We need one. Ten to one either Nordra or Viper is already up here."

"Are you sure there's only one way in?" Kyle asks him.

Sam shakes his head. "There might be an opening on the inside of the volcano, but unless you can swim through boiling lava, I'd advise against searching for a back door."

"If I were Viper and I was waiting to ambush us," I say, "I'd cloak and hang near the opening but stay outside. No way I'd let myself get cornered inside the cave, not when it's three against one."

"Hey, don't I count?" Chad complains.

"Sorry," I mutter.

"Good point," Sam agrees. "The interior of the cave has fresh air but there's still plenty of hot springs and lots of steam. We'd spot Viper in a second in the steam, cloak or no cloak."

"What about Nordra?" Kyle asks.

"I doubt Nordra would allow himself to get cornered either," Sam says.

"I'm not so sure," I say. "Nordra's advantage is his size and strength. The cave's got a narrow opening. If you go by history, it's always been easier for a small army to defend itself against a large army if it had a narrow pass to defend."

Chad pats me on the back in approval. "You're thinking of the Battle of Thermopylae. When a few hundred Spartans held off a hundred thousand Persians at the pass. That battle strategy could apply here, but only if Nordra believes we're determined to get inside the cave."

"Are we?" Kyle asks.

"Gimme a break," I snap. "It was your idea to hike all the way up here in the first place."

"It was Sam's idea!" Kyle complains. "He's the one who told me how amazing it is inside."

"Let's stop the bickering and make a decision," Sam replies. "I think Jessie's right and there's a good chance Viper's hanging somewhere near the entrance, cloaked. If that's the case, we should wait here for the moon to rise higher and shine on the cave. That'll give us a much better chance of spotting her."

"To hell with that," Kyle growls. "I'm not standing on the side of this freezing sand castle for another hour. I say we suck it up and go over and have a peek inside."

They all turn to me, like always, to decide.

"Ordinarily, I'd agree with Sam," I reply. "The moonlight's our best defense against Viper. But Marc's in bad shape. I've got to get him inside and out of the cold. I say we go for it."

"Fine," Sam agrees reluctantly. "But we've got to free up our hands if we're going to fight and the only way we can do that is by leaving Marc, Chad, Li, and Jelanda outside."

"No way," I say. "We did that last time and look what Nordra and Viper did to us. We can't make the same mistake twice."

"She's got a point," Kyle says. "Who knows if Nordra's in front of us or behind us?"

"Chances are he's already here, in front of us," Sam says.

"I can set Marc down in an instant if I have to," I say. "As for Chad and Li, they can walk the rest of the way to the cave. And Jelanda . . . I don't know what to do with her."

"I'll slice her Achilles tendons again and tie her to a boulder outside the cave, no problem," Kyle says.

"Then it's settled," I say, not happy about his tendon slicing but too worried about Marc to waste time on another argument. "Everyone draw their weapons and scan for any sign of movement. Search the ground for prints. Listen for breathing." I nod. "Let's do it."

We start for the cave, passing out of the moonlight half-way to the entrance. The sudden dark is unsettling, and as if it senses my fear, the volcano suddenly belches out a shower of red sparks, several of which land only a few feet to our right side. A rumbling starts deep beneath us and the ground seems to shake. The King of the Field, I think, with his burning red crown, knows the climax of the contest is near at hand. I could swear the flashes of fire cannot be a coincidence. The volcano must be alive.

We stop ten yards shy of the opening, searching for signs of Viper and Nordra, and the ghosts for that matter. There *are* prints in the ash, but as far as we can tell they were created by a person hiking from the other side of the volcano, who stopped at least thirty yards shy of the cave before reversing direction and walking back the way he came.

The prints are huge; I'm confident they belong to Nordra. His pattern has always shown a lack of subtlety. He prefers the straight attack, never mind what Cleo told me. Viper's been the opposite; she's always snuck up on us. Which makes me fear that she might have brushed away her tracks as she neared the cave.

All of us, we exchange looks, but there's nothing to say.

We need to go forward.

Up close the circular nature of the cave opening is beyond dispute—it's ridiculously symmetrical. It looks as if the entrance was cut into the side of the cinder cone using a gigantic drill bit. Since nature doesn't work with such preci-sion, the entrance to the cave, at least, is artificial.

We step to the opening and peer inside.

There's light. It's a soft red but it's enough to see by. We don't need to light a torch. Nevertheless, Kyle holds up an unlit torch and gestures with his fingers, indicating he wants to light it once we're inside. In response I point to Jelanda and motion for him to tie her up—now. No way I'm bringing her inside with us.

Kyle nods and drags her off to a nearby rock, wraps her with multiple layers of vines and cloth, casually slices the heels of her feet wide open, and returns to where we wait.

He's taking a terrible risk. If the rest of the ghosts are nearby and suddenly swoop in, they might be able to free their leader. Yet, since we started up from the base of the cinder cone, we've lost all sight of them.

We step inside. The first hundred feet are perfectly circular. The giant drill must have been shoved in deep, I think. Care-fully touching the walls with my fingertips, I'm struck by their hard blackness, their smoothness, and their warmth. Already the temperature and humidity have increased dramatically.

None of us has to search far to see why. Sam was right; the interior's filled with pools of steaming water and glowing baths of molten lava. We come upon them abruptly, as the nar-row entrance expands into a cavern as large as my childhood church.

An uncluttered gray path leads down the center and the high ceiling has a gentle arc to it, but I couldn't swear the cavern itself is artificial. The pools of water and lava are haphazardly placed and the walls are riveted with deep grooves; the erosion probably the result of the swirling steam and repeated tremors. Once again I feel as if the ground beneath my feet trembles but it might be my imagination.

Kyle signals to me with his torch. I nod and he lights it and holds up the bright orange light, which contrasts sharply with the somber red. Chad lights a torch as well and takes a step forward to explore before I grab his arm and give him a sharp look. I want us to stay close together until I'm sure we have the place to ourselves.

Yet the light from the twin torches is reassuring. They create such a bright glare, I find it hard to believe Viper could be cloaked inside the cave and we couldn't spot her. The cavern is only two hundred feet deep and half that wide. It doesn't take us long to explore it, and realize the back wall holds the most fascinating riddles.

First there's an icy stream that strangely comes out the base of one wall and mysteriously disappears into the base of another. Then there're the rows of petroglyphs above the stream, alongside a tall wall of writing.

The petroglyphs—or images—and the ancient language are two separate things, and yet I've seen both before. They are definitely related to the symbols and writing I saw on a wall overlooking a secret pool concealed in a rocky hill in the desert outside Las Vegas. Kendor took me to the spot to swim in the pool and to show me a prophecy that related to my daughter, Lara. Kendor had told me the site had once been considered sacred to the Paleo-Indians who had lived in the area centuries before the white man arrived.

Gently, I set Marc down against a wall beside the stream and cup a handful of the cold water in my palms and pour it over his head. He stirs and opens his eyes briefly before closing them again. Yet he smiles faintly.

"More," he whispers.

"You can have all you want," I say, relieved to see him awake. I continue to splash his head and even mange to get him to take a few sips. It's as if the stream is as magical as the desert pool Kendor took me to. Marc's fever goes down at least two degrees in the short time I treat him.

"Obviously this is written in a different language than the plaque," Kyle says. "But I'd swear the style of writing is the same."

Before I can tell them what Kendor told me about the old language, and the petroglyphs, Sam speaks.

"This language is called Tarora. It's known only to the oldest of the Tar and it's directly related to these petroglyphs. My mother taught me a few of the Tarora's characters when I was a kid but I can't remember well enough to decipher any of these words. Too bad she's not here, she could probably translate this entire wall for us."

"A pity," Kyle says with a hint of sarcasm in his voice, like he doesn't believe Sam—which makes no sense considering the fact that Sam didn't have to volunteer the information. Nevertheless, our paranoia being what it is, I, too, begin to wonder if Sam is lying, if he knows exactly what it says on the wall and is keeping it to himself. Hell, maybe the Tarora writings do explain a secret way of getting off the island.

"Let's study the pictures," I say, standing and taking a step away from Marc, scanning the images more closely. Whoever drew them had a skilled hand and access to a variety of colored paint or chalk. The symbols take up more space than the writing and are arranged in four distinct rows.

The first image in the top row shows a diagram of our solar system. The sun is depicted as a bright white star, with only a faint hint of yellow, which I know from my high-school astronomy class to be accurate. I find the attention to detail interesting, as well as the fact that there are ten planets circling the sun instead of nine—never mind that poor Pluto is technically no longer supposed to be called a planet. Between Mars and Jupiter is a blue-white planet that resembles the Earth. It occupies the orbit of what is now the asteroid belt.

The fifth planet intrigues me. I know that many astronomers believe that the asteroids were created in the distant past when an unfortunate fifth planet exploded. It is in fact the leading theory for the existence of the space rubble.

It makes me wonder how old these images are. And if the

artist who created them had a different set of science books than modern man has.

In the second picture we see a close-up image of Venus, Earth, Mars, and the unnamed fifth planet. There are signs of green on all of them except Venus, which all modern astronomers agree has too hostile an environment to support life. Yet, as a semiscience nerd, I find the image exciting because a large number of scientists do speculate that Mars had life on it in the past.

Also, it's fascinating, although frightening, to think the mysterious fifth planet could also have supported life. I wonder if it was inhabited.

The third image is strange.

It shows a featureless black wall ringing half the fifth planet. I say half because only half the planet is depicted in the picture. The other half is just . . . gone. It doesn't exist.

The image makes no sense.

How could half a planet orbit the sun?

Maybe it couldn't. In the fourth and final image of the top row, the mysterious fifth planet is nothing but rocks tumbling through space; the rocks obviously representing the asteroid belt. Basically, the fourth image is a diagram of how the solar system looks today.

The second row starts with an overhead painting of the Field. I can tell it's our island because half of it is identical to the half I've seen. There's the volcano, the huge valley, the raging river, the smaller valley where we landed, the cliff with the cave where we first slept, the rocky beach, and so on.

The six following images show close-ups of six spots on the island. I immediately recognize two of them. They show where Sam's group and our group landed. Yet I'm confident the third image is Kyle's landing spot based on the description he gave me of where they set down on the beach.

That leaves three pictures of the island that depict spots I've not been to but nevertheless vaguely recognize. Two appear to be set in the forest where Shira died, where I first encountered the ghosts and Nordra. The third location is on the barren side of a hill, which I only spotted in the last hour when we neared the top of the volcano.

The superficial meaning of the pictures is clear. They list where we, the contestants in the Field, were placed on the island. A deeper meaning is implied, however—that *every* contestant, throughout time, is placed at one of these six spots. Certainly, whoever created these pictures knew these six locations were important.

But why were they important? And why were none of the six landing spots located on the other side of the island? The third row, which has only one image, might provide an answer to my second question.

Like the picture at the start of the second row, it shows an overhead view of the island. But only half the island is present, the half we've been running around on for the past three days. The other half is missing. It's just gone, there's nothing there.

The fourth and final row has three images in it. The first shows the black wall that was depicted in the picture of the mysterious fifth planet. Only here, the image is a close-up of our volcano and the wall. The picture appears to have been cropped for some reason; it doesn't extend far in either direction.

But it is drawn from the perspective of someone staring at the wall from roughly our position on the side of the volcano, or at least from our altitude. And it makes it clear that if we hike farther around the cinder cone, we'll run into the wall.

The next image shows a female, who bears a resemblance to Cleo, approaching the wall and pressing a red bracelet to its side. The picture gives the impression this is the proper way to touch the wall, instead of with one's fingertips.

The third and final picture in the bottom row is odd. It shows the same young woman as before, holding her bracelet to the wall, only now there are countless images of other people who overlap with each other as they stretch alongside the wall. These people are drawn more like ghost figures—we're able to see through them. The original female remains clear, only now there's a faint white light around her head, something akin to a halo.

"What the hell?" Marc mutters from his place on the

floor. I was so busy studying the images that I hadn't noticed he had reopened his eyes and was doing the same thing. I kneel by his side.

"How do you feel?" I ask.

"Would you please quit asking me that." Marc points to the pictures. "We came all the way here for that?"

I have to smile. No matter how dire the situation, Marc is always still Marc. "Got any profound insight on what the pictures mean?" I ask.

Marc closes his eyes and leans his head back. "It means that black wall is one freaking weird barrier," he mumbles.

I stand and look at the others. "I agree with Marc."

"You're saying it's not a way off the island?" Kyle asks.

"I'm saying we're not going to figure out what it is by standing here and talking about it," I reply.

"I've already been to the wall," Sam says suddenly, his voice anxious. "I'm not going back."

"What?" Kyle exclaims. "You're the one who told us about it! Who got us all excited about it! Now you just want to chicken out and stay here?"

Sam shifts uneasily, lowers his head. "It's different once you've touched it. It gets under your skin. It's hard to explain but I sort of forgot about it after I left this place. But now that we're back here—I don't know, the thought of getting near it creeps me out."

Kyle shakes his head. "I can't believe this."

I speak to Sam. "Are you saying you're not going with us to check it out?"

Sam hesitates. "I don't want to go."

"You don't have a choice!" Kyle snaps. "We don't know where Viper and Nordra are, but we have to assume they're close. We have to stick together. It's the only way we stand a chance of fighting them off."

Sam turns to me and points to Marc. "He's in no condition to hike, not at this altitude. And Li's in bad shape. She's hardly said a word all day. If you two are serious about going to the wall, then I can stay behind and guard them. I can keep an eye on Jelanda as well. Someone has to—you can't take them all with you."

Sam has his eyes fixed on me, waiting for my approval. He must know I have doubts about him. He may even suspect I've heard about his history with his murdered boyfriend.

My gut is still too twisted in knots to tell me whether I can trust him or not, but what he says makes sense. Marc can't travel and Li's a mess. At least one witch has to remain behind.

If we are determined to study the wall.

It's a big if. Our first priority is survival and we're stronger if we stick together. But what's the point of remaining in the cave? Sure, it can provide shelter for the night. But then what? Are we going to huddle here forever and wait for Nordra and Viper and the ghosts to attack?

No, I have to make a choice. A tough choice.

"Kyle and I will go to the wall," I say. "Sam and Chad will stay here and keep an eye out for you know who. At the first sign of trouble scream at the top of your lungs. Kyle and I will be traveling light and we'll be able to get back here in a hurry."

Chad raises his arm like he's in class. "Excuse me, Jessie, I have a suggestion."

"Don't say it," I warn.

Chad continues. "I respect you're in charge and all that but you have to take me. This wall—it's obviously a phenomenon mankind's never run into before. And by 'mankind' I'm including witches, too. It's an enigma and I'm the only scientist in this group who's been trained to study enigmas. You need me."

Kyle glances at me. "He might be useful."

I'm a far from objective leader. I don't want to take Chad because I want him to stay and keep an eye on Sam, to make sure he doesn't harm Li or Marc. Yet, if Sam is a traitor, he'll have no trouble overpowering Chad, so in a way leaving Chad behind is an exercise in futility.

Once again paranoia fills the air.

"Fine, you can come," I say.

As we hike toward the back of the volcano, what we call the west side, we angle for greater altitude. According to Sam, the wall is higher than the cave. The moon has climbed farther into the sky since we entered the cave, and to our night-adjusted eyes we have all the light we need.

That's why we can't understand why we have yet to catch a glimpse of the wall. Granted, Sam told us he didn't notice it until he stumbled upon it. Yet once he did find it, he realized it stretched for miles, north and south.

Talk about a confusing story.

The volcano's molten crown continues to throw out streams of red flares, and the guys begin to joke that it's happy to see us. But the sudden activity continues to haunt me. Besides, I don't like them talking and tell them to hush.

We hike for half an hour straight, no breaks.

Then we see it. No warning. It's just there.

It's tall and dark and at first glance it appears to be massive. There's no question it stretches for many miles in both directions. I wouldn't be surprised if it divides the island in half. But I don't see anything supernatural about it and wonder why it spooked Sam so much.

Until I take a closer look.

From our position on the side of the cinder cone, we should be able to see over the wall, even though it's far taller than Sam described. Still, we've hiked way up and we definitely should be able to see the wide ocean far beyond the western edge of the island, especially in the brilliant glow of the moon. East of us the sea is sparkling like a veritable lunar field.

Yet we can see nothing above and beyond the wall.

We can't even decide how tall it is. Chad says two hundred feet. Kyle says it's over four hundred feet. The guys both believe we're not seeing over it because it's too tall. Yet we all agree we can see the top of it—sort of. Kyle and I turn to Chad for an answer.

"You're the science nerd," Kyle says. "Explain how it's screwing with our eyesight?"

Chad frowns. "I wish we'd come here during the day. We'd probably spot the problem in a minute. There's something about the way it reflects light or the angle it's built at that throws off our sense of perspective."

"Hate to break it to you, mate," Kyle says, "but that wall ain't reflecting no light. It's swallowing the bloody moonlight whole."

"I think Kyle's right," I say.

Chad holds up a hand. "Let's not jump to any conclusions. There are plenty of objects in nature that, at first sight, give the wrong impression of what they really are."

"Name one that's as big as this fucker," Kyle says.

"I can't, not off the top of my head," Chad says, turning to me. "We have to examine it."

"Maybe I should go alone," I say.

"Jessie, this is every scientist's dream," Chad pleads. "It's a genuine enigma. To the naked eye, it makes no sense. But our eyes are only one sense. I need to touch it, I need to examine it."

I nod. "All right, we'll go closer, all of us together. But no one lays a hand on it until I say so. Agreed?"

We walk toward it until we're standing thirty feet away.

That would be a first down in football. Stretching our necks back, we have even more trouble figuring out exactly where the top is.

Again, we turn to Chad for an explanation.

"It's definitely hard to estimate its height. Our main problem is a lack of proper tools. You need a microscope to see germs or a telescope to see galaxies. In the same way, if we just had a long measuring tape . . ."

Kyle interrupts. "Smart boy, we're stranded on a tropical island. We don't have any special tools to work with. But I can tell you something—my whole life, I've never needed more than my eyes and my wits to tell how tall a building is. What's so special about this thing that we can't even guess at a height?"

"Well?" I say finally, when Chad doesn't answer. But then I realize we might be putting too much pressure on the poor guy. He suddenly takes a step toward it.

"Fair enough," he says. "Let me at least figure out what it's made of."

I grab his arm. "I just told you, no one touches it until I give the okay."

"At least let me feel for its temperature. I can do that without actually touching it."

"Fine," I agree reluctantly.

Chad and I step to within three feet of it. Kyle stays where he is. He says he doesn't care if it makes him look like a coward, he knows when something isn't natural. This is from a witch with supernatural powers.

Chad raises his hand, moves his palm toward the surface.

"Careful," I warn.

Chad brings his palm within three inches and stops. He frowns.

"What's wrong?" I ask.

"It has a normal everyday temperature."

"Normal is good. Why are you frowning?"

"Because it's freezing up here. When I said it has a normal everyday temperature, I should have said it's at room temperature."

"Are you sure?"

"Yes. I can feel its warmth."

"How's that possible?" I ask.

"It must have an internal heat source. Or . . ." Chad doesn't finish.

"Or what?" I ask.

"It's not really here. Not in the conventional sense."

"That doesn't sound very scientific."

Chad shrugs. "You wouldn't say that if you were a student of string theory, which I am. Modern physics believes there are a lot more dimensions than the standard three. In fact, your witch world is proof that physicists are on the right trail. For all we know this wall is the product of a highly developed civilization."

"We talking aliens here? 'Cause I'm not into aliens."

"You spoke about how your witch's Council knows about advanced races that lived here before us. And back in that cave, the drawings clearly showed a depiction of our solar system with an unknown fifth planet."

"Not following you, mate!" Kyle calls.

"Will you get over here," I snap.

"Happy where I am!" Kyle replies.

Chad continues. "What I'm saying is that it's possible that human beings lived on more than one world in our solar system in the past. The idea isn't as far-fetched as it sounds. There are many signs that Mars had a thick atmosphere and open water in the past. And when it comes to the fifth planet, even the most conservative astronomer will admit the asteroid belt was probably a complete world thousands or millions of years ago."

"And you're saying this advanced race of people built this wall?" I say.

Chad nods. "It's more likely than saying aliens built it."

"Interesting," I mutter.

Kyle snorts. "If they did build it, their wall didn't do the people on the fifth world any good. Since their planet exploded."

"You're missing the point," Chad says. "Whatever this structure is, it's amazing."

Kyle grumbles. "Who gives a shit? All I want to know is if we can use it to get off this island."

"Let me do another test," Chad says, lifting up his spear. He looks to me for approval.

"You can touch it with the tip as long as you keep as far away from it as you can," I say.

Chad grips the spear by the end and tries to scrape it against the wall. But the instant the wood touches the dark material, his face goes blank and he stops moving. I immediately shove him aside and he drops the spear and lands on his butt. Kyle runs over as I kneel by Chad's side.

"What happened?" Chad mumbles.

"You tell us," I say.

Chad looks around as if surprised at his surroundings.

"How long was I gone?" he asks.

"You didn't go anywhere," Kyle says. "You just fell on your ass."

Chad stares at me. "That makes no sense. I remember doing things. Going places and talking to people."

"Who? Where?" I demand.

Chad goes to speak and stops. "I'm not sure. But I know I left here and was gone for a while." He looks around some more. "It's dark."

Kyle groans loudly. "Now we know what the wall's good for. Shorting out your brain. I've got pills back home that can do the same thing, only they take a little longer and they give you a lot more pleasure."

"Can you recall one clear memory?" I ask.

Chad brushes himself off and I help him stand.

"I remember watching TV and a U.S. senator and a Supreme Court justice had just died," Chad says.

Kyle and I exchange a startled look.

Chad notices our surprise. "What is it?"

"Those events happened in witch world," I say. "But they haven't happened in this world yet." I turn to Kyle. "He definitely experienced witch world. And he didn't have to die to go there."

Kyle is suddenly interested. "Are you saying we can reach witch world by using this wall?"

I consider. "That should be impossible. Our real-world bodies can't physically survive in witch world, at least according to the Council. But clearly the wall's connected to it. At the very least Chad's mind went there." I put my hand on Chad's shoulder. "You feel all right?"

Chad tries stretching, then grimaces. "Now that you mention it, I'm sore all over, like I just went twelve rounds in a prizefight." He rubs his temples. "I have a dull headache."

"All that because you touched the wall with the tip of your spear," I remark. "What does the scientist in you think of that?"

"That this wall isn't interested in science as we know it. The thing is already breaking a half dozen physical laws by warping all our senses."

"All our senses," I mutter to myself. I grab Kyle's arm. "What do you hear?"

"What do you mean? I don't hear anything."

I strain to reach with my ears. "Not the wind. Not the rumbling of the volcano. Nothing." I stop. "Nordra and Viper could be attacking the cave right now, the others could be screaming for help, and we wouldn't know it."

"Do you want me to back away from the wall?" Kyle asks hopefully. "At least to where I can hear normal sounds again."

"That's very thoughtful of you," I say.

Kyle begins to back away. "I told you, I'm as bad as Sam, that thing gives me the creeps. I'm happy to get away from it."

"Don't go too far," I say.

Kyle suddenly stops. "What are you going to do?"

"You know."

"What the woman in the picture did," Kyle says. "Press your bracelet to the side of the wall."

"Someone has to try it. It may as well be me."

Chad speaks. "Bad idea. You're our leader, the strongest one we've got to protect us. You're the last one we should risk."

"A witch drew the images in the cave," I say, thinking of Cleo. "I can tell. The lines are too perfect. That means the woman in the picture was a witch."

"Your logic is weak," Chad says.

"I know who the witch was." I speak seriously. "If I freeze up when I make contact with the wall, don't push me away. Let me be."

"For how long?" Chad asks.

"As long as it takes."

"Bullshit," Kyle interrupts. "A minute, tops. We're not going to let it fry every synapse in your brain."

"You're supposed to be backing off," I tell Kyle.

Kyle points at Chad. "Give her sixty seconds, no more."

Kyle walks away while I mentally try to prepare myself. A talk Kendor and I had in training comes back to me.

"People will tell you that all fear is based on the fear of death. It is not true. People only imagine they fear death. Because they are afraid it will be painful. Pain is the source of fear. Once you accept that you will suffer in life no matter how hard you try to avoid it, the fear vanishes."

"Why? How?"

"Because that is when you stop running from it."

His words were simple but they had a profound effect on me.

They calm me as I turn toward the wall. "Wish me luck."

"Good luck, Jessie. I . . ." Chad doesn't finish.

"What?"

He stammers. "I know you're in love with Marc and that he loves you. I just want you to know that . . . I think you're amazing."

I lean over and kiss his cheek. "Thanks. That means more to me than you know."

The kiss takes him by surprise. He blushes, nods.

I walk toward the wall, staring up at it as I approach. I can't see the top. It might be because of the steep angle or it might be because it has no top. No other side. Is that the secret of the wall? That it's a doorway to nothing?

I wish I could stop the urge to run from my fear.

The moon shines bright in the sky but not a single white ray reflects from the wall's dark surface. Staring at, into it, I search for my reflection but find no one.

Waiting will not help.

Raising my left arm, I press my bracelet to the wall.

I sit at a blackjack table in a smoky casino. It's late at night, the joint is practically empty, and except for the dealer I'm the only one at my table. A tall drink sits beside my cards and I know it's a Cuba libre—Coke, rum, and lime, a favorite of mine.

The dealer has just dealt me a ten and an ace, twenty-one, and I'm glad my last bet was a hundred bucks because now I'm going to get paid one and a half times that amount.

Yet the dealer waits for me to tell him whether I want another card or not and I don't know why. He should have paid up the moment he saw my cards.

"You want me to hit you or not?" he asks.

I smile. "You're kidding, right?"

"Nope."

"I've got twenty-one. Pay up."

He grins easily. "You've only got eleven, sister. You can do better than that. Why don't you take another card?"

I know he must be teasing but I don't mind, probably because I'm a little drunk and feeling fine, maybe more than fine. So far my trip to Las Vegas has been a total blast, just what I needed. But I could swear I've met the dealer before, he looks familiar. Then again, it might just be wishful thinking.

He's a handsome devil: six-two, in his mid-twenties, muscular, tough looking, but cool, too, someone who'd be just as comfortable as a cop working the streets late at night or as a high-priced lawyer shooting the breeze with celebrities over lunch at the Four Seasons in Beverly Hills.

He's got a hot body but it's his eyes that intrigue me—a kind of blue that's so close to black, they remind me of the sky when the first faint hint of dawn starts to erase the stars. I feel a little starry-eyed staring at him. He must have noticed my interest because his smile widens.

"So what are you going to do?" he asks.

"I'm going to stand, you ape. I've got blackjack. Give me my money before I report you to your boss."

He leans toward me over the green felt table and gently taps the red card beside the wooden shoe that holds the decks of cards. "You can see by the sign here that you're not playing twenty-one. You're playing twenty-two, red queen, and that ace you're holding is only worth one point." He pauses and asks casually, "You remember now, sister?"

I giggle, suddenly feeling like a fool. Of course he's right, I've got my games mixed up. I still do that sometimes when I come to Las Vegas, ever since . . . well, ever since the last time I was here, which was a while ago, I suppose, since I'm having trouble remembering when it was. I reach for my glass and take a hit of my rum and Coke, but if I'm hoping for it to clear up my memory, I'm as dumb as the dealer must think I am. Still, the liquor tastes good going down and even though it's late, the night feels young to me and full of possibilities. I wonder when Mr. Dealer gets off work, if he'd like to have a drink with me. He might if I lie about my age.

"I'm sorry!" I gush, picking up my cards and scratching the table with the corner of my pitiful hand. "Hit me, baby."

He chuckles as he tosses me a card, a goddamn two, probably the worst card I could have got. "Did you just call me baby?" he asks.

"Yeah. But don't let it go to your head." I tap the two angrily. "Why do you keep giving me such shit cards?"

He lowers his tone and for once speaks seriously. "Because red queen is a hard game. It's kind of like life in that way. You can never see what's coming next. All you can do is play the cards the universe deals you."

"The universe. Gimme a break. It's you who's dealing and it's you who's taking my money. Hit me again."

"Are you sure? Get a ten and you bust."

"Well, I can't stand at thirteen. That's a total shit hand."

He taps his own cards. "Sister, you're not thinking. You haven't even stopped to look at what I'm showing."

I peer over the green table, forcing my eyes to focus, and I realize I'm probably more than a little drunk. When I think about it, which is not easy, I vaguely recall ordering four or five of the Cuba libres since I sat down. Everyone says the casinos water down their free drinks, but I think this dealer has been telling the bar girl to serve me the hard stuff, not that I'm complaining.

It feels good to sit at this table with this hot guy and argue about this stupid card game. I really hope he gets off work soon, and that he doesn't have anyone at home waiting for him. If we do have a drink I'm not sure if I'd go to bed with him, since I'm not that kind of girl, but it's fun to think about. I wouldn't mind a long hot make out. Hell, I wouldn't mind a short one. He's got the sweetest smile.

But I manage to tear my eyes away from his mouth to study his cards, but only because he told me to. "Christ, you've only got a six!" I exclaim.

"That's right. It's looking like I've got a total shit hand as well." He stops to smile again. "Of course, you don't know what my hole card is. Say I've got another six under there. That adds up to twelve and when I take a card there's a good chance I'll get a ten or a picture card and then you'll owe me two hundred dollars. And you'll have to bet two hundred again to try to win back your original bet."

I stop smiling. "That don't seem fair."

"Those are the rules. Told you, red queen is a lot tougher than blackjack. You shouldn't sit at the table unless you're ready to gamble."

A wild idea suddenly hits me. When he originally dealt the first four cards, two to each of us, he automatically checked his hole card, like most dealers do. Which means he knows whether he has a lousy hand or not. The guy is obviously flirting with me, and if I play my cards right—no pun intended—I suspect there's a good chance I can get him to tell me whether I really should hit again or not. I lean a little closer in his direction.

"The reason I came to this table is because I saw you," I say.

He laughs. "Now I see! You're not worried about the rules or your money. You're just worried about whether I like you or not. Is that what you're saying, sister?"

I blush. I can blush on cue but I don't have to fake it this time. "Yeah, kind of. I mean, let's be straight with each other, you know you're hot. And me, well, what do you think of little old me?"

Once again he leans over the table, this time bringing his face so near I can feel the warmth of his breath on my skin and see the sparkle in his dark eyes.

"You really want me to be honest with you, Jessie?"

"Huh? How do you know my name? I didn't tell you my name."

"It doesn't matter. You've got a decision to make and you asked me a question. You asked because you're a little drunk and you're a little young. And you asked because you're hoping I'm going to tell you whether I have a shit hand or not, but I'm not going to do that because that would be cheating. And no one who cheats at red queen ever gets away with it. Never."

I blink, trying to keep up with everything he's saying. But he seems to be talking kind of fast, kind of serious, and I suddenly realize he's not flirting anymore. "Who are you?" I mumble.

He stands back. "You know who I am."

I squint through the smoky haze. Casinos—they're supposed to have no-smoking sections but no one pays attention to the signs. I'm trying my best but it's hard to focus on his face.

Not that I can't identify him by his voice. I know that voice. I know him, I'm sure of it now. Only I can't remember his name.

"Just tell me," I plead.

"No. You've got to stop and think. It's important. This game is important. I told you, it's like your life. You've got to watch everything that's happening around you, every little detail, and you've got to stop and think what it means. Otherwise, it's like the bet you've got on the table right now. You'll lose it and you'll have to play another hand just to try to get even. But right now you can improve your chances by stopping and figuring out what the odds are. That's the smart thing to do, Jessie."

"But if I just knew what your hole card is . . ."

He speaks sternly. "That would be cheating and you know it. But that's your problem right now. You're playing with a weak hand and you're hoping your magical abilities will solve your problems. They won't. It doesn't matter how powerful you are, how many witch genes you've got. If you don't look at what's right in front of you, like what my hand is, then you're going to end up losing."

"Russ!" I gasp, finally recognizing him, while wondering why it took me so long. "What are you doing here?"

He smiles faintly, sadly. "You ask like you're surprised. Of course I'm here. I'm here to help you win."

I frown. "But you just said . . . ah, never mind. I'm confused. You shouldn't be here. Something happened to you. I'm trying to remember. . . ."

"Jessie . . ."

"You're dead!" I exclaim. "Christ! I remember now, it was awful, and I was so sorry. You've got to know I didn't want to do it. I was just trying to protect my daughter. You know about Lara, you saw her just before I killed you."

Russ nods. "Don't worry about it, Jessie. You were strong that night. You did what you had to do. But you've been slipping since you took down Syn. You've been running away from who you are."

"I don't understand. I'm a witch. That's who I am. And a witch has powers so he or she can use them to help people. As a matter of fact, I'm using them right now to help save . . . Wait a second, this doesn't make sense! What am I doing here? I was on an island with Marc and the others. Now I'm in a casino in Las Vegas with you and you're dead. Answer that, Russ—how in God's name can you be here if you're dead?"

"So you believe in God now."

"I do if you're dead and He brought you back to life."

Russ shakes his head. "Nothing with me's changed. Things are good where I'm at. But I still worry about you. I don't think you're taking this game seriously enough."

"You mean the Field, not red queen, right?"

"The Field and red queen are related but that's a long story. Right now you've got to treat the Field like the card game. Don't just rely on the strength of your hand. Look at what's in front of you, what you've got, then look at what everyone else has got. Count up what's there. That's the only way you'll know what to do next."

"But even if I do all of that, I can still lose."

"True. Life's a gamble, there are no guarantees."

"You can't just tell me who my enemy is?"

"Sorry. That would be like telling you what my hole card is. It would be cheating."

"But, Russ! I have so much I need to talk to you about!"

I reach out with my hands, hoping he'll reach back and take them. He remains standing behind the red queen table, though, and I get the impression it's a barrier neither of us can cross. I know it's true because finally my head has cleared.

Again, he flashes a sad smile. "I wish you could stay and we could talk all night. We were together only a short time but it meant a lot to me. I miss you."

I stand from the table. I don't know how but I know our time together is over. "I miss you, too. Is there any way we can meet again?"

He goes to shake his head but then stops. "There is one way, but I want you to fight, Jessie. Do what Cleo and Jimmy told you to do. Stay alive. Do it for me, please."

I hesitate to promise him and I know why.

"Thank you, Russ."

He nods. "Good luck, Jessie."

Luck. He says it because it's key.

I can play the odds perfectly and still lose.

I wake up on the ground, staring up at the sky, Chad standing over me, Kyle yelling for help from far off. Chad stares down at me anxiously.

"Are you okay?" he cries.

I stick up my arm. "Help me up."

He pulls me to my feet as I shake off a wave of dizziness.

The shift from a smoky casino back to a freezing mountaintop is disorientating. I wish I had a chance to process what I experienced while in contact with the wall, but now I have to help Kyle.

Yet my ability to focus is off. Even though I scan the area I don't understand what's happening. Beside me, Chad raises his arm and points me in the right direction.

It's Nordra. He's still high on the volcano, off to our left, but he's heading toward Kyle. The fact that he hasn't tried to take us by surprise tells me he still wants to make a deal.

He doesn't move with the authority he had the last two times we met. It's possible he's faking the weakness—his shoulders are hunched and he's bent forward—but if he is it's a masterful job of acting. I don't know if the last blow I dealt him sapped his strength or if he's suffering from a fresh wound. The moon is bright but he has his back to it; as a result, his front is shadowed and it's hard to make out details. Yet it does appear as if his blue uniform has large dark spots on it, particularly the shirt, and that his clothes are stained with blood. The stains look wet.

Viper. She must be in the area.

She must have attacked him.

Perhaps another reason he's not attacking us. Yet.

"Stay where you are!" I call, and watch as Nordra hears and obeys. He pauses fifty yards above, staying to our left, which makes me worry he might be sending someone to flank our right. My eyesight is returning to normal and I scan in that direction but see no one.

I turn to Chad. "How long was I out?"

"Two seconds."

"That's impossible."

"That was it. How long did it feel?"

"We'll discuss it later." I grab him by the shoulders. "I'm going to tell you something you're going to hate but you have to listen. You need to sit this one out."

He stiffens. "I can't do that."

"Please, you can't help. You can only distract me."

Chad remains firm. "You fight, I fight. I'm not a coward."

I can see he's determined. Perhaps a compromise will satisfy his male need for glory. "All right, here's what you can do. Head to the right and lay down three spears pointed at Nordra, spread equidistant apart, the last one at his present altitude. Do it casually, try to drop them when he's focused on us."

"Jessie . . ."

I shove the spears into his hands, holding on to my machete. "Go! Hurry!" I snap.

Chad nods, takes the weapons, and moves toward our right. In reality I'm not hopeful I can repeat the same trick twice. It only worked the first time because I caught Nordra off guard. It's why I didn't set the spears on the ground when we arrived at the wall. Nordra will be wary of flying objects and with his reflexes he'll have no trouble swatting the spears aside. Still, I might be able to use them to distract him at a critical moment.

I hike to Kyle's side.

"Took your bloody time," he grumbles.

"He looks wounded."

"Probably an act."

"I don't know. He doesn't seem so cocky."

"Give him time," Kyle says, gripping his machete tightly. He's scared; I can smell the sweat on his palms. Nevertheless, he's brave; I can't imagine him running from a fight.

"Jessica Ralle!" Nordra calls. "I'm here to make you an offer!"

"It'd better be a new one!" I call back. The wind has suddenly picked up, the ash whirls around us like snowflakes. It annoys us both because the ash keeps getting in our eyes. Adding to the distraction, the molten crown behind Nordra sends forth the largest shower of sparks yet, for a short time making him look like a red demon fresh out of hell.

That damn volcano, I swear to myself.

It's not on my side, I can feel it.

"Let us create a temporary alliance!" Nordra calls. "You and your people help me destroy Viper and the ghosts! Then, when they are dead, we end the alliance and fight to the death!"

"Let me talk it over with my partner!" I turn to Kyle. "What do you think?"

"No way. We drop our guard and he'll chop us to pieces."

"He sounds sincere. And there's something else in his voice. I think he's hurting."

Kyle is adamant. "He's still a barbarian. Think about how it would feel to turn your back on him in the middle of a fight. We can't do it, I won't do it," he adds. "Besides, if he really is hurt, now's the time to take him down."

I nod reluctantly. "You're playing the odds."

"That's all I've been doing since I got here."

I hesitate. "Is that a warning?"

Kyle smiles. "Maybe."

I think of Russ then. Is Kyle telling me he has a hole card he has yet to show? And if he does have one, why warn me about it?

My emotions of trust and fear embrace and somersault.

Not a good state of mind to enter battle with.

"No deal!" I call to Nordra.

He doesn't look surprised or disappointed. From behind, he draws two machetes, larger and sharper weapons than we've seen before.

"Then we fight!" he yells.

I hastily whisper marching orders to Kyle. "First thing we do is go for the high ground. I'll approach on our right, you on our left. We trade a few blows then we quickly circle around until we're above him. He'll try to get the high ground back and we'll let him—but slowly. Then, when we're opposite each other, keep fighting until I say 'bastard.' Follow my lead, but roughly three seconds after I yell out that word, I'm going to leap over him and go for his head. You do the same. We have to decapitate him. But remember to veer to your right when you leap so we don't smash into each other in midair."

"Got it. What if that fails?" Kyle asks.

"I'll launch Chad's spears. Be sure to drop down when I yell 'shit.'"

Kyle nods his approval. "One last point. I'm taller than you. Better I swing at his top while you concentrate on his legs."

"Agreed. Let's kill this asshole," I say.

Our fighting surface couldn't be worse. Not only do we have the steep angle to contend with, the ash is so damn thick. It's like we've been ordered to fight in a Colosseum that's been flooded with three feet of water. The same old gladiator analogy keeps coming back to me. Everyone must fight to the death and there can be only one winner. Damn the Romans for inventing the idea.

Our approach to Nordra is defensive. We're hoping to take him out with our leaps in the air. Unfortunately, Nordra doesn't seem to know the meaning of the word "defense." His first shots are brutal—"killer blows." He goes for our necks with synchronous swings and it takes all my strength to repel his machete. He's a hundred percent ambidextrous. He strikes at Kyle with equal strength and our plan to gain the high ground has to be put on hold for the moment.

Each time Nordra strikes, he takes a huge step back, but he's not technically retreating. Fighting us from above adds to his natural height. I soon see that the only way to get around him is to hurt him.

I've been going for his left knee, hacking at it after every blow he takes at my head or heart. It's his most vulnerable target, especially with Kyle doing a great job of swinging at his head. But now I decide to take a risk and alter my strategy.

Nordra swings at my neck, his blade slicing toward my throat like a horizontal guillotine. Rather than block his blade with my own, I duck. My trick almost backfires—I feel the tip of his machete take off the hairs at the back of my head. I luck out but don't take time to celebrate. His wild miss causes him to momentarily lose his balance, and for an instant his left side is wide open.

I swing at his ankle.

It's the last place he expects me to strike. He recovers fast from his wild swing and manages to position his machete to protect his knee. Yet when I strike at his ankle, I know it's one of the few open shots I'll get so I put everything I have into the blow.

I hear a loud cracking noise as Nordra's ankle breaks and he staggers forward, down the slope. I rush around him, securing my half of the high ground. To my dismay I see that Kyle believes he has a chance to end the fight once and for all and swings at the top of Nordra's skull.

It's a mistake. Kyle doesn't know Nordra as well as I do; plus he's disobeyed my instructions. Nordra's an experienced fighter. Wherever home is, he must practice hours a day, probably with live targets. Even when off balance he knows how to protect himself. I can't really blame Kyle—he saw an opening and took it. But Nordra has his machete up to cover his head even before Kyle finishes his windup.

Kyle's killer shot bounces harmlessly off Nordra's blade.

"Move!" I yell at Kyle. He's still below Nordra, still hoping to take him out while Nordra's injured. What he doesn't realize is that Nordra may have already healed. "Hurry!" I scream.

Finally, Kyle tries circling around to where I'm standing but Nordra will have none of it. First blocking Kyle's path, Nordra suddenly turns and comes after me, both his machetes swinging. I have the high ground and I'm not hurt—those are my advantages. But I have only one blade to repel his two and he's swinging like a madman.

For a moment I feel doomed.

It's only then I notice that Nordra's blows are not quite as fast and accurate as the first time we met. He's still formidable, he's still stronger than Kyle and me put together, but something's wrong with him. Again, I note the bloodstains on his blue uniform, how wet they are. At first it makes no sense.

Any wound he might have gotten earlier should have healed by now.

Then I realize the obvious.

Viper not only attacked him.

Viper poisoned him the same way she poisoned Marc!

That's why Nordra wanted the alliance and that's why his balance is off. After being stabbed at the hot springs, the first thing Marc complained about besides feeling feverish was dizziness. Does Nordra feel dizzy? For sure, the bastard is going to trip and fall if he keeps swinging at me the way he is.

"I'll take his head!" I shout to Kyle. Calling out the change in our strategy will give nothing away. Nordra will see in a second that we've switched roles. Because I have the high ground, I think, it's only natural that I focus on his upper body.

Knowing Nordra isn't at full strength gives me confidence. It helps that Kyle is chasing after Nordra from below. Even though he failed to gain the high ground with me, Kyle keeps poking at Nordra enough that our foe is forced to quit chasing me with two blades and reverts to keeping Kyle at bay.

Slowly, I can feel the tide turning.

We're going to win this battle.

Yet Kendor's words come back to warn me.

"Overconfidence is usually a warrior's greatest weakness. I've killed far more cocky men than fearful ones."

I still want to employ our planned "knockout blow." Catching Kyle's eye, I slowly begin to move back down the incline, all the while swinging at Nordra's arms and throat. Nordra is glad to see me giving up the high ground—so glad, he doesn't notice that Kyle is creeping up the incline on his side.

It doesn't take long until Kyle and I are directly opposite each other, with Nordra in the middle. More and more, it's obvious he is not himself. Nordra is gasping for air; his skin is tinged blue, and I can't imagine how he could fake that.

No, I reassure myself, he's ripe for a fall. We've just got to time everything perfectly. Again I catch Kyle's eye and nod.

"Bastard!" I shout at Nordra. Counting to three and bending my knees, I prepare to use the full strength of my legs to leap over his head. Kyle does likewise and my heart pounds with excitement. Time for the giant to drop!

We leap together, Kyle and I, in perfect rhythm. On the way up I feel a rush of adrenaline as I see Kyle lift up across from me. He has his machete raised high, ready to strike. Mine is also above my head. I visualize splitting Nordra's head open like a coconut. It's obvious we've caught him off guard. Why, he's looking around stupidly.

"Obvious." A favorite word of the overconfident.

We haven't caught Nordra off guard at all. He must have noticed us both bending our knees. To an experienced fighter that would be a sure sign that we were planning a simultaneous leap. And what would we aim for with our leap but his head?

Nordra slashes at the space above his skull with both machetes. Crossing in midair, just when Kyle and I should be reaching down to slice off Nordra's head, we're forced to snap our legs back at the knees so we don't lose a foot. Unfortunately, my leg bangs into Kyle's and he doesn't get his foot up in time.

Nordra's machete strikes home. It's a brutal blow. It slices through Kyle's boot, his flesh, his bone, everything. His severed left foot flies sadly through the air, landing somewhere down the incline. Stunned, Kyle lands awkwardly and rolls through the ash.

Nordra swoops in for the kill.

"No!" I scream, chasing after him, drawing my machete all the way back so I can chop him in half. I should have kept my mouth shut. Again Nordra anticipates my move and whirls and stabs me in the belly just while I'm cocking my arm. I feel an explosion of agony; I feel like I've been gutted.

Yet in reality I'm almost out of Nordra's reach and it's only the tip of his machete that penetrates, an inch or two, no more. It hurts, though; I stagger back and plop down on my butt. Seeing a chance to kill me instead of Kyle, Nordra reverses direction and rushes toward me.

"Shit!" I call out, and mentally lock on all three spears Chad's laid out for me. I know exactly where they are; I don't need my eyes to get a fix on them. And I know Kyle's lost his foot; I know he's down for the count. I'm not worried about hitting him. All I care about is ramming all three spears into Nordra's chest.

Yet I don't know why I reach for all three. In practice with Kendor, I've never lifted more than one object at a time. I have no experience with telekinetic multitasking. I think I just grab all the spears with my mind because I'm pissed off and I want to make a pincushion out of Nordra.

I don't have to look, I *feel* the spears fly toward us.

But Nordra is looking and he ducks. Even poisoned, wounded, he's still fast. He crouches down and manages to dodge two of the spears. The third one catches him hard inside the right shoulder. It's not a fatal wound but it's not going to heal anytime soon—not with the tip sticking out his back. He staggers to the side and drops the machete in his right hand.

It's only then I see what's going on behind him.

Kyle is standing on one foot. I can only surmise he jumped up to protect me when Nordra stabbed me. What with his missing foot and a selfless desire to protect me, I can understand why he forgot about my warning to duck when I said the word "shit."

It's a pity, really, it's a fucking shame.

One of the third spears hit Kyle.

Stuck him right in the center of his gut.

The spear also protrudes from his back.

Seeing Kyle totally helpless, Nordra takes a quick look at me still sitting on my ass and veers toward what he figures will be easy pickings. He probably thinks he can kill Kyle and take care of me afterward. I did, after all, just get stabbed in the stomach. It's doubtful Nordra knows how deep he struck.

Furious, I *rise* to my feet. I don't recall standing, I'm just up. Before Nordra can reach Kyle, I let fly with my machete, repeating the same trick I used on Viper. The tip of my weapon sinks into Nordra's right hip and he staggers and I pounce. He falls to his knees and I'm on him in an instant, grabbing the two sides of his skull near his ears.

"Now you die," I swear, ready to rip off his head.

From behind me, Chad screams.

I turn and freeze.

Viper has suddenly appeared.

She has ahold of Chad, a black blade at his throat.

Her tactics have not changed. She's timed her attack to the second. Let our fight with Nordra distract us, wait for it to reach its climax, then slip in and kill the helpless.

Viper's smart. Even if I had been told ahead of time what she had planned, I couldn't have stopped her. On the other hand, for a witch-bitch with such a badass rep, she sure fights like a coward.

Of course she's handicapped now.

I see a stump where her left hand used to be.

"Well?" she says.

She's waiting for me to kill Nordra. He's waiting for me to kill him. He knows I've got him; he's doesn't move an inch. He knows if he does, I'll break every bone in his neck.

"What do you want?" I ask Viper.

"Kill him and we'll talk."

"Let my friend go and I'll kill him."

Viper nicks Chad's throat. A red line trickles onto his collar. Viper grins. "No," she says.

Frantically, I try to think of a way to use Nordra's life as a bargaining chip to save Chad. I find it difficult to think with all the blood that's been spilled. Glancing toward Kyle, I see him kneeling in the ash, his hands wrapped around the pole I drove through his guts, a red circle growing across his shirt. The amount of blood he's losing from his severed foot is worse. The light brown ash at the end of his stump is black. His eyes are closed; he's in terrible pain.

My own wound is healing rapidly. I've stopped bleeding and feel only tenderness where Nordra stabbed me.

I turn back to Viper and make an offer.

"You don't let Chad go and I'll release Nordra," I say. "You know he's wanted to form an alliance with me from the start. Well, I'll form one with him right now." I shake Nordra. "Want to help me kill this bitch?"

He grunts. "It would be my pleasure."

"You're bluffing," Viper says. "The instant you let go of him I slit your friend's throat. Then he's dead and you still have Nordra and me to deal with. But you kill him now and it's down to you and me."

I don't like how she's not worried about Sam.

Has she already been to the cave?

Are Marc and Li dead?

"Jessie," Chad says calmly. "You have to let me go."

"Shut up!" I snap at him before speaking to Viper. "All right, say I kill Nordra. How do I get my friend back?"

Viper speaks. "Simple. Kill him and back away from your weapons. That's all you need to do."

"What guarantee do I have you'll let Chad go?"

She nicks his throat again. "None."

Viper reeks of deception. I doubt she's going to release Chad. She just wants Nordra dead. And the truth is, Nordra's bad for both us. Killing him is the logical thing to do.

However, there could be a danger in walking away from my weapons. Viper has practiced telekinesis for years. Her skill has to be superior to my own. If it came to a psychic tug-of-war over the machetes, I'd lose.

I can see Chad thinking the same thing.

"You're not giving up your weapons for me," he says.

"I told you . . . ," I begin.

"Don't feel bad, Jessie," he interrupts. "There's no way I was ever going to leave this island alive."

With that Chad twists against Viper, snarling like a wild animal in her grip, and she's forced to slit his throat just to stop him from hurting her.

Which is exactly what he wanted her to do.

"No!" I cry.

Nordra sees I'm crushed. He reaches up with his hands and . . .

I snap his neck. I twist his head so far around he's facing forward when I'm finished. Every cervical vertebrae in his neck cracks. He slumps to the ground, dead.

Viper drops Chad's lifeless body and vanishes.

I can see her outline in the moonlight, though, and can follow her footsteps in the heavy ash. There's no question of her destination. She's heading for the cave.

I hurry to Kyle's side. He's still on his knees, the spear poking out both sides of his body. "I'm so sorry," I moan.

"Not your fault," he gasps. "I forgot about the 'shit.'"

"Should we try to remove it? Can you heal fast enough?"

"I think it's the only thing that's keeping me from bleeding out." He coughs weakly, spitting up blood. "I need to get back to the cave."

"What's in the cave?"

He peers at me through agony and smiles. "I didn't want you guys to know, but I can read Tarora. The petroglyphs—I know what they say. And I know the water there, in the stream, has powerful healing properties." He adds, "You must have noticed when you splashed it on Marc's head, how his fever went down. That wasn't a coincidence."

"You should have told me. I would have had him drink it. It could have saved him."

"He did drink it."

"Well, I would have had him drink more," I say.

Kyle nods, sweat pouring off his face. "When we first met, it was all an act from my side. I planned to kill you all. I thought I had to. I thought that's what you had to do in this kind of place. I didn't trust anyone." He struggles to breathe. "I'm sorry, I didn't know."

"What didn't you know?"

"How wonderful you are."

I feel foolish how much his words mean to me. Sure, he's on the verge of death and he's telling me that all along he planned to kill me and my friends. I should feel nothing but scorn for him. And yet I understand. Because I had the identical thoughts—kill Kyle and Sam before they kill me. I doubt that anyone who's been sent to the Field hasn't thought the same.

Of course, it doesn't mean I suddenly trust him.

Tearing off strips of his uniform, I make a crude tourniquet for his leg and then a bandage. The bleeding slows but doesn't stop. The only way I can get him to the cave is to carry him. I tell him as much and he nods.

"It's probably too late anyway," he says with a sigh.

Slipping Nordra's machete through the back of my belt, I heave Kyle into my arms. "There's hope. Just don't black out. Don't go into shock."

His eyes wander in the direction of Chad.

"He was a sweet kid," Kyle says.

The sweetest. Tears roll over my cheeks.

But there's no time for grief.

All I can do is keep moving forward and pray Marc's alive.

The hike back to the cave is an ordeal. I move too fast, I jar Kyle and the spear stuck in him, and he cries out in pain. But when I move too slowly, I'm forced to watch the blood leaking from his body. I don't even know how many quarts of blood the human body holds, but I keep thinking he's got to run out soon.

Kyle's conscious when we reach the cave.

We stop behind a boulder and peer around.

All six ghosts guard the entrance.

And they're armed. They have made the impossible.

All six are equipped with bows and arrows.

"Ora swore there was nothing to make bows and arrows with," I say.

Kyle speaks in a feeble voice. "They're industrious critters. I'm not surprised they found a way."

I study his pale face in the moonlight. His skin is as white as the moon. "Is that why you dragged their leader up here? Or was there another reason you never told us about?"

Kyle grins slyly. "To use the ghosts to kill you all?"

"Was that your reason?"

He shakes his head. "Nothing so dark, I'm afraid. I captured Jelanda because I know more about the ghosts than I let on. They can form a group mind only when close together and only when they're next to their leader."

"Like now."

"Exactly. Look at them—for the first time they're ready to fight. It's ironic, though, at this moment they're also vulnerable." He struggles to breathe. "I dragged Jelanda here because I knew she was the key. I knew if I survived and had only the ghosts to contend with, she'd be my ticket off this island."

"How so?"

"We can only imagine what a group mind's like, but it's probably safe to assume that what one feels, they all feel. Hold on to that idea. And keep in mind that Jelanda is the glue that keeps them linked together."

"Are you saying the ghosts cannot survive without a witch for a leader?"

"That's what my Lapra friends taught me. Don't look surprised, I told you I have a foot in both worlds. It might be the reason the ghosts have survived for so long, I don't know and I don't care. What matters is that if you kill their leader while they're fused as one mind . . ."

"You kill them all," I finish.

"That's it."

I study the path of Viper's footprints that we've followed back from the wall. They appear to sweep right past the ghosts and enter the cave. I share the information with Kyle, but he doesn't seem surprised.

"She might have got here before the ghosts arrived," he says. "They might not be able to see her while she's invisible. What difference does it make? We knew she'd get to the cave before us."

I slump low, the constant stress of worry I've felt in my chest all day swelling with each painful beat of my heart. I feel I've come so far only to fail those I care most about.

"It makes a lot of difference," I say bitterly. "There's no reason for Viper to keep Marc or Sam or Li alive."

Kyle winces and I don't know if it's because of his wounds or my words. "You're wrong. There's not a chance in hell she'll hurt Marc. Viper's watched us, studied us. She saw you practically beg Nordra for Marc's life. She knows you're attached to him. He's the only lever she's got when it comes to you."

"What does she need with a lever?"

Kyle shakes his head. "Jessie, for a smart girl you're pretty dumb sometimes. Viper's terrified of you. You cut off her hand. She saw you kill Nordra. She'll do anything to avoid having to face you one-on-one. At least on an even playing field." He pauses. "Marc's her ace in the hole."

"Almost worthless," I mutter.

"Huh?"

"Just something a guy named Russ told me."

Kyle stares at the spear sticking out his front. "To think, last week I was worried about how to choreograph my next video. Pretty hilarious if you think about it." He wipes away the blood that continues to leak from his mouth. "I don't want to rush you or anything but I need to get in that cave."

I nod and study the organization of the ghosts' defense. It's pretty basic. Jelanda and another ghost are focused on the interior of the cave. The other four stand poised with arrows in their bows, facing outward. I can see only one way to approach without being seen.

I explain my plan to Kyle and he nods his approval. He's closed his eyes again and is having trouble staying awake. I warn him again about going into shock and he just grunts and tells me to hurry.

The ghosts are looking everywhere but above. I retrace the first part of the path we took to the wall and then veer off and head straight up the side of the cinder cone before cutting back toward the cave. Soon I'm a hundred yards above the entrance, hugging the side of a very steep incline.

I know I can creep silently down to the entrance, without sliding off, but I worry about the ash I'll knock loose before I reach my goal. The stuff is everywhere: in my hair, my eyes, my mouth, my nose. Bump it and a tiny cloud inevitably floats in the air. I'm not sure how intelligent the ghosts are, but if they're suddenly hit with an avalanche of ash, I'm sure at least one of them will turn his or her eyes upward.

I have no course but to move slowly, to waste time, the one

commodity I can't afford to waste. Crawling down the cinder cone on all fours, I have to fight the temptation to just scream at the top of my lungs and drop in on them with my machete swinging. Yet if I do that, I know what they'll do. Circle the leader, protect her at all costs. Hell, they've already formed a ring around Jelanda. All I'm hoping for is one clean shot at her brain.

Fifteen minutes later I'm in position, crouched above the entrance, peering down at the four ghosts guarding against a frontal attack. I can't see Jelanda and her partner but I'm not surprised. Unless they've moved, they were so close to the opening, they should be directly beneath the stone ledge where I'm perched.

I've managed to stir up a handful of ash but none of the ghosts pays it any heed. But suddenly I have a more urgent problem.

I have to sneeze.

I try to stop it and fail. I let out a loud one.

All four of the ghosts start to turn. I don't give them time to point their arrows at me. Pressing my palms flat on the ledge, I do a backflip over the edge and land cleanly on my feet less than five feet from Jelanda.

She blinks in shock. I smile.

"All of *you* are going to die," I say as I step forward and cut off her head. Even before her skull hits the ground, the other five ghosts start to fall like puppets whose strings have been cut. In two seconds all six lie motionless on the ground.

I don't waste any more time on them. Quickly, I check on Kyle, find he is still alive but slipping in and out of consciousness. Then I stride into the cave.

The cavern has changed since I was last here. The lava pools have risen and like a dozen campfires fed by a fresh supply of logs, they throw off continuous showers of sparks. More important, the hot springs bubble with renewed ferocity and the steam is so thick, I can't see the rear of the cavern from the front. I can't even find the walls and am forced to stalk forward at a cautious pace.

It's at the back of the stone chamber where I find the last of my foes. Once again, Viper stands with a knife to the throat of a friend of mine—Sam. She doesn't act so casual as she did with Chad, no surprise. Holding a witch instead of a human being in her hands is different and she knows Sam might break free at any second.

But I wonder if there isn't more to Viper's lack of confidence. I notice her hand trembling and a vein pulsing fast on her left temple. Her eyes are bloodshot, although the smell of sulfur inside the cavern is not strong.

A simple explanation would be to say Viper is exhausted.

Yet my intuition says no. Her weakness goes deeper.

Still, she holds the advantage. She's cornered Sam with a knife and Li, as usual, stands helpless.

Yet Viper's hold over me relies on Marc and she knows it. The bitch has shoved him into the stream and keeps a grip on him by pressing her bare foot to his head, wedging his skull in place with the help of a stone.

Since I splashed Marc's face with the same water less than two hours ago, I know how cold it is and how fast he must be losing his body heat. He could be dead for all I can tell; his skin is icy blue.

"He's still alive, barely," Viper says, answering my unspoken thought.

Her voice is soft, somehow lonely, and it occurs to me that I've never seen her people. Perhaps Nordra killed them. Perhaps she killed them herself. Nothing would surprise me when it comes to Viper.

"I killed Nordra, now what do you want?" I ask, acting bored.

"Throw down your weapons."

"In exchange for what?"

She strokes Sam's hair, trying to mock both of us. But the gesture is wasted on me since all she has to brush his locks with is a crusty stump.

"In exchange for Sam's life and your boyfriend's life. Drop your machete into the lava. We wouldn't want it to suddenly fly off the floor and hurt someone, would we?"

"Don't do it, Jessie," Sam calls.

"She slit Chad's throat by the wall," I say.

Sam sighs. "She's going to slit mine. You know you can't bargain with a monster like her." He adds, "Where's Kyle?"

"Dead," I say.

"Nordra?" Sam asks.

I nod. Better Viper think Kyle's no longer in the picture.

"Sam's wrong," Viper interrupts. "I am here to bargain. I want off this island as much as you do, Jessica."

"I'm sure you do," I reply. "But since the rules of the Field say there can be only one winner, I can't see us forming a partnership."

Using her stump, Viper points to the petroglyphs on the wall behind her. "Tell me what these mean."

I take a step forward. "I can't."

"They must mean something!" Viper cries, sounding like she's trying to convince herself. "You speak to the Council. You know Cleo. She must have told you a secret way off this island."

There's no question Viper is under immense strain and handling it badly. She looks and sounds nothing like the ruthless girl Cleo described or the lava-spewing creature who attacked us by the hot springs. She keeps putting her stump to her forehead as if trying to halt a pressure that's building inside.

"There's no secret," I say. "The last one left alive wins and is allowed to leave the island. You've known that since the moment you arrived here. What I don't get is why you suddenly want to change the rules."

"Don't come any closer!" she warns, pressing her knife deep into Sam's throat. She's already broken his skin and I see blood spilling over her blade.

I take a step closer. "Why are you afraid to fight me one-on-one?"

"Back up or I'll kill both of your boys!"

I take another step toward her and chuckle. "Go ahead and try. I'll kill you before you can finish with the first one."

Viper is scared but still shrewd. She's not going to fall for a simple bluff. Her eyes fall on Marc, who floats on the surface of the stream beneath the heel of her foot.

"You forget how well I know you," Viper says, changing her tone. "I have to kill only one to destroy you." She pauses. "Dump your weapons in the lava. Now."

"No!" Sam hisses.

I shrug as I toss the machete I used to decapitate Jelanda in the lava. The wood ignites in a line of fire before sinking beneath the somber surface.

"It doesn't matter. I only need my hands to kill you," I say.

"Your knives, too, both of them," Viper orders.

I hate giving up my knives. Whether using my mind or my hands, I had hoped to plant one between her eyes. She must have seen them on me back at the wall.

I toss Ora's favorite blades into the lava.

I sneer. "What's next? Want me to strip down?"

Viper hardens her voice despite the fact that sweat drips from her face. Her eyes meet mine through the red steam. Her knife hand continues to tremble; if she presses any harder, she'll open Sam's jugular.

"Last chance," she tells me. "What are the secrets of this cave and that wall out there?"

"I have no idea," I say.

"Die, you bitch!" Sam cries as he suddenly rams an elbow into Viper's gut, causing her to double up, and spins away from her knife. His neck bleeds freely but he's full of fire and ready to fight. Rather than retreat to my side for support, he stands over her slight figure with arms and hands outstretched, ready to strangle the breath from her body.

Off balance, with the wind knocked out of her, Viper struggles to stand upright. For a moment I see a chance to take her out. But Sam's blow has forced her to release her hold on Marc, who floats over the top of the stream toward the spot where the water disappears beneath the wall. It's obvious the water that keeps him afloat has only appeared for a brief stretch and that it's about to return to its natural state as an underground stream.

And that it's going to take Marc with it.

I want to rush Viper. Like Sam, I want to rip off her head. Instead, I have to race toward the other side of the cavern to catch Marc. But out of the corner of my eye, I see everything that happens.

Sam has definitely caught Viper by surprise and it looks like he stands an excellent chance of killing her. She's only a few feet away and has only one working hand. But I should know better. Viper's never used her hands to torment us, not without telekinetic sparks flying through her fingers.

Sam takes a bold step forward before suddenly becoming aware of a thin but bathtub-size-wide sheet of lava slowly rising from a molten pond on his left. I say slowly because it takes far longer to stand than the sheet of lava Viper drenched Ora with the last time we fought her. Indeed, I feel the sight has Sam hypnotized. He's close to Viper. He needs to kill her before . . .

The lava suddenly flies toward Sam, drenching him from head to toe. In an instant he's transformed into a human torch. He opens his mouth to scream but inhales lava and his throat swells like a balloon. His skin drips off like melting wax, changing to black ash before dripping to the floor, and I'm bitterly reminded of the way Russ died last month.

Nothing could be worse.

But again, I'm given no chance to grieve.

Somehow I manage to catch Marc and pull the top half of his body out of the icy water and into my lap. He's not breathing! Why isn't he breathing? His skin is so cold. But before I can warm him up, even give him mouth to mouth, Viper stalks toward me.

Li continues to stand uselessly. Granted, Li's psychologically shorted out but I wish she could at least wake up long enough to give Viper a kick in the ass and knock her in the water.

Li does nothing and Viper keeps coming.

Viper stands over me and nods at Marc's frozen body.

"I'm not the one who put him in the water," she says.

"Who did?" I ask.

"Sam told me he crawled in before I arrived." Viper shrugs. "That poison makes a person so hot they'll do anything to cool off."

"You're lucky you were able to find it on this island."

"I heard stories about the Field growing up. I knew where to look."

"Like I said, you're a lucky girl."

Viper stares down at me. "I was sure you'd put up more of a fight. I had no idea the loss of Romeo would take the heart out of you."

I stare back at her. "Marc knew what he was doing when he climbed in the freezing water. And I know how to kill you with a mere flick of my wrist."

Viper feigns amazement. "Pray tell, Syn Killer."

"Funny you should bring Syn up. I took her down the same way I'll take you down."

"How?"

"With knowledge. You're sweating, your hands are shaking, your eyes are bloodshot. You're a mess."

Viper fumes. "I was strong enough to fry Sam and I'm

strong enough to defeat you! You coward—sitting there holding your dead lover like he's going to save your ass! You make me sick!"

I smile. "In a way I'm the one who made you sick. When I chopped off your left hand."

Viper hesitates. "Huh?"

"You honestly don't know why you're falling apart, do you?"

"I'm not falling apart."

"It started when you lost your bracelet. It was right in front of you. You picked up your hand but left it for me to find." I pull the red bracelet from my pocket. "That was a mistake."

She hesitates. "That thing is useless."

"When I told you I didn't know any secrets about the wall, I lied. I know a few. One is that it makes this island a pretty weird place. A place where we can't even walk around and kill each other unless a piece of the wall is in contact with our skin." I show her the dark stone on the inner lining of her bracelet. "Be honest with me, Viper. I'll bet that since you lost this little piece of rock you've been stumbling around in a daze."

She sucks in a breath. "You're babbling."

"I'm being insightful. I don't know what this rock and that wall are made out of, but the material has a powerful effect on our minds. I even suspect that wearing a piece of this rock next to where the veins in our wrist pump our blood around and around every few minutes synchronizes our mind and body with our bracelet."

"You're making this up!" Viper cries.

I continue in a calm voice. "Not at all. To test my theory, I tried your bracelet on my right wrist for a few minutes and got a whopping headache. That tells me these bracelets are like dog tags. Once one's been made for you, it's personal and without it you're bound to get lost."

Viper loses it; she screams. "You're full of shit! I'm still here!"

"Not for long," I say casually as I toss her bracelet into a pond of lava six feet off to my left. The red plastic flares as it ignites and begins to melt before sinking from view.

Viper tries to inhale but gags as if she's got a rock stuck in her windpipe. Her black eyes bulge and she shuffles backward like a broken robot. Then she raises both her arms above her head and dances like a demented marionette before crumbling to the floor. Dead.

Jumping up, I pull Marc the rest of the way out of the stream and begin mouth-to-mouth resuscitation. But he doesn't respond; he doesn't start breathing. Putting my ear to his chest, I listen for a heartbeat but there's nothing. I finally sit back and cry.

Li touches my shoulder. "I can help," she says.

"Go away."

"Jessie, I can save him. I have my powers back."

I turn and give her a long look.

She just said more words than she's said all day.

"Why are they back?" I ask.

"Lula is inside me again. I can heal."

I gesture to Marc's dead body. "Do what you can."

Li searches the area. "I need to study the poison she put inside him. Where's the knife she stabbed him with?"

"There," I say, pointing to the knife that spilled from Viper's belt when she dropped dead.

Li picks it up and kneels beside me, staring down at Marc's peaceful face. She reaches for my hand. "Our power will be greater if we work together like we did before," she says.

I stare at her and in an instant I understand everything.

Absolutely everything.

Every piece of the puzzle suddenly fits together and I see a face.

The face of my true enemy.

Since arriving at the Field, I kept checking my own cards but never the dealer's. That's why Russ came to me when I contacted the wall. It's what he tried to teach me over a game of red queen. Of course Russ loved me. Like Jimmy and Cleo, he was desperate for me to survive the Field.

Yet there are more important things in life than survival.

There's what's right and wrong; and then there's love.

Love. Love. Love.

Despite what I know, I decide not to change my bet.

I offer Li my hand. She takes it, squeezing it hard.

The physical contact links me to Li in a profound way. It's

like two wires have been crossed; I can feel her body almost as well as I feel my own. Her touch reminds me of a trick Syn taught me while she grilled me on how to mimic another person's appearance. If you can touch the one you need to copy, Syn had told me, you can copy them so perfectly even another witch will have trouble telling you from the real thing.

If nothing else, Syn has been an excellent teacher.

"Let's close our eyes and concentrate on saving Marc," Li says.

I close my eyes. I know what comes next.

Li doesn't surround us with white light.

Nor does Li invoke her sister.

Instead, she tries to stab me in the lower back with Viper's poisonous knife. She aims for my kidneys, with good reason. The kidneys filter a person's blood and if she were to shred them, and fill them with poison, then I'd start to burn immediately, much worse than Marc. And the pain would be unbearable.

But I catch Li by the wrist before she can touch me.

I open my eyes and stare at her. "I don't blame you," I say.

Her face twists into that of a rabid animal and she fights me, struggling with all her strength to force the tip of the blade into my body. But her effort is wasted on me and I finally tire of her futile attempt and snap her wrist, breaking the bone. Viper's knife falls from Li's grasp and bounces on the floor.

Li stares down at the knife as if it were more important to

her than her broken wrist. She reaches for it again but before she can get to it I pick it up and slide it in the back of my belt. Li crumples as if shot.

"I honestly want to help you," I say.

She stares at me with hollow eyes, empty eyes.

"Is Kyle dead?" she whispers.

"Yes," I lie. "You don't have to think about Kyle any more. Do you hear me, Li? He no longer has any power over you."

Li is a mass of confusion. She keeps blinking, looking around in short jerky movements, avoiding my eyes.

"I don't know what I'm supposed to . . . ," she begins, before breaking off into sounds that can only be described as psychotic babbling.

I want to pat her on the back, embrace her, tell her it's not her fault. But I suspect if I so much as touch her she'll scream bloody murder. Her programming runs deep.

I speak gently. "Li. Listen to me. You don't know what to do and that's understandable. You've been subjected to a terrible form of psychic attack. But the person who attacked you can no longer harm you. You no longer need to listen to what he told you to do. You're free now, do you understand?"

"Free?" The word seems to catch in her throat and in her brain and at last she looks in my direction. "Free?"

I smile warmly, feeling a wave of relief.

I reach out and squeeze her hand.

"Yes, you're free to do whatever you want," I say.

Li recoils in horror, jumps to her feet, stares at her hands as if they're soaked in blood, then stares at me as if I'm the one who forced her to commit the bloodshed. She moves so fast, like a witch, probably as fast as her sister in witch world, and I'm not given a chance to stop her, to save her.

"Free!" she screams, her eyes no longer empty but filled with the anguish of everyone she saw tortured to death in the prison camps in North Korea, her sister included. Her pain is suicide pain, the type that cannot be borne; and she won't bear it. Turning, she leaps into the pool of lava that swallowed Viper's bracelet and I hear one final scream, loud and short, and a massive flare rises to the ceiling but it doesn't last. In seconds there's no trace left of Li.

I wish I could have stopped her.

But maybe there was no point.

Maybe she was too far gone.

Leaning over, I kiss Marc on the lips and speak softly to him. "It's you. It was you from the start," I say, and even though his body is colder than ice, and his heart no longer beats, and he no longer breathes, I know I can heal him.

Impossible, you think? Think again. . . .

Only one will survive.

Which is another way of saying one MUST survive.

I kiss Marc again and whisper in his ear. "I want it to be you."

Standing, I close my eyes and visualize Li in my mind's eye.

Once again, I feel her body as if we're still holding hands, every nerve and muscle and inch of skin that made her look the way she looked. Then I feel a wave of power sweep over me and know that from the outside I look exactly like her.

I stagger outside and find Kyle waiting behind the boulder where I left him with a spear poking out his front and back, and a tourniquet tied tight to his leg to stop his bleeding.

Only, the spear is missing because it never struck him.

Clever Kyle. He never forgot my instruction to duck.

The impaled spear had been an illusion.

Yet his leg is still bleeding and I realize that Nordra did wound him, after all, and seriously. The wound has caused him to pale. He stares up at me, or rather at Li, and nods without surprise.

"Did you take care of them?" he asks, his voice flat.

I nod mechanically. "Viper killed Sam. I killed Jessie."

"And Marc?" Kyle asks.

"He's dead."

Kyle gestures to a spot beside him. "I need your healing touch. Come, sit here and invoke your sister's power."

As Li, I sit beside him but act like I'm hesitant to touch him.

"What will become of me after you're healed?" I ask.

He acts annoyed, for a moment, before he focuses on my eyes, locking his gaze on mine. He speaks in a soft, persuasive tone.

"When you've healed me, you'll return to the cave and

jump in the lava. You'll die but in dying you'll be reunited with your sister. Do you understand?"

"Yes," I say.

Kyle lies his head back on the boulder. "Heal my leg now."

I reach out with my left hand to touch his leg, while with my right hand I pull Viper's poisonous knife from my belt, the blade that had been designed by Kyle to kill me.

I raise the knife to stab him.

But to my dismay his relaxed victorious demeanor suddenly vanishes. I'm confident he hasn't penetrated my disguise, but it doesn't matter. He's seen my raised knife, and his reflexes are staggering, faster than my own. The instant I move in for the kill he grabs his machete and raises it above his head to strike.

Yet I still have the advantage; his machete is still above his head when I bury Viper's poisonous knife in his diaphragm, six inches beneath his sternum. Above me his machete trembles and falls from his fingers as I push the blade in deeper, making sure his system absorbs every last drop of the burning pain the poison will bestow on him. Indeed, that's why I don't just stab him in the heart and end it. I want him to feel the kind of pain he has caused all of us.

Kyle gasps as I yank out the knife.

"Feel all better now?" I ask. I've dropped my disguise, although I can't say when I did so.

The rear of his head falls back on the boulder with a thump.

"Fuck you," he mutters.

"Are those to be your last words? You're dying, Kyle."

"Tell me something I don't know."

I crouch by his side. "You're a master hypnotist, aren't you? That's what you were trying to tell us when you bragged about having the cloaking gene. But you've also got the telepathy gene, which you didn't tell us about. That's why you can stare someone in the eye and get them to do pretty much anything you want. True?"

Kyle grimaces. "That sort of sums it up."

"You killed Pierre and Keb to make me suspect Sam."

"Sure."

"How?"

Kyle feigns boredom. "There was a back entrance to that cave none of you knew about."

"They meant nothing to you?"

"Gimme a break," Kyle says.

I nod. "You started your attack on our group when you took Li with you to heal your buddies. It was then you planted the time bomb in her to kill me when all your other enemies were dead. That means you were banking on me being the last one alive." I pause. "I suppose I should feel flattered."

"I knew you had it in you," Kyle says.

"Maybe. But you thought I was too naive to figure out your plan until too late."

"I was a fool. I underestimated you."

I reach out and squeeze his arm. "Don't be so hard on yourself. You have no idea how close you came to fooling me."

"How did you figure it out?"

I lean over and whisper in his ear. "I finally took a good look at your hole card."

He's bitter. "You didn't know. I had you fooled. It was that wall, that damn wall, it warned you somehow."

I wipe the blood from the blade on my pants leg. "In a sense it was the wall. In another sense it was the love of a dear friend I lost in Las Vegas that came to my rescue."

The burning is already beginning to spread through his blood. He shakes with pain and trembles with fear. His bitterness appears to grow and I realize that this is a first for him. No one has ever defeated him before.

"Too bad you're not going to have a chance to celebrate your victory with your lover boy," Kyle chokes, managing to flash a satisfied grin. I stand and slap him in the face.

"How little you understand love," I say.

His whole body is suddenly racked with tremors as blood leaks from his gut and sweat drips off his face. The *real* pain from the poison has finally hit, I realize. His cocky attitude vanishes in an instant. Suddenly he is just a pathetic beaten asshole, and I pity him. But only a little. . . .

"Jessie, please, at least stop the pain. Kill me," he begs. "I can't bear it."

Leaning over with the knife, I use the sweat dripping off

his face and his shirt collar to wipe away any last remaining residue of poison from the blade.

"Do it!" he cries, thinking I'm about to cut his throat.

"I will, I will," I say, even though I have no intention of stopping his pain. I hold up my naked wrists for him to see. I actually smile. From reading, I know the best way to open the veins is to cut from the wrist up the center of the inside of each arm. Feeling not a shred of fear, I press the blade deep into my flesh and swiftly make the incisions in front of Kyle and then toss the knife over my shoulder.

"Do you understand love now?" I ask.

Kyle gasps in disbelief. "Why?"

I smile. "Because only one can survive."

I walk away without another word. My destination is the wall and I know it will be a hard hike at the rate I'm losing blood. I'd like to bury Chad, although I doubt I'll have the strength, and I'd like to have another quiet chat with Russ before I go. I always loved Russ and wish he hadn't left my life so soon.

But Chad is already half covered with ash by the time I reach the wall, and a stream of molten red lava has spilled over from the volcano's crown and is slowly creeping toward Nordra's body and the black wall. Nordra being the warrior he was, I doubt he'll mind having his remains incinerated.

I'm not surprised the volcano has sent out lava to cover the area. It will probably pile up against the wall and cremate me as well. But it's only a narrow stream and it will take time. The one thing the king of the island has, though, is time. I was right to mistrust it. I knew it would claim me for its own in the end.

I'm only ten feet from the wall when I stumble and fall and can't get up. Rolling onto my back, I stare up at the stars and the edge of the wall and try to figure out if it really has a top. The pain in my wrists has subsided and I no longer feel as if I'm squirting blood onto the ground. Considering that I don't have long to live, I feel pretty good.

Time goes by and I think of everything that has happened in the past few days. As the old song says, "Regrets, I've had a few, but then again, too few to mention." I'm pleased that in the end I had the courage to do what I thought was right. The only thing that makes me sad is that I'd like to shake the hand of the winner of the Field. Maybe even give him another kiss.

And of course I miss Lara and Jimmy. God do I miss them . . .

I close my eyes and drift. When I open them, there's a hint of light in the sky and the narrow stream of lava has reached the wall. I doubt it will have much effect on it.

A figure climbs over the hill and waves to me.

I wish I could wave back but I can't move.

He walks to where I lie and kneels by my side, brushing my sticky hair from my eyes. I can't remember the last time I showered.

I smile. "You woke up on your own."

Marc nods. "I was lucky."

"That's because you're a lucky guy. I knew it the first night I dreamed about you."

He smiles. "If I knew you were watching I would have behaved better."

"No, it was fun. You had everything planned."

His smile fades. "What happened?"

"Kyle and I had a final showdown. He betrayed us all in the end, the bastard. Luckily, I was able to kill him."

"How do you feel?"

"Happy. Sad. That's life, I guess, and death."

Marc's eyes water and he tries to blink away the tears but I see them. "Is there anything I can do for you?" he asks.

"Hold me. Hold me in your arms."

He leans over and picks me up and presses his head to my head. "I wish you could do this with me."

"You'll feel more confident when you press your bracelet to the wall. You have to do it—the pictures in the cave made that clear. It's the final step in winning the Field. You'll instantly remember the experiences of every witch who fought on this island and was victorious here. You'll even get acquainted with that friend I told you about, Cleo."

"She sounds like a special woman."

"Like you, she only changed into a witch when she came here. Her mentor was the one who helped her."

"Her mentor was your inspiration?" Marc asks.

"In a way. But the more I got to know you, I knew it had

to be you. Don't ask me to explain. The Council will be lucky to have you." I add, "Just don't let anyone boss you around."

His face darkens. "But won't you be there when we're in witch world? You told me when a person dies in the real world, it's not such a big deal."

I wish I had the strength to reach up and touch his cheek.

"I don't know where here is but it's not the real world," I say.

"So you don't know if we'll meet again?"

"I'm sorry, I don't," I say past a painful lump in my throat. A shudder goes through my body. I want to try—I should be crying. But a part of me feels everything has worked out for the best, the way it was supposed to. Even if that best means I am about to die.

Still, another part of me does not want to let go—not to life, not to Marc. It's sad it's taken me so long to realize how I truly feel about him. Jimmy will always be my first love, it's true, but Marc will be my last.

My words are hard on Marc and he holds me tighter.

"It's time," I whisper.

His tears flow freely now. "Did I ever tell you that I love you?"

"Once or twice but you can tell me again."

"I love you, Jessie. I'll love you forever."

I smile. "I love you more."

He kisses me. I feel his lips touch mine.

Then I feel myself floating upward, like people talk about when they have a near-death experience. But I also feel like I'm levitating up the side of the wall so I'm not sure if my body is making the trip or if it's just my spirit.

Once I reach the top, I stand at the edge and look out over the island. I see Marc down below, pressing his bracelet to the wall, standing as still as a statue, and it's like I can see the whole of the Field at once.

A long time seems to go by.

I stand and wait, although I know not what for.

Then I hear a sound and I am no longer alone.

A woman clears her throat behind me. "Having fun yet?"

I whirl. "Who are you?" I ask.

"You don't recognize me?"

"You look familiar. Sort of like my mom."

"I'm not your mother, Jessie."

Then I recognize her.

I'm looking at an older version of myself.

I gasp. "So it isn't over?"

"Not by a long shot. It's just begun." She offers her hand and I take it. "Where would you like to go first? Or maybe I should say when?"

"Can we go back to when Columbus discovered America?"

"Columbus didn't discover America. The Vikings did."

"I know that. Wherever he came ashore—whenever—I'd like to go back and greet him. If that's okay?"

The woman smiles and leads me over the top of the wall.

"I remember asking that same question," she says.

EPILOGUE

THE MEMORIAL SERVICE WAS FOR CLOSE FRIENDS AND family so Marc decided to sit at the back. He hoped no one would notice him and ask a bunch of questions. He wouldn't have come except he felt compelled. It seemed already his intuition was guiding his steps.

Jessica Ralle's father stood and gave a long talk about how special his daughter was and how he would miss her. Jessica's mother was going to speak after him but got choked up and was unable to talk. But a string of friends spoke next: Alexis, Herme, Debra. James went last and his talk was the only one Marc could relate to.

"Jessie hated funerals," he began. "She often told me she wasn't going to show up at her own. And now that she's gone and we have no body to bury, I'm sure she would laugh and say, 'See, I got my last wish.' Many people might have thought her sense of humor strange and it was, because she was a strange girl. I mean that in a good way. When we first met, I knew she wasn't like anyone I had ever met before. It took me a little time to realize just how wonderful she was but she gave me that time and for that I'll always be grateful. Our relationship started with a few bumps but Jessie always had faith in us. She had faith in love itself. I know that might sound corny but it sums up her approach to life. There was nothing she wouldn't do for someone she cared about. There was nothing she wouldn't do for someone she had just met. Even though we may never know the circumstances surrounding her death, I suspect she died so that others could live. Like a wise man once said, there can be no greater love."

That was it, that was all he had to say. Marc was surprised at James's brevity but appreciated it as well. He knew he couldn't have described her better.

On the way out of the church, Marc made a beeline for his car but heard someone call his name before he could make his escape. Since there was only one person at the memorial who could have recognized him, he was not surprised to see James walking his way. But he was shocked to see him holding Jessica's daughter, Lara. Marc had known about Lara, of course, although Jessica had told him little about her except to say she was "special."

At the time Marc had assumed she was saying what all moms said about their kids, but one look at Lara and Marc felt a wave of something so unique, there hadn't been a word invented to describe it. Whoever the kid was, she was going to have an amazing future.

James offered his hand. "It's Marc, isn't it?"

Marc nodded. "Jessie always called you Jimmy."

James smiled. "She never got used to witch world. She kept saying she only felt at home in the real world. I'm not sure why when her powers worked so much better here than there."

Marc gestured. "I'm no different. This world is interesting but it's not home."

"Trust me, it grows on you over time."

"Is it true you spend every day here?"

James kissed the top of his daughter's head. "Lara and I both. We're the odd couple when it comes to witches."

Marc was surprised. "I'm sorry, I heard about your sacrifice and how you ended up on this side of the curtain. But Jessie never told me that your daughter had been killed in the real world."

"She wasn't. She was never born there." James paused and looked around the parking lot to make sure they had privacy. "But my son was. That's one of the reasons I wanted to speak to you."

Marc hesitated. "Go on."

"I know you don't know me and that I'm in no position to ask a favor of you, but I was wondering if you could check on him from time to time. Jessie took care of him before we lost her but his mother's grandparents have him now. He lives in Apple Valley and his name is Huck Kelter."

Marc frowned. "How come Jessie's father and mother don't have him?"

"Jessie wasn't his mom. And his own mother is dead."

"I see," Marc said, although he wasn't sure he did. "If Jessie cared about him so much, he must have been important. I promise to check on him for you."

James studied him. "You're not just saying that. You really mean it."

"You seem surprised."

James shook his head. "I'm sorry, I'm just used to people not caring about Huck. It's an old story with me, I won't bore you with all the details."

A silence settled between them. Marc was surprised he didn't feel more uncomfortable. James's grief was clearly overwhelming, although he was doing his best to hide it. He kept rubbing his nose against the top of Lara's head, which made the child giggle. Marc loved the sound of her voice, but wasn't sure why. There was just something magical about it.

He could sense magic these days. Ever since he had put his green bracelet to the black wall as the victor of the Field. He could sense many things he never could before. Sometimes he felt as if his life had just begun. It was sad Jessie wasn't around to share it with him. Even if they could only be friends. . . .

"I should probably let you go," James said finally.

Marc glanced at his watch. "Have you had lunch yet? I'm feeling kind of empty. Would you like to meet somewhere and talk?"

"Talk about what?"

Marc shrugged. "You know."

James glanced in the direction of the scattering family and friends and pulled his daughter close to his chest. "I'd like that. Where would you like to meet?"

"How about that deli where you spied on the two of us?"

"She told you about that?"

"Yes."

James chuckled. "You going to head straight there?"

"I was going to Malibu to drop off a piece of jewelry that belongs to an actress. But I can always do that later. Yeah, I can head straight there." Marc paused and stuck his finger near Lara. It felt pretty cool when she grabbed it. "But only if you bring this little angel with you."

"I don't go anywhere without her," James said as he turned in the direction of his car. But he stopped and glanced back at Marc. "Do you mind telling me one thing? Before we eat?"

"Not at all."

"Do you think we'll see her again?" James asked.

"No one's seen her in over a month."

"I know. Tell me what you think."

Marc considered. "She's not gone."

I am a vampire, and that is the truth. But the modern meaning of the word *vampire,* the stories that have been told about creatures such as I, are not precisely true. I do not turn to ash in the sun, nor do I cringe when I see a crucifix. I wear a tiny gold cross now around my neck, but only because I like it. I cannot command a pack of wolves to attack or fly through the air. Nor can I make another of my kind simply by having him drink my blood. Wolves do like me, though, as do most predators, and I can jump so high that one might imagine I can fly. As to blood—ah, blood, the whole subject fascinates me. I do like that as well, warm and dripping, when I am thirsty. And I am often thirsty.

My name, at present, is Alisa Perne—just two words, something to last for a couple of decades. I am no more attached to them than to the sound of the wind. My hair is blond and silklike, my eyes like sapphires that have stared long at a volcanic fissure. My stature is slight by modern standards, five two in sandals, but my arms and legs are muscled, although not unattractively so. Before I speak I appear to be only eighteen years of age, but something in my voice—the coolness of my expressions, the echo of endless experience— makes people think I am much older. But even I seldom think about when I was born, long before the pyramids were erected beneath the pale moon. I was there, in that desert in those days, even though I am not originally from that part of the world.

Do I need blood to survive? Am I immortal? After all this time, I still don't know. I drink blood because I crave it. But I can eat normal food as well, and digest it. I need food as much as any other man or woman. I am a living, breathing creature. My heart beats—I can hear it now, like thunder in my ears. My hearing is very sensitive, as is my sight. I can hear a dry leaf break off a branch a mile away, and I can clearly see the craters on the moon without a telescope. Both senses have grown more acute as I get older.

My immune system is impregnable, my regenerative system miraculous, if you believe in miracles—which I don't. I can be stabbed in the arm with a knife and heal within minutes without scarring. But if I were to be stabbed in the heart, say with the currently fashionable wooden stake, then maybe I would die. It is difficult for even a vampire's flesh to heal around an implanted blade. But it is not something I have experimented with.

But who would stab me? Who would get the chance? I have the strength of five men, the reflexes of the mother of all cats. There is not a system of physical attack and defense of which I am not a master. A dozen black belts could corner me in a dark alley, and I could make a dress fit for a vampire out of the sashes that hold their fighting jackets closed. And I do love to fight, it is true, almost as much as I love to kill. Yet I kill less and less as the years go by because the need is not there, and the ramifications of murder in modern society are complex and a waste of my precious but endless time. Some loves have to be given up, others have to be forgotten. Strange as it may sound, if you think of me as a monster, but I can love most passionately. I do not think of myself as evil.

Why am I talking about all this? Who am I talking to? I send out these words, these thoughts, simply because it is time. Time for what, I do not know, and it does not matter because it is what I want and that is always reason enough for me. My wants—how few they are, and yet how deep they burn. I will not tell you, at present, who I am talking to.

The moment is pregnant with mystery, even for me. I stand outside the door of Detective Michael Riley's office. The hour is late; he is in his private office in the back, the light down low—I know this without seeing. The good Mr. Riley called me three hours ago to tell me I had to come to his office to have a little talk about some things I might find of interest. There was a note of threat in his voice, and more. I can sense emotions, although I cannot read minds. I am curious as I stand in this cramped and stale hallway. I am also annoyed, and that doesn't bode well for Mr. Riley. I knock lightly on the door to his outer office and open it before he can respond.

"Hello," I say. I do not sound dangerous—I am, after all, supposed to be a teenager. I stand beside the secretary's unhappy desk, imagining that her last few paychecks have been promised to her as "practically in the mail." Mr. Riley is at his desk, inside his office, and stands as he notices me. He has on a rumpled brown sport coat, and in a glance I see the weighty bulge of a revolver beneath his left breast. Mr. Riley thinks I am dangerous, I note, and my curiosity goes up a notch. But I'm not afraid he knows what I really am, or he would not have chosen to meet with me at all, even in broad daylight.

"Alisa Perne?" he says. His tone is uneasy.

"Yes."

He gestures from twenty feet away. "Please come in and have a seat."

I enter his office but do not take the offered chair in front of his desk, but rather, one against the right wall. I want a straight line to him if he tries to pull a gun on me. If he does try, he will die, and maybe painfully.

He looks at me, trying to size me up, and it is difficult for him because I just sit here. He, however, is a montage of many impressions. His coat is not only wrinkled but stained—greasy burgers eaten hastily. I note it all. His eyes are red rimmed, from a drug as much as fatigue. I hypothesize his poison to be speed—medicine to nourish long hours beating the pavement. After me? Surely. There is also a glint of satisfaction in his eyes, a prey finally caught. I smile privately at the thought, yet a thread of uneasiness enters me as well. The office is stuffy, slightly chilly. I have never liked the cold, although I could survive an Arctic winter night naked to the bone.

"I guess you wonder why I wanted to talk to you so urgently," he says.

I nod. My legs are uncrossed, my white slacks hanging loose. One hand rests in my lap, the other plays with my hair. Left-handed, right-handed—I am neither, and both.

"May I call you Alisa?" he asks.

"You may call me what you wish, Mr. Riley."

My voice startles him, just a little, and it is the effect I want. I could have pitched it like any modern teenager, but I have allowed my past to enter, the power of it. I want to keep Mr. Riley nervous, for nervous people say much that they later regret.

"Call me Mike," he says. "Did you have trouble finding the place?"

"No."

"Can I get you anything? Coffee? A soda?"

"No."

He glances at a folder on his desk, flips it open. He clears his throat, and again I hear his tiredness, as well as his fear. But is he afraid of me? I am not sure. Besides the gun under his coat, he has another beneath some papers at the other side of his desk. I smell the gunpowder in the bullets, the cold steel. A lot of firepower to meet a teenage girl. I hear a faint scratch of moving metal and plastic. He is taping the conversation.

"First off I should tell you who I am," he says. "As I said on the phone, I am a private detective. My business is my own—I work entirely freelance. People come to me to find loved ones, to research risky investments, to provide protection, when necessary, and to get hard-to-find background information on certain individuals."

I smile. "And to spy."

He blinks. "I do not spy, Miss Perne."

"Really." My smile broadens. I lean forward, the tops of my breasts visible at the open neck of my black silk blouse. "It is late, Mr. Riley. Tell me what you want."

He shakes his head. "You have a lot of confidence for a kid."

"And you have a lot of nerve for a down-on-his-luck private dick."

He doesn't like that. He taps the open folder on his desk. "I have been researching you for the last few months, Miss Perne, ever since you moved to Mayfair. You have an intriguing past, as well as many investments. But I'm sure you know that."

"Really."

"Before I begin, may I ask how old you are?"

"You may ask."

"How old are you?"

"It's none of your business."

He smiles. He thinks he has scored a point. He does not realize that I am already considering how he should die, although I still hope to avoid such an extreme measure. Never ask a vampire her age. We don't like that question. It's very impolite. Mr. Riley clears his throat again, and I think that maybe I will strangle him.

"Prior to moving to Mayfair," he says, "you lived in Los Angeles—in Beverly Hills in fact—at Two-Five-Six Grove Street. Your home was a four-thousand-square-foot mansion, with two swimming pools, a tennis court, a sauna, and a small observatory. The property is valued at six-point-five million. To this day you are listed as the sole owner, Miss Perne."

"It's not a crime to be rich."

"You are not just rich. You are very rich. My research indicates that you own five separate estates scattered across this country. Further research tells me that you probably own as much if not more property in Europe and the Far East. Your stock and bond assets are vast—in the hundreds of millions. But what none of my research has uncovered is how you came across this incredible wealth. There is no record of a family anywhere, and believe me, Miss Perne, I have looked far and wide."

"I believe you. Tell me, whom did you contact to gather this information?"

He enjoys that he has my interest. "My sources are of course confidential."

"Of course." I stare at him; my stare is very powerful. Sometimes, if I am not careful, and I stare too long at a flower, it shrivels and dies. Mr. Riley loses his smile and shifts uneasily. "Why are you researching me?"

"You admit that my facts are accurate?" he asks.

"Do you need my assurances?" I pause, my eyes still on him. Sweat glistens on his forehead. "Why the research?"

He blinks and turns away with effort. He dabs at the perspiration on his head. "Because you fascinate me," he says. "I think to myself, here is one of the wealthiest women in the world, and no one knows who she is. Plus she can't be more than twenty-five years old, and she has no family. It makes me wonder."

"What do you wonder, Mr. Riley?"

He ventures a swift glance at me; he really does not like to look at me, even though I am very beautiful. "Why you go to such extremes to remain invisible," he says.

"It also makes you wonder if I would pay to stay invisible," I say.

He acts surprised. "I didn't say that."

"How much do you want?"

My question stuns him, yet pleases him. He does not have to be the first to dirty his hands. What he does not realize is that blood stains deeper than dirt, and that the stains last much longer. Yes, I think again, he may not have that long to live.

"How much are you offering?" he ventures.

I shrug. "It depends."

"On what?"

"On whether you tell me who pointed you in my direction."

He is indignant. "I assure you that I needed no one to point me in your direction. I discovered your interesting qualities all by myself."

He is lying, of that I am positive. I can always tell when a person lies, almost always. Only remarkable people can fool me, and then they have to be lucky. But I do not like to be fooled—so one has to wonder at even their luck.

"Then my offer is nothing," I say.

He straightens. He believes he is ready to pounce. "Then my counteroffer, Miss Perne, is to make what I have discovered public knowledge." He pauses. "What do you think of that?"

"It will never happen."

He smiles. "You don't think so?"

I smile. "You would die before that happened."

He laughs. "You would take a contract out on my life?"

"Something to that effect."

He stops laughing, now deadly serious, now that we are talking about death. Yet I keep my smile since death amuses me. He points a finger at me.

"You can be sure that if anything happened to me the police would be at your door the same day," he says.

"You have arranged to send my records to someone else," I say. "Just in case something should happen to you?"

"Something to that effect." He is trying to be witty. He is also lying. I slide back farther into my chair. He thinks I am relaxing, but I position myself so that my legs are straight out. If I am to strike, I have decided, it will be with my right foot.

"Mr. Riley," I say. "We should not argue. You want something from me, and I want something from you. I am prepared to pay you a million dollars, to be deposited in whatever account you wish, in whatever part of the world you desire, if you will tell me who made you aware of me."

He looks me straight in the eye, tries to, and surely he feels the heat building up inside me because he flinches before he speaks. His voice comes out uneven and confused. He does not understand why I am suddenly so intimidating.

"No one is interested in you except me," he says.

I sigh. "You are armed, Mr. Riley."

"I am?"

I harden my voice. "You have a gun under your coat. You have a gun on your desk under those papers. You are taping this conversation. Now, one might think these are all standard blackmail precautions, but I don't think so. I am a young woman. I don't look dangerous. But someone has told you that I am more dangerous than I look and that I am to be treated with extreme caution. And you know that that someone is right." I pause. "Who is that someone, Mr. Riley?"

He shakes his head. He is looking at me in a new light, and he doesn't like what he sees. My eyes continue to bore into him. A splinter of fear has entered his mind.

"H-how do you know all these things?" he asks.

"You admit my facts are accurate?" I mimic him.

He shakes his head again.

Now I allow my voice to change, to deepen, to resonate with the fullness of my incredibly long life. The effect on him is pronounced; he shakes visibly, as if he is suddenly aware that he is sitting next to a monster. But I am not just any monster. I am a vampire, and in many ways, for his sake, that may be the worst monster of all.

"Someone has hired you to research me," I say. "I know that for a fact. Please don't deny it again, or you will make me angry. I really am uncontrollable when I am angry. I do things I later regret, and I would regret killing you, Mr. Riley—but not for long." I pause. "Now, for the last time, tell me who sent you after me, and I will give you a million dollars and let you walk out of here alive."

He stares at me incredulously. His eyes see one thing and his ears hear another, I know. He sees a pretty blond girl with startlingly blue eyes, and he hears the velvety voice of a succubus from hell. It is too much for him. He begins to stammer.

"Miss Perne," he begins. "You misunderstand me. I mean

you no harm. I just want to complete a simple business deal with you. No one has to . . . get hurt."

I take in a long, slow breath. I need air, but I can hold my breath for over an hour if I must. Yet now I let out the breath before speaking again, and the room cools even more. And Mr. Riley shivers.

"Answer my question," I say simply.

He coughs. "There is no one else."

"You'd better reach for your gun."

"Pardon?"

"You are going to die now. I assume you prefer to die fighting."

"Miss Perne—"

"I am five thousand years old."

He blinks. "What?"

I give him my full, uncloaked gaze, which I have used in the past—alone—to kill. "I am a vampire," I say softly. "And you have pissed me off."

He believes me. Suddenly he believes every horror story he has been told since he was a little boy. That they were all true: the dead things hungering for the warm living flesh; the bony hand coming out of the closet in the black of night; the monsters from another page of reality, the unturned page—who could look so human, so cute.

He reaches for his gun.

ABOUT THE AUTHOR

Christopher Pike is a bestselling author of young adult novels. The Thirst series, *The Secret of Ka*, and the Remember Me and Alosha trilogies are some of his favorite titles. He is also the author of several adult novels, including *Sati* and *The Season of Passage*. Thirst and Alosha are slated to be released as feature films. Pike currently lives in Santa Barbara, where it is rumored he never leaves his house. But he can be found online at christopherpikebooks.com.

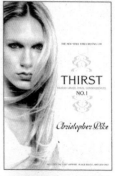
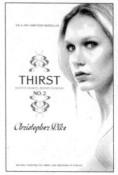

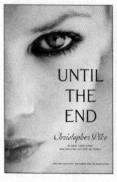
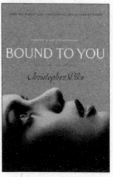
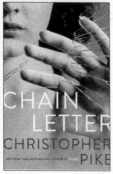